3/20 c2

About the Author

Georgie Lee loves combining her passion for history and storytelling through romantic fiction. She began writing professionally at a local TV station before moving to Hollywood to work in the entertainment industry. When not writing, Georgie enjoys reading non-fiction history and watching any movie with a costume and an accent. Please visit www.georgie-lee.com for more information about Georgie and her books.

Regency Rogues

Regency Rogues:

Rescued by Temptation

GEORGIE LEE

MILLS & BOON

First Published in Great Britain 2020
By Mills & Boon, an imprint of HarperCollinsPublishers
1 London Bridge Street, London, SE1 9GF

REGENCY ROGUES: RESCUED BY TEMPTATION © 2020
Harlequin Books S.A.

Rescued from Ruin © 2014 Georgie Reinstein
Miss Marianne's Disgrace © 2016 Georgie Reinstein

ISBN: 978-0-263-27951-1

MIX
Paper from
responsible sources
FSC
www.fsc.org **FSC™ C007454**

This book is produced from independently certified FSC™ paper to ensure responsible forest management.

For more information visit: www.harpercollins.co.uk/green

Printed and bound in Spain
by CPI, Barcelona

RESCUED
FROM RUIN

I'd like to thank my husband, parents and in-laws for all their support, childcare, dinners, and patience while I worked on this book. I couldn't have done it without all of you.

Chapter One

London 1816

Randall Cheltenham, Marquess of Falconbridge, looked down the length of the salon, his chest tightening as if hit by a low branch while riding.

Cecelia Thompson stood in the doorway, just as she had so many times in his dreams.

When was the last time he'd seen her? Ten years ago? For ever?

Her eyes met his and the image of her standing in a field, the acrid smell of cut grass and damp earth blending with the warmth of the late afternoon sun, overwhelmed him. He was eighteen again and she was here.

Once, he would have sold his soul for this moment. Now, he waited for the tenuous connection to snap and for her soft look to turn hard with disdain. In his experience, it was a rare woman who forgot past slights. He'd played no small part in her decision to leave England; driving people away was a talent he'd possessed in spades back then.

He stood rock-still, anticipating the sneer, but it never came. Instead her face remained soft, her smile easy and genuine. Her brown hair was a shade darker and her hazel eyes, flecked with green, held something of the girl he'd once known, but with an unmistakable maturity. In other women it made them seem hardened by life, but in Cecelia it increased her beauty, surrounding her with an air of mystery more fascinating than the innocence he remembered so well.

Then old Lord Weatherly shuffled between them to greet her and she looked away.

'You already know the young woman?' Madame de Badeau gasped, her thick voice pulling his thoughts back to the room. He looked down at the mature French woman standing beside him in her lavender dress, her dark eyes dancing with the thrill of having discovered something new about him after all their years of acquaintance.

'If you call conversing with her at my uncle's estate knowing her,' he said abruptly, uneasy at the obviousness of his reaction and eager to distract his former lover from it. 'What's she doing here? I thought she lived in America?'

'She's here to find a husband for the cousin.'

Randall finally noticed the young woman standing beside Cecelia. 'And her husband is with her?'

'No. He's dead.'

Randall's muscles tightened more at the news than the callous way Madame de Badeau delivered it. Cecelia was here and a widow. He swallowed hard, remembering the night Aunt Ella had told him of Cecelia's marriage to the colonial landowner, his aunt's soft words raining down on him like the blows from his father's belt. The wrenching pain of having lost Cecelia so completely was almost the only thing he remembered from that night. The rest was blurred by the haze of alcohol. It was the last time he'd allowed himself to drink.

'How do you know Mrs Thompson?' he asked, looking around the room and accidentally catching the demure Miss Thornton's eye. Lady Thornton, her dragon of a mother, shifted between them to block his view and he met her warning glare with a mocking grin. He wasn't about to trouble with a green girl. They weren't worth the effort, not with so many willing widows aching to catch his notice.

'Cecelia's mother and I attended the same ladies' school in France, the one your aunt attended when your grandfather was ambassador there. Cecelia's family was in the silk trade, quite wealthy at the time. They did a great deal of business with my father, back when the country was civilised. Dreadful revolutionaries.'

He clasped his hands behind his back, uneasy at the idea of Madame de Badeau having any connection with Cecelia, no matter how tenuous. 'It's difficult to imagine you in a ladies' school.'

'I had my pleasures there, too. Ah, the curiosities of young girls. Most delightful.' She swept her fingers over the swell of breasts pressing against her bodice, adjusting the diamond necklace resting in the crevice of flesh. Though old enough to be Cecelia's mother, Madame de Badeau was still a stunning woman with a smooth face and lithe body. Young lords new to London often fell prey to her beauty and other, more carnal talents.

He glanced at the full bosom, then met her eyes. His passion for her had faded long ago, but he maintained the friendship because she amused him. 'And now?'

She snapped open her fan and waved it over her chest in short flicks. 'I'm helping her launch her cousin in society.'

'Why? You never help anyone.'

Madame de Badeau's smile drew tight at the corners before she covered her irritation with a light laugh. 'Lord Falconbridge, how serious you are tonight.' Her hand slid around his arm, coiling in the crook of his elbow like a snake. 'Now, let me reacquaint you with the little widow.'

They strode across the room, past the pianoforte where Miss Marianne Domville, Madame de Badeau's much younger sister, played, her head bent over the keys, indifferent to the crowd of young bucks surrounding her. The room hummed with the usual assortment of intellectuals and friends Lady Weatherly regularly gathered for her salons. Randall cared as much for them as the poet in the corner sighing out his latest drivel. Only Cecelia mattered and he focused on her, wondering what she would think of him after all these years. Madame de Badeau must have told her of his reputation and all the scandals surrounding him. The woman took pride in spreading the stories.

Of all the disapproving looks he'd ever caught in a room like this, Cecelia's would matter the most.

He ground his teeth, the failings he'd buried with his father threatening to seize him again. A footman carrying a tray of champagne flutes crossed their path, the amber liquid tempting Randall for the first time in ten years. He ran his thumb over the tips of his fingers, wanting to take one smooth stem in his hand and tip the sharp liquid over his tongue, again and again, until everything inside him faded.

Instead he continued forward, shoving down the old craving and all the emotions fuelling it.

They passed a clutch of whispering ladies, the women's fans unable to muffle their breathy exclamations as they watched him.

'…he won a duel against Lord Calverston, drawing first blood…'

'…he and Lady Weatherly were lovers last Season…'

He pinned them with a hard look and their voices wilted like their folding fans.

As he and Madame de Badeau approached Cecelia, Lord Weatherly took his leave and Cecelia's eyes found his again. An amused grin raised the corner of her lips, almost bringing him to a halt. It was the same smile she used to taunt him with across the card table at Falconbridge Manor. Back then, she could send him into stutters with a look, playing him like Miss Domville played the pianoforte, but not any more. No one could manipulate him now.

'My dear Mrs Thompson, I'm sure you remember Lord Falconbridge,' Madame de Badeau introduced, a strange note of collusion in her voice, as though she and Randall shared a secret of which Cecelia was not aware. Randall narrowed his eyes at the Frenchwoman, wondering what she was about, before Cecelia's soft voice captured his attention.

'Lord Falconbridge, it's been too long.' The hint of a colonial twang coloured the roll of his title across her tongue, conflicting with the tones he remembered so well.

'Much too long.' He bowed, taking in the length of her body draped in a deep red dress. Cut straight across the bodice, the gown was modestly high by London standards, but still displayed the white tops of her pert breasts. He longed to drop light kisses on the tempting mounds, to find a secluded bedroom where they might while away the evening in more pleasurable pursuits, finishing what they'd started so long ago.

He straightened, hating the vulnerability in this wanting. 'My condolences on the loss of your husband.'

'Thank you.' She fingered the gold bracelet on her wrist, her smile fading before she bolstered it and motioned to the young woman standing beside her. 'Allow me to introduce my cousin, Miss Theresa Fields.'

With reluctance, Randall tore his eyes away to take in the cousin. She was pretty, but not ravishing, and met his appraising look with an air of confidence most green girls lacked. Her dress was made of fine cotton, but simply cut and lacking the ruffles and ribbons preferred by the other young ladies this Season.

'It's a pleasure to meet you, Lord Falconbridge,' she replied, the Virginia twang strong in her speech.

'Miss Fields, I know my sister is dying to see you again.' Madame de Badeau took Miss Fields by the arm and drew her out from between Cecelia and Randall. Madame de Badeau threw him a conspiratorial look as she passed, as though leaving them alone together in a bedroom and expecting nature to take its course. He wondered what scheme she had in mind for him and Cecelia. Whatever it was, she was mistaken if she thought to manipulate him like one of her country lords new to London.

'You're the Marquess of Falconbridge now?' Cecelia asked, her voice flowing over him like the River Stour over the rocks at Falconbridge Manor and all thoughts of Madame de Badeau vanished.

'Yes, Uncle Edmund couldn't keep it for ever.'

'My condolences on your loss,' she offered with genuine concern. 'I remember him fondly.'

'You were one of the few people he truly liked.'

'Then I'm even sorrier to hear of his passing.'

'Don't be.' Randall smirked. 'He died as he lived, with a large appetite for the pleasures of life.'

'And no doubt still railing against society. What is it he used to say?'

'"Nothing to be gained by chasing society's good opinion",' Randall repeated Uncle Edmund's words, remembering the old man sitting at the head of the table thumping his large fingers against the lacquered top. '"All it does is make you a slave to their desires and whims"—'

'"Be your own man and you'll be the better for it",' she finished, her voice deepening to mimic Uncle Edmund's imperious tone.

Randall laughed at the accurate impression. 'I wanted to engrave it on his headstone, but Aunt Ella wouldn't allow it. She said it wasn't how she wanted to remember her brother.'

'How is Lady Ellington?' Cecelia accepted a glass of champagne from a footman.

'She's quite the mistress of Falconbridge Manor.' Randall waved away the offered drink, making Cecelia's eyebrows rise in surprise. 'She decided to live there after Uncle Edmund passed. It amuses her to manage the house.'

'Will she come to London for the Season?' There was no mistaking the eagerness in her voice and it grieved him to disappoint her.

'Aunt Ella is as likely to venture to town as Uncle Edmund was to live as a respectable country gentleman.'

'Nor are you likely to live so quiet a life. I hear enough stories about you to make your uncle proud.' She touched the glass to her full lips and tilted it, letting the shimmering liquid slide into her mouth.

He focused on her moist lips, almost jealous of the glass. 'As Uncle Edmund also used to say, a touch of scandal lends a man a little mystery.'

Cecelia laughed, wiping away a small drop of champagne from the corner of her mouth. 'From what Madame de Badeau tells me, you have more than a touch.'

He stiffened, struggling to hold his smile. 'You shouldn't believe everything you hear, especially from her.'

'Do my ears deceive me or is the notorious Marquess of Falconbridge embarrassed?' she gasped in mock surprise and Randall's jaw tightened. He couldn't remember the last time a woman had dared to tease him like this.

'Do you have a reputation, Mrs Thompson?' he asked, determined to take back the conversation, the old familiarity too easy between them.

Darkness flickered through her eyes and she fiddled with her gold bracelet, turning it on her wrist. Whatever suddenly troubled her, he thought it would bring the discussion to an end. Then she raised her face, bravely meeting his scrutiny, her smile alight with mischief. 'If I do, it is far behind me in Virginia and unlikely to be discovered until well after the Season.'

He stepped closer, inhaling her warm skin combined with a heady, floral scent he couldn't name. 'Perhaps I may discover it sooner?'

She met his low voice with a heated look from beneath dark lashes. 'Only if you have a very fast ship.'

'My ship is never fast, but lingers upon the salty water,' he murmured, his body tightening with desire. 'I'd be most happy to take you sailing.'

Her tongue slid over her parted lips, moistening the red bud, daring him to be bold and accept the invitation in her eyes. Then, like a wave rushing out to sea, the hungry look disappeared, replaced by her previous mirthful smile. 'A very tempting offer, but I fear being disappointed so early in the Season.'

Randall coughed to suppress a laugh and a bitter sense of loss. 'The Season will disappoint a spirited woman like you much quicker than I.'

'After enduring such a difficult crossing, I can only hope you're wrong.'

'I'm never wrong.'

'Then you're a very fortunate man.'

'Not entirely.' For a brief moment, the hard shell he'd cultivated since coming to Town dropped and he was simply Randall again, alone with her in the Falconbridge study, free of a title and all his London escapades. 'Even the life of a Marquess has its dark moments.'

Her teasing smile faded and a soft understanding filled her eyes. 'Everyone's life does.'

He'd watched stone-faced while mistresses wailed on their *chaises* and stepped casually to one side to avoid the errant porcelain figure lobbed at him. None of these overwrought reactions cut him to the core like her simple comment. For the second time in as many minutes, the shame of his past gnawed at him before he crushed it down.

'Good.' He smiled with more glib humour than he felt, clasping his hands behind his back. 'Because in London, I'm a very good acquaintance to have, especially for someone who's left her reputation across the Atlantic.'

'I shall keep it in mind. Good evening, Lord Falconbridge.'

She dipped a curtsy and walked off across the room to join a small circle of matrons standing near the window.

He watched her go, the boy in him desperate to call her back, the man he'd become keeping his shoes firmly rooted to the floor.

'Quite the morsel, isn't she?' a deep voice drawled from beside him, and Randall's lip curled in disgust. Christopher Crowdon, Earl of Strathmore, stood next to him, a glass of claret in his thick fingers.

'Careful how you speak of her, Strathmore,' Randall growled, hating the way Strathmore eyed her like a doxy in a bawdy house. 'She's an old acquaintance of mine.'

'My apologies,' Strathmore mumbled, trilling his fingers against the glass, a rare fire in his pale eyes as he studied Cecelia. 'Is it true she has extensive lands in the colonies?'

'Why? Are you in such dire straits as to chase after heiresses?'

'Of course not,' he sputtered, the claret sloshing perilously close to the side of the glass before he recovered himself. 'But there's something to be said for a widow. They know the way of things, especially when it comes to men. Best to leave such a prize to a more experienced gentleman.'

'Should I find one, I'll gladly step aside.' Randall turned on one heel and strode away.

Cecelia stood with the other matrons, trying to concentrate on the *on dit,* but she couldn't. Randall's rich voice carried over the hum of conversation and she tightened her grip on the champagne glass, willing herself not to look at him.

When she'd first seen him standing in the centre of the room, as sturdy as a wide oak in the middle of a barren field, she'd been torn between fleeing and facing him. The girl who'd once pressed him about their future together in the Falconbridge conservatory, only to be sneered at by a man unwilling to debase the family name with a poor merchant's daughter, wanted to flee. The woman who'd helped her husband rebuild Belle View after the hurricane demanded she hold steady. The wealth and plantation might be gone, but the woman it had made her wasn't and she'd wanted him to see it.

She finished the drink, the biting liquid as bitter as her present situation. Despite her time at Belle View, she'd returned to London no richer than when she'd left, her future more uncertain now than it had been the day she'd climbed aboard the ship to Virginia, the husband by her side as much of a stranger as the people in this room. She might shine with confidence in front of Randall, but everything else—the land in the colonies and her wealth—was a lie. She wondered how long her fine wardrobe and the width of the Atlantic would conceal her secret and the nasty rumours she'd left behind in Virginia. Hopefully long enough for either her or her cousin Theresa to make a match which might save them.

She deposited the empty champagne glass on the tray of a passing footman, the crystal clinking against the metal. As the footman reached out to steady it, she glanced past him to where Randall stood with a group of gentlemen, his square jaw and straight nose defined as much by his dark hair as the practised look of London ennui. Then he turned, his blue eyes meeting hers with a fierceness she could almost feel. Her thumb and fingers sought out the gold bracelets on her wrist while her lungs struggled to draw in an even breath. For a moment she was sixteen again, desiring him beyond reason, and nothing, not the long years of her marriage or the hours she'd spent managing Belle View, seemed to matter. She'd loved him, craved him, needed him, and in the end he hadn't experienced the same depth of feeling for her.

She looked away, shaken by how, after all these years, he could still needle her, and chastising herself for speaking so freely with him tonight. No matter how easy it was to tease and flirt with him as she used to, she couldn't afford to be bold with a man like him. It might ruin her.

'Mrs Thompson, I hear you've been living in America,' a woman's distant voice intruded, snapping Cecelia's attention back to the circle of ladies.

'Yes. I have a plantation in Virginia.' Her stomach tightened with the lie.

'What brings you and Miss Fields back to London after all this time?' Lady Weatherly asked.

Cecelia met their curious looks, the same awkwardness that nearly stole her tongue the night Daniel had presented her to the Richmond families at the Governor's ball stealing over her. She squared her shoulders now as she had then, defiant against her unease and their scrutiny. 'I brought my cousin back to London in the hope of seeing her settled.'

'Did she not have suitors in Virginia?' Lady Weatherly pressed like a small terrier determined to dig out a rat and Cecelia bit back the desire to tell the Countess to keep to her own affairs. Despite a dubious reputation, the statuesque young woman draped in gauzy silk was a fixture of society whose good opinion Cecelia needed to keep. Swallowing her pride, Cecelia repeated the story she and Theresa had practised during the crossing.

'She did, but when the British burned Washington, we were no longer warmly received, despite having known many of the families for years. It wasn't suitable for her to look for suitors under such hostile circumstances. When I suggested a Season in London, she was thrilled with the chance to come home.'

'Speaking of gentlemen—' Lady Weatherly waved away her interest in Cecelia with one gloved hand '—here is Lord Strathmore.'

'Good evening ladies.' Lord Strathmore bowed before fixing Cecelia with a smile more snakelike than charming. 'Mrs Thompson, would you care to join me for some refreshment?'

'Thank you, but I have no appetite tonight.' His smile faltered and she widened hers. She didn't relish the Earl's company, but it would prove less irksome than Lady Weatherly's questions. 'If you'd care to escort me to the pianoforte, I'd like to see how my cousin is faring.'

'It would be my pleasure.'

As she and Lord Strathmore crossed the room, she hazarded a glance at Randall, startled by the glare he fixed on Lord Strathmore. As fast as the look came it was gone and he turned back to the man next to him and resumed his conversation.

Cecelia wondered what about the man raised Randall's hackles. Lord Strathmore had no reputation she could discern, or none Madame de Badeau had seen fit to reveal, and the woman delighted in revealing a great many things about a number of people.

'May I be so bold as to say how radiant you look tonight?' Lord Strathmore complimented, his serpentlike smile returning to draw up the small bit of skin beneath his round chin.

'You're too generous.' She untwisted the strap of her fan, shaking off the strange reaction to his look. With so many things worrying her, she must only be seeing trouble where none existed.

'Madame de Badeau tells me you have no horse in London at your disposal.'

'No. I had to leave my beautiful horse in Virginia.' Anger burned through her at the thought of the stables, Daniel's stables, the ones he'd worked so hard to establish, now under the control of her selfish stepson Paul.

'It'd be my pleasure to accompany you and your cousin in Rotten Row. I keep a few geldings in London suitable for ladies to ride.'

'You're most kind.' The idea of riding properly in Rotten Row beside Lord Strathmore dampened her enthusiasm. However, borrowing horses from his stable would spare her the expense of hiring them and allow her and Theresa to be seen during the fashionable hour.

Cecelia stepped up to the pianoforte and touched Theresa's elbow. Her cousin turned, frowning at Lord Strathmore, and Cecelia shot her a warning look. In their present situation, Cecelia didn't have the luxury to refuse any man's attention. Except Randall's.

Only then did she notice the absence of his voice beneath the melody of the pianoforte. She glanced around the room, expecting to meet his silent stare, but saw nothing except the other guests mingling. Relief filled her, followed by disappointment. He was gone, his conversation and interest in her as finished tonight as it was ten years ago. Yet something about their exchange continued to trouble her. Beneath Randall's rakish smile and desire to capture her notice, she'd sensed something else, something all too familiar. Pain.

Polite applause marked the end of Miss Domville's piece and Cecelia clapped along with the two young men standing on the other side of the instrument.

'Play again, Miss Domville,' Lord Bolton, the taller of the two, urged. 'We so enjoy your fingerwork.'

Instead of blushing, Miss Domville rose and coolly lowered the cover on the keys.

'I'm afraid you'll have to make do with your own fingerwork for the rest of the evening,' she answered in a sweet voice before coming around the piano and taking Theresa by the arm. 'Miss Fields and I are going to take a turn around the room so we may discuss all of you in private. May we, Mrs Thompson?'

Cecelia studied Miss Domville, debating the wisdom of letting Theresa associate with such a bold young woman. However, Miss Domville's sense of confidence and the gentlemen's sudden notice of Theresa overcame her doubts. 'Of course.'

'Wonderful. We'll discuss how much we dislike London.' Miss Domville led Theresa away, chatting merrily, and Cecelia noticed the genuine enjoyment spreading over her cousin's face.

If only all our worries could be so easily soothed.

Lord Strathmore lingered beside her and she struggled to ignore her discomfort as she faced him. 'Tell me about your horses.'

He spoke more to her bosom than her face as he launched into a droll description of his stables. She forced herself to appear impressed, rubbing the gold bracelet again and hating this act. Speaking with him was like stepping up on the bidding block to be inspected by the first man who showed a modicum of interest in her. It made her feel cheap and deceitful, but what choice did she have?

The memory of Randall's hooded eyes teasing her sent a wave of heat across her skin and her fingers stopped.

Yes, there was another option, the same one General LaFette had suggested when he'd cornered her at the Governor's picnic, eyeing her breasts the way Lord Strathmore did now, but she refused to entertain it. She hadn't scorned one man's offer only to take up another's. She wasn't so desperate, at least not yet.

Chapter Two

'Good evening, my lord,' Mr Joshua, the wiry young valet, greeted as Randall entered his bedroom. 'You're in early tonight.'

'So it seems.' Randall stood still while Mr Joshua removed his coat, the skin along the back of his neck tightening as a chill deeper than the cool night air crossed him. He moved closer to the marble fireplace, the warmth of it doing little to ease the lingering tightness from his encounter with Cecelia.

She was back, the wealth and confidence of her experiences in Virginia circling her like her perfume, making her more beautiful then when she'd stood before him as a young girl with the weight of sorrow on her shoulders.

It seemed marriage had benefited her.

He grabbed the poker from the stand and banged it against the coals, trying to ignite the heat smouldering in their centres. A splash of sparks jumped in the grate, followed by a few large flames.

He didn't doubt she'd benefited from the marriage. She'd practically rushed at the colonial after Aunt Ella made the introduction, fleeing from Randall and England as fast as the ship could carry her.

She'd escaped her troubles, and left Randall behind to be tortured by his.

He returned the poker to the stand, his anger dying down like the flames.

After everything that had passed between them, when he'd been foolish enough tonight to show weakness, she hadn't belittled him. Instead she'd displayed an understanding he hadn't experienced since coming to London. Considering the way they'd parted, it was much more than he deserved.

The squeak of hinges broke the quiet and the bedroom door opened.

'Hello, Reverend.' Randall dropped to one knee and held out his arms.

The black hunting dog ran to him, his long tongue lolling out one side of his mouth. Randall rubbed Reverend's back and the dog's head stretched up to reveal the wide band of white fur under his neck. 'And where have you been?'

'Probably in the kitchen hunting for scraps again,' Mr Joshua answered for the dog while he brushed out Randall's coat.

'I'll hear about it from cook tomorrow.' Randall scratched behind the dog's ears, the familiar action soothing away the old regrets and torments.

'A message arrived while you were gone.' Mr Joshua held out a rose-scented note, a cheeky smile on his young face. 'It seems Lady Weatherly is eager to renew last Season's acquaintance.'

Randall's calm disappeared. He stood and took the note, skimming the contents, the sentiments as trite as the perfume clinging to the envelope.

'Good dalliance, that one. Obliging old husband with more interest in the actresses of Drury Lane than his wife,' Mr Joshua observed with his usual candour. No one else in London was as honest with Randall as the valet. Randall had encouraged it from the beginning when he'd taken the labourer's son into his service and saved his family from ruin. 'Lord Weatherly isn't likely to object to your lordship's continued acquaintance with his wife.'

'Yes, but I've had enough of Lady Weatherly.' Randall tossed the paper in the grate. 'If she calls again, tell her I'm engaged.'

'Yes, my lord.'

Randall leaned against the mantel, watching the letter curl and blacken. He dropped one hand to his side and Reverend slid his head beneath it. Randall rubbed the dog behind his ears, despising Lady Weatherly and all those of her ilk. They never flattered him without an eye to what they could gain. Yet he tolerated them, enjoyed what they eagerly gave because they demanded nothing more of him than the esteem of being his lover.

The image of Cecelia danced before him, her lively voice ringing in his ears. She'd entered Lady Weatherly's salon, a butterfly amid too many moths, standing alone in her beauty while the rest flapped around the candles. She didn't need light, it was in her eyes, her smile, the melody of her voice, just as it was ten years ago. Her responses to his amorous suggestions were playful and daring, but tinged with an innocence women like Madame de Badeau and Lady Weatherly had abandoned long ago. He grieved to think what London might do to her. What had it done to him? Nothing he hadn't wholeheartedly embraced from his first day in town. Nothing his father hadn't feared he'd do.

You're as bad as your uncle, his father's deep voice bellowed through the quiet, and the faint scar on his back from where his father's belt used to strike him began to itch.

Randall closed his eyes, seeing again his father waiting for him in the vicarage sitting room, the darkness of the window behind him broken by small drops of rain flickering with the firelight.

You think your Uncle Edmund has all the answers, but he hasn't, his father sneered from his chair. *All his wine and women, they're only to fill the emptiness of his life. You can't see it now, but some day you will, when your own life is as hollow as his.*

At least he accepts me, Randall spat, his uncle's port giving him courage, anger giving him words. Reverend stood next to him, the puppy's tense body pressed against his leg.

I'm hard on you for your own good. He slammed his fist against the chair, then gripped the arm as a raspy cough racked his body. He stood, his skin ashen, and he closed his eyes, drawing in a few ragged breaths as he steadied himself.

Randall braced himself for the usual onslaught of insults, but when his father opened his eyes they were soft with a concern Randall had only experienced a handful of times, yet every day craved. *I want you to be more of a man than Edmund. I want to know your mother's death to bring you into this world was worth it.*

His father's eyes drifted to the portrait of Randall's mother hanging across the room, the concern replaced by the constant sadness Randall loathed, the one which always pulled his father away. Randall tightened his hands at his side, wanting to rip the portrait from the wall and fling it in the fire. *Why? No matter what I do, it's never enough for you.*

And what do you do? Drink with your uncle without a thought for me. His father's face hardened with disgust. *You're selfish, that's what you are, only ever thinking of yourself and your future riches instead of being here and tending to the vicarage like a proper son.*

Randall dropped his hand on Reverend's head, anger seething inside him. He'd obeyed his father for years, taken every insult heaped on him and more, thinking one day the old man would look at him with the same affection he saved for the portrait, but he hadn't, and tonight Randall realised he never would. *I'm not staying here any longer. Uncle Edmund has invited me to live at the manor. I'm going there and I'm not coming back.*

You think because you'll be a Marquess some day, you're too good for a simple vicarage. Well, you're not. His father snatched the poker from the fireplace and Randall took a step back. *You think I don't know how you and my brother laugh at me, how you mocked me when you named that wretched dog he gave you.*

He levelled the poker at Reverend and a low growl rolled through the gangly puppy.

Well, no more, his father spat. *You killed the one person I loved most in this world, then turned my brother and sister against me. You have no idea how it feels to lose so much, but you will when I take away something you love.* He focused on Reverend and raised the poker over his head.

No! Randall rushed at his father, catching the poker just as his father brought it down, the hard metal slamming into his palm and sending a bolt of pain through his shoulder. He tried to wrench the iron from his father's hand, but the old man held on tight, fighting with a strength fuelled by hate. Reverend's sharp barks pierced the room as Randall shoved his father against the wall, his other arm across his chest, pinning him like a wild animal until his father's fingers finally opened and the poker clattered to the floor.

I hate you. You killed her, he hissed before the deep lines of his face softened, his jaw sagged open and his body slumped forward on to Randall's chest.

Randall struggled to hold his father's limp weight as he lowered him to the floor, then knelt next to him, panic replacing his anger as he patted his face, trying to rouse him. *Father? Father?*

A faint gurgle filled his father's throat before his eyes focused on Randall's. Reverend whimpered behind him, as if he, too, sensed what was coming.

Father, forgive me, Randall pleaded.

You aren't worthy— he slurred before his head dropped forward and he slumped to the side.

The room went quiet, punctuated by the crackling of the fire and Reverend's panting.

Randall rose, stumbling backwards before gripping a table to steady himself. Reverend came to sit beside him and he dropped his hand on the dog's soft head. *I didn't mean to hurt him, I didn't mean to—* kill him.

A gust of wind blew a fury of raindrops against the window, startling Randall. He couldn't stay here. He had to get help, to tell Aunt Ella and Uncle Edmund.

The poker lay on the floor next to the wrinkled edge of the rug. With a trembling hand, he picked it up and returned it to the holder. With the toe of one boot, he straightened the rug, careful not to look at the dark figure near the white wall. Then he turned and left, Reverend trotting beside him out into the icy rain.

* * *

Randall opened his eyes and knelt down next to Reverend, rubbing the dog's back, struggling to calm the guilt tearing through him. He'd walked through the freezing rain back to the manor, then stood dripping and shivering as he'd told Aunt Ella he'd come home to find his father collapsed. The doctor had said it was his father's heart that had killed him. Randall had never told anyone the truth, except Cecelia.

His hands stopped rubbing Reverend and the dog licked his fingers, eager for more. Randall noticed with a twinge of sadness the grey fur around Reverend's black muzzle. 'I wonder if you'd remember her.'

'Did you say something, my lord?' Mr Joshua asked.

'No, nothing.'

The small clock on the side table chimed a quarter past twelve.

'Will you be going out again tonight, my lord?'

'Perhaps.' Randall stood, shaking off the memories, but the old emotions hovered around him, faint and fading like the waking end of a dream: vulnerability, uncertainty, innocence, regret. In the end, he'd driven Cecelia away, too horrified by what he'd done to keep close the one person who knew his secret. His father had never forgiven him. Would Cecelia have forgiven him back then? He'd never had the courage to ask her.

'Keeping such hours, society will think you've gone respectable,' Mr Joshua joked, 'then every matron with a marriageable daughter will be here at the door. I'll have so many cards stacked up we won't need kindling all winter.'

Randall frowned, hearing the truth in his jest. No, he wasn't going to spend the night wallowing in the past like his father used to do. Those days were far behind

him, just like his relationship with Cecelia. At the end
of that summer, they'd both made their choices. He refused to regret his.

'I'm going to my club.' He patted Reverend, then
flicked his hand at the bed. 'Up you go.'

The dog jumped up on the wide bed, turning around
before settling into the thick coverlet, watching as Mr
Joshua helped Randall on with his coat.

Randall straightened the cravat in the mirror, then
headed for the door. 'Don't expect me back until morning.'

Cecelia sat in the turned-wood chair next to the small
fireplace in her bedroom, staring at the dark fireback.
Still dressed in her evening clothes, she shivered, having forgotten how cold London could be even in the
spring, but she didn't burn any coal. She couldn't afford it.

She closed her eyes and thought of the warm Virginia
nights heavy with moisture, the memory of the cicadas'
songs briefly drowning out the clop of carriage horses
on the street outside.

The sound drew her back to Lady Weatherly's and
the sight of Randall approaching from across the salon.
He'd moved like the steady current of the James River,
every step threatening to shatter her calm like a tidal
surge driven inland by a hurricane. She'd known he'd
be there tonight. Madame de Badeau had mentioned
it yesterday, leaving Cecelia to imagine scenario after
scenario of how they might meet. Not once did she picture his blue eyes tempting her with the same desire she
used to catch in the shadowed hallways of Falconbridge
Manor. Back then every kiss was stolen, each moment
of pleasure fumbling and uncertain.

There was nothing uncertain about Randall tonight, only a strength emphasised by his broad shoulders and the height he'd gained since she'd last seen him. Her body hummed with the memory of him standing so close, his musky cologne and hot breath tempting her more than his innuendoes and illicit suggestions. Yet she'd caught something else hovering in the tension beneath his heated look—a frail connection she wanted to touch and hold.

She opened her eyes and smacked her hand hard against the chair's arm, the sting bringing her back to her senses. There'd never been a connection between them, only the daydreams of a girl too naive to realise a future Marquess would never lower himself to save her. He hadn't then and, with all his wealth and privilege, he certainly wouldn't now, no matter how many tempting suggestions he threw her way. No, he would be among the first to laugh and sneer if the truth of her situation was ever revealed, and if she could help it, it never would be.

She slid off the chair and knelt before the small trunk sitting at the end of the narrow bed, her mother's trunk, the only piece of furniture she'd brought back to London. The hinges squeaked as she pushed opened the lid, the metal having suffered the ill effects of sea air on the voyage from Virginia. Inside sat a bolt of fabric, a jumble of tarnished silver, a small box of jewellery and a stack of books. It was the sum of her old possessions and the few items of value she'd managed to secrete from Belle View after Paul had taken control. They sat in the trunk like a skeleton in its coffin, reminding her of everything she'd ever lost. For a brief moment, she wished the whole lot had fallen overboard, but she needed them and the money they could bring.

She pushed aside the silver, the metal clanking as she lifted out one large book on hunting from beneath a stack of smaller ones. It had been Daniel's favourite and the only one she'd taken for sentimental reasons. She opened it and, with a gloved finger, traced a beautiful watercolour of a duck in flight, remembering how Daniel used to sit in his study, his brown hair flecked with grey falling over his forehead as he examined each picture.

Guilt edged her grief. In the end, this book would probably have to be sold, too.

She snapped it shut and laid it in the trunk next to the velvet case that had once held the gold bracelet she wore. It had been a gift from her father, given to her the Christmas before his ship had sunk off the coast of Calais, taking with it his life and the merchandise he'd needed to revive his business. Moving aside the silk, she caught sight of the small walnut box in the corner. She reached for it, then pulled back, unable to open it and look at the wispy curl, the precious reminder of her sweet baby boy.

Squeezing her eyes tight against the sudden rush of tears, she fought back the sob rising in her throat and burning her chest with grief. Her hands tightened on the edges of the trunk, the weave of her silk gloves digging into her fingertips. Loss, always loss. Her father, her mother, her infant son, Daniel… Would it never end?

She pounded one fist against the open trunk lid, then sat back on her heels, drawing in breath after breath, her body shaking with the effort to stop the tears.

Why did she have to suffer when people like Randall found peace? Why?

A knock made her straighten and she rubbed her wet face with her hands as the bedroom door opened.

Theresa appeared, a wrapper pulled tight around her nightdress. 'I heard a noise. Are you all right?'

'I'm fine.' She looked away, trying to hide her tears, but Theresa saw them.

'You aren't missing Daniel, are you?' The girl knelt next to her and threw her arms around Cecelia.

'No, I'm angry with him.' Cecelia pulled herself to her feet, not wanting anyone's pity or comfort tonight, not even Theresa's. 'When he recovered from the fever eight years ago, I asked him, begged him to write his will, to provide for me, not leave me at the mercy of Paul, but he wouldn't. All his superstitions about making a will inviting death, his always putting it off until next month, next year until it was too late. Now, we're lost.'

'We aren't lost yet.'

'Aren't we?' She slammed the lid down on the trunk. 'You saw everyone tonight, treating us like nothing more than colonial curiosities. How they'll laugh when the money runs out, scorn us the way Paul did when he evicted us from Belle View and refused to pay my widow's portion. Not one of them will care if we starve.'

Theresa fingered the wrapper sash. 'I think one person will care.'

'You mean Lord Strathmore?' Cecelia pulled off the damp gloves and tossed them on the dressing table. 'It seems I can attract nothing but men like him and General LaFette.'

'I didn't mean Lord Strathmore. I meant Lord Falconbridge.'

Cecelia gaped at Theresa. The memory of Randall standing so close, his mouth tight as he spoke of the difficulties of life flashed before her. Then anger shattered the image. She shouldn't have bothered to comfort him.

He wouldn't have done the same for her. 'I assure you, he'll be the first to laugh at us.'

'I don't believe it. I saw the way he watched you tonight. Miss Domville did, too. She said he's never looked at a woman the way he looked at you.'

'I hardly think Miss Domville is an expert on Lord Falconbridge.' Cecelia crossed her arms, more against the flutter in her chest than the ridiculous turn of the conversation. 'And be careful what you tell her. We can't have anyone knowing our situation, especially not Madame de Badeau.'

For all the Frenchwoman's friendliness, Cecelia wondered if the lady's offer to introduce Cecelia and Theresa to society had an ulterior motive, though what, she couldn't imagine.

'I don't like her and I don't like Lord Strathmore.' Theresa wrinkled her nose. 'He's worse than General LaFette. Always staring at your breasts.'

'Yet he's the man we may have to rely on to save us.' She paced the room, the weight of their lot dragging on her like the train of her dress over the threadbare rug. She stopped at the window, moving aside the curtain to watch the dark street below. 'Maybe I should have accepted General LaFette's offer. At least then we could have stayed in Virginia.'

'I'd starve before I'd let you sell yourself to a man like him,' Theresa proclaimed.

Cecelia whirled on her cousin. 'Why? Didn't I sell myself once before to keep out of the gutter?'

'But you loved Daniel, didn't you?' Theresa looked stricken, just as she had the morning Cecelia and Daniel had met the newly orphaned girl at the Yorktown docks, her parents, Cecelia's second cousins, having perished on the crossing.

Cecelia wanted to lie and soothe her cousin's fears, allow her to hold on to this one steady thing after almost two years of so much change, but she couldn't. She'd always been honest with the girl who was like a daughter to her and she couldn't deceive her now.

'Not at first,' she admitted, ashamed of the motives which drove her to accept the stammering proposal of a widower twenty years older than her with a grown son and all his lands half a world away. 'The love came later.'

Yet for all her tying herself to a stranger to keep from starving, here she was again, no better now than she'd been the summer before she'd married. Even Randall had reappeared to taunt her and remind her of all her failings.

She dropped down on the lumpy cushion in the window seat, anger giving way to the despair she'd felt so many times since last spring when General LaFette had begun spreading his vicious rumours. The old French General had asked her to be his mistress. When she'd refused, he'd ruined her with his lies. How easily the other plantation families had believed him, but she'd made the mistake of never really getting to know them. Belle View was too far from all the others to make visiting convenient, and though Daniel was sociable, too many times he'd preferred the quiet of home to parties and Williamsburg society.

'Now I understand why Mother gave up after Father died.' She sighed, staring down at the dark cobblestone street. 'I had to deal with the creditors then, too, handing them the silver and whatever else I could find just so we could live. I used to hide it from her, though I don't know why. She never noticed. I don't even think she cared.'

'She must have.' Theresa joined her on the thin cushion, taking one of her cold hands in her warm one.

'Which is why she sent me to Lady Ellington's?'

'Perhaps she didn't want you to see her suffer.'

'No. I think all my pestering her to deal with the creditors bothered her more than the consumption. The peace must have been a relief when she sent me away.' Cecelia could only imagine how welcome the silence of death must have been.

Theresa squeezed her hand. 'Please don't give up. I don't know what I'd do if you lost hope.'

Cecelia wrapped her arms around her cousin, trying to soothe away all her fears and concerns the way she wished her mother had done for her, the way her father used to do.

'No, I won't, I promise.' She couldn't give up. She had to persevere just as Daniel had taught her to do when his final illness had begun and she'd had to run Belle View, to pick up and carry on the way her father used to after every blow to his business. 'You're right, all isn't lost yet. We'll find a way.'

We have no choice.

Randall sat back, his cards face down under his palm on the table. Across from him, Lord Westbrook hunched over his cards, his signet ring turning on his shaking hand. A footman placed a glass of wine on the table in front of the young man and he picked it up, the liquid sloshing in the glass as he raised it to his lips.

Randall reached across the table and grasped the man's arm. 'No. You will do this sober.'

Lord Westbrook swallowed hard, eyeing the wine before lowering it to the table. Randall sat back, flicking the edges of the cards, ignoring the murmuring crowd circling them and betting on the outcome. In the centre of the table sat a hastily scribbled note resting on a pile of coins. Lord Westbrook's hands shook as he fingered his cards and Randall almost took pity on him. If this game were not the focus of the entire room, he might have spared the youth this beating. Now, he had no choice but to let the game play to its obvious conclusion.

'Show your cards,' Randall demanded.

Lord Westbrook looked up, panic draining the colour from his face. With trembling fingers he laid out the cards one by one, leaving them in an uneven row. It was a good hand, but not good enough.

Randall turned over his cards, spreading them out in an even row, and a loud cheer went up from the crowd.

Lord Westbrook put his elbows on the table and grasped the side of his head, pulling at his blond hair. Randall stood and, ignoring the coins, picked up the piece of paper. Lord Westbrook's face snapped up, his eyes meeting Randall's, and for a brief second Randall saw his own face, the one which used to stare back at him from every mirror during his first year in London.

'I've always wanted a house in Surrey,' Randall tossed off with a disdain he didn't feel, then slid the note in his pocket. 'Come to my house next week to discuss the terms.'

Turning on his heel, he left the room, shaking off the many hands reaching out to congratulate him.

Chapter Three

Cecelia shifted the white Greek-style robe on her shoulders, the wood pedestal beneath her biting into the back of her thighs, the sharp odour of oil paints nearly smothering her as she struggled to maintain her pose. Pushing the wreath of flowers off her forehead for the third time in as many minutes, she sighed, wondering how she'd ended up in Sir Thomas Lawrence's studio in this ridiculous position.

'Lord Strathmore was right. You make the perfect Persephone,' Madame de Badeau complimented from beside the dais, as if answering Cecelia's silent question.

Cecelia shifted the bouquet in her hands, feeling more like a trollop than a goddess. Lord Strathmore wanted a painting of Persephone to complement one he already possessed of Demeter. Madame de Badeau had convinced Cecelia to pose, all the while hinting at Lord Strathmore's interest in her. If it weren't for the need to maintain his interest, Cecelia never would have agreed to this ridiculous request.

Her spirit drooped like the flowers in her hand, the weariness of having to entertain a man's affection out of necessity instead of love weighing on her. Thankfully, business prevented Lord Strathmore from accompanying them today and deepening her humiliation.

'Have you heard the latest gossip concerning Lord Falconbridge?' Madame de Badeau asked, as if to remind Cecelia of how her last affair of the heart had ended.

'No, I have not.' Nor did she want to. She'd experienced enough cruel gossip in Virginia to make her sick whenever she heard people delighting in it here.

'Lord Falconbridge won Lord Westbrook's entire fortune. Absolutely ruined the gentleman. Isn't it grand?' She clapped her hands together like a child excited over a box of sweets.

'What?' Cecelia turned to face Madame de Badeau and the wreath tumbled from her head.

'Mrs Thompson, your pose.' Sir Thomas hurried from behind his easel to scoop up the wilting wreath and hand it to her.

She repositioned it on her head, her hand shaking with the same anger she'd known the morning Paul had turned them out of Belle View. 'How could Lord Falconbridge do such a thing?'

'My dear, he prides himself on it.' The smile curling Madame de Badeau's lips made Cecelia's stomach churn. 'The losses aren't the worst of Lord Westbrook's problems. Now that he's penniless, the family of his intended has forbidden the match.'

Cecelia's fingers tightened so hard on the bouquet, one flower snapped and bent over on its broken stem. She more than anyone knew the hardships Lord Westbrook now faced. 'Surely Lord Falconbridge must know.'

'Of course he does. All society knows. I think it most fortunate. Now Lord Westbrook will have to marry for money instead of love. I abhor love matches. They are so gauche.'

As Madame de Badeau launched into a description of the now-infamous card game, Cecelia fought the desire to rise and dismiss her. If she didn't need Madame de Badeau's connections in society, she'd have nothing to do with the shallow woman. Despite being an old friend of her mother's, Cecelia sensed the Frenchwoman would gladly push her into poverty if only to provide a few witty stories for the guests at her next card party.

Cecelia thought again of Lady Ellington and all the unfinished letters she'd drafted to her since returning to London. The sweet woman had been such a comfort ten years ago, listening while Cecelia poured out her heartbreak over losing her father, her mother's illness and, in the end, Randall's rejection. The Dowager Countess was the only other connection she still possessed in England, though it was a tenuous one. They hadn't exchanged letters in over eight years.

Cecelia shifted again on the dais, pulling the robe tight against the cold grief which had ended the correspondence. During her first two years at Belle View, she'd sent the Countess so many letters filled with the details of her life, from surveying her own fields to dining with the Governor. She'd written each with the hope the lady might share them with Randall and show him how far the 'poor merchant's daughter' had come.

Then, after the loss of her little boy and the near loss of Daniel to the fever, all her girlish desires to impress someone half a world away had vanished.

Stinging tears filled her eyes and she blinked them back, determined not to cry in front of Madame de Badeau and risk the woman's mocking laughter. Like her heartache, the sense of isolation from anyone of decency sat hard on Cecelia's chest. She pressed her thumb into one of the thorns on the stem, forcing down the encroaching despair. She would not fail, nor give up on Theresa the way her mother had given up on her. The Season was still young. They would make new friends and meet the man who'd save them before the truth of their situation became impossible to conceal.

'Madame de Badeau, I'm surprised to see you here. I didn't think you a patron of the arts,' a familiar voice called out from behind her.

Cecelia's back stiffened with a strange mixture of excitement and anger and the sudden movement made the garland tumble to the floor.

'Hello, Mrs Thompson.' Randall came to stand in front of the dais, towering over her, his tan pants covering his long legs while one hand grasped the silver head of his ebony walking stick. His other hand rested on his hip, pushing back his dark coat to show the grey waistcoat hugging the trim waist underneath. With an amused look he took in her draping-goddess dress and the basket of fruit at her bare feet.

'Lord Falconbridge,' she greeted through clenched teeth, annoyed at having to face the man whom, at the moment, she very much detested.

He bent down to pick up the garland, his hot breath caressing the tops of her toes and making her skin pebble with goose bumps. 'I've never thought of you as a muse.'

She pulled her feet back under the robe. 'You haven't thought of me at all.'

'Oh, I have, many times.' His beguiling eyes pinned hers and she shivered. 'But more as an adventurous Amazon in the wilds of America.'

He held out the wreath, the simple gesture more

an invitation to forget herself than a desire to aid the painter.

She snatched it from his hands and pushed it down on her head. 'How flattering.'

Randall straightened and for a brief moment appeared puzzled, as though surprised by the edge in her words. He quickly recovered himself, tossing her a scoundrel's wink before strolling off to stand behind the easel.

'I heard the most delicious news about you,' Madame de Badeau congratulated, her wicked cheer grating. 'You must tell me all about the game with Lord Westbrook.'

'The subject bores me and I'm sure you already know the most interesting parts.' Randall watched Sir Thomas work, irritation sharpening the lines of his face.

Cecelia wondered at his reaction. She expected him to boast about his win over Lord Westbrook, or revel in Madame de Badeau's praise, not dismiss it as if he weren't proud of what he'd done.

'Then you're the only one.' Madame de Badeau sniffed. She wandered to the tall windows and peeked through a crack in one of the shutters covering the bottom and shielding Cecelia from the people passing outside. 'Ah, there is Lady Thornton. I must have a word with her. Lord Falconbridge, please keep Mrs Thompson entertained until I return.'

His hot eyes pinned Cecelia's. 'It would be my pleasure.'

'I don't need company.' Cecelia fixed her attention on a small crack in the plaster on the far wall, trying to avoid Randall's suggestive look.

'Tilt your head a little to the left, Mrs Thompson,' Sir Thomas instructed and she obliged. Randall continued to study the portrait and Cecelia, but said nothing. Only the sound of the painter's pencil sketching across the canvas, combined with the muffled clack of passing coaches outside, filled the room.

'I have not seen the likeness yet,' Cecelia remarked, the quiet making her restless. 'Tell me, Lord Falconbridge, is it favourable?'

'Hmm.' He stepped back to examine the portrait and the subject. 'It's an excellent likeness. My compliments to the artist. However, the original is still more stunning.'

Cecelia arched one disbelieving eyebrow at him. 'Thank you, my lord, but be warned, I won't succumb to such obvious flattery.'

'It's the truth.' His soft protest was like a caress and her heart ached to believe him, to know again what it was like to be valued by a man, not sought after like some prized cow.

She adjusted one hairpin at the back of her head, unwilling to believe that a man who'd bedded a number of society women possessed any real interest in her. 'Tell me, Sir Thomas, how many times have you heard such compliments made in your presence?'

'Many times,' the painter chuckled. 'But Lord Falconbridge's are the most sincere.'

'There you have it,' Randall boasted. 'I'm not lying.'

'Or you're simply better at it than most.'

They fell silent and the sketching continued until Randall said something to the painter in a low voice. She strained to hear, but the laughter of two men on the street muffled the words. Then, Sir Thomas rose from his stool.

'If his lordship and the lady will excuse me, I need another pencil. I shall return in a moment.'

'Don't hurry on our account,' Randall called after him.

'You asked him to leave, didn't you?' Cecelia accused, wary of being left alone with him.

'You really think I'd stoop so low?' He came closer to the dais, moving with the grace of a water snake through a lake in Virginia.

She struggled to remain seated, eager to place the distance of the room between them as he rested one elbow on the half-Corinthian column beside her. 'Based on the gossip I hear attached to your name, it seems you're fond of ruining people.'

He dropped his chin on his palm, bringing his arrogant smirk so close, all she needed to do was lean in to feel his mouth against hers. 'You think a moment alone with me will ruin you?'

She glanced at his lips, wondering if they were as firm as she remembered. 'It's possible.'

'I shouldn't worry.' His breath brushed her exposed shoulders and slid down the space between her breasts. 'Sir Thomas is a very discreet man.'

Neither of them moved to close the distance, but she felt him waiting, expecting her to weaken under the strength of his charm and throw herself at him like Lady Weatherly and heaven knew how many others. She wouldn't give him the satisfaction of meeting his expectation.

'You, however, enjoy boasting of your conquests.' She leaned away and Randall jerked up straight.

'You're truly mad at me?'

'Why shouldn't I be?'

'Why should you be?'

'Because you ruined Lord Westbrook.'

'Lord Westbrook?' He had the audacity to look surprised before a scowl replaced the suggestive smile of only a moment before. 'What interest do you have in him?'

'None, but I can sympathise with his plight, something you're obviously incapable of doing.'

'How can a rich widow sympathise?'

Cecelia looked down, pulling the cloak closer around her shoulders. Her situation was already precarious. She needn't arouse suspicion by showing so much emotion. 'Whether I can sympathise or not doesn't matter. What you did to him is still wrong.'

'Is it?' Randall paced the studio, swinging his walking stick in time with his steps. 'Lord Westbrook is a man with responsibilities and capable of deciding whether or not to risk his future at the gaming table. You should be happy it was I who played him. Others wouldn't have been so kind.'

'You believe ruining him is kind?'

He halted, jabbing his stick into the floor. 'I haven't ridden to his estate and turned him out as I assure you is quite common. Nor have I forced him to the moneylenders and outrageous terms.'

'Yes, he's very fortunate indeed. It's a wonder people don't speak more favourably of you when you're obviously such a generous gentleman.'

A muscle in his jaw twitched and shame flashed through his eyes before he looked away. For a moment she felt sorry for him. She'd seen this expression once before, ten years ago, when they'd stood together under the large ash tree at Falconbridge Manor, the shadows shifting over his father's plain headstone. Like then, the look didn't last, but fled from his eyes as fast as he'd fled back up the lawn, hard arrogance stiffening his jaw.

Footsteps sounded in the hall outside the studio.

'Sir Thomas is returning,' Randall announced, moving to examine a large landscape near the window, his back to her as Sir Thomas's footsteps grew louder. He stood still except for his fingers. They toyed with the walking-stick handle, betraying a certain agitation, as if her words had struck a chord. Did he feel some guilt over what he'd done to Lord Westbrook? No, surely it was only the shock of being dressed down by a lady, something she was sure he rarely experienced.

'Are you ready to continue?' Sir Thomas asked, taking his place behind the easel.

'Yes, please.' Cecelia resumed her pose just as the curtain flew open and Madame de Badeau swept into the room.

'You won't believe what Lady Thornton just told me. Lord Falconbridge, you'll think it sinfully good when you hear it.'

'I'm sure, but for the moment, you'll have to entertain Mrs Thompson with the story. I have business to attend to.' He snapped his walking stick up under his arm and made for the door.

'What a bore you are,' Madame de Badeau chided, then turned to Cecelia. 'My dear, wait until you hear what's happened to Lord Byron.'

Randall barely heard two words of Madame de Badeau's gossip as he stormed from the room, catching Cecelia's reflection in the mirror near the door, disapproval hard in her eyes before she looked away.

He passed through the dark shop and out into the sunlit street beyond, tapping his walking stick in time with his steps.

He hadn't expected to meet her in the studio today, especially not in a silky robe wrapped tight around her narrow waist, exposing the curve of her hips and breasts and making him forget all business with the painter. Once together, he hadn't been able to resist tempting her with a few words, or trying to draw out the alluring woman who'd met his daring innuendoes at Lady Weatherly's. Who knew his efforts would be rewarded with a reprimand?

Randall sidestepped two men arguing on the pavement, a crate of foul-smelling vegetables smashed on the ground between them.

Who was she to chastise him? What did she know of London habits? Nothing. She'd spent the past ten years among provincials, cavorting with heathens and who-knew-what society. Now she seemed to think it her duty to shame him the way his father used to

He slammed his walking stick against the ground, the vibration shooting up his arm.

Why didn't she stay in America?

Instead she'd returned to London, dredging up old memories like some mudlark digging for scraps along the Thames, determined to berate him like some nursemaid. She was mistaken if she thought she could scold him with a look, or if her chiding words meant anything to him. He wasn't about to change because of her or anyone else's disapproval.

He swatted a tomato with his walking stick, sending it rolling into the gutter, trying to ignore the other, more dangerous feeling dogging his anger. He'd caught it at the salon the other night and again today when he'd complimented her and for a brief moment she'd almost believed him. It was the faint echo of the affection they'd once enjoyed. Whatever she thought of his behaviour, somewhere deep beneath it, she felt the old connection, too.

He turned a corner into a square of fine houses, trying to concentrate on the bright sun bouncing off the stone buildings and the steady clop of horses in the street, but his thoughts remained stubbornly fixed on Cecelia.

His anger changed to interest as he walked, twirling his stick. He'd ached to trace the line of her shoulders with his fingers, push back the tumble of brown hair sweeping her neck and draw her red lips to his. Even angry she was beautiful and he wanted her, more than he'd ever wanted any woman before.

His pace slowed and he trailed his walking stick along the wrought-iron fences surrounding the houses, the quick clicks echoing off the buildings.

What weakness kept bringing him back to Cecelia? He'd enjoyed and left a number of women over the years without regret. Why couldn't he forget her?

Because at one time, he'd loved her.

He stopped, his walking stick pausing against the metal before he snapped it up under his arm.

Love, he snorted, resuming his walk. This had nothing to do with love or any other ridiculous sentiment, but the excitement of a challenge. There wasn't a woman he'd known who hadn't thrown herself at him once he made his interest clear. Until today. He'd nearly forgotten the excitement of the pursuit and the pleasure of the capture.

Despite Cecelia's caustic words, he'd caught the flashes of desire his suggestions brought to her eyes and how her parted lips practically begged for his kiss. He recognised her reprimand for what it was—an obstacle to overcome. After all, most women found it necessary to put up some charade of resistance, even after showing up at his house in the middle of the night wearing little more than a pelisse.

He turned a corner, stepping out on to busy Great Russell Street, the energy of the people rushing past him feeding the anticipation building with his determination. She might sneer at his reputation today, but once she surrendered to him, and she would, they'd enjoy enough pleasure to ensure she forgot all about his previous escapades.

He tapped his fingers against his thigh, eager to feel her soft skin against his and taste the lips which had been so tantalisingly close to his in the studio.

It would be so different between them this time. With her wealth, she wouldn't demand more of him the way she had before, and when the passion faded, as it always did, they could part without regret, all the old sins forgiven and forgotten.

For the first time in a long time, he looked forward to the chase.

Chapter Four

Cecelia and Theresa sat astride two geldings from Lord Strathmore's stable, slowing their horses to match the leisurely pace of Madame de Badeau and Lord Strathmore's mounts as they entered Rotten Row. It was the first ride for either of them during the crowded fashionable hour. Cecelia sat up straight in the saddle, savouring the gentle gait of the horse beneath her and the fine spring evening. It was well worth the pain of enduring Lord Strathmore's endless chatter about his carriage to be on horseback again.

'I painted it red and ordered gold crests to match the gilding along the top,' he explained to Madame de Badeau, who offered a perfunctory nod, her attention on the riders surrounding them. 'I'm also rebuilding the carriage house in stone. I much prefer the smooth texture. It's quite alluring, especially when rendered into the curves of the female form.'

His hungry eyes fixed on Cecelia, sliding down the length of her. She offered him a wan smile, then leaned back in the saddle so Madame de Badeau and Theresa blocked her from his view. Theresa rolled her eyes at

Cecelia, who shot her cousin a reprimanding look betrayed by the smile sneaking in beneath it.

'Look at Lord Penston's mount,' Madame de Badeau interjected, inclining her head at a round man with white hair riding past them. 'What a shame. Someone of his standing should invest in a better bit of blood.'

Lord Strathmore responded with an 'hmm' before returning to the topic of his carriage, his words keeping pace with the horses as they continued down the Row.

Cecelia smiled at two passing gentlemen, grinding her teeth as their stony faces stared past her. One would think all London were afraid to crack a smile for fear of sending the city sliding into the Thames. Adjusting the reins, she wanted to tap the horse into a sprint and ride like she used to at Belle View. Let the spectacle of a horse truly exercising bring some emotion to the other riders' staid faces. Instead, she rested her hands on her thighs, rocking with the horse and settling into her thoughts, the mounting pile of bills at home preying on her.

She'd spent the better part of the morning calculating the value of her few possessions against their mounting debts, her depression growing by the minute. The one small ray of hope was the inheritance payment she'd soon receive. It was the only money left to her by her father, his share of a sugar plantation in Barbados, the single investment to have ever made him any money. The payments were never large because there were so many other investors, but even the paltry amount would be enough to ease some of her present worry.

She ran her hand over her wrist, feeling the small bump of the gold bracelet beneath the velvet, not wanting to think about the last time she'd so desperately needed the money. Her mother hadn't been able to rouse herself for even two hours to see to this small matter and Cecelia had ventured alone to Mr Watkins's office to collect the payment. Cecelia had railed at her mother afterwards, no longer capable of holding back all her fears and frustration, wishing her mother would wrap her arms around her and tell her everything would be all right. She hadn't.

Not long afterwards, she had told Cecelia to pack for Lady Ellington's.

Cecelia's shoulders sagged, the pain and loneliness of then mirroring her life now. She wanted to slide off the gelding and crawl beneath a bush, curl up in a ball where no one and nothing could bother her. Then she forced back her shoulders and raised her head high, smiling at a passing gentleman. Was his name Mr Hammerworth or Mr Passingstoke? She couldn't remember and it didn't matter, nor did she let it trouble her when he trotted past without so much as a glance. She would not give up, she would not leave Theresa alone to face an uncertain future the way her mother had left her.

'Look—' Theresa's voice pierced Cecelia's thoughts '—there's Lord Falconbridge.'

Cecelia's body tensed as she watched Randall ride towards them, his eyes fixed on her, his smile wide and inviting. She struggled not to frown, frustrated to know she could elicit smiles from no one in Rotten Row except him.

'Good evening, Lord Falconbridge,' Madame de Badeau sang, more cheerful than she'd been the entire length of the ride.

'Falconbridge,' Lord Strathmore mumbled.

'Isn't it lovely out, Lord Falconbridge?' Theresa greeted in a bright voice, arching a suggestive eyebrow at Cecelia with an obviousness as chafing as Randall's presence.

'Yes, it is, Miss Fields.' Randall turned his horse, bringing it alongside Cecelia's. 'No greeting from you, Mrs Thompson?'

'Hello, Lord Falconbridge.' She tried to focus on the path instead of him, but she couldn't. Atop the brown stallion, he looked like a fine sculpture, his confidence as solid as any bronze casting. He wore a dark riding coat tailored close to fit the strong angles and broad expanses of his torso. The cut of the coat was nothing compared to the close fit of his breeches. His stallion danced and Randall's thigh muscles tightened as they gripped and eased to control his mount. She followed the line of them up to a more enticing muscle before a rumbling laugh made her eyes snap to his.

'I see you're enjoying all the sights of the Row,' he teased.

She swatted a fly from her skirt, annoyed at having been caught staring at him.

'I'm enjoying the ride, not the sights, Lord Falconbridge.'

'Randall, please, like in old times.' He placed one hand over his heart, the gesture genuine and matched by the sincerity in his eyes. She caught in their depths the young man who'd once sat beside her on the banks of the River Stour, listening while she cried out her anger at being sent away and her worries over the future. It touched the cold, lonely place inside of her, the one growing like a tumor since Daniel's death.

'I'm surprised to see you out riding,' she commented, eager to thwart the encroaching pensiveness. His comfort had been fleeting and hardly worth remembering.

'Why aren't you home resting for another long night of ruining people?'

The teasing remark came out sharper than intended and she steeled herself, expecting a cutting response. Instead he laughed, the barb rolling off him like water off a fine saddle. 'Contrary to what you believe, I don't spend every evening ruining young gallants who possess more money than wits.'

'How do you spend your evenings, then?' She was truly curious.

He shrugged. 'Much the same as you do.'

'I doubt it.' *Since I don't bed half the widows in society.* Lady Ilsington rode by on her chestnut gelding, eyeing Randall with a hungry look, then frowning when he failed to acknowledge her. 'With the exception of balls, it isn't my habit to keep late hours.'

He leaned towards her, his thighs tightening beneath the buckskin, their hardness carrying up through the solid centre of him to his blue eyes shaded by his hat. 'Then we must cure you of such a strange malady.'

Her hands tightened a little too hard on the reins and the horse began to veer towards Randall.

'An interesting proposition, but I think your cure might be worse than the disease,' she rushed, correcting the horse.

'You would die a thousand little deaths.'

His low voice twined around her and her knee bent harder around the pommel, her pulse fluttering against the tight collar of her habit as she slowed the horse to drop behind the others, ignoring Theresa's questioning look.

Randall slowed his stallion to keep pace, loosening his grip on the reins as the horses ambled along.

'Shall we dismount here and wander off into the

bushes?' she suggested. 'Or would you prefer a more clandestine meeting— your town house, perhaps—late at night? I could wear a veil and arrive by hackney, most sinful and nefarious indeed.'

His finger trilled slowly over his thigh. 'You make it sound so sordid when it could be so beautiful.'

She ran her tongue over her lips, noting with triumph how it drew his eyes to her mouth, her power over him driving her boldness. 'Am I really an illustrious enough candidate to bestow your favours on?'

'Who could be more illustrious than an old friend?'

Friend. She brought the gelding to a stop, the word snapping her out of the seductive haze. They'd been more than friends once, or so she'd believed until the end. He was mistaken if he thought he could charm her into forgetting. It was time to bring his teasing to an end. 'As an old friend you will understand when I politely decline.'

He turned his horse, walking it back to her as the others rode on. 'And you will understand when I ask again tomorrow, or perhaps the day after.'

'No, Randall, I won't.' The gelding shifted and she tugged the reins to steady it, the animal's agitation adding to her own. 'Why do you continue to pester me when I've made my position clear?'

'Because you captivate me, more than you realise.'

The revelation nearly knocked her from the saddle and she shifted her foot in the stirrup to keep her seat. Did he really care for her or was this all part of his game, his ego's desire to capture the adoration of every woman in London, even an insignificant widow? Her horse shook its head and she turned it in a circle, eager like the animal to vent the energy building inside her.

She positioned her riding crop over the horse's

flank, mischief creeping in beneath her resentment. If he wanted the thrill of the chase, she'd give him one, along with a beating solid enough to end his interest in her. 'Do you still race, my lord? I remember you were the best in the county.'

'I was eighteen.'

'Then I expect you've improved with age. To the statue and do not disappoint.'

She snapped the crop against the horse and it shot off down Rotten Row. Behind her, the stallion's hooves drummed a steady beat on the packed dirt path and in a moment Randall was beside her. They raced side by side, the horses nearly in sync as they flew past geldings shying off the path or rearing up in surprise, their wide-eyed riders hanging on tightly. She turned the horse to the right to avoid a curricle, the driver's curses lost in the pounding of the gelding's hooves. Randall dodged around a group of riders and fell back until the path cleared and his stallion picked up speed. The statue came into view and his horse pulled ahead. She dug her heel into the side of the gelding and the horse leapt forward, passing the statue a nose length before Randall's.

'Now there's the woman I remember,' Randall congratulated, his thick voice echoing through her, infectious and alluring as they slowed their horses to a walk.

'It's been ages since I've ridden like that.' Her heart raced in her ears and Cecelia lifted her face to catch the stiff breeze sweeping over her damp skin.

'Shall we canter to the lake?' He circled her with his horse, tempting her with the energy radiating between them. 'Put that horse of yours through its paces?'

'I think it's you who'll be put through his paces. You pulled back, just like you always used to do.'

'I did no such thing.'

'You did, I saw it, and I'll see it again at the lake.' She raised the reins, ready to snap the horse back into action, when three old matrons crossing their path in the curricle stopped her. The tallest one glared at her from beneath a dark parasol while the other two whispered behind their hands. Only then did Cecelia notice the other riders watching them, their faces pinched and disapproving. What little she'd accomplished with all her smiles, she'd just undone in a moment of rashness.

She swallowed hard, the riders' scrutiny too much like the morning she'd entered Bruton Parish Church to meet the cold stares of every family who believed General LaFette's lies. It would happen again here in London if she wasn't careful. Only this time, there was nowhere else for her and Theresa to go.

'What's wrong?' Randall asked.

She wrapped the reins around one hand, eager to be away from him, the Row and everyone who'd seen them. 'Once again I've forgotten myself in your presence.'

Randall scowled, bringing his horse close to hers. 'Don't worry what they think.'

She pulled her horse's head to one side, forcing him away from Randall's mount. 'Unlike you, I must.'

'What happened to the brave girl I remember?'

'As you said, I was a girl. A lady must mind her behaviour.'

'No, you have the means to be free. Don't let these people make you afraid.'

'Don't seek to counsel me, Lord Falconbridge,' she snapped. 'You know nothing of me or my life.'

She kicked her horse into a trot back up the path, her habit itchy under the rising heat of her embarrassment and anger. How dare Randall sit on his horse with all the privileges of his sex, title and wealth and instruct her on how to behave? How dare he try to tempt her into an indiscretion, then chide her for wanting to protect her reputation? He'd abandoned his so long ago, it was clear he couldn't fathom why anyone would want to keep theirs.

The animal tried to gallop, but she kept him at a trot, despite wanting to let it run, to carry her away from all the heartless people and her own troubles. Ahead, Madame de Badeau and Lord Strathmore came into view, their faces hard. Madame de Badeau walked her horse out to meet Cecelia.

'A splendid display of horsemanship.' It was a warning, not a compliment. 'I don't know how ladies ride in Virginia, but here they don't race through Rotten Row.'

'I'm sorry. I quite forgot myself.'

'I don't recommend forgetting yourself again.' She inclined her head at Lord Strathmore, his snub nose wrinkled in disapproval. 'Not all gentlemen appreciate such spirited public displays.'

Anger burned up Cecelia's spine and she wanted to turn and gallop back to Randall, dismiss them both and embrace the freedom he offered. Only the sight of Theresa beside the Earl kept her from snapping the horse into a run. It wasn't freedom Randall offered, but an illusion as fleeting as those her father used to create before every failed trip to Calais, and as likely to sink her as her father's ship had sunk him and his business.

'Come along, then.' Madame de Badeau escorted Cecelia back to Lord Strathmore, riding beside her like a guard.

Cecelia felt like a prisoner to her debt and to every bad choice made by her father, her mother and even Daniel. They'd all escaped the ramifications of their decisions, leaving her, always her, to deal with the consequences.

Resignation extinguished her anger and she let the horse, Lord Strathmore's horse, continue forward. It wasn't just her future at risk, but Theresa's. If she lost the Earl's good opinion, and the opinion of who knew how many others, Theresa would suffer, too, and she refused to allow it. Fingering her gold bracelet, she tried to look contrite while thinking of all the simpering words she might say to soothe the hard set of Lord Strathmore's lips. Each turn of phrase burned her tongue like hot water, but she would say them. Life was what it was and she must make the best of it. Nothing good could come from wishing for it to be any different.

Chapter Five

Randall stood on the staircase, watching the elite men of London snigger and cough as they examined the selection of paintings arranged on easels across his wide marble hall. A fine collection of art base enough to make a bawd blush was on display. It was the last of Uncle Edmund's collection, which used to hang in the entrance hall of Falconbridge Manor, his uncle's defence against respectable ladies attempting to cross the threshold and land a Marquess.

'Impressive works, Falconbridge,' Strathmore mumbled as he walked past, looking a little red around the collar, as if this much flesh so early in the day was more than even a man of his tastes could tolerate.

The footmen carrying trays of Madeira were also having trouble maintaining a steady course in the face of so much painted flesh. For the second time in five minutes, Randall watched as the wiry-haired Duke of St Avery nearly collided with a gaped-mouth footman.

'You'll gain quite the reputation as a collector after this,' Lord Bolton offered with a touch of reverence as he stopped to examine a nearby portrait.

'I don't think that's the reputation I'll gain.' Randall

smirked with more arrogance than he felt. The exhibition might titillate society, but today, the excitement of shocking their sensibilities left him flat. Instead all he could think about was Cecelia and their encounter yesterday in Rotten Row. His agitation was exacerbated by the ridiculously early hour he'd arisen. Not even Reverend had deigned to join him to watch the sun rise and tease out why Cecelia, after flying like a mad woman down the row, all lively laughter and glowing skin, had shrunk back into herself like some scared turtle at the sight of a few old matrons.

It wasn't the Cecelia he remembered, the one who used to laugh boldly at these paintings in front of Uncle Edmund instead of averting her eyes.

What had dulled her bravery and made her more afraid of a few old crows than she'd ever been of Uncle Edmund? Perhaps the husband was to blame.

Randall tightened his hands into fists behind his back, imagining the colonial's face twisted in disapproval. Cecelia might have stood up to such scrutiny at first, but over time it would have chipped at her, like his father's constant reprimands ate at him.

Randall cracked the knuckle of one finger.

The colonial was a fool if he'd failed to cherish Cecelia's spirit or revel in her sweet laughter the way Randall had yesterday.

The art dealer, a short man with a wide forehead, approached, tugging at the knot of his cravat, his discomfort no doubt eased by the tidy profit waiting for him at the end of the sale. 'I know I objected to your lordship displaying such a…' he paused, searching for the proper word '…unique collection in an open exhibition, but you were right. The interest this showing has generated is stunning. I don't expect one painting to remain unsold.'

'Good. I want them gone by the end of the day.' For years, they'd kept Aunt Ella ensconced in the dower house until a fire the spring before Cecelia had come to visit made it unlivable. The morning after Uncle Edmund's funeral, she'd demanded the paintings be taken down and Randall had agreed. He possessed no more desire than she did to live in a manor house decorated like a bordello.

Strathmore, standing before a painting of two naked women wrestling for the amusement of several soldiers, waved the dealer over.

'If you'll excuse me, Lord Falconbridge, I believe we've made another sale.' The dealer hurried off to join the Earl.

Randall watched as Strathmore pointed a thick finger at first one and then another of the most sordid of the lot. All at once, he imagined Strathmore sitting close to Cecelia, his dry lips hovering near her ear as he relayed with delight the dirty details of every picture, relishing the chance to poison her against him.

Randall took a step down, ready to grab the Earl by the collar and toss him out of the house, but he stopped, regaining his imperious stance and wiping away all traces of annoyance from his expression. Strathmore was beneath his notice and his anger.

A footman pulled open the front door and Lord Weatherly, Lord Hartley and Lord Malvern entered, their loud voices dropping at the sight before them.

'Heavens,' Lord Weatherly mumbled as he stepped up to the nearest painting, an explicit depiction of an ancient Roman man and woman watched by their curious servants. It used to hang in Uncle Edmund's study, a strange complement to the paintings of birds and hunting dogs.

Behind him stood Lord Hartley, Marquess of Hartley, a stately man of forty-five and a fixture of society whom Randall liked and respected. He could not say the same about his dolt of a nephew, Lord Malvern. The young Baron in the tight blue silk coat possessed more words than brains and little knew how to wield either.

The fop gaped at the paintings before catching Randall's eye. He made for Randall, his poor uncle following behind like a tired governess chasing after a wayward charge. If it weren't for Lord Hartley, Randall would have cut his nephew. Instead, he remained standing on the steps, looking down at the rail-thin Malvern.

'Lord Falconbridge, with so much interesting art for sale, may we assume you have a new conquest, one who is making you part with your precious collection?' His weak lips drew up into a grin Randall assumed was meant to be haughty, but it only made him look as if he'd smelled curdled milk.

Behind him Lord Hartley rolled his eyes.

Randall twisted the signet ring on his small finger, looking over the stupid man's head. 'You may assume whatever you like.'

'Don't disappoint, Lord Falconbridge.' He lifted one foot to step up and Randall pinned him with a look to melt ice.

Malvern lowered his foot back to the floor. 'Tell us who she is. All society wants to know.'

'If by all society, you mean the betting book at White's, don't think I'll give you the advantage. We aren't on familiar enough terms for such confidences.'

Lord Malvern's lips twitched as if trying to form a retort when his uncle dropped a restraining hand on his shoulder. 'Spare the Marquess any more of your wit, Morton. Go see the paintings and enjoy the only visit you'll likely make to the Marquess's house.'

Lord Malvern sneered at his uncle, but shuffled off to join a group of similarly dressed young men crowding around a painting of nymphs and satyrs engaged in an orgy.

'If he wasn't my wife's nephew, I'd have nothing to do with him.' Lord Hartley shook his head, leaning one elbow on the wood balustrade. 'He thinks his mouth will make him a reputation, but it won't be the one he wants. I don't suppose you'd consider calling him out, aim wide and send him scurrying back to the country?'

'As tempting as it is to draw first blood on him, he's hardly worth the effort or the bullet.' Randall stepped down to join the Marquess. 'Besides, with his lack of wit, you won't be saddled with him for long.'

'Ah, how I look forward to the day he leaves.' Lord Hartley laughed before he sobered at the sight of his nephew making a rude gesture to one of the other fops. 'I'd better see to it he doesn't embarrass himself further. Good day, Lord Falconbridge.'

Lord Hartley walked off to rejoin his nephew near the Roman painting.

The fops crowded around it, laughing into their hands like a gaggle of school girls before one of them reached out to run a gloved finger over the Roman woman's arm.

Her arm is too long, Cecelia's voice rang through his mind, the memory of her laughing at the painting bringing a smile to his face, but it faded fast. Her innocence felt too pure for a display like this.

The fops moved on to a similar Egyptian painting, leaving the Roman woman and her lover to their joy.

Randall followed the line of the Roman woman's arm and the long strokes of cream paint giving it a fleshlike texture. He stopped at the smudge of black in the corner of her elbow, the same speck of paint he'd fixed on the morning Uncle Edmund had called him into the study.

I like Cecelia, she's a good girl, full of spirit. Uncle Edmund rubbed the wood of the hunting rifle lying across his lap, the smell of oil mixing with the dust of old books. *But she's poor and you'll be a Marquess some day. Don't think she doesn't know it and won't try to land you. Don't let her, my boy, don't let any of them ever trap you. Bored wives and widows, that's what you need to keep you amused. They ask less of a man.*

Randall had refused to believe him, until the morning in the conservatory when Cecelia had pressed him about their future together.

Randal dropped his hands to his sides, trying to laugh as another footman collided with the Duke of St Avery, but the little joy he'd gleaned from this ridiculous display was gone. He hated it and everyone here. For all the sideways glances and whispered remarks they made about him, he might as well crawl up on a dais like Cecelia, wrap his body in a toga and display himself to the crowd.

He clasped his hands tight behind his back, wanting to knock the filthy art off the easels and toss everyone from his house. Let them find some other fool to feed their need for amusement. He was tired of performing for them.

He turned and started up the stairs before stopping on the landing, his hand tight on the banister. No, he was not part of their amusement, but the lord and master of this game. He turned, resuming his imperious stance, meeting Lord Bolton's eyes and smirking in triumph when the young lord dropped his gaze into his drink. The Marquess of Falconbridge would not run from society like some coward, no more than he'd run from Cecelia's rebukes. Let them whisper and gawk at him, it was to his benefit, not theirs.

'You mean I won't receive a payment from my father's inheritance until December?' Cecelia blurted across the desk at Mr Watkins, the solicitor responsible for distributing the Barbados payments. In the chair next to hers, Theresa squeaked out a worried gasp and Cecelia reached over, giving her cousin's hand a reassuring squeeze.

'I'm afraid so.' Mr Watkins sat back, his leather chair creaking. 'And perhaps not even then. The hurricane devastated the harvest and though it's expected to recover, as is always the case with crops, there is no guarantee.'

'Perhaps I may receive an advance on future earnings?' Cecelia asked, struggling to keep the desperation from her voice, feeling the blow to her situation as if Mr Watkins had struck her. 'My income from Virginia has also been delayed. I was counting on this money to see me through until it arrives.'

It was a plausible enough lie, for there were many in London who received income from abroad and often found regular payments interrupted by storms or pirates.

'There's nothing I can do. The plantation doesn't have the money to spare and there are other recipients waiting to be paid as well. If there are no further disasters, the harvest will recover and you may see a payment in December.' He flicked the file on his desk closed, making it plain he intended to do no more for her than deliver this devastating news. Even if he wished to help them, what could he do? He couldn't make the crops fruitful or force the ships transporting the money to sail faster.

'I look forward to speaking with you then.' She nodded for Theresa to rise, the strain on her cousin's face striking Cecelia harder than Mr Watkins's news. It ripped at her to see Theresa so worried instead of carefree and happy like she used to be before Daniel's death. It reminded her too much of herself at sixteen.

'I don't normally recommend this measure, but I sense you may be in need of such services.' Mr Watkins's words stopped them and they settled back on the edges of their chairs. He removed a slip of paper from the desk drawer, laid it on the blotter and began to write. 'This is the name of a gentleman who may be able to help you.'

He handed the paper across the desk. Cecelia took it and looked at the name and address.

Philip Rathbone, 25 Fleet Street.

'A gentleman? You mean a moneylender.'

Mr Watkins nodded. 'I would not recommend him except among his class he is exceptional.'

'You mean he doesn't ruin people as quickly as the others.'

Mr Watkins steepled his fingers in front of him. 'He'll deal fairly with you, more so than any other man in the Fleet.'

'I'll take it into consideration.' She slipped the paper into her reticule. 'Thank you for your help, Mr Watkins.'

The solicitor escorted them through the front room past two clerks copying documents. 'I'll notify you if anything changes.'

She caught a slight sympathy in the older man's

words and, though she appreciated it, hated being in a position to need it. 'Of course, you'll be discreet concerning this matter.'

'I'm always discreet.'

'Thank you. Good day.'

Cecelia slipped her arm in Theresa's and guided her down the pavement.

'What are we going to do?' Theresa whispered, looking nervously over the passing people as if expecting someone to stop, point and announce their secret.

She didn't blame her for being nervous. There were many times when she had wondered if everyone already knew and if that's why they kept their distance.

Cecelia clutched the top of the reticule and the paper inside crinkled. Having Mr Rathbone's name in the bag made it, along with all the other burdens she carried, seem heavier. She stood up straight, trying not to let this new setback weigh her down, to be brave for Theresa's sake and ease some of her cousin's fears. 'I may have to visit the moneylender.'

'But you can't.' Theresa's voice rose high with panic before she clamped her mouth closed, leaning in close to Cecelia. 'We haven't the means to repay a man like him.'

'I know, but it's better to owe one discreet man than to have the butcher and grocer declaring our debts through town. I can make arrangements with Mr Rathbone, then only use the money if things turn dire.' Though at the moment, they were teetering precariously close to dire.

London was proving far more expensive than she'd anticipated. They reworked old dresses, made do with only Mary, shivered through the night to avoid burning coal and relied on refreshments at soirées and dances to help keep them fed, yet still it wasn't enough. She'd sold the silver yesterday, the small amount it brought already spent to secure their town house for the next three months. Hopefully, it would be enough time for either her or Theresa to find a husband. If not, she wasn't sure how they would survive. Except for their simple jewellery, fine clothes and the books, there was little left to sell.

'Miss Domville told me all sorts of horrible stories about people being threatened by creditors,' Theresa protested, stepping closer to Cecelia when the pavement narrowed and the crowd thickened. 'It isn't safe to deal with them.'

'What does Miss Domville know except gossip?' Cecelia scoffed, wondering if Madame de Badeau's sister was the best influence for Theresa. 'I've dealt with creditors before. I know how they conduct business.'

'But I thought Daniel didn't believe in credit?'

'He didn't, but after the hurricane, when the harvest was destroyed, we had no choice, not if we wanted to rebuild. If Mr Rathbone is as honest as Mr Watkins says, then his money will give us the time we need.' She said it as much to convince herself as Theresa.

'And if he isn't?'

'Then we can hardly be any worse off than we are now.'

They paused at the corner, waiting for a break in the carriages and carts to cross. Cecelia covered her nose with her hand against the stench of the filth littering the street. The fresh air of Belle View, the bright sun hanging over the lush green trees and reflecting off the red brick seemed so far behind her, and with it all the strength of Daniel's patient smiles and tender ways. Daniel might have failed to provide for her after his death, but alive he had always been a rock, steady and calm beside her. Even after the loss of their little boy, Daniel, despite being weak from the fever, had held her and let her pour out her heart and her grief.

Tears blurred Cecelia's vision, and she let Theresa pull her across the street, fighting the heaviness settling over her to reach the other side before a large carriage passed. Exhaustion pulled at her until she wanted nothing more than to sit on the stone pavement and surrender to her troubles, let them press down on her until she could do nothing except pace the hallways and cry, just like her mother.

'Cecelia, I've been thinking. If the Season ends and neither of us are settled, I'll become a governess,' Theresa said as the clatter of the street faded behind them.

The announcement snapped Cecelia out of her fog. She couldn't give up, not with Theresa depending on her. 'Certainly not.'

'Why? My wages could support us.'

Cecelia pulled her into the quiet of a small space between two shops, not wanting to discourage the girl's spirit, but unwilling to let her live in ignorance of the realities of life. 'You don't speak French and you know nothing of music. Who but the most questionable of families might hire you and then where would you be? A stranger in a strange house, always hovering between a paid servant and an unwanted member of the family, perhaps suffering the inappropriate attentions of the gentleman?'

'Yet you'll let men like Lord Strathmore pester you?'

'If it means seeing you happy and safe, then, yes.'

'I won't let you, not with him. Miss Domville says he may not even be rich and she tells me the most awful things about him. Please, promise me you won't marry him.'

Cecelia laid her hands on either side of Theresa's face, smoothing away the tight lines at the corners of her mouth with her thumbs. 'Even if Miss Domville's stories are true, I can't promise not to marry him. His title will keep us from debtors' prison, and a poor Countess is still more respected than a poor colonial.' She smoothed Theresa's dark hair from her forehead. 'I saw so many of my father's business associates driven into poverty by shipwrecks or war. Once they were poor, almost everyone turned their backs on them just like they did to us in Virginia, except here it'll be worse. I know, because I saw what happened to the daughters of more than one of Father's old associates. If tying myself to Lord Strathmore means saving us from a life uglier than you can imagine, then I'll do it.'

'What about Lord Falconbridge? He seemed quite taken with you when we were riding and you certainly enjoyed his company.'

'Lord Falconbridge is only interested in me as a diversion, nothing more, and I was foolish to forget myself with him.' Cecelia dropped her hands to Theresa's arm and drew her back onto the busy pavement, her embarrassment rising at being reminded of her behaviour, and his. 'You have no idea the damage it might have done.'

'I know you told me about what he did to you before, but perhaps he's changed.'

'The only thing that's changed is his conceit, which is worse now than ever. Trust me when I tell you, Lord Falconbridge is not the man to save us.'

'Then why can't we save ourselves, if not as governesses, then perhaps as a lady's companion?'

Cecelia thought again of Lady Ellington, wondering if the Dowager Countess would be kind enough to take Cecelia on in such a position. She imagined the scorn

Randall would heap on her then, assuming he allowed his aunt to employ her. 'I'm sure we'll find a way to survive, but let's not think about it until we have to.'

'Some days, I think that moment is coming faster than we'd like.'

Cecelia wrapped one arm around Theresa's shoulders, drawing her close. 'Please, don't worry. Everything will be fine, you'll see. You forget, this isn't the first time I've been in this situation and pulled through.'

Hopefully, it would be the last.

Chapter Six

Cecelia laid down the winning card, able to breathe again as the other players erupted in begrudging congratulations. Reaching into the centre of the table, her hands shook as she scooped up the small pile of coins. She shouldn't have taken a chance with her money, but Lady Thornton's card party was no place to be frugal, not when pretending to be wealthy. Palming one coin, she examined the face imprinted on the surface. For a brief moment during the play, the thrill of risking her money had proved as exciting as racing Randall in Rotten Row. Thankfully, the win meant she didn't have to go home and explain to Theresa why she'd gambled away the butcher's payment.

'You've been very lucky tonight,' Lady Weatherly observed as she gathered up the cards. 'Will you play again?'

Cecelia looked at the eager faces of the other players, tempted to try to win enough of their blunt to relieve some of her troubles, then changed her mind. When it came to risking money, like her father, luck never seemed to stay with her for long.

She dropped the coins into her reticule, then rose. 'I believe I'll stop while I'm winning.'

'As we all should, but we won't, will we?' Lady Weatherly laughed, wasting no time dealing another hand to the players who remained.

Cecelia tightened the strings of her reticule and walked away, her excitement fading, the mask of calm respectability she'd worn since the incident in Rotten Row smothering her again. If only she could be as carefree about losing money as Lady Weatherly, play with abandon and enjoy herself without her heart stopping at every turn of the cards, but she couldn't. She could barely afford a ride in a hackney, much less a gambling loss.

She dropped her hands to her side, working to appear the cheerful, wealthy widow. Handwringing and dejection would get her nothing, not even pity, and what she needed now as much as money were friends and introductions and all the possibilities they carried.

At the door to the adjoining gaming room, she paused on the edge of a group of matrons deep in conversation. Madame de Badeau had introduced her to Lady Thornton, but the other two, Lady Ilsington and Lady Featherstone, she knew only by sight. She stood on the periphery of their circle, catching Lady Thornton's eye. The woman gave her a nod of acknowledgement, but nothing more, and Cecelia moved off, wanting to stamp her foot in frustration. She might as well try to widen the English Channel for all the success she enjoyed trying to widen her circle of friends.

A number of grim-faced people leaving the table in the corner blocked her progress. They avoided her eyes as they passed, or offered only the slightest acknowledgement, despite the wide smiles she threw their way.

'Attempting to storm the city gates?' Randall's voice

pierced her frustration, the deep tones rumbling through her like thunder.

Her hand went to her bracelet as he rose from his chair on the far side of the table. When had he joined the card party? He hadn't been here when she and Madame de Badeau had arrived or she felt sure she would have noticed him, felt his presence permeate the air like a vase of fresh-cut flowers on a hot day.

He wore a dark coat with a white waistcoat beneath shot with gold. The subtle yellow threads caught the candlelight, bringing out the ring of yellow in his blue eyes. Gold buttons to match the thread rose up in a straight line to his cravat and she imagined them undone, the silk discarded, the shirt gaping open to reveal the sweep of chest and hair beneath.

Another thrill more potent than the draw of the cards raced along the edge of her spine, surprising her with its intensity before she banished it. 'The gates are proving most formidable.'

'My gates are wide open.' He motioned to the empty seat across from him, his confident smile as irksome as the large pile of coins in front of him. Why did men like Randall always win while people like her seemed doomed to struggle? 'Will you tempt fate with me, Mrs Thompson?'

She traced the edge of a coin through the velvet reticule, wanting to sit down and put a large dent in his winnings and his ego. Maybe he'd let her win in the hopes of currying favour. Remembering the way they used to play at Falconbridge Manor, the stakes low but the competition fierce, she knew better than to expect much lenience. 'I don't think my meagre shillings can compare to an estate.'

'No, but your company is far preferable to any man's,

as I imagine mine is to his.' He nodded to the doorway and Cecelia looked through it to see Lord Strathmore watching them from across the drawing room, his lips pulled down at the corners. Having been noticed, he looked away, raising a hand in greeting to another gentleman before hurrying off to speak to him.

'Yes, those gates continue to meet me with an open invitation.' She frowned, then silently chastised herself for speaking so meanly of the Earl. With no other prospects appearing, he was fast becoming her and Theresa's only hope for salvation. She dropped her hands to her sides, hating the hopelessness of it all.

'Don't look so troubled,' Randall's voice cut through her gloom as he gathered up the discarded cards. 'I won't tell him. I don't want to deprive you of the opportunity of disappointing him yourself.'

'You're too kind.' She laughed, his devil-may-care attitude infectious and easing her dark mood before the memory of all the disapproving faces in Rotten Row sobered her. 'But his good opinion isn't the only one I'm interested in maintaining.'

'Have you ever considered how a connection with me might benefit you?' Randall tapped the cards into a neat rectangle.

'Like it benefited Lord Westbrook?'

The cards stopped. 'He was a fool to risk so much.'

'And what would I risk?'

'Catching the attention of Lady Thornton and who knows how many others, perhaps even the mother of some young gentleman looking to marry an heiress like your cousin.'

Cecelia fingered the back of the chair in front of her, remembering the hard looks of the women in the curricle. They had not been impressed when Cecelia had forgotten herself with Randall. No doubt they'd snatch up their marriage-minded sons and run in the opposite direction if they saw her playing cards with him now.

He leaned forward on his elbows, the same annoying smirk he'd worn while teasing her in Sir Thomas's studio dancing on his lips. 'They aren't even looking.'

She turned to the door. The ladies were gone, drawn into the sitting room to listen to a singer with a tall feather in her hair perform a surprisingly good aria. In fact, very few people remained in the card room except for a handful of men huddled around the far table, so engrossed in their play, they barely noticed the footman setting down glasses of Madeira at their elbows.

There was opportunity in the absence of people, but not the kind Randall thought.

'Now, sit and play,' he invited. 'I promise not to bankrupt you.'

She pulled out the chair and sat down, not sure if it was bravery or foolishness urging her on. However, if she wanted to be free of Randall, this might be her only chance.

He took his seat and began to shuffle the deck. 'I knew you couldn't resist playing me.'

'I can't, but I don't want to play for money.'

He maintained the steady rhythm of shuffling, the cards moving fast between his hands. 'Then what do you wish to wager?'

She traced a triangle inlay in the table, debating her next words. She should throw down her shillings and take her chances with the money and nothing else, but there was so much more at stake tonight. 'If I win, you leave me in peace. No more innuendoes, no more suggestions. We see each other in a room and nod our greetings, but nothing more.'

He placed the deck on the table in front of her. 'And when I win?'

'If you win,' she corrected, cutting the deck.

'If I win…' he stacked the cards, then swept his hand over them, fanning them out in a row across the table '…I continue my pursuit until you relent.'

Beneath the table, her fingers found her bracelet before she steadied herself. She'd begun this game, she couldn't withdraw now. 'I hope you don't think I'll marry you because you win a hand of cards.'

He placed his fingers beneath the last card and, in one quick motion, slid them all together again. 'I never mentioned marriage.'

She stiffened, her daring twisting into an old anger tinged with humiliation. She wanted to sweep the cards off the table and rage at him for what he'd said to her ten years ago, chastise him for the callous way he'd treated her and the way it echoed through those four words. Instead, she fixed him with the same smile she used to flash the insolent Belle View foreman when she gave directions for planting and he sneered at her—sweet but with an edge of poison. 'No, I don't suppose there's a woman in England who can snare the illustrious Marquess of Falconbridge.'

The small muscles beneath his eyes pulled tight. 'Shall I deal?'

'Please.' Her anger eased at having registered a blow and some of her former daring returned. 'I can't wait to give you a good thrashing like I used to in your uncle's drawing room.'

'Don't be so confident. I let you win back then.'

'Liar.' She picked up the cards, careful to keep her disappointment from showing. With a hand like this, he'd be trailing her through the entire Season.

Over the repeating notes of the singer's aria and the loud laugh of a gentleman from the table behind her, she heard Randal flick the edge of his cards. He used to do this when they played before. Did it mean he held a good hand or a poor one? She struggled to remember and sneaked a glance at him, her ire rising at the sight of him sitting back in the chair, self-assured and cocky.

He must have a poor hand. Or maybe not. Why couldn't she remember what the flicking meant? She laid down a card and chose another from the deck, taking her time, trying to match his calm and confidence while wishing she knew some way to knock his down a peg or two. She looked at her new card, the queen of hearts, struggling to suppress a smile as a wicked idea came to mind.

She waited until he reached for the deck, then opened her cards like a fan and peered over the tops, tilting her head to one side and looking up at him through her lashes.

His hand paused, the selected card dangling from his fingers. In the piercing hold of his gaze, she saw the hungry boy who used to sit across from her in the Falconbridge drawing room, every emotion registering on his smooth face. Only he wasn't a boy any more, but a man capable of doing to her all the things she'd known nothing about as a girl and now missed. Beneath the table, her toes curled in her slippers, eager to shake off the satin and slide up the hard length of his leg to tease him out of sight of the room. She flicked her top teeth with her tongue and watched with glee as his chest rose with a deep breath, his fingers so tight on the card, they creased the stiff paper. Her skin grew moist as she continued to hold his desiring look, fearing she might be burned by the heat of it, but unwilling to turn away. This was a reckless, dangerous game for a woman in her position to play, but his reaction was too exquisite for her to stop.

'You have a good card, good enough to beat me?' Randall asked, sitting back, his tight voice an encouragement when it should have been a warning.

'Perhaps I don't or perhaps I do.' She lowered her eyes, trying not to gloat at the small victory as she slid the queen of hearts from her hand and laid it on the table.

'I think not.' He laid his card on top of hers. The ace of spades.

The heat in her went cold, the worried widow rushing in to replace the daring coquette.

'You cheated,' she blurted without thinking.

'Careful, Cecelia, or I'll demand satisfaction.' The dark suggestion deepened the shadows of his eyes and played on the desire still smouldering in her body. He looked like a wolf ready to pounce and she felt the tide of power turn, trapping her.

'You have the humour of a schoolboy,' she hissed.

'And the skills of a man.' He reached across the table, took her hand and turned it over.

His thumb slid slowly across her palm, the movement subtle but strong as it made small circles on her hot skin. She struggled to breathe, barely noticing how he plucked the cards one by one from her fingers with his other hand. All she could sense was the gentle sweep of his skin against hers, his touch reaching to her very core.

Her fingers tightened over his thumb, covering and capturing it within the hollow of her palm, willing it to be still and to stop the aching tease. With a sly wink, he slid his hand out from beneath hers, his fingernails raking the skin on the back of her hand, his thumb caressing her fingers as he withdrew.

She laid her palms on the cool table, easing the heat

which still burned her skin. Pushing against the solid top to steady herself, she rose. He matched her movement, towering over her as she struggled to maintain her dignity against the butterflies warring inside her. 'Thank you for a spirited game, Lord Falconbridge.'

He leaned towards her with a bow more predatory than polite. 'We have not yet begun to play.'

She grasped her reticule as she backed away, moving as slowly as she had the morning she'd stumbled on the copperhead snake coiled in the sun behind the brew house. Only when she was a safe distance did she turn her back on him, feeling more vulnerable than when she'd faced him.

He'd be relentless in his pursuit now.

She froze, her panic taking off like a pheasant scared out of the grass, the Season spreading out before her as one constant effort to dodge his advances, her time and energy devoted to keeping him away instead of encouraging any man who took an interest in her or Theresa.

This was how it had started with General LaFette.

She flicked open her fan, waving it furiously in front of her face, trying to calm her racing heart. Would Randall be as cruel as the General when she spurned him, spreading vicious lies and ruining all her and Theresa's chances at happiness?

'Are you all right, Mrs Thompson?' Lord Strathmore's voice made her jump and she whirled to find him behind her.

'Yes, I'm fine.' Her glance flicked over his shoulder to the table where Randall sat, only to find it empty. 'I'm just very hot.'

'Then let me fetch you a glass of punch.'

She didn't have the stomach for Lady Thornton's tart

punch, but if it kept the Earl away until she could calm herself, she'd gladly drink a cup. 'Thank you.'

He made for the refreshment table and she bolted for the open balcony doors, trying not to run, yet eager to reach the cool of the darkness where she could be alone and think.

Her fingers tapped an uneven beat on the stone as she stood at the railing, drawing in deep breaths of the cool night air. Staring at the tendrils of smoke rising over the London roofs and illuminated by the low moon, she felt her panic settle and with it her thoughts. Whatever happened between her and Randall, she knew he wouldn't be as cruel as General LaFette. Despite all the scandals attached to his name, not one ever accused him of spreading vicious rumours. He might have ruined Lord Westbrook, but Randall was right, the young man should have stopped the game before betting his estate.

Just as I should have stopped the game before it began. She hadn't, she couldn't, not with her ego pushing her to get the better of him, not with his wicked smile tempting her. Beneath the desire to best him lingered another truth, one she was loath to admit, even to herself. She'd enjoyed playing him more than anything else in London, and for the length of the game, she'd felt like a young woman in love again, the possibility of happiness as real as Randall's thumb against her palm.

She turned over her hand, the skin cold from the stone. Opening and closing her fingers, she wished she were rich enough to accept everything hinted at in Randall's touch. Even if his adoration proved fleeting, for a while she could enjoy the long-forgotten feeling of being wanted.

Footsteps sounded behind her and her fingers tightened into a fist. She turned, expecting to see Lord Strathmore, and gasped.

'Randall.'

He stood in the doorway, the angles of his shoulders silhouetted by the light from the room behind him. Without a word, he slid one arm around her waist and drew her into the shadows next to the door, out of sight of the drawing room.

In the faint light, his eyes held hers, the desire smouldering in their depths burning away the cold loneliness which gripped her. Need and fear pulled her in opposite directions and she didn't know which urge to follow. He wanted her and, for the moment, it was the only thing that mattered.

She tilted her face to his and he kissed her, his mouth demanding she relent and she did, all reasons against it fading as his tongue swept over her lips. She opened her mouth, accepting the penetrating caress, and his arms tightened around her, his body steady against the tremors racking hers. This was the Randall she remembered, his soft touch strong enough to make all the troubles of her life fade like the far-off voice of the singer. If he sought to possess her now, she'd gladly surrender, if only for the chance to know again something more tender and beautiful than heartache and loss.

'Mrs Thompson?' A male voice sounded from somewhere in the distance.

Randall's hands tightened on her back and she clung to him, refusing to relinquish this moment of happiness to the reality beyond the balcony doors.

'Mrs Thompson?' Lord Strathmore's voice rang out again like some clanking dinner gong and she felt her bliss slipping away.

'Randall.' She turned her head and his lips brushed her cheek. 'Please, I must go.'

'No, not to him,' Randall growled, his teeth taking in one sensitive earlobe, his heavy breath in her ear making her nearly forget herself and Lord Strathmore.

'Mrs Thompson?' The Earl called again, shattering the illusion of peace created by Randall's embrace.

'Yes, I must.' She pushed against Randall and he let go.

Cold surged in where his warmth used to be, bringing with it all the reality of her position and his, the truths she'd allowed herself to forget under the sweet pressure of his lips.

'Why? What is he to you?' Randall hissed.

'And what am I to you? Nothing more than a plaything to tease with all your suggestions and—' She flapped one hand at him, lost for words, more flustered by her own actions than his. 'I'm not one of your society ladies, someone to amuse yourself with until the shooting season begins, nor will I let you treat me as such.'

'But you'll let him treat you like that?' Randall jabbed one finger at the door.

She clenched her hands at her sides. 'Whatever you think of him, at least his intentions are more honourable than yours.'

She fled back into the light of the drawing room, pausing just inside to compose herself, afraid Randall's kiss still lingered on her lips for all to see. Thankfully, the singer and the cards held almost everyone's attention, except Lord Strathmore's. He stood in the centre of the room, a glass of punch in each hand, lighting up at her appearance. 'There you are.'

He made for her, his eyes focused on her décolletage. She covered her chest with her hand, wanting to pull the dress up to her chin and walk away from his crass appraisal. It felt too much like the day General LaFette had first leered at her from across the lawn at the Governor's picnic.

'What were you doing out there?' he asked as he handed her the punch.

She took the glass, careful to avoid his round fingers. 'It's so warm in here. I had to step outside for a moment.'

'On the balcony?' His eyes flicked with suspicion to the darkened doorway and her hand tightened on the crystal.

'Where else is one to go for fresh air?' She struggled to keep her voice steady as she moved to his side, looking at the dim outline of London. Randall was still out there, waiting in the shadows. He could step from them at any moment and make his presence on the balcony with her known. She held her breath, expecting him to reveal her indiscretion and ruin all her chances with the Earl. Time seemed to stretch out as she waited, but only a light breeze drifted in through the open door, ruffling the lace curtains hanging on either side.

Her hand eased on the glass. He hadn't revealed himself. He could have, but he didn't. She sensed the effort to protect her in his choice and the realisation proved more startling than his appearance on the balcony and nearly as touching as his kiss.

'Shall we listen to the singer?' Lord Strathmore asked.

'Yes.' She accompanied him into the drawing room, struggling to put Randall out of her mind, but his warmth still lingered on her lips. He wanted her and for a moment, she'd wanted him enough to risk a very public indiscretion. She shouldn't have trifled with him, it only added fuel to his fiery pursuit, threatening to burn her and all her carefully laid plans. She rubbed the bracelet, wondering why he was so determined to claim her when a relationship with her would bring him nothing. Whatever Randall's motives, she sensed they were more for his benefit than hers. In the future, she must be more careful when dealing with the Marquess.

The singer's voice crawled up Randall's spine. He stood in the darkness of the balcony, feeling as if he'd been cut. He tugged his wrinkled coat straight. She'd even had the audacity to rail at him as if he'd attacked her in an alley when all he'd done was answer the challenge she'd tossed at him from across the table. The image of her alluring eyes, more green than brown, the dark lashes curling above the wide pupils, seized him, twisting his frustration.

The singer's shrieking ceased and the guests applauded. Randall clasped his hands behind his back and strode inside, not about to linger in the darkness like some weeping girl left out of a dance.

At the edge of the audience, Strathmore clapped like a trained monkey. Cecelia stood next to him, the roundness of her buttocks hinted at beneath the wide skirt of her pale yellow dress. The alluring blush along the sweep of her exposed shoulders didn't escape his notice. Neither did the flutter of her pearl earrings as she leaned away from Strathmore when he moved closer to speak. Her distaste for the man was obvious in the weakness of her smile, yet the moment the fool had caterwauled for her, she'd wrenched herself away from Randall, the passionate woman receding once again into the frigid widow.

I should have followed her and killed Strathmore's

interest. But he hadn't. He wasn't about to lower her opinion of him just to best a fool, not after he'd felt such wanting when his tongue swept the sweet line of her mouth. She craved his touch, no matter what she believed about his intentions, or Strathmore's. He cringed to think about the Earl's intentions, yet Cecelia believed Strathmore more worthy of her affection than him.

You're not worthy. His fists tightened before he crushed the memory down like he had the first day of his first Season when he'd stepped out of the carriage and on to the London street, refusing to let it control him.

Then Madame de Badeau stepped between him and Cecelia, jostling him from his thoughts. The Frenchwoman looked at Cecelia, then Randall, condescending amusement dancing in her brown eyes.

Only then did he realise how he stood in the centre of the room, mooning at Cecelia like some sad puppy. He scrutinised each face near him as people moved to fill the empty tables, wondering who else had noticed his moment of weakness. No eyes met his, but it didn't lessen his unease. The art of observing without being observed was well practised in society.

He turned and, without so much as an answering nod to Madame de Badeau, strode from the room, refusing to let the Frenchwoman or even Cecelia make a fool of him. He more than any other man in London was worthy of Cecelia and he'd be damned if he let her or anyone else make him think otherwise.

Madame de Badeau stood with Cecelia and Lord Strathmore on Lady Thornton's front portico, watching as her carriage pulled to a stop before the house, ready to convey the widow home before returning for her.

'I would be more than happy to escort you home,' Lord Strathmore offered to Cecelia as he handed her into the vehicle. 'It worries me to know you're not feeling well.'

'You're very kind, but I can't impose or ruin your evening,' the little widow answered, more play-acting in her simpering smile than in half the performances in the Theatre Royal.

'Indeed, you cannot.' Madame de Badeau laughed, stepping forward, eager to see the slut off. 'Lord Strathmore has promised me a game of piquet and I'm eager to win back the five shillings I lost to him last week.'

'Quite right.' Lord Strathmore bent over Cecelia's knuckles and Madame de Badeau caught the flicker of disgust in Cecelia's eyes. Apparently, Strathmore saw only what he wanted for he closed the carriage door, waving it and Cecelia off with a self-satisfied grin.

'I think I'm making great strides with her.' Lord Strathmore hooked his thumbs in his waistcoat, trilling his fingers over the silk. 'I can count on you to keep recommending me to the lovely, wealthy woman?'

'Of course. Nothing would bring me greater pleasure than to see the two of you together.' *And the whore suffering under your depravity while you both sink into poverty.*

Suspicion darkened his brow. 'I'm surprised you're being so helpful, considering what happened before.'

'My dear, you know I care nothing for the past, or revenge.' She fought to keep from laughing at her own lie. No, she hadn't forgotten the horrid way he'd treated her the night he'd thrown her over for that actress. She touched her cheek where the bruise had formed after he'd struck her. The bruise might have faded, but not her hate, nor her craving for revenge. It burned as bright as her desire to bring low the daughter of the woman who'd stolen away her first love. Losing him had forced her at sixteen into the protection of old Chevalier de Badeau and years of vile treatment at the Frenchman's gnarled hands before the Terror took off his head.

She touched her neck, shivering at how close she'd almost come to losing hers. Robespierre's execution had saved her from the blade, but not the destitution afterwards, or everything she'd been forced to do to survive.

'Shall we return?' He held out his arm, and she took it, dismissing the past as he led her back into Lady Thornton's.

She'd waited a long time for the perfect revenge to reveal itself and her patience was about to be rewarded. She caressed the diamonds against her breasts, thinking how delightful it would be to see both Lord Strathmore and Cecelia brought low. Cecelia might be innocent of her mother's sins, but there were debts to be repaid and if the mother wasn't alive to pay them, then it fell to the daughter to suffer.

Innocent, Madame de Badeau sneered behind one gloved hand. The tart was hardly innocent, throwing herself at Randall, playing him with a talent she might admire if it didn't made her sick. To see a man of Randall's reputation humbled by a nobody was more than she could stomach.

She shrugged off her disgust, knowing his infatuation wouldn't last. When it ended, he'd see once again how she alone among all the others continued to stand beside him. Some day, her loyalty would be rewarded, but for the moment she concentrated on the other matter, waiting for the right moment to strike. She smiled up at Lord Strathmore, smirking as his eyes fixed on her breasts. After all these years, she would finally see her enemies crushed.

Chapter Seven

Randall raised his arm as Mr Joshua fastened the cuff-link, shaking his head at the selection of bracelets the jeweller held up for his inspection. 'No, none of these.'

'Perhaps you'd like to see something with sapphires?' the jeweller suggested, returning the velvet-lined tray to the wood case, then withdrawing another and holding it up.

'I have no interest in rings,' Randall snapped. 'I wish to show the lady the seriousness of my intentions, not give her ideas about marriage.'

'Of course, my lord. I have another collection which I think might suit your needs.' He fiddled with the trays in the case.

Mr Joshua finished with the cufflink and Randall dropped his arm, opening and closing his hand, the feel of Cecelia's back against his palm as vibrant this morning as it had been last night. He could still hear her sighing as her sweet lips opened to him, the weight of her body soft against his, surrendering until he'd thought his conquest complete.

How wrong he'd been.

He smoothed the crease out of one cuff, another long

night without sleep, the hours of darkness consumed by thoughts of Cecelia, dragging on him. In the early hours of morning, when he'd paced the halls chewing over last night, he'd come to realise she was right. Cecelia wasn't like all his other conquests and it was a mistake to treat her like one. He'd approached her with all the finesse of a battering ram, expecting her defences to collapse simply because he knocked at her gates. The same tactics might have worked with women like Lady Weatherly, but with Cecelia they only strengthened the wall keeping him out. It was time for the softer, more delicate approach.

'Here you are, my lord. A selection of necklaces from Italy.' The jeweller held up another tray with gold pendants arranged on the velvet. 'Perhaps one of these will suit.'

A square pendant in the middle caught his attention. He picked it up, admiring the fine etching of ivy leaves covering an exposed brick wall. It reminded him of the old mill at Falconbridge Manor where the stucco had fallen away from the stone. The mill was gone now, damaged in a storm five years ago and rebuilt in stone. In the gold, he could almost see again the old one and the way the bricks used to glow in the late afternoon sun while he and Cecelia had floated over the pond in the miller's boat, her hem wet, the red highlights in her hair sparkling in the low sunlight.

He met the jeweller's eager eyes over the tray and, turning, carried the pendant to the window. It weighed nothing, but felt as heavy in his hand as the solid end of the oars had when he'd rowed, choking out his secret to Cecelia, the truth of his father's death too heavy for him to carry alone.

He swept the fine lines of the design with his thumb, the gold glinting like the fish had done as they swam beneath the boat. He'd watched them flitting over the rocks, too ashamed to look at Cecelia, too afraid of seeing in her sweet face the same hate and disgust that used to fill his father's eyes. Then she'd touched his cheek with an understanding he'd never known before and certainly not since.

His fingers closed over the pendant, filled again with the same desolation he'd felt every time he stood at the pond after she'd left.

She knew his secret. Perhaps it was the real reason she continued to push him away.

He forced down the loneliness as he strode back to the jeweller. No, that wasn't the reason. She'd told him why last night when she'd accused him of being insincere. He was about to show her depth of his sincerity. 'This one will suit.'

'Thank you, my lord.' The salesman produced a velvet box from the case and arranged the pendant inside. He handed it back to Randall, then packed up the case and followed Mr Joshua out of the room.

Randall took a seat at the wide writing desk, laying the case on the blotter as he withdrew a sheet of paper. He dipped the silver pen in the inkwell and began a note to Cecelia to accompany the gift. The words tangled together as he wrote, nothing making sense. Frustrated, he scrapped the paper from the blotter, wadded it up and tossed it in the fire. He pulled another sheet from the pile, laying it down next to the box and tapping his fingers on the leather before returning the pen to its stand.

Let the pendant speak for him.

Mr Joshua returned and Randall rose, sweeping the box from the desk and holding it out to him.

'Take this to Mrs Thompson. Tell her it's a token of my friendship and ask permission for me to call to see how well it fits her. Wait for an answer.'

* * *

Cecelia opened the slim box and drew in a sharp breath.

'Lord Falconbridge hopes you find the gift acceptable,' the valet announced.

'It's beautiful,' she murmured breathily in spite of herself. Removing the necklace from the velvet, she held it up, letting the light from the windows play off the gold. The image of the Falconbridge mill where the plaster had fallen away from the bricks came to mind. The hours she and Randall had spent floating in the miller's boat were some of her fondest. More than once during her time at Belle View, she'd passed the small lake between the fields in the late afternoon and thought of Randall, wondering if he ever thought of those days, too.

Perhaps he did.

She laid the pendant in her palm, the cool metal warming like his cheek had when she'd laid her hand aside his face all those years ago. Sitting across from him, the water lapping at the rough sides of the boat, the pain and loss in his eyes had mirrored her own. They'd shared so much then, the small space protecting them from all the problems and heartache waiting on the shore.

Or so she'd once believed.

She lowered the necklace back into the box, her excitement tarnished by both the past and the present. Even if the gift was a reminder of their time together, she knew he didn't send it for any emotional reasons. She'd rebuked him last night and this was his attempt to flatter his way back into her good graces. It'd almost worked.

'Lord Falconbridge asks permission to call, to see

how well you wear the necklace.' The valet's voice jostled her out of her thoughts.

She looked at the lean young man in the fine coat, his hands laced behind his back, his stance betraying nothing, but she sensed this wasn't the first time he'd watched a woman open one of Randall's tokens.

She looked at the pendant again and considered keeping it, wearing it once in front of Randall and then pawning it, but changed her mind. No matter how misguided his intention, she couldn't take advantage of Randall's generosity.

'Lord Falconbridge is very kind.' She closed the box and, with a surprising tug of regret, handed it back to the young man. 'But I can't accept such a gift. Please return it to him with my thanks and my apologies.'

The valet's mouth dropped open before he snapped it shut and she guessed this was the first time he'd witnessed a woman refuse a gift.

'I'll convey your message. May I also tell Lord Falconbridge he has your permission to call?'

After last night, the idea of being alone in her house with Randall didn't sit well and for more reasons than she cared to ponder. However, if he came to tea, it would save her the trouble of explaining her refusal in public. Also, for all her chastising of Randall, he was as much a fixture of society as Lord Strathmore or Lady Weatherly. To alienate him completely might cause more harm than good, though she wasn't sure to whom. 'Yes, Lord Falconbridge has my permission to call.'

The valet bowed, then left.

Cecelia returned to her desk and dropped into the chair. Opening the account book, she snatched up the pen, trying to remember where she was in her calculations and which bills in the pile above the ledger could be paid and which could be left until she sold something else.

She opened the brass ink jar, moving the metal lid back and forth on its hinges. Even in the sunlight, it didn't gleam like the pendant. She dropped the pen and closed the book, Randall's persistence more irritating than Lord Strathmore's, and far more flattering.

No wonder Randall enjoyed great success with women like Lady Weatherly.

Jealousy flared inside her and she wondered if his gifts to other ladies were as personal. No, of course not, and she was a fool to think Randall chose the pendant for sentimental reasons. His motives, as well as his request to call, were only a part of his silly game to capture her attention. Last night on the balcony, and again today, he'd almost succeeded.

Flipping open the account book, she returned to her sums, determined to put him from her mind. In time, he'd tire of this game and move on to a more willing woman. The thought should have comforted her, but it didn't.

'What's your interest in Mrs Thompson?' Madame de Badeau asked, lounging on the silk-covered chaise across from him in her morning room, déshabillé as was her custom during the day. 'Why are you running after her?'

Randall lay back against the sofa. He should have skipped this weekly engagement, but there was little else to amuse him while he waited for Mr Joshua to return from Cecelia's. 'I'm hardly running.'

'I saw you in Rotten Row. You've chased foxes with less enthusiasm.'

He threw one arm over the back of the sofa and fingered the gilded edge. 'A little chase makes a woman seem more like a conquest and more entertaining than all my past dalliances.'

'All of them?' She leaned forward to pick up a teacup from the low table between them, her wrap falling open to reveal the tops of her generous breasts, her eyebrows raised with the slightest hint of invitation. When he was a young lord new to London, the look would have made his blood boil with desire. Not today.

'All of them.'

She sat back, pulling the robe closed and sliding her feet beneath her. 'If you want the thrill of the chase, then you need a few more obstacles in your path.'

'If you're speaking of Lord Strathmore, don't trouble yourself. She isn't interested in him.'

'Or she's interested in his title and a manor house in the country.'

Randall's fingers tightened on the back of the sofa, one fingernail finding the rough edge of a chip in the smooth paint. 'One mortgaged up to the gables?'

'Her money for his title. She wouldn't be the first colonial to make such an exchange.'

Randall picked a slice of paint from the chip, wondering if Cecelia was seeking more than a husband for the cousin. She'd once asked for the protection of his title, just as Uncle Edmund had predicted she'd do, but she'd been desperate back then. She was rich now and there was no reason for her to debase herself with Strathmore just to force people she disliked to bow to her. It was only Madame de Badeau's wicked tongue seeking to turn him against any woman but her. The Frenchwoman was overestimating his esteem if she thought she could trifle with him. 'I'd prefer if you didn't interfere with me and Mrs Thompson.'

'Oh, but I must. After all, she is my friend.'

'You don't have friends.'

'Nevertheless, I'm already involved and, since nothing else has arisen to amuse me this Season, I have no choice.' Her narrow eyes met his with a challenge and he wished again he'd skipped this little ritual.

'But how serious you are this morning.' She laughed, trying to break the sudden chill between them and not succeeding. The sound of the front door opening caught their attention and, a moment later, Miss Domville attempted to slip past the door. 'Marianne, come in here and greet Lord Falconbridge.'

With the pursed lips of a petulant child, Miss Domville stepped into the room. Despite her fine features and well-formed figure, she wore a plain grey pelisse lacking decoration and style. It stood in direct contrast to her sister's lavish ruffles and lace and Randall sensed the girl had deliberately chosen it to irritate her sister.

'Good day, Lord Falconbridge,' Miss Domville offered tersely, one foot turned to leave.

'Whatever are you wearing?' Madame de Badeau scolded before Randall could return the greeting. 'Take it off at once.'

'I like it.'

'That was an order, not a suggestion. Dalton, come in here.' The thick-necked butler, smelling faintly of brandy, stepped into the room. 'Please help Miss Domville out of that awful pelisse and give it to the poor.'

Dalton took the pelisse's collar and Miss Domville shrugged out of the garment, the walking dress beneath no fancier.

'I don't see why you insist on hiding your body beneath such ugly clothes,' Madame de Badeau chided as

Dalton left. 'No gentleman will look at you if you keep dressing like a nun.'

'Better a nun than a strumpet,' Miss Domville sneered.

'You hate me. Good. Then you'll marry faster and be gone from the house.' Madame de Badeau stirred her tea, the silver spoon clinking against the flowery cup. 'I only hope you aren't foolish enough to wait for love. Find a rich, accommodating husband, like Lady Weatherly did, one who won't trouble you too much. After all, with a figure like yours, you might enjoy any number of young men once you're settled.'

'May I go?' Miss Domville seethed.

'Yes.' Madame de Badeau waved a dismissive hand. 'Hurry off and do whatever it is you do all day.'

Miss Domville fled the room.

'Silly child. One would think she didn't want her freedom.'

'She's young. In time, she'll see how the world is and adapt,' Randall said carelessly, covering a yawn with the back of his hand.

'Perhaps what she needs is someone to introduce her to the finer points of conducting herself in matters of love.' Madame de Badeau eyed him over the cup.

'An amusing prospect.' Randall stood, disgusted and eager to be free of the house. 'But I'm not about to start ruining young ladies, with or without their guardian's permission.'

Madame de Badeau set her cup on the table, the effect of Randall's rebuff evident in the rattle of the china. She stood, fingering the lace of her robe. 'Are you attending Lady Ilsington's ball tomorrow night?'

'I am.' He was tired of these society rounds, but

knew Cecelia would be there. It was the one bright spot in what looked to be a dull evening.

'Good, then we'll both be able to play our little games. Until tomorrow night.'

She held out her hand and Randall nodded over it instead of kissing the knuckles. Irritation hardened her eyes and not even her charming smile could hide it. Randall dropped her hand, straightened and left the room, not giving a fig for her mood or her desire to meddle.

In the hall, he expected to see Dalton waiting with his hat and walking stick, but the butler was nowhere to be seen.

Where is the man?

He stormed to the window, flicking aside the curtain to see Mr Joshua pacing back and forth in front of the carriage.

Footsteps sounded behind him and he turned, eager to collect his things and go, only it wasn't Dalton, but Miss Domville who appeared.

She hurried up to him, carrying his hat and walking stick, shooting a cautious glance at the morning-room door as she approached.

'I know more than she realises,' Miss Domville whispered.

'Yes, I've gathered as much from the way you listen at doorways.' He adjusted his hat over his hair.

She held out the walking stick. 'You're a friend of Mrs Thompson?'

'I am.' He reached for the stick, but she pulled it back.

'Then tell her to be careful. My sister does not have her best interests at heart.'

'She's never had anyone's best interests at heart except her own,' he snorted, wondering what the chit was about. Other than pleasant civilities, he'd never had so much as three words from her.

'Marianne, are you out there?' Madame de Badeau called from the morning room. 'Come in here at once.'

'Good day, Lord Falconbridge.' She shoved the stick at him, then trudged into the morning room.

Randall pulled open the front door and stepped outside, Miss Domville's odd warning nagging at him. Madame de Badeau had been kind enough to introduce Cecelia to society and the woman wasn't one for kindness, but he couldn't imagine what she might gain by ruining Cecelia. No doubt Miss Domville's cryptic words were only an attempt to stir up mischief in order to spite her sister.

Randall twirled his walking stick as he stopped beside the carriage.

'Well?' he asked Mr Joshua, eager to hear about Cecelia's reaction to the necklace.

Mr Joshua held out the box. 'She sent it back.'

'What?' Randall snatched it from him, his fingers crushing the velvet. 'Why?'

'She said she couldn't accept such a gift.'

'Of course she could. What woman doesn't accept jewellery?'

''Tis a rare one indeed, my lord.'

'Apparently, I've found her.' Randall shoved the slender box in his coat pocket. 'Did she at least like it before she sent it back?'

'I'd say so.'

'Then why did she send it back?'

'I don't know, but you have her permission to call.'

'How generous of her.' Randall climbed into the carriage and tossed his hat on the opposite seat. He settled on the squabs, his hands planted on top of his walking stick, his fingers tight on the silver handle. He should have known she'd reject his gift. She'd done nothing but toss him aside since Lady Weatherly's salon.

Mr Joshua picked up the hat, brushing it off with his hand as he sat down across from Randall.

'Where to, my lord?' the groom asked.

'To Mrs Thompson's, my lord?' Mr Joshua hazarded from across the carriage.

'No.' If he walked into her sitting room now, she'd know at once the effect she had on him. Most likely it was the real reason she'd refused the necklace. She'd challenged him to a game last night and now they were playing it.

'My lord?' the groom pressed.

'Home,' Randall commanded.

The groom started to close the door, but Randall stuck his walking stick between it and the jamb.

'No. To Mrs Thompson's.' He would be the one to set the rules, to make the moves, not her.

Mr Joshua's eyebrows rose in surprise, but he said nothing as the groom closed the door.

The carriage set off and Randall sat up straight, balancing himself with his walking stick. Mr Joshua kept his thoughts to himself and Randall was glad. He was in no mood for the man's humour.

What the devil was he doing going to Cecelia? Sending the gift back was a message and his visit would be an answer. He should wait a few days, then call upon her without a hint of agitation. He could go to White's, but after his win against Lord Westbrook, the club and the company were proving tedious. Too many men like Lord Malvern kept hoping to make a name for themselves by challenging him to a game of cards. Though at the moment, the social upstarts' nagging seemed more preferable than a widow determined to annoy him.

He raised the walking stick, ready to bang it against the roof, but stopped.

'Is there something you need, my lord?' Mr Joshua asked as Randall lowered the stick.

'No, nothing.' There was no reason to appear agitated and it didn't matter if she'd refused his gift. He could purchase a hundred such tokens and distribute them throughout London without a second thought.

The carriage turned a corner and the houses became more simple and understated. He settled back against the leather and stretched out one leg across the floor. He was not about to let her see the effect she had on him. This was his game and he would run it.

Cecelia rubbed her forehead with her fingers, unable to write any more. It was the third letter she'd drafted to Paul asking, then demanding, now pleading with him to pay her widow's portion. The other two letters smouldered in the grate, the heavy scent of smoke echoing her mood. She snatched the letter from the blotter, crumpled it and tossed it in with the others. No, she wouldn't beg. She might ask and insist, but she would not beg. She took up her fourth sheet and in simple words made her case for the payment, reminding him of Daniel's desire to see her taken care of and a son's duty to obey his father's wishes. She paused at the end of the letter to look at the slanting lines, knowing nothing she wrote would make a difference. Virginia law might demand he pay her, but there was no one in England or Virginia willing to help her press her case. All the people who'd flocked to Belle View after Daniel's death had closed their doors in her face.

Paul might respond if the crest of Falconbridge were etched on the top of the paper.

She stuck the pen back in its holder, nearly laughing aloud at the thought. She wasn't likely to get any help from Randall, only more trinkets and the start of a questionable career as a courtesan. Things were not desperate enough to place her feet on such a road. At least not yet.

She sealed the letter, summoned Mary and gave her instructions for its delivery. Mary was not two feet out of the room when the front doorknocker sounded through the hallway.

'Mary, if that is Lord Strathmore, please tell him I'm out,' Cecelia called, hearing footsteps in the hallway and assuming they were the maid's.

'It's not Lord Strathmore and I can see very plainly you're in.' Randall came around the corner and the room seemed to shrink as he entered, his presence filling the small space. He wore a cinnamon-coloured coat, which added to his size, while the black waistcoat cut close to his stomach emphasised his lean strength. Cecelia braced herself as he strode towards her, waiting for his arms to press her against the firmness of his chest and for his mouth to claim hers as it had last night. She fingered her gold bracelet, her whole being scared tight by his approach, yet ready to melt into his calming embrace.

He stopped before her, sweeping off the hat and handing it and the walking stick to Mary, who hurried up behind him, red faced with embarrassment.

'I'm sorry, Mrs Thompson, he came in as I was leaving to post your letter,' the flustered girl explained.

'It's all right.' The anticipation drained from her,

the lack of his embrace leaving her as unsettled as her strange craving for it. 'Please see to the letter.'

The maid dipped a curtsy and hurried away.

'I'm glad to hear you're putting Strathmore off. I thought you two were becoming quite close.' Randall laughed, a noticeable edge to his jest.

'Lord Strathmore and I are not close.' Despite the initial rush of excitement, she didn't relish seeing Randall on the heels of her letter to Paul. It only heaped one insult on top of another.

'Cecelia, have you seen my fan?' Theresa called out before she stopped at the morning-room door, her lips forming an O as wide as her eyes. 'Good afternoon, Lord Falconbridge.'

She dipped a curtsy, teetering with barely contained giggles as he answered it with a respectful bow.

'Good day to you, Miss Fields.'

'Theresa, your fan is on my dressing table,' Cecelia answered, eager to send the girl and her giggles away, but Theresa lingered in the doorway.

'I'll fetch it at once. I'll probably be upstairs for a very long time,' she announced, looking back and forth between them as if helping to plot an elopement.

'Yes, thank you.' Cecelia's terse dismissal did nothing to dampen her cousin's conspiratorial smile and Theresa floated out of the room, her giggles fading as she hurried up the stairs.

Cecelia turned back to Randall, wishing she could dismiss him as easily as Theresa, especially since he wore the same annoying smile as her cousin.

'Miss Fields is a charming young lady,' he complimented. 'Quit bold and spirited.'

'I'm afraid I've allowed her more freedom than I

should have, but it was different in Virginia. I find it difficult to be strict with her now. It's not our habit.'

'It's charming to see. Not everyone I know is as kind or loving with their charges.' His smile faded into something more serious, like a man watching a child play with a wooden top and wishing he could find the same joy in something so simple.

'But I suspect you didn't come here today to discuss my cousin.'

'No. I didn't.'

Cecelia motioned to the chairs near the table. He chose the sofa in front of the window instead, dropping on to the cushion at one end. She looked at the other end, empty and inviting, and chose the small chair across from it.

'Why did you refuse my gift?' he asked with startling directness.

'Did you really drive all the way here to ask me that?'

'I drove here because you said I could.'

'I didn't think you'd call so soon.'

'Are you disappointed?'

'No. Surprised.' He'd been so eager to be rid of her ten years ago. Why was he so persistent now?

'Good, I like to surprise you. It amuses me.'

And there was her answer. 'Surely there are other people in London to amuse you.'

'Perhaps, but they aren't as kind and honest as you.'

She swallowed hard. Honest was the one thing she hadn't been since coming to London. 'You are too kind.'

'And you are determined to avoid answering my question.'

'Not at all. I shouldn't have been so bold with you last night. In the spirit of the evening, I forgot myself, which I can ill afford to do, not with Theresa to think about. I must safeguard my reputation as well as hers if she's to find a husband, and accepting expensive gifts from gentlemen is no way to do it.' This was as close to the truth as she was willing to venture.

'What about accepting a gift from a friend?'

'Are we friends?'

'I'd very much like it if we could be.'

'Why?'

Randall shifted on the sofa, looking uncomfortable for the first time since she'd seen him at Lady Weatherly's. 'As you've discovered, London is full of shallow people and while, on more than one occasion, I've sought nothing but to cultivate their respect, I'd be lying if I told you it brings me great joy. It did once, but not any more.'

He pulled the thin box out of his pocket and removed the lid. 'You're not like everyone else, you aren't impressed with my title and you don't hunger after all the things you think I can give you.' The chain sparkled as he took out the pendant and laid it in the palm of one hand, cradling it like a delicate seashell. 'I know I've been brusque, if not inappropriate with you, and it was a mistake. Please believe me when I say I wish us to be real friends.'

He held out the pendant and she stared at the warm gold, wanting to believe in the sincerity behind his offer, but too afraid of being disappointed. He'd let her down once before, like almost everyone else in her life, and with so many troubles already plaguing her, there was little room for one more. 'I'm not sure we can be friends.'

'If you aren't ready to accept my friendship, then please do me the honor of accepting the gift and giving me the pleasure of seeing you wear it.'

Before she could object, he was on his feet and behind her chair.

Her skin tingled as he came close, anticipation building with each sweep of his breath over the back of her neck. He lowered the necklace on to her chest, his fingers so close to her cheeks, he only needed to stretch them out to caress her. As the warm pendant touched the tops of her breasts, she drew in a long breath, catching faint traces of almond above the sharp metallic scent of silver from where he'd gripped the walking-stick handle. The chain draped up the length of her chest, feathery against her flesh like his fingers brushing the back of her neck when he fastened the clasp.

Then he laid his hands on her shoulders and one thumb slipped beneath the fabric, his touch as soft and gentle as the weight of the pendant. She closed her eyes, gripping the chair cushion as she waited for him to slide his hands down her arms and lower his face to hers so she might know again the feel of his tender lips.

'Now, let me see it.' His deep voice plucked the tension building inside her before his hands slid over the curve of her shoulders as he slowly moved away.

She opened her eyes and allowed herself to breathe again. Pushing against the chair's sturdy arms to steady herself, she rose and turned, surprised by what she saw.

His eyes were serious and unsure, like the moment before he'd first kissed her at Falconbridge Manor. She felt it, too, the wanting mixed with the fear of risking too much and being rejected. Her heart caught in her chest, the pendant heavy around her neck.

'Do you like it?' he asked, all his London airs gone.

She lifted the necklace, running one finger over the finely etched ivy clinging to the brick. 'Yes, it's lovely. It reminds me of the old mill at Falconbridge Manor and the way the sun used to strike the bricks in the afternoon.'

'Yes, I thought so, too.' His words were so quiet, she almost didn't hear them. 'It suits you.'

Her eyes met his and it was as if they were alone again in the little boat, the ripples from the mill wheel pushing them into the centre of the pond, away from everything and every problem waiting for them on the shore.

He reached out and lifted the pendant from her fingers, the metal catching the light behind him and sending a slash of gold across his cheek. In the soft sweep of his hand over hers, she knew there was more to this gift than simple friendship and more to Randall than the jaded Marquess. He was just a man standing before her, hoping she treasured his gift.

'If only you could be this kind with everyone all the time,' she offered, trying to draw out more of the considerate man, the person he struggled so hard to hide.

He laid the pendant gently against her chest and she tensed, eager for the soft press of his fingertip against her skin, but he was careful to avoid touching her this time. 'Not everyone deserves it.'

She glanced at the grate with the letters to Paul smouldering inside, disappointment replacing her anticipation. 'No, some people don't.'

'Do I?'

She wanted to trust him and in this moment she almost did, but the charred papers in the fireplace and the bills littering her desk made her hesitate. 'I don't know yet.'

'Then perhaps some day soon you will.' He stepped back, clasping his hands behind his back, and the old

Randall was gone, leaving the man of London standing before her once again. 'Now, I have to go.'

'Must you?' It surprised her how much she wanted him to stay.

'I'm afraid I have other business to attend to today.' He bowed, then made for the door, fleeing more than leaving, and she wondered who he feared more, her or himself.

'Thank you for the present, Randall.'

He stopped, his stiff shoulders relaxing. 'It was my pleasure.'

Then he left.

She paced the room, her steps taking her close to the window before she whirled around and walked away, refusing to watch him leave. The carriage equipage jangled and the rhythmic clop of hoofbeats began. She turned to see the dark green carriage pass by outside, nothing inside visible through the leaded glass. He was gone, but his absence didn't put her at ease, or answer all her lingering questions. One moment he was the rake she detested, the next he was the man she'd first fallen in love with. She wished he'd choose who to be so she might know how to behave. Though it was possible he no longer knew the difference between the real Randall and the fake.

'I've come to settle my debts,' Lord Westbrook announced. He stood before the wide oak desk in Randall's office, his appearance as neat as expected for such a meeting. However, heavy circles hung beneath the Baron's light eyes and Randall tapped the wood, realising how much the debt must be weighing on him.

'Have you now?' Randall motioned for him to take

a seat, then lowered himself into his own chair, waving at Reverend to lie down on the floor beside him.

'A gentleman always pays his debts.'

'Even when they'll ruin him?'

Lord Westbrook studied the floor. 'Yes.'

Randall leaned back against the leather, seeing something of his young self in the Baron's discomfort. He'd taken the same idiotic risks his first year in London, daring the ghost of his father to strike him down for doing everything the old man used to rail against, and more. If Lord Westbrook's reasons were as shallow as Randall's, he deserved this punishment. 'Why did you wager so much?'

Lord Westbrook met Randall's question with a defiant look. 'You wouldn't understand.'

Randall laced his hands over his stomach. 'Try me.'

'I did it for love.' Lord Westbrook sat up straight, showing a bit of pluck for the first time since he'd sat down across from Randall at the card table. 'My income is not substantial and, though my title assures me certain privileges, the family of my intended raised objections to the match. I'd hoped to win enough to allay their fears.'

'But instead you lost everything.'

'Everything was already lost.' Lord Westbrook ran his fingers through his straight hair, his anguish over losing the woman he loved greater than the pain of losing his estate. 'Now, may we proceed with the formalities? I've brought the deed.'

He pulled a yellowed paper from his coat pocket and laid it on the desk. Randall eyed it, but didn't move.

If only you could be this kind with everyone all the time.

He looked across the polished oak at Lord Westbrook, whose one leg bounced nervously. No, not everyone deserved his kindness, but not everyone deserved to be crushed simply because he could, especially when their motives were more noble than any of his had ever been. 'Let me offer you another proposition.'

'You have everything of mine. What more do you want?' Lord Westbrook cried, jumping to his feet, as panicked as a rabbit caught in a snare.

'Your time and patience. Please, sit.' Randall motioned the man back into his seat. 'Despite a well-cultivated reputation, it's not my desire to ruin young lords new to London. Therefore, I'll return your land to you along with your winnings on two conditions.'

Lord Westbrook's jaw fell open in surprise. Randall could understand his disbelief. He barely believed what he was saying.

'First, you leave London today and not return for at least three years. That should prove sufficient time to make society forget about you and your losses and believe whatever story you decided to concoct about how you regained your fortune.'

'And second?' Lord Westbrook asked, hope colouring his voice.

'You don't make public what I've done. If you do, I'll spread such malicious rumours about your ungentlemanly conduct regarding the debt, you'll never be able to show your face in society again. Do you understand?'

'Yes, yes, I do. Thank you, Lord Falconbridge.' Lord Westbrook stood and extended his hand across the desk. Instead of taking it, Randall picked up the deed and laid it in the Baron's palm.

'Allow me to suggest, instead of gambling, an investment in the Maryland Trading Company. I have it on good authority it will turn a profit. Go to their offices and speak to a Mr Preston regarding the matter. Tell him I sent you with discretion.'

'I will indeed, my lord. Thank you. You don't know how much this means to me.'

Yes, I do. 'Good day, Lord Westbrook.'

Randall rang the hand bell on his desk and a moment later the butler appeared and escorted Lord Westbrook out of the room.

Randall stared at the closed door, noticing the scratches at the bottom where Reverend had pawed to get out. No doubt the youth was practically singing in the street with joy. As long as he kept his end of the bargain, Randall didn't care what Lord Westbrook did.

He looked down at Reverend, who stretched, then came to sit beside him. Randall scratched behind the dog's head, making the dog's nose point in the air. 'I suppose you think Cecelia had something to do with my decision.'

The dog's ears shifted forward.

'She didn't. I simply have no desire to maintain a house in Surrey.'

Despite what Cecelia thought of him, this wasn't the first kindness he'd performed since she'd last known him. There were others, legions of them, but not for the men or women of society. It was the rare one who deserved it.

Including Randall.

He moved to the table near the window. A ceramic jar sat on it next to a decanter of brandy he kept for guests and as a reminder of his strength in refusing it. He ran his hand over the top of the cold crystal stopper, the old unease pushing him to remove it, pour himself a deep draught and savour the burning flavor. It would kill the regrets and confusion churning inside him, just as it'd killed his innocence and his father.

He jerked his hand away and snatched up the lid to the jar. The clink of the porcelain brought Reverend to his side, his wagging tail making the fringe on the carpet flutter. Randall took out a couple of hard biscuits, then replaced the lid.

If Cecelia learned of his kindness to Lord Westbrook, would she consider him worthy of friendship, or search for something more selfish in his motives?

'Sit.' The dog obeyed and Randall tossed him the treat. Reverend caught it in midair, then eyed him, waiting for more, and Randall tossed him another.

Cecelia wasn't going to learn about it. If he told her the story and it got out, every man he'd ever played would be at his door begging for their losses back and people like Madame de Badeau would laugh at his lenience.

He turned the last biscuit over in his palm. At one time, Madame de Badeau's skill with gossip had added to his reputation, helping him cultivate the image he craved, the one which kept everyone at bay. Now he felt the mistake in letting people like her define him.

He tossed the last biscuit to Reverend, then marched to the French doors and threw them open. The dog shot past him and down the stairs, scaring up the birds picking through the grass.

A breeze shook the pink roses growing along the edge of the portico where Randall stood. The blush of the petals reminded him of Cecelia's smooth skin beneath his fingers when he'd clasped the pendant around her neck. Her shoulders had teased him as they had in Sir Thomas's studio, only this time there were no reprimands to keep him from feeling the heat of her skin, despite the risk of her pushing him away.

Then she'd stood and faced him. In her full, parted lips there'd lingered an anticipation he could almost touch, and he'd realised it was no longer his ego driving him to capture her attention. He wanted her friendship, as much as he'd once wanted the adoration of society, and he craved the freedom to take her hand, draw her down on the sofa and reveal how memories of his father sometimes haunted him at night.

She, more than anyone else, would understand.

Reverend bounded up to him with a stick and Randall took it and flung it across the garden, sending the dog running after it. What did it matter if she understood or not? He wasn't about to throw himself on her sofa and moan over his father like some weak fop. Instead, he'd enjoy the peace and tranquillity of her house and the brief respite it offered from all the machinations of society and people like Madame de Badeau.

Chapter Eight

Cecelia fell back against her chair, tossing the letter down next to the grocer's bill that arrived with it in the morning post.

Theresa looked up from her breakfast. 'What is it? What's wrong?'

'I should have saved my shilling instead of mailing the letter to Paul. He's already sent us more excuses as to why he can't pay my widow's portion.' She shoved the letter across the table to Theresa, who scowled at the contents.

'I hope the crops fail,' she blurted, the letter shaking in her hand. 'I hope another hurricane flattens the house and all the fields. I'd rather see it in rubble than know he has it.'

Cecelia agreed, but didn't say it, afraid of what other hate might spill from her if she let even this little bit slip out. 'Let's hope it doesn't come to that, or we may never see a shilling.'

'I don't see how we will anyway.' She snatched up a piece of toast and began to butter it.

'Perhaps one of our future husbands will be kind enough to hire a solicitor to press our case.' She rose from the table, weary after another long night of fitful sleep.

'Where are you going?'

'Upstairs to fetch the books. I have an appointment with the bookseller.'

'So early?'

'It's my best chance to sell them without being seen. Few in society rise before noon.'

Theresa's hand tightened on her knife and butter dripped on to her plate. 'You're going to sell them all, even Daniel's?'

'It's the most valuable of the lot.' She patted Theresa's shoulder, trying to offer her the courage she fought to rouse within herself. 'It's only a book. We still have our memories.'

Theresa looked down at the toast, but not before Cecelia caught the shimmer of tears in her cousin's eyes. Cecelia squeezed her shoulder, then headed for the stairs, pausing at the sight of Mary waiting there, her fingers twisting her apron.

'Mrs Thompson, might we now discuss my unpaid wages?'

'Not now, but I'll have some money by this afternoon and can offer you something.'

'Thank you, Mrs Thompson. Oh, and the baker is demanding his pay or he'll give us no more bread.'

'I'll see to him as well when I return.'

Cecelia started up the stairs, each step heavy on the treads. Paul's letter was nothing more than she'd expected from him, but seeing his refusal to pay written in a plain hand made the cut deeper.

On the upper landing, exhaustion settled over her like the darkness in the hallway. Pushing open the door to her room, she eyed the chest, then walked past it, sitting down in the window seat, reluctant to open the lid and look again on her dwindling possessions and all the sad reminders of her past.

She touched the pendant resting on her chest beneath her dress, tempted to sell it and keep the books, but she couldn't. In the warm gold she felt the first kindness she'd experienced since coming to London. Randall wanted her friendship and the wounded woman in her wanted to curl up next to him on the sofa and cry out her troubles. For a brief moment yesterday, she felt he would have listened, put aside all his airs and schemes and arrogance, and comforted her the way Daniel used to during the nights when she awoke, thinking she'd heard the faint cry of her buried little son.

Sobs tore at her chest and the tears burned her eyes as they rolled down her cheeks, dropping on to her lap.

Why is Randall doing this to me? Why is he bothering me? She balled her hands against her temples, bending forward beneath the weight of her pain and slamming her fists into the cushion. He wanted her to open herself up to him, lay herself bare once again and hope he didn't crush her. How could he ask such a thing of her? *Doesn't he know what I've been through?*

He didn't know. No one did except Theresa.

She pushed herself up, the tears falling silently as she sat in the window, weak and drained, wanting only to lie down and close her eyes and not rise from the cushions again. It was too much, all of it: the loss, the worry, the memories and how even those were being torn from her by poverty or faded by time. Daniel's face was no longer clear, not even in dreams, and she'd tossed last night, struggling through the mud of the dark images to see him again. The memory of Randall's hands on her shoulders had finally pulled her from the cloying dream, but even this comfort proved fleeting as all her worries rushed in to fill the night silence. They tormented her as much as the longing to accept Randall's kindness and the unspoken peace it offered.

Peace, she sniffed, wiping her wet cheeks with the back of her hands—for all the peace Randall was likely to offer, she might as well tell society the truth and expect them to rush to help her. No, trusting him was like trusting Paul, fruitless and futile.

The sun peeked over the top of the house across the street. It was getting late and there was still an appointment to keep.

Randall entered the quiet bookshop, thankful to leave the bright sun out on the street for a while. Another early morning kept him from his bed, the need to do something, anything, driving him out of the house when most of society was still asleep.

'I brought these with me from Virginia.'

He heard her voice before he spied her at the counter. Cecelia stood with a small stack of books, watching the bookseller thumb through a large one with interest. Randall moved along the edge of the room, enjoying the way the light from the large windows fell in patches on the yellow cloak draped over her neck, making the amber threads in her hair sunlight could the subtle waves, a sadness note noticed the redreach darkened her ex to a child and not a bound ness of her even her books? It wasn't unusual for held, as satisfy gambling debts by exchanging coins, but there seemed little reason for a wealthy widow to do the same. He'd seen her gambling at Lady Thornton's. Perhaps she'd wagered too much.

He thought of slipping out before she noticed him. Whatever her reasons for being here, they were none of his business and there was no reason for him to interfere. Let her handle her affairs as she saw fit, they did not concern him. However, the deep furrow above her eyes and the tight line of her pretty mouth kept him from leaving. He edged closer, listening to their conversation, careful not to draw attention to himself.

'If you have more editions like this one, I'll gladly purchase them. Hunting books of such quality command a good price,' the bookseller offered.

'These are the only ones I have. I wouldn't even part with them now except I'm a widow and no longer in the country and I have little use for them.' Cecelia flashed the bookseller an innocent smile, but Randall caught the lie in the way her fingers worried her gold bracelet.

'Of course. Please excuse me while I confer with my associate on a fair sum.' He laid the book on the stack and walked off down the counter.

Cecelia pulled the book to her and ran one finger over the leather, tracing the gold-tooled title. Her chest rose and fell with a heavy sigh and Randall took one step, soothe way to stride to her, take her in his arms and not in such the shadows in her eyes, but he couldn't,

He glanced a place.

go, but he wasn't a

misery. ondering again if he should

'Good morning,' he gre her here alone in such

'Randall.' She jumped, a

over her pale cheeks, as if he'd

ding

over the counter with her hand in the till. 'What are you doing here?'

'You sound surprised to see me in a bookseller's shop.'

A tiny smirk raised one corner of her lips. 'If I remember correctly, you were not one for scholarship.'

'People can change.'

The faint humour faded. 'Yes, of course, but in my experience, they rarely do.'

The bookseller returned with a slip of paper and passed it across the counter to her. 'Is this satisfactory?'

She glanced at the sum with a frown. 'They are fine books.'

'Yes, but it's a fair price,' he countered.

'Is it?' Randall asked and both Cecelia and the seller stared at him. Randall opened the large book and turned the pages, admiring the watercolours of pheasants and ducks. 'I can't remember when I've seen such an excellent book. Any gentleman would pay a top price for it.'

He pinned the bookseller with a pointed look. The man shifted on his feet, looking nervously back and forth between them, and Randall could practically hear his purse strings loosening.

'Of course. Let me speak with my associate and see if we can do better.' The bookseller hurried away.

'Randall, this isn't necessary. I only wish to be rid of the books, not fleece the gentleman for every shilling.' The lie lingered in the hope which brightened her eyes and the fast movement of her fingers on the bracelet. At this rate, she would soon wear the gold through.

The bookseller returned and handed her another folded paper. 'Will this do?'

She read the note, her eyebrows rising at the new amount. 'Yes, this will do.'

The bookseller handed a small envelope across the counter. 'It was a pleasure doing business with you. If you receive any more books from Virginia, I'd be most happy to have them.'

'Thank you, and you, too, Randall. Good day to you both.' She slipped the envelope into her reticule and turned to leave, but Randall stepped between her and the door.

'Perhaps I can tempt you with tea. I know a place not far from here. It's a respectable establishment and I promise not to do anything scandalous.'

Her lips drew up in a little smile, but it could have been pure joy for the way it brightened her face. However, even this slight break in the clouds of her unease did not calm her restlessness. 'I'm sure you'd be quite well behaved, but I'm afraid I can't. I have other things to attend to today.'

'I see.' He didn't protest, not wanting to press her as he had at Lady Thornton's. 'Good day, then.'

He stepped aside and she hurried to the door, pausing to allow an incoming gentleman to hold it open. She cast one last look at Randall before stepping out into the street.

'How may I assist you, Lord Falconbridge?' the bookseller asked, drawing Randall's attention across the counter.

'I wish to purchase the large book the lady just sold. I'll take it with me now. Charge it to my account.'

Randall picked up the book, tucked it under his arm and left. No doubt the man would charge him double what he'd just paid Cecelia for it, but Randall didn't care.

Outside, Randall approached the carriage and the groom standing by the open carriage door, Mr Joshua standing next to him. Down the street, the slash of Cecelia's yellow cloak caught Randall's attention. He watched the bright cape move through the growing crowd of people, the book beneath his arm heavy. Her troubles were not his, but he couldn't let her go.

He handed the book to Mr Joshua. 'Take this and put it somewhere where it can't be seen and wait here with the carriage.'

'Yes, my lord.'

Randall hurried down the street after Cecelia, keeping the cloak in sight over the heads of passing men and women. An unmistakable heaviness slowed her pace and it wasn't long before he was next to her.

'A beautiful day for a walk, isn't it?'

She whirled to face him, her wide, startled eyes narrowing. 'Did you follow me?'

'I can't be denied the pleasure of your company.' He laid one hand on his heart, determined to charm her, but it only deepened her scowl.

'Then I'll have to disappoint you.' She started off again, faster this time.

Randall paused for a young soldier leaning heavily on a cane to pass, then caught up to Cecelia. 'At least allow me to accompany you.'

'No.' She turned on him so fast, he took a step back. 'Now leave me be, I have no patience for your games today. Find someone else to trifle with.'

'I'm not trifling with you.' His hands tightened at his sides and he nearly left her standing on the pavement stewing in her anger. However, the pain lacing her words kept him still. Whatever her troubles, they ran deeper than her suspicion of his motives and he opened his fingers, letting his concern soften the chafe of her reprimand. 'I'm worried about you. I haven't seen you this upset since…' He paused, not wanting to deepen her wounds by reminding her of the last time they'd been together at Falconbridge Manor. 'I followed you because I wanted to make sure you're all right. Forgive me for going about it the wrong way.'

'I'm sorry.' With one shaking hand, she rubbed the back of her neck. 'I received some bad news from Virginia this morning. A dear friend of mine is very sick.'

'Then allow me to see you home in my carriage. The street is no place to be when you're upset.'

She moved closer to him, then stepped back as if changing her mind about accepting his offer. 'I don't think I should. It wouldn't be proper.'

'You needn't worry.' He held out his arm. 'There isn't anyone up this early to see us.'

She eyed it as if it were a rotten log wedged in a stream waiting to snag an unsuspecting swimmer, her fingers moving fast on her bracelet. Then she tucked the gold beneath her sleeve and slid her hand under his elbow. 'Thank you.'

He examined the slender fingers resting against his dark blue coat, wanting to raise them to his lips and kiss each one, lay her palm against his cheek and listen while she told him her troubles. Instead, he guided her back to the carriage, aware of every rustle of her skirts, each time her cape brushed his hand and the wind slid her perfume over him.

The groom pulled open the door and Mr Joshua stepped out.

'Mr Joshua, ride with the groom,' Randall instructed.

'Yes, my lord.'

Randall handed Cecelia in, then took the seat across from her, noting the weary way she rested against the squabs and stared out the window. He sensed something deeper in her melancholy than the illness of a friend.

The carriage rocked into motion, the jangle of equipage steady beneath their silence. Despite the bright cloak falling over her arms, she looked small and lonely against the dark wood behind her, her vulnerability bringing Miss Domville's warning to mind.

'May I offer some advice?' he ventured. 'Guard yourself around Madame de Badeau. She isn't the friendly woman she appears.'

'Yes, I know,' she answered with a deep sigh. 'Theresa and Miss Domville are of the same opinion, but I assure you, I've been careful around her.'

'You shouldn't trouble with her at all.'

She frowned. 'I thought she was your friend?'

He flexed his fingers over his knees. 'More of an old acquaintance.'

'You mean lover.'

He threw back his head and laughed. 'With such a bold tongue you worry about *my* reputation?'

'No, only mine.' She folded her hands in her lap and his amusement faded. 'I would distance myself from her, but I need her help to secure invitations.'

'I can provide all the connections you need.'

She didn't look impressed. 'Imagine how people would whisper if you suddenly took such an interest in me.'

'Yes, they're so simple minded that way,' he sneered.

She cocked her head to study him. 'You have so much disdain for society, yet you do everything you can to cultivate its opinion. I wonder how much you truly despise it.'

'More than you realise. As for cultivating its opinion,

I prefer it to think little of me. It keeps the sycophants and marriage-minded matrons at bay.'

'If that's your goal, then why not retire to the county like your uncle and be done with it?'

He tapped his knee. 'Because, even as you've discovered this Season, society is the devil we know.'

'Yes, it is.' Her agreement whispered the same longing to be free of society he sometimes experienced before his pride reared up to remind him why he stayed.

The carriage turned a corner, leaving the busy street for Cecelia's small neighbourhood before drawing up to her door.

The groom handed Cecelia down and Randall followed her out, stepping on to the pavement and taking in the square. He'd been so focused on the gift yesterday, he'd failed to notice the dark soot staining the stone and how the park in the centre was more natural than even the current fashion allowed. In a few weeks, it would border on unkempt. This was not a part of London he frequented and it seemed a touch too shabby for a widow of Cecelia's worth.

He joined Cecelia at the bottom of the steps leading to her door, studying the small house wedged in between the others. It was neat, but the dull paint on the railing and the small triangles of dirt in the corners of the windows were too obvious to overlook.

'Thank you, Randall, for your kindness.' She turned, hands in front of her, ready to dismiss him, but he wasn't ready to go.

'Tell me, why did you sell your books? Are you in need of money?'

'No.' She clutched the reticule ribbons as if they were a horse team on the verge of bolting. 'I mean, well, my funds from Virginia have been delayed and it's been so long since I've managed my own affairs. In my excitement to enjoy London, I overspent.' The words came out in a rush.

'I didn't think you were enjoying London quite so well.'

'I am—I mean we are, what with all the new gowns and diversions of the city.' She moved one step higher, as if trying to slide away from him. 'I can't believe I was so foolish with my money, but in a very short while, I'll receive my income from Virginia and have nothing to worry about.'

'I see.' Nothing about her plain yellow cloak or the house and neighbourhood spoke of lavish spending. However, he could easily believe her income from abroad being delayed. His payments from the Maryland Trading Company were often late. 'When your income arrives from Virginia, you should consider more fashionable lodgings.'

'I will. We were so eager to be settled after arriving in London, I'm afraid I chose the first place available.' She clasped the key to her chest before lowering her arms. 'Thank you very much for accompanying me home and for your concern.'

Her explanations didn't completely ease his concern. Everything she told him made sense, but not the frightened way she watched him or the strained, nervous way she spoke. It all hinted at something more serious.

He stepped closer and she took one step up, bringing her face level with his. 'Cecelia, please believe me when I say I want us to be real friends again. If there is anything I can do for you, you only have to ask.'

'Whatever do you mean?' Her voice trembled.

'I mean, if you're ever in need of assistance, you have only to come to me for help.'

She pressed her lips together as though stopping herself from saying something. He drew closer and the heady scent of her flower perfume surrounded him as he waited, willing her to believe him, to tell him her real troubles and ease both of their worries. She tilted her face to his and he raised his hand, aching to trace the sweep of pink along her cheek, to twine his fingers in the soft hair at the nape of her neck, pull her to him and comfort her with a kiss when the flick of a curtain over her shoulder made him freeze. Miss Fields watched them from the window, not bothering to conceal her interest.

He straightened and stepped back. In the middle of the street in front of prying eyes was no place to gain Cecelia's trust.

She noticed her cousin in the window, the hesitant yearning he felt in her replaced by the stoic widow he'd come to know so well. 'I assure you, I'm in no trouble at all, but thank you for your concern. Good day.'

He didn't stop her as she hurried up the steps and pushed open the door, pausing a moment to look back at him before she slipped inside.

When it closed, the tarnished knocker clanked against its equally tarnished strike plate. Whatever Cecelia's situation, it wasn't as rosy as she'd tried to make him believe.

Randall strode to the carriage where Mr Joshua stood beside the groom next to the open carriage door.

Randall was about to climb inside, but the sight of the hunting book lying on the squabs made him pause. He trilled his fingers against the wooden side, the condition of Cecelia's lodgings and her reaction to the sale of the books nagging at him.

'Mr Joshua, Mrs Thompson mentioned another matter she's attending to today. I want you to follow her and see where she goes. Be very discreet.'

'Yes, my lord.'

Guilt followed Randall into the carriage. He should trust her and not interfere in her private affairs, but the pain on her face in the bookseller's haunted him too much to ignore.

Cecelia leaned against the front door, the cloak tight around her neck, its weight oppressive. Through the wood, she heard the equipage of Randall's carriage and the steady clop of the horses as it drove off down the street.

She slapped her palm against the wood, the sting not nearly as sharp as her frustration.

Of all the booksellers in London, she'd chosen the one Randall frequented. She could have stood anyone else seeing her; their words would be vicious but not as searing as the pity in Randall's eyes.

'I thought you went to the bookseller's, not out with Lord Falconbridge,' Theresa remarked from the morning-room door, more amused than curious.

Cecelia marched to the hall mirror and tugged at the cloak ribbons, eager to be free of the heavy garment. 'I did, but Lord Falconbridge saw me.'

Theresa's amusement disappeared as she rushed to Cecelia's side. 'What did you tell him?'

'I said I wasn't used to managing my money and my payments from Virginia were late.' She tugged at the stubborn strings, ready to snap them in order to free herself.

Theresa gently moved Cecelia's hands aside and began to work the knot loose. 'Do you think he believed you?'

Not at all. 'I'm not sure, but I think he did.'

'Maybe if you tell him the truth then he can help us,' Theresa hazarded.

'I'm not about to tell Randall anything so personal or damaging.'

Theresa's eyebrows rose with surprise. 'Randall?'

'Lord Falconbridge.' She pushed the girl's hands away and pulled off the cloak, tossing it over the banister and storming into the morning room. She paced across the rug, anger, worry and fear swirling in her until she thought she might be sick.

'He's not as bad as you think,' Theresa offered from the doorway.

'You're so sure? You know him so well?' Cecelia snapped, but Theresa didn't flinch.

'No, but I see the way he looks at you.'

'Please, spare me any more of your romantic notions.' Cecelia marched to the desk and pulled the reticule from her wrist. 'Randall is charming and polite and I can see how you've been fooled into thinking he cares, but believe me, Randall is not a man guided by emotion, especially not love.'

'If so, then why did he drive you home today? Why did he give you the pendant?'

'Because he only wants another wealthy widow to dally with.' She slammed the reticule down on the blotter. 'You've heard the rumours and the way people talk about him. You know what he did to Lord Westbrook. Do you truly believe he'd risk such a carefully cultivated reputation for us?'

'I think you're being unfair.'

'Because you don't know Randall the way I do.'

Theresa stuck out her chin like a stubborn child.

'Maybe I don't, but I know a gentleman doesn't buy a woman jewellery unless he's truly interested in her.'

Cecelia crossed her arms, matching Theresa's determination. 'What about all of General LaFette's trinkets?'

'His gifts were never as valuable or as pretty as Lord Falconbridge's and he never looked at you the way Lord Falconbridge did just now.'

Cecelia touched the pendant, tracing the sturdy square hidden beneath her dress. Theresa was right. The General's gifts were never so personal or bestowed with the sincerity she saw in Randall's face yesterday, and again today. On the stairs, with his hand so close to her cheek, he'd asked her to trust him and for one fleeting moment she'd almost believed the caring in his eyes. Cecelia pinched the bridge of her nose, wishing she knew what to think of him and whether or not she could trust him. It had taken so long to get over the last hurt he had caused and she feared suffering the pain all over again.

'You don't have to tell him the truth,' Theresa said. 'But I think you should give him the chance to be kind to you. Maybe he's sorry for what he did and this is his way of making it up to you.'

Cecelia looked down at the reticule on the desk, thick with the money from the sale of the books. He'd already helped her today without asking for anything in return except her faith in him. It seemed ludicrous to believe Theresa might be right, but the weight of the pendant around her neck made the idea too tempting to dismiss.

'I don't know, but I can't think about it now.' She dug the money out of the bag and slid it into the desk drawer, unable to ponder Randall's motives, Theresa's suggestion or anything except the more pressing problems facing her. 'I must keep my appointment with Mr Rathbone.'

'But if you sold the books, we don't need him.'

'The money from the books won't last for ever, and I'd rather see Mr Rathbone now and bargain for good terms than turn to him when we're desperate and accept poor ones. Besides, if all goes well, we may not need Mr Rathbone's money.'

'You mean if Lord Strathmore proposes,' Theresa stated flatly.

'Him, or another gentleman.' She wasn't quite ready to believe Randall was that sincere in his pursuit. 'Now, I must go.'

Cecelia headed for the door, but Theresa stepped between her and it as though stopping an errant husband from visiting the public house. 'Promise me, no matter how desperate things become, you won't marry Lord Strathmore.'

The concern in Theresa's voice sent a stab of guilt through Cecelia. She couldn't blame her for not understanding, or for hoping. 'You know I won't make such a promise. Now, don't worry so much. The Season is young and we still have options open to us.'

Cecelia stepped out into the fine weather, shielding her eyes from the sun with her hand. What she wouldn't give for a thick fog, something to match her mood and hide her from anyone else who might be out today. Hopefully, no one from society would be at Mr Rathbone's.

A brisk breeze played at the hem of her skirt as she moved from the quiet of their neighbourhood to the busy main street, her pace slowing as she drew closer to the Fleet. The imposing front of the gaol came into view and Cecelia paused to watch a soldier in a tattered red uniform, one sleeve pinned up at his side, step through the iron gate. Catching a glimpse of two women washing inside, their lives confined by the gaol and their debts, Cecelia knew she couldn't place her faith in Randall the way Theresa did. If Theresa was wrong, if Randall proved to be no better now than he'd been ten years ago, Cecelia and Theresa might spend the rest of their days languishing here, if not somewhere far worse. He'd asked for her friendship and she'd give it, but it would not be a deep one. She couldn't afford it.

'She went where?' Randall snapped the hunting book closed and rose from his chair, stepping over Reverend, who slept on the rug in front of him.

'Mr Rathbone's, my lord,' Mr Joshua repeated.

'Surely she can't have overspent that much?' Randall shoved the book in between the others on a shelf, but it stuck out, breaking the clean line of spines along the library wall.

'Might get herself in real trouble if she isn't careful,' Mr Joshua warned, echoing Randall's thoughts.

'Or if her money doesn't arrive in time to pay the debt before the interest increases it.' Randall dropped the book into an opening on a lower shelf, but it was too small for the space and he took it up again.

'Mr Rathbone's better than most, my lord, but he doesn't shrink from sending people to the Fleet if they don't pay.'

Randall tapped the book against his palm, pacing before the shelves. Cecelia was intelligent and he didn't doubt she'd be cautious in her dealings with the moneylender, but he'd seen more than one young lord fall prey to such men and all their games. It wouldn't take long for Mr Rathbone to trap her and turn the small debt into a crushing one. 'If she knows her payments are coming from Virginia, then why did she turn to a moneylender? Why not a friend?'

'Being from the colonies, maybe she doesn't know better. And I don't expect the likes of Madame de Badeau to help her. Dalton asked her for money once, flew at him like a cat, despite all his years of servin' her.'

Then why didn't Cecelia come to me? The memory of her face in the conservatory, her hands balled at her sides, her lips trembling while she struggled to stand up beneath his barrage of heartless words flashed before him.

She didn't trust him.

The realisation burned a hole in his gut. He tossed the book across the tops of others on the shelf and marched to the desk. He might have handled their break poorly, but it didn't lessen his present concern, or his desire to see to her safety.

Removing a key from his waistcoat pocket, he slid it into the lock on the top drawer. 'I know a little something of Mr Rathbone, he isn't likely to tell you his client's business.' He removed a leather pouch from the drawer and tugged open the drawstring, then counted out a number of coins. 'See if his servants have anything to say on the matter.'

Mr Joshua opened his hand, his eyes neither greedy nor scheming as Randall dropped the money into his palm. 'Why not ask him yourself, my lord?'

'And do what? Purchase her debts? Have her know I'm sneaking around prying into her personal affairs?' He could well imagine her lack of faith in him after that little row. Even if he bought the slip anonymously, with all his questions today, it wouldn't be long before she discovered it was him. Lord Strathmore wasn't likely to be so generous. He probably owed the man himself, and Mr Joshua was right about Madame de Badeau's unwillingness to help.

'If her mistress is visiting a moneylender, Mrs Thompson's maid probably hasn't been paid her wages,' Mr Joshua suggested. 'She might be willin' to take a little blunt in exchange for information.'

'Make sure she's discreet before you offer it.' Randall dropped a few more coins into the valet's hand, then pulled the drawstrings closed. 'I don't want her alerting her mistress.'

Mr Joshua slipped the coins in his waistcoat pocket. 'Why are you so keen on this one, my lord?'

Randall returned the bag to the drawer and locked it. 'I have my reasons.'

Mr Joshua nodded, accepting the answer as Randall knew he would. It was only the second time since Mr Joshua had begun working for him that he'd been less than candid with the valet. The young man knew enough secrets about Randall and a number of highborn ladies to scandalise society. It was the other lesson from Uncle Edmund he'd taken to heart—one loyal servant was worth his weight in gold.

'Mr Joshua, you don't have any plans to take up a trade, do you?'

'No, my lord, I enjoy workin' for you, though some day I'd like to have a son and set him up fine. Maybe send him to Oxford, raise him up like Mr Brummell was raised.'

'Then when the time comes, we'll have to see what we can do.'

'Thank you, Lord Falconbridge.' Mr Joshua bowed, then left.

Randall stared at the empty doorway and the large painting of Falconbridge Manor hanging in the hall across from it. The tall columns of the front portico stood proudly in the foreground, but little of the land surrounding the house was visible, not the stables, the river nor the mill wheel turning lazily at the edge of the pond.

He'd been a fool to think he could secure Cecelia's confidence with a few well-chosen words and jewellery. She'd seen through his ruse and, despite his efforts today, the damage was done. Randall settled back into his chair and Reverend rose and laid his head on Randall's leg. He scratched behind the dog's ear. Despite the past hanging between them, he had to find a way to earn her trust, to make her see there was more to his interest than a rake's desire. Then she'd tell him the truth and he'd help her, whatever her problem.

Chapter Nine

The thump of the front-door knocker echoed through the house and Cecelia and Theresa caught each other's eyes in the dressing-table mirror.

'It's too early for Madame de Badeau,' Cecelia said. A little light still filled the sky outside the window. 'We're not due at Lady Weatherly's until eight.'

'Perhaps it's Lord Falconbridge.'

Cecelia pursed her lips at Theresa, amazed at how the girl continued to cling to the idea of a romance between her and Randall. 'I doubt it, but I'll go see.'

'I'll come with you.'

Cecelia didn't wait, but made her way out of the room, stopping at the top of the stairs.

'Please tell Mrs Thompson that Mr Rathbone is here to see her.' The clipped voice trailed through the hall and sent a shot of panic through Cecelia.

Theresa grabbed her arm, her fingers tight. 'What's he doing here?'

'I don't know.'

'What if someone sees him?'

'Stay here while I deal with him.'

Theresa released her and Cecelia descended the

stairs, gripping the banister to settle herself and regain her courage. She was once the mistress of Belle View, responsible for managing all sorts of matters high and low. She would not be rattled by a moneylender.

'Good evening.' She clasped her hands in front of her and fixed him with the same smile she once reserved for insolent foremen. 'I know you said you'd call, but I didn't think it would be so soon.'

'I make it a habit to surprise potential clients who don't possess property. It keeps them from hiding the valuables they didn't offer as collateral, the ones I might seize if they default due to interest.' He bowed and she was struck again by his youth. He was no more than thirty, tall and lean with the matter-of-fact air of a businessman. He wore a fine brown redingote, the full lapels and generous skirt adding a little bulk to his slender frame. If she'd seen him in a sitting room, she wouldn't have guessed him for a moneylender, but the son of a well-to-do merchant. 'The house is hired?'

'It is.'

He peeked into the morning room, his sharp eyes taking in the furnishings and calculating in an instant their worth and hers. 'And the furniture?'

'It is let with the house.'

'Is there a dining room and library?'

'There's no library and the dining room is this way.'

She led him down the narrow hall and into the dining room, seeing the plainness of the furniture through his eyes and hating the cheapness of it all. Her dining room at Belle View had been three times the size and the walnut table used to shine in the candlelight.

He walked around the table in the centre before stopping at the narrow buffet to look over the pewter. 'And there is no silverware or china?'

'No, I sold it in Virginia to pay for our passage.'

'So you have no more collateral than the jewellery and clothes we spoke of this afternoon?'

'That's correct. Would you care to come to the morning room to discuss it?'

He shook his head. 'Our discussion will be brief. Given your lack of collateral, I cannot advance you the full sum we discussed.'

Cecelia swallowed hard, fighting to maintain her composure. 'I'm expecting an inheritance payment in December.'

He smiled to reveal white, even teeth. 'Most people in need of my services are expecting some kind of payment. Rarely does the money arrive. I can provide half of what you requested.'

'And if I need more in the future?'

Mr Rathbone made his way around the table, running one finger over a long scratch in the surface. 'I've heard rumours of a titled gentleman who's taken an interest in you.'

'You presume a great deal.'

'I make it my business to know the affairs of my clients. Is it true?'

Cecelia offered a terse nod.

'Once you and the gentleman have an understanding, I'll advance any additional sums you require for your cousin's dowry or other debts.'

'You wish me to borrow money without my potential husband's knowledge?'

'You wouldn't be the first lady to do so, nor the last to appeal to her husband's good graces to see it repaid.'

'No, I suppose not.' She'd heard stories of ladies losing vast sums at the gambling tables and borrowing money from friends and others to cover their losses.

Some of them were the wives of great men and were obliged to retire from society until their husbands could settle their debts.

'It isn't my intention to ruin you, Mrs Thompson, but like any man of business, I must protect my investments.'

'Yes, of course. Thank you, Mr Rathbone.' She led him out of the dining room and down the hall when, to her horror, Mary opened the front door and Madame de Badeau and Lord Strathmore entered. In the dining room, so far from the front of the house, she hadn't heard Madame de Badeau's carriage arrive.

Her heart began to race. If Madame de Badeau saw Mr Rathbone, she might guess the reason for his presence. Cecelia looked around for somewhere else to lead the moneylender, but there was nowhere, not even a linen closet in which to stash him. All she could do was continue forward, though she slowed, forcing Mr Rathbone to come up short behind her and then step back to avoid colliding. Though Mr Rathbone was not the most sought- after moneylender among the *ton,* he dealt with enough people in society to be known. Hopefully, Madame de Badeau would not recognise him and Cecelia could safely see him out with little question or concern.

'There you are,' Madame de Badeau called with a wide smile before she glanced over Cecelia's shoulder. Her smile remained fixed, but a cat-like glee filled her eyes and Cecelia's heart dropped. She recognised him.

Cecelia summoned again her mistress-of-the-plantation facade. Whatever secret Madame de Badeau thought she'd discovered, Cecelia would use confidence to dampen its impact. She stopped and stepped to one side, giving Madame de Badeau a full view of the moneylender. 'Madame de Badeau, Lord Strathmore, allow me to introduce Mr Rathbone.'

Madame de Badeau's eyes darted back and forth between Cecelia and Mr Rathbone as if observing something so wicked, not even her skills as an actress could hide her curiosity. 'We have already been introduced. It was in Brighton, was it not?'

'I do not recall.' The clipped words made it clear the moneylender didn't share her interest in their former meeting. Madame de Badeau shot him a scathing look, but it failed to humble him or change his attitude and Cecelia silently applauded the young man. He was the first person she'd met, besides Randall, who cared nothing for the woman or her opinion.

Whatever Lord Strathmore thought of the encounter he kept it well hidden as he examined a poorly executed landscape near the foot of the staircase.

'Good evening, Mrs Thompson.' Mr Rathbone tipped his hat to her and left.

As soon as Mary closed the door behind him, Madame de Badeau began her second act, appearing all concern and care as she took Cecelia's hands.

'My dear, you aren't in trouble, are you?'

'Of course not.' Cecelia laughed, sliding her hands out of the woman's tight grip. 'I only consulted him on the advice of my solicitor. It seems money from Virginia takes a great deal longer to reach London than I realised and I overspent. My husband used to manage such affairs. I fear without him, I'm simply lost, though I am improving.'

At last Lord Strathmore joined the performance, his face long with sympathy. 'I know how hard it can be for a woman without a man to guide her. Please allow me to send my man of affairs to help you. It would save you the trouble of dealing with unsuitable people like Mr Rathbone.'

He laid one hand on his heart, his sickeningly sweet look of pity making Cecelia want to scream. 'You're most generous and kind, but I assure you, I'm in no need of such services. My money from Virginia arrived this morning, Mr Rathbone has been repaid and I shall have no more dealings with moneylenders. Please allow me to collect Theresa and then we may go.'

'Of course,' Madame de Badeau agreed. 'We can't keep such an *eligible* lady from all the young men.'

Madame de Badeau's words followed Cecelia up the stairs to where Theresa stood, pressed against a far wall, out of sight of the hall. Her eyes were wide with worry and Cecelia took her arm and pulled her back into her room.

'She didn't believe you, I could tell by her voice,' Theresa whispered as Cecelia closed the door. 'How long until she tells everyone?'

Cecelia fixed a small flower in Theresa's hair. 'We aren't interesting enough to society for her to bother spreading rumours. If anything, she'll only whisper nasty things to Lord Strathmore and his loss, as you've pointed out before, would not be a tragedy.'

Theresa's body eased, her worried frown softening. 'No, it wouldn't be.'

'Now smile and put on a brave face. We can't have Madame de Badeau and Lord Strathmore suspecting more than they already do.'

Randall stepped into Lady Ilsington's crowded ballroom, conscious of, but ignoring, the many people watching his entrance. Hushed conversation trailed him as he made his way to the garland-draped balcony overlooking the dance floor. Beneath the high crystal chandeliers, men and women moved in circles and twirls over the polished dance floor while the ones along the sides performed as many intricate steps for those around them. None of them interested him. Cecelia was the only person he wanted to see.

He looked over the tall feathers marking the coiffures of a group of matrons and Cecelia's soft features came into focus. He strolled down the wide staircase, then twisted past a few soldiers standing together, exchanging greetings with numerous gentlemen before stopping a short distance from the feather-bedecked matrons. He ignored their disapproving looks, knowing how fast they'd bow and scrape to him if he showed an interest in their daughters, the old hypocrites. If it weren't for Cecelia, he'd leave them all to their quadrilles.

Cecelia stood alone across the room on the edge of the dance floor, watching Miss Fields perform a chasse with Lord Bolton. She wore a dress of deep purple shot with silver thread and the gown sparkled as she shifted to better see her cousin between the guests. A fine strand of pearls draped down her chest, their roundness echoed in the curve of her high breasts. The gold clasp shone at the nape of her neck and above it bounced the few curls not contained by the thick ribbon wound through her coiffure. Against the dark of her silk gown, the smooth skin of her shoulders curved to tempt him and his palms burned at the memory of her warmth. He rarely danced at balls, but tonight he wanted to press her body against his, feel the soft contours of her hips as they waltzed, exchange witty remarks and enjoy again the same light-heartedness they'd shared during the race in Rotten Row.

The dancers parted into two lines, giving Randall a

clear view of her, and she finally noticed him. A stunning smile illuminated her eyes with a power he felt in his chest. He nodded to her, afraid to return the smile for fear everyone around them would notice her effect on him. He could sense her disappointment from across the room as he wound through the guests, willing himself to not stare at her.

The dance ended and the crowd grew thick as young people changed partners and their mothers jockeyed for better positions along the perimeter of the dance floor. Randall made a wide arc through the room until he was behind Cecelia. He listened while she offered her cousin a few words before Lord Bolton escorted Miss Fields out for another dance. When the music rose to begin the set, Randall stepped up next to her, inhaling her flowery perfume as he bent down close to her ear. 'I wouldn't allow her to dance with Lord Bolton again.'

She startled, a pink flush spreading over her creamy skin, her finger and thumb finding the gold bracelet on her wrist. 'Why not? He seems like an affable young man.'

'He plays a good game, but he has a pack of debts and is a regular customer at a house of ill repute in Covent Garden. One more dance and people will assume they have an understanding.'

'It wasn't like that in Virginia,' she stammered, worrying the bracelet. 'And I didn't know Lord Bolton was so disreputable.'

'Which is why he's paying her so much attention. You're the only matron not aware of his situation.'

Her lips drew tight as if debating marching into the middle of the dance and removing her cousin from her partner. 'Thank you very much for your warning and your concern. No one else here...' she nodded at Madame de Badeau, who stood laughing with Lady Weatherly on the balcony '…saw fit to enlighten me about Lord Bolton's true situations or the etiquette concerning dancing partners.'

'And you think *my* friendship questionable?' He laughed, twisting his signet ring on his finger, waiting for her answer.

'I wouldn't say questionable, only, unexpected.' She let go of the bracelet, her hands dropping in front of her as she laced her fingers together, the relaxed gesture giving him hope. 'Now, since you've warned me off Lord Bolton, perhaps you know of someone more suitable for my cousin?'

'Let me see.' He looked over the guests at the group of young bucks laughing together near a column. 'See the tall gentleman with the brown hair near the fireplace? That is Mr Menton. His grandfather was a merchant who amassed a nice fortune in the islands and purchased a baronetcy. His father, Sir Walter Menton, continued the business and Mr Menton enjoys a tidy income from his colonial holdings. He isn't likely to look down on your cousin's background or lack of station.'

'A most amusing and blunt way to assess his potential, and Theresa's,' Cecelia replied. 'How do you know the gentleman?'

'His father purchased Hallington Hall, the estate adjacent to Falconbridge Manor. He's quite affable, though his mother is a mushroom and might be the only obstacle should the two enjoy an affection.'

'I never would have believed it, but you almost possess the skills of an accomplished matchmaker.'

He brought his lips close to her ear, the flicker of her pulse beneath the sweep of her hair tempting him to near distraction. 'I have many skills of which you are not aware.'

She flashed him a teasing sideways look, not rising to his bait, but not shrinking from it either. 'Does one of them involve arranging an introduction with the young man?'

He wanted to laugh, but restrained himself to a wide smile. 'It would be my pleasure.'

He slid his fingers beneath hers and raised them to his lips. The satin carried the smell of her perfume and he drank it in as he laid a firm kiss across the back of her hand.

The catch of her breath was more beautiful than the notes of Handel floating through the room. With regret, he stepped away, hating to break the moment, but not trusting himself to linger longer.

Cecelia clutched her fan as if the thin wood could steady her as she watched Randall head off through the crowded ballroom. He stood taller than the other men, his confidence keeping her eyes riveted to him as he approached the group of young gentlemen. They were equally impressed, jumping to attention at the appearance of the notorious Marquess.

She snapped open her fan and waved it in front of her, her attention darting to the people around her, wondering if anyone had noticed her and Randall conversing in such an intimate manner. If they did, they didn't reveal it, neither meeting her eyes nor returning her nervous smile. Not even Madame de Badeau seemed to notice, her attention focused on something of interest near the musicians.

The small breeze from her fan did little to cool her skin or calm her worries. It seemed every time Randall came near her, she forgot herself and in the most public of places. She should have stepped away, placed some distance between them, but his low voice curling around each word had turned her feet to lead.

Theresa and Lord Bolton passed by in a promenade, reminding her of Randall's warning. It seemed both she and Theresa were destined to make spectacles of themselves tonight with inappropriate men. Cecelia closed the fan, wishing the dance would hurry and come to an end. The dances in Virginia never seemed to last so long, yet this one felt like it would continue for ever.

She turned back to Randall, watching him speak with Mr Menton to the visible jealousy of the young man's acquaintances. Randall wasn't just conversing with a neighbour, he was vetting a possible suitor for Theresa, going out of his way to secure an introduction which might help them.

Why? What does he hope to gain?

Guilt pricked at her and she reached up to touch the pendant before realising she'd left it at home. Maybe Theresa was right and she had been unfair to him. He'd warned her about Lord Bolton and helped her at the bookstore, yet Cecelia continued to look for something wicked in his deeds. The only thing wicked was the way her body responded to his words and his touch.

She twisted the pearls around one finger, the sweep of his dark hair over his forehead while he spoke, his confidence as steady as the pillar behind him feeding the hunger he'd created when he'd kissed her hand. It pulled her towards temptation like the current of the James River used to draw small boats out from the shore. The pearls tightened around her knuckle. She wanted to fall into him like she used to fall into the river on hot days and quench the heat which stole over her body in a light sweat every night.

He motioned to her and she looked down at a small smudge on her slipper, fearing the hold he had over her. If she relented to his pursuit, it might cool her need, but drown any chance of a respectable future.

She disentangled her finger from the strand, raised her head and pushed back her shoulders as Randall approached with the young man.

'Mrs Thompson, may I present Mr Menton.'

'It's a pleasure to meet you, Mrs Thompson.' Mr Menton bowed, friendly in a way she hadn't seen in either Lord Bolton or any of the other young bucks who'd deigned to dance with Theresa. When he straightened, it revealed his height and, though his nose was a little too large and his jaw too wide to make him devilishly handsome, he possessed a certain appealing charm.

'Mrs Thompson is an old friend of my family's,' Randall explained. 'I was just telling her about your estate.'

'I know the land well, it's an excellent property. Your father was wise to buy it,' Cecelia flattered.

Mr Menton stood a little taller. 'Mother was against it at first and Father was afraid of taking on such a burden, but I convinced them in the end.'

'I've advised them on a number of improvements,' Randall added.

'He did and we're grateful. The estate has prospered and put all my father's fears to rest.'

'And does your mother enjoy the country?' Cecelia asked.

'It's too far from London for her tastes, but it suits her sense of how a baronet should live.'

The dance ended and Lord Bolton escorted Theresa back from the dance floor, a catlike smile on his round face. When they were close, Cecelia nearly reached out to snatch Theresa away, but Randall acted first.

'Lord Bolton, may I have a word?' He stepped between the two young people.

'Yes, of course,' Lord Bolton mumbled, unable to refuse the request, and followed Randall out of earshot.

'Mr Menton, may I present my cousin, Miss Theresa Fields.' Cecelia nudged Theresa forward. 'We have recently arrived in London from Virginia.'

'I visited there once on my way to Bermuda. It's beautiful.'

'What business did you have in Bermuda?' Theresa asked, her Virginia accent stronger than usual and Cecelia knew her cousin was happy and relaxed.

'My family has an interest in a shipping company based there.' He made the statement without ego or arrogance and Cecelia detected in his countenance a genuine kindness lacking in other gentlemen. While he and Theresa discussed Virginia and the rigours of sea travel, Cecelia felt the spark between them and, for the first time in days, hope. Though one conversation did not mean an engagement, especially with the possibility of obstacles, this was more progress than they'd made since the start of the Season.

Behind Mr Menton, Randall spoke to Lord Bolton. Judging by the young man's long face, he was taking a dressing down from the Marquess. If so, it seemed strange for a man of Randall's reputation to chide another for indulging in the same pastime he surely enjoyed. Or did he?

She'd heard many stories attached to Randall's name, but nothing so nefarious as brothels. If he were a well-known patron of bawdy houses, she felt sure Madame de Badeau would have related the story with glee. Whatever the truth of his nocturnal habits, for the moment she didn't care. He was helping her and she appreciated it.

'May I have the pleasure of this dance?' Mr Menton asked as the musicians began the next set and the couples started to form up.

Theresa looked to Cecelia for approval and she readily gave it. He offered Theresa his arm and their lively conversation continued as they walked out on to the dance floor.

'See, friendship with me has its advantages,' Randall boasted, resuming his place beside her. She shivered at the closeness of him, wishing he would offer his arm and lead her on to the floor, sweep her along in time to the music and lull her with his deep voice. She would willingly surrender to his lead if it meant feeling weightless and free of cares, comforted and protected, if only for a few minutes.

'Don't congratulate yourself yet. One dance is not a proposal.'

'Then you have set me quite a challenge.'

'Wonderful, for I long to see Theresa settled before—' *we are ruined.* Cecelia caught herself.

'Before what?'

'Before the Season is over.' She worked to cover the worry with a light tone. 'For even I know enough about society to know a young woman's chances diminish each Season she is not settled.'

'Then let us increase her value in society's eyes. May I have the pleasure of this dance?' Randall held out his hand and Cecelia's heart jumped in excitement before stopping in fear. Despite her former daydream, the idea of promenading with him in front of everyone made her nervous. However, after his kindness, it would be rude to refuse.

She took his hand and his fingers closed around hers with a subtle possessiveness she sensed but couldn't fully comprehend. She followed him on to the dance floor, feeling as if all eyes were upon them, weighing them down with their opinion. She only hoped Randall was right and Mr Menton saw advantage in a connection to people on such intimate terms with the Marquess of Falconbridge.

As they positioned themselves for the allemande, Theresa spied them through a gap in the partners. She threw her a questioning look, but Cecelia ignored it. There would be ample time to explain the decision to dance later.

Then the music began and she and Randall moved forward and back in time with the others. The dance turned them to face one another and the closeness of him, more than the pace of the steps, made her breath quicken and her heart race. Studying the shiny buttons on his waistcoat, she didn't dare look up and reveal her nervousness. Instead, she glanced across the room, catching Lord Strathmore's narrow eyes. The disapproval on his face annoyed her, as did the realisation that, for all his fawning and flattering, he'd never done half as much for Theresa as Randall had tonight.

Theresa was right. Cecelia had misjudged him.

'You're still worried about being seen with me publicly,' Randall challenged, mistaking her silence.

She faced him, raising her chin in determination. 'No, I'm proud to be seen with you.'

He pulled back in surprise. 'Quite a change from before.'

'You helped me when others wouldn't and you've

been nothing but kind, even when I haven't been.' She raised her hand above her head for the turn and he grasped it, his grip firm, his thumb sliding over hers to nestle against her palm.

'Then I'll do my best to deserve your newfound faith in me.'

His heat spread through her hand, undiminished by the thin satin glove separating their skin. It trailed down her arm, wicking through her as they moved in a circle together.

'What scent are you wearing?' he asked in a low voice. 'I always notice it on you, but don't recognise it.'

'Magnolia flower.'

The candles burning overhead brought out the subtle ring of yellow surrounding the centre of his blue eyes. 'It's intoxicating.'

'I'm glad you like it.'

'There's nothing about you I don't like.'

Her face grew hot and humour rose to cover her embarrassment. 'Even when I tease you?'

A smirk pulled up one side of his mouth. 'Especially when you tease me.'

'You never used to like my teasing.'

'I was young and stupid. I've matured since then.'

'You make yourself sound like a cheese.'

He snorted a laugh. 'I should think myself more of a fine wine.'

'If you like, but I'll think of you as a Stilton.'

'As long as you think of me. It's all that matters.'

She tightened her grip on his hand, forcing her feet not to lose their steady rhythm as they turned out for a promenade. 'Why?'

He let go of her as they each travelled around another couple. When they faced each other again, she saw his

London mask slide to reveal the man who'd stood with her in the morning room, then again yesterday on the front stairs. 'You remind me of better times.'

'Were they better?'

'In many ways.'

She looked down, studying the subtle weave in the grey threads of his waistcoat. Perhaps it was time to completely forgive him, but she hesitated, the wronged girl in her unable to let go of the hurt, still waiting for an apology which would never come. The musicians brought the piece to a close and all around them people stepped apart and clapped, but they remained together. His thumb pressed her palm again, the subtle touch making her feel calm and beautiful, even in the midst of so many people. She drank it in, wanting to hang on to him even as etiquette demanded she let go. As couples jostled past them, she felt the frail connection break and reluctantly allowed him to lead her back to her previous spot.

'Thank you very much for the dance.' He bowed, friendly but reserved, with none of the passion she'd sensed in him a moment before. The London facade had returned and the intimacy they'd enjoyed was gone. 'Now I must go.'

She wondered at the change in him, but in some small way understood. After all, she wore a mask for society, too. 'I wish you would stay.'

'My goal is to make you visible, not a spectacle. Besides, you must attend to your cousin and we must see if my attention has raised or lowered you in everyone's eyes.'

'Thank you again, Randall.'

'It was my pleasure.' With a wink, he left just as Theresa and Mr Menton returned. They were barely with her a moment before Mr Menton offered to escort them to the refreshment room. Cecelia agreed, following a step behind as they left the ballroom. Once they had their lemonade, she watched the couple, keeping a slight distance to give them privacy and enjoying their enthusiastic conversation.

'Mrs Thompson, you look lovely tonight,' Lady Thornton complimented, appearing at her side with Lady Featherstone. These ladies had barely acknowledged her at the card party; now they surrounded her with wide smiles, as if they'd all taken lessons from the same dancing master as green girls. Cecelia was polite, accepting their compliments about her dress with grace, Randall's influence in their sudden interest in her unmistakable.

Randall watched with amusement as women continued to approach Cecelia. He knew they'd speculate about his relationship with her, but they'd also accept her more readily than before. It would widen her circle of London acquaintances and hopefully dilute some of Madame de Badeau's influence.

'Careful, Randall, or you'll make our little widow the talk of society.' Madame de Badeau slid up beside him like the devil after hearing his name called.

'She appears to be handling the attention admirably.'

'And what of your attentions? Has she surrendered to your charm yet?'

He laced his fingers behind his back, the woman's presence grating. 'Contrary to what you believe, my personal life is not fodder for your amusement.'

'It is when you're on the verge of making a fool of yourself with a woman who is clearly trying to snare you.'

Randall twisted his signet ring. 'Mrs Thompson is no more interested in me than she is in Strathmore.'

'I don't think so, she's only better at luring you in than all the others, more subtle, and you won't see her plan until she has you before the vicar. Imagine how people will talk when the Marquess of Falconbridge marries a nobody.'

His jaw tightened at the nastiness in her remark. She was trying to coerce him with her wicked suggestion, bend him to her will and turn him against Cecelia, but he wouldn't be manipulated, not by her or anyone else. 'You overestimate society's interest in me and Mrs Thompson.'

'And you underestimate it and the damage it'll do to your little widow.' She snapped open her fan, waving it over her breasts. 'I should hate to see her driven to Italy by vicious gossip. I hear it's quite a haven for those who've been disgraced.'

'Careful how you speak of Mrs Thompson,' Randall growled, raising a warning finger between them. 'Because if you damage her reputation in any way, I'll make sure you're driven from London.'

He strode off, confident his threat would keep the Frenchwoman silent, but the malice she'd tossed at him made him wary. As a woman, there was little she could do to hurt him, but he knew she wouldn't shrink from attacking others to get at him. He climbed the stairs to the balcony, looking out over the guests to where Cecelia stood, surrounded by a number of society ladies. They clamoured after her now, but they'd turn on her as fast as lightning if Madame de Badeau whispered against her. He would not see Cecelia hurt because of him, and a plan began to form to protect her.

It was time to remove Cecelia from London.

Only years of practice kept Madame de Badeau from following Randall and shrieking at him. How dared he threaten her or act the chivalrous knight with Cecelia? He possessed no notions of chivalry.

Madame de Badeau gathered up her train and wound her way through the room, her hand so tight on the beads, the glass grated together. She'd tell him the truth about the two-faced harlot if it didn't mean Lord Strathmore might find out, too. Between the heads of two gentlemen, she spied Cecelia standing with her cousin and some nobody. She stopped, her lips curling in disgust as the two women surrounded the gentleman, trying to trap him with their lies like Cecelia was trying to trap Randall.

Just like her mother.

She heard the crack of glass and opened her hand to let the pieces of broken bead clatter to the floor.

A short distance away, she spied Lord Strathmore watching Randall leave the room, the irritation as plain on his face as if it were painted on. She approached him, the hint of a smile raising her lips as his eyes flicked to her breasts with ill-concealed appreciation.

She stopped beside him, dropping her train. 'You look as though you're not enjoying the evening.'

'I'd enjoy it better if Mrs Thompson weren't making a fool of herself with Falconbridge.'

'Stand up with her now and you'll start people speculating.'

'They'll only think I'm picking at his crumbs.'

'Perhaps, but think what a fool you'll make of him when you marry the woman everyone saw him dancing with tonight.'

Lord Strathmore's face brightened and he puffed out his chest at the imagined victory.

'Yes, you're right.' He trilled his fingers against his stomach. 'Ah, there is the end of the dance. Please excuse me.'

He hurried off to Cecelia, and Madame de Badeau relished the uncomfortable smile tightening Cecelia's features as the Earl asked her to dance. If all went well, it would only be the first of many uncomfortable, if not painful, moments for the little harlot.

Randall might threaten and dismiss her now, but he'd thank her once Strathmore and Cecelia were married and the truth was revealed. Then he'd come crawling back to her, begging for her to restore his ruined reputation and she'd bind him to her with her help, never letting him free again.

Chapter Ten

Cecelia poked at her meagre breakfast, spreading the last of her eggs around the plate with a fork, her plain toast and sugarless tea forgotten on the table beside her. 'I hope you enjoyed the cakes at Lady Featherstone's dinner last night, we can't afford such delicacies at home.'

'I can't dream of food.' Theresa threw out her arms with a theatrical sigh. 'Not when I have love.'

'Think of the money we'll save.' Cecelia rolled her eyes, wishing she could greet the morning with such excitement. Despite the relief of finally widening their circle of acquaintances, it wasn't enough to dampen the impact of the new bills delivered this morning. Not even Mr Menton's continued attention to Theresa during the past week had been enough to take Cecelia's mind off her worries, or Randall. She touched the pendant beneath her dress, disappointed at not having heard from or seen him since the ball. At every dinner and gathering over the past few days, she'd searched for him, disappointed by his absence and all the while convincing herself it was for the best. His influence in the arrival of so many new invitations was unmistakable and troubling. The more he helped her, the stronger his friendship became, weakening her determination to keep him at arm's length.

The sound of a carriage on the street outside echoed through the room and Cecelia looked up from her tepid tea. 'Who can that be? I thought Mr Menton left for the country this morning.'

'He did. It seems there is some social obligation his mother needs him to attend and he won't be back for a week.' She picked up the small stack of invitations beside her plate. 'How am I going to face all these soirées without him?'

'You'll find a way to manage.' Cecelia chuckled, trying to hide her own disappointment. The Season was slipping away fast enough without them wasting too much time on one young man who might forget Theresa the moment he left town.

The front doorknocker thumped and Theresa went to the window to look outside. 'Oh, my goodness, Lord Falconbridge is at the door.'

Cecelia stopped midsip of her tea. She set the cup down, nearly tipping both it and the saucer before steadying them.

Out of the corner of her eye, she saw Mary hurry by to answer the door. Cecelia rose and brushed the crumbs off her dress, then stepped up to the mirror over the mantel and smoothed her hair.

'You seem eager to greet him,' Theresa teased.

Cecelia settled her shoulders and faced her cousin. 'Of course. I must thank him for the introduction to Mr Menton.'

'Of course.' Theresa nodded with a wry grin.

The front door creaked open, followed by a strange scratching on the wood. Then a large black dog with a greying muzzle dashed into the room and straight at Cecelia. She backed up, her shoulder catching the marble mantel as the animal rose up on its back legs, placed his paws on her stomach and revealed the band of white fur beneath his neck.

'Reverend, is it you?' The dog licked Cecelia's face and hands as she rubbed his back, his body shaking with his wagging tail. 'I can't believe it. You were just a puppy the last time I saw you.'

'He remembers you. I knew he would.' Randall strode into the room.

'I certainly remember him. Oh, how wonderful it is to see him.' Almost as wonderful as seeing Randall.

He stood in the doorway, his affection for the dog evident in the warm way he watched them. He wore a brown redingote with a matching hat, which he removed and handed along with his walking stick to Mary. Beneath his hat, his dark hair lay matted and he raked his fingers through it, tousling it and making it fall over his forehead.

She wanted to run her own fingers through the thickness and push it away from his face, clasp her hands behind his neck and draw him down into a deep kiss. Instead, she scratched Reverend harder, making the dog's eyes close in delight. 'Good morning, Randall. It's a pleasure to see you.'

From behind him, Theresa mouthed 'Randall' with a questioning rise of her brows, her eyes sparkling like a child who'd just overheard a secret. Cecelia stood and flicked the look away with her hand before motioning Randall to the table. 'Would you like to join us for breakfast?'

'No, I already ate, but please, don't let me disturb you.'

With relief, Cecelia took her seat along with the others. She didn't relish inventing lies to explain the poor bread, bland tea or the absence of sugar. Reverend sat next to her, laying his head on her lap and looking back and forth between her and the plate. She broke off a small piece of bread and offered it to him.

'Miss Fields, I hear you and Mr Menton are getting along quite well,' Randall remarked.

'Very well, only he has gone to the country.'

'Which brings me to the reason for my visit.' Randall reached into his coat and removed an envelope. 'I've been in the country this past week on business. When I told Aunt Ella of your return to England, she insisted I bring you back with me for a visit.'

He held the letter out to Cecelia, his wide hand almost covering the small missive. She took one edge, trying to avoid his fingers, but she felt the subtle sweep of his thumb against her fingertips as he released the paper. It was almost imperceptible, but it sent a shock through her equal to a lightning bolt striking a mast. Her eyes met his, searching for the same reaction in their blue depths and meeting a penetrating stare she could not read.

Taking the letter, she opened it and read the contents. True to his word, his aunt expressed great excitement at the prospect of seeing Cecelia again. She stroked Reverend's head. A week in the country with Randall, away from the restraining influence of society, made her nervous. It smelled of a trap, but just how much did she want to step into the snare? The chance to see Lady Ellington again might be worth the risk and perhaps she could find a way to confide in the Dowager Countess the same way she had ten years ago. Maybe the kind woman could offer some solution to Cecelia's dilemmas.

Cecelia folded the letter, not sure if she wanted another marriage of convenience, though at this moment, any marriage besides one to Lord Strathmore was appealing.

She laid down the letter and peered up at Randall. To her shame, she wondered what he hoped to gain from a country visit. 'How very kind of Lady Ellington, but we can't impose.'

'It's no imposition at all.'

'Isn't Mr Menton's estate close to Falconbridge Manor?' Theresa interrupted. 'If we go to the country, then we can see him.'

'Theresa, we can't simply stroll over to his house and ring the bell,' Cecelia chided.

'Aunt Ella knows the Mentons well,' Randall added, selecting a slice of toast from a plate in the centre of the table. 'She could arrange for Theresa and Mr Menton to meet.'

'Please,' Theresa begged.

Cecelia frowned as Randall spread a large slice of butter on the bread. A visit to Falconbridge Manor might further Mr Menton's interest in Theresa, but she wasn't sure what it would do to her relationship with Randall.

She folded her hands over the letter. They had no relationship. They were friends and as a friend he was trying to assist her and Theresa again. It seemed wrong to refuse his help. 'I'll write to Lady Ellington this morning to accept her invitation.'

'There isn't time to write,' Randall announced, taking a bite of toast. Cecelia thought she saw him wince before he swallowed. 'If you'd please be ready by one, I'll collect you in my carriage.'

Cecelia sat back, aghast. 'So soon?'

'My business there cannot wait.' Randall dropped the

unfinished toast on the plate in front of him and rose. He snapped his fingers and Reverend's eyes shifted back and forth between Cecelia and Randall, but the dog didn't move.

'But we're expected at Lady Thornton's tonight,' Cecelia protested, irritated by his heavy-handed treatment. That he should come here unannounced and expect them to cancel their plans to journey with him to the country was ridiculous and flattering.

'Then you must send your excuses.' He snapped his fingers again, but Reverend remained by Cecelia's side, this time not even bothering to look at his master.

'We have other engagements beside Lady Thornton's.'

'Then you'll have many letters to write before we leave.'

'I'll start on them at once.' Theresa jumped up from her seat. 'Thank you, Lord Falconbridge.'

'My pleasure.'

'You've made her one of the happiest young ladies in London,' Cecelia observed drily as Theresa's quick footsteps faded up the stairs.

'And what of your happiness?' Randall asked with a seriousness she found unsettling.

She wished she could share her cousin's excitement.

'I'll be very happy to see Lady Ellington again.' If the Countess could be as influential with Mr Menton and Theresa as she had been with Cecelia and Daniel, it might solve all of their problems.

'And you'll see her soon enough, which is good because I'm not sure how else to get my dog back. I think he's quite taken with your company.' He took his hat and walking stick from Mary. 'I'll collect him when I collect you.'

'Aren't you worried about leaving him here?'

'Not at all. I know he's in capable hands. I'll see you both at one.' He slipped out the door.

Reverend yawned, smacking his mouth as he trotted to the hearth rug and stretched out under a strong shaft of sunlight. Cecelia watched the dog, irked at Randall, but touched to know he trusted her enough to leave his beloved dog with her. She drew the pendant out from beneath her dress and rubbed the smooth gold, unsure what the next few days might bring. With any luck, Lady Ellington would help Theresa make progress with Mr Menton. As for her and Randall, she was afraid to think about it, but with Theresa there, she could easily find ways to avoid him and the warm feelings building inside her.

'All the money you had to throw about and you've discovered nothing about why Mrs Thompson was visiting a moneylender?' Randall leaned over his desk, his fingertips pressed into the smooth surface.

Mr Joshua stepped forward and placed the coins in a neat stack on the desk. 'Never seen such a loyal group of men around a moneylender. Not one of them and none of the maids would say a word about his business. Seems Mr Rathbone pays them too well to risk takin' a bribe.'

'And Mrs Thompson's maid? Certainly she isn't paid so well?'

'Skitterish girl, that one, came over with Mrs Thompson and Miss Fields. Don't think she's ever been in a big town before. I tried speakin' to her, but she was suspicious of me, as if I planned to eat her for lunch.'

'No doubt her employer has cautioned her about London ways.'

'Should have cautioned herself about dealin' with the likes of Mr Rathbone.'

'Unless she has no choice.' Randall resumed his seat behind the desk and reached down to pet Reverend, his hand meeting only air. Out of habit he looked to the hearthrug before remembering the way the dog had clung to Cecelia that morning. He tapped his knee, the dual discomfort of Reverend's absence and the knowledge Cecelia might be in real distress making him restless.

The lack of food on Cecelia's table this morning hadn't escaped his notice, nor the poor quality of the butter and bread she ate. Even the furniture seemed out of sorts. Though he couldn't point to anything specific, no fraying rugs or worn cushions, something about the suite of furniture looked tired.

Randall rose and went to the window, reaching for the ceramic jar before catching himself again. Whatever the truth of Cecelia's situation, it was definitely worse than she wanted him or anyone else to believe.

Randall returned to the desk and scooped up the coins. He counted out a generous amount and handed them to Mr Joshua. 'These are for you.'

'Thank you, my lord.'

He handed him another small pile. 'These are for the maid. When we leave for Falconbridge Manor, I want you to stay behind for a few days. With her mistress away, the maid might be more willing to speak. In the meantime, send the carriage to Mrs Thompson's with my regrets for not joining them for the journey. It's time I paid a call on Mr Rathbone and got to the heart of this matter.'

Cecelia watched out the carriage window as Falconbridge Manor came into view. It stood on a small hill framed by large trees on one side and a wide expanse of rolling land on the other. The last of the late evening sun threw long shadows over the light stone, making the rows of windows sparkle. With its large front columns and classical lines, the house was stately and strangely understated for a family of Marquesses who enjoyed living in a grand style.

'What a magnificent house,' Theresa gasped from beside Cecelia.

'It is.' She ran her hand over Reverend's head, his soft fur easing the tightness in her stomach. He'd lain at her feet during the drive and now, sensing they were close to his home, sat up, panting as he stared out the window.

All during the rush to pack this morning, Cecelia had debated the wisdom of staying at Falconbridge Manor. She'd considered sending Theresa alone, entrusting her to Lady Ellington's care and asking the Countess to do what she could to further a match with Mr Menton. However, every time she'd moved to take the clothes from the trunk, intending to write her instructions and stay behind, she'd stopped. The chance to see Lady Ellington again and, to her shame, enjoy Randall away from the eyes of society proved too tempting. Here in the country, she could enjoy a brief respite from all the play-acting and perhaps know again the man who'd danced with her at the ball and whose pendant she wore so close to her heart.

The carriage stopped at the base of the large front staircase and Reverend whimpered in excitement until the groom opened the door. The dog shot out of the carriage and up the stone stairs to greet Lady Ellington at the front door. The Dowager Countess patted the retriever's head, then motioned for him to go inside, instructing a footman to take care of him.

Following Theresa out of the carriage, Cecelia drew

in a deep breath of the clean country air. The dry dust of the driveway mingled with the fresh cut grass and Lady Ellington's roses. The scent took her back to evenings with the dowager, waiting for the carriage, or mornings riding with Randall through the woods. Old emotions began to creep over her, but she forced them back. It wasn't a lie when she'd told Randall her memories were both good and bad, but while she was here, she didn't want them pulling at her like the thick mud of a marsh. She had enough troubles now without reviving the old ones.

'Cecelia, how wonderful to see you again.' Lady Ellington hurried down to greet them, her blond curls streaked with grey bouncing as she rushed forward to embrace Cecelia.

Cecelia held the woman tightly, inhaling her rosewater perfume and the hint of her favourite plum wine clinging to her fine dress. In a strange way, the scent smelled more like home than the bottle of her mother's old perfume at the bottom of her trunk. Lady Ellington caressed her back, the way she used to do when Cecelia had cried, and Cecelia's eyes filled with tears. The longing to sink down into the woman's ample chest and cry out all her stress and frustration almost made her forget Theresa, the footmen, driver and maid all standing around them.

'I am so sorry to hear about Daniel,' Lady Ellington whispered.

Cecelia squeezed her eyes shut and hugged the woman closer. To her shame, it wasn't the memory of Daniel which upset her so much at this moment. She took a step back, wanting to speak, to thank Lady Ellington for her kindness, but she couldn't for fear of releasing the sobs caught in her throat.

Lady Ellington cupped Cecelia's face in her soft, ring-clad hands, brushing away the tear slipping down Cecelia's cheek. 'It's more than Daniel, isn't it?'

Cecelia nodded.

'Don't worry, my dear. When you're settled in, we'll have a good long chat like we used to and work out what's to be done.' She smiled in her motherly way and Cecelia couldn't help but smile back, knowing deep down coming here had been the right choice.

Lady Ellington squeezed her hands, then turned to Theresa.

'And you must be Miss Fields.' Lady Ellington clapped her hands together, the large diamond ring from her late husband, the Earl of Ellington, sending a splash of rainbows across her face. 'I hear you've caught the eye of a certain young neighbour of mine.'

Lady Ellington hooked her arm in Theresa's and drew her up the stairs to the house, Cecelia following on her other side. 'I hope you don't mind, but I've taken the liberty of arranging many, shall we say, "chance" encounters between you and Mr Menton while you're here. The first will be a country ball at the assembly room. Won't he be surprised when I arrive with you?'

They entered the manor and walked through the high-ceilinged hall. Marble busts on half pillars between the tall windows watched them, the classical lines echoed in the numerous landscapes hanging in large gilded frames on the plastered walls.

'I don't know how well you remember the house, Cecelia, but I've made a number of improvements since Edmund passed.' Lady Ellington let go of Theresa, waving her jewelled hand over the hall and the large wooden staircase leading upstairs. 'For one thing, I changed the subject matter of the paintings.'

'Yes, all London was talking of Lord Falconbridge's art exhibition.'

Lady Ellington sighed. 'Sometimes Randall has Edmund's flair for the theatrical, but I'm relieved to see the last of them gone. I could live with the memory of my brother, but not those paintings. However, the statue garden is almost as he left it, though Randall has made a few changes and it's much improved. Now, follow me, there's a light supper waiting for you in the sitting room.'

Lady Ellington strolled off and Theresa hurried to Cecelia's side. 'What's in the statue garden?'

'Nudes,' Cecelia whispered. 'Enough to make a bawd proud.'

Cecelia drew a stunned Theresa forward, following Lady Ellington into a sitting room adorned with red-silk wallpaper and gilded trim. On a small table in the centre, an assortment of meats, cheeses, fine bread and cakes waited for them.

They sat down to enjoy the food, Cecelia relishing the strong brew and spooning a large helping of sugar into her cup. While they ate, Lady Ellington outlined their week, a lively mix of dances, dinners and rides, most of which, in some way, would include Mr Menton.

'When will Lord Falconbridge be joining us?' Theresa asked, shooting Cecelia an impish look before turning innocent eyes back to Lady Ellington.

'If he sent Reverend ahead, then he can't be far behind.' She looked at the dog, who leaned against Cecelia's leg, watching every bite of cake. 'I know more about Randall's comings and goings because of his dog than any letter he ever sends me. Reverend, come here and stop pestering Cecelia.'

The dog's eyes shifted to Aunt Ella before resuming their steady stare at Cecelia.

'He's all right. I don't mind.' She rewarded his patience with a piece of cake.

'He's quite taken with Cecelia,' Theresa added.

'He isn't the only one.' Lady Ellington smirked before hiding it behind a long sip of tea.

Cecelia focused on Reverend, adjusting his collar to keep her embarrassment from showing. She hoped Lady Ellington didn't intend to play matchmaker with her and Randall.

'You've arrived at a very fortunate time.' Lady Ellington set down her cup, then sat back with no small measure of pride. 'A young lady from one of the nearby families ordered dresses for her wedding trousseau, then eloped. Her family refused to pay for them, so I purchased the lot. The modiste will be here tomorrow morning to alter them for Miss Fields.'

'Oh, but Lady Ellington, I couldn't, I mean—' Theresa stammered, shooting Cecelia a panicky look. They couldn't afford new dresses, much less a modiste to alter them.

'Your clothes are quite fine, but I'm told they lack the fashion and I want you to look your best for Mr Menton,' Lady Ellington explained.

'You're too kind,' Cecelia stepped in. 'But we can't impose.'

'Nonsense. The dresses and modiste are already paid for so I'll hear no refusals.' Lady Ellington patted Theresa's arm. 'Since I have no daughter of my own, I shall simply adopt you. Now, tell me about your beau.'

Lady Ellington listened with rapture while Theresa told her all about her time with Mr Menton, leaving Cecelia to her thoughts.

Cecelia finished her tea and set down the cup, noticing the large portrait of Randall hanging across the room near the door. Judging by the style of his clothes and the smoothness of his face, it must have been painted not long after her summer here, perhaps during his Grand Tour. His eyes held not the surety of the present, but the same false arrogance she remembered. Like her, he'd been struggling with his own grief and searching for a sense of his place in the world, puffing himself up to hide the pain lying just below the surface, a pain she knew too well.

She picked up her tea and took a long sip, the deep flavour helping put off the memories. With any luck Randall would stay in London and she could focus on Theresa and Mr Menton. As much as she wanted to see him again, his absence would give her a chance to enjoy the quiet of the country and regain something of the woman who'd once managed Belle View.

Chapter Eleven

Cecelia walked down the line of horses in the Falcon-bridge stable, admiring the fine selection of horseflesh. Reverend trotted at her heels and a groom followed close behind. Most of the horses were meant for the carriage, but she passed two fine stallions shifting in their stalls, one tall with a brown coat, the other black with a white nose. Just past them stood a pied gelding waiting patiently, a fine horse, but nothing like the stallions. Since Lady Ellington no longer rode, Cecelia could only imagine why Randall kept the more docile animal.

'Shall I saddle the gelding for you, ma'am?' the groom asked.

'No, I'll ride the black stallion.' She wasn't about to join the no doubt long line of ladies who'd ridden the gelding before.

'Ma'am, he isn't a suitable horse for a lady.'

'Why? Is he unruly?'

'No.'

'Is he prone to jump or bolt?'

'No, but—'

'Then he's perfect for me. Please saddle him at once.'

With an 'it's your neck' shrug, the groom led the

horse out of the stall and saddled him. He worked at a snail's pace, the whole time throwing out instructions for managing the horse. Cecelia heard little of it, wishing she could push him aside and saddle the animal herself, itching to be off.

Finally, he finished adjusting the stirrups, but his suggestions seemed to have no end.

'Keep a tight grip on the reins. Never let your control slack.' He boosted her into the saddle, then stepped back. 'Would you like me to ride with you?'

'No, thank you.' She settled her knee around the pommel, arranged the skirt of her grey riding habit over her legs, then took up the reins. 'I believe I can manage.'

With an unladylike hoot, she kicked the horse and they bolted out of the paddock, Reverend running beside them. The horse raced down the riding path, kicking up dust and sending birds flying from the grass. She leaned over the horse's strong neck, urging him on, the speed more thrilling than the race in Rotten Row. Here there were no frowns of disapproving matrons to stop her, nor worries over her reputation and Randall, only rolling hills and wide open fields. She rode faster and harder, her body tight and alive.

The horse sped up the path to the crest of a small hill before beginning to slow and she eased him into a walk, his steady rocking as relaxing as one of the old porch chairs at Belle View. Reverend bounded through the long grass beside the packed dirt, flushing out rabbits and a few quails before picking his way back to her. Beneath her, the horse ambled along, oblivious to the dog panting beside him, pieces of grass and twigs stuck in his dark fur.

From the small hill, she could see the manor house, but not the rooms at the back where Lady Ellington

and Theresa were busy with the modiste. They'd spent
most of the morning selecting the first gowns to be
altered, Theresa as giddy as the day of her thirteenth
birthday when Cecelia had taken her to Williamsburg
to purchase her first grown-up dresses. As much as Cecelia enjoyed seeing her cousin happy, all the talk of
ribbons and trim could not hold her attention. Instead,
she'd sat in the window seat, petting Reverend, her ears
and the dog's perking up each time a footman passed
in the hallway, both of them waiting for the sound of
Randall's arrival.

By midday, he had yet to appear and, unable to sit
still any longer, Cecelia had made her excuses, changed
into her habit and fled to the stables, Reverend determined to remain at her side.

Ahead, another horse and rider appeared on the crest.
Reverend stopped, his sharp noise pointing at the rider,
his ears twitching forward before he took off in a run.
Cecelia froze in her saddle.

Randall.

He trotted forward on the brown stallion and her fingers sought out the gold bracelet, but she couldn't find
it. She looked down in a panic, thinking it lost until
she remembered leaving it on her dressing table so it
wouldn't catch in the buttons of the habit. Her nervous
fingers toyed with the riding-crop loop instead.

'My aunt said you were out riding.' Randall cocked
one finger at the stallion. 'An interesting choice for a
lady.'

'You and your groom are of the same mind.' She sat
up straighter, frowning at the dust rimming the edge of
her habit. 'You're back from London so soon?'

'I concluded my business and saw no reason to stay

away.' His horse flicked its ears, shooing off a small fly. 'Shall we ride together?'

She hesitated, not wanting to be alone with Randall, but unwilling to return to the house and more talk of dresses. 'Of course.'

Randall heard the stallion snort as Cecelia brought it into step beside his mount.

'I've missed views like this so much since coming to London.' She followed the flight of a bird as it dipped down over a field, genuine delight brightening her face.

'I miss it, too. The peace and quiet. When I'm here, I'm a different man.' Randall took in the wispy clouds passing above the gnarled oaks on the hillside. 'There's a calm here sorely lacking in London.'

'Do my ears deceive me or is the notorious Marquess of Falconbridge pining for the pleasures of the country?' Cecelia laid one hand on her chest in feigned surprise. 'Society would be shocked to discover it.'

He shrugged. 'Perhaps I no longer care what society thinks.'

'Liar.'

'It's the truth.'

Mirth danced in her eyes. 'I don't believe it.'

'Why? Can't a man change?'

'If he has a compelling enough reason to, but you, my lord, have none.'

'How do you know? Can you read minds now?'

'One has only to look at you to see it. You aren't ill and therefore not afraid of dying, nor has the fear of God struck you from your horse.'

'Perhaps it's a deeper emotion compelling me?' His humour dimmed with the truth of his statement.

'Such as?' The question was drawing instead of teasing and he answered it more honestly than he should have.

'Seeing the man I've become through another's eyes.'

Her smile faded. 'I've been very bad about that, haven't I, especially since you've been nothing but kind. I'm sorry. It's not my place to tell you how to live or behave, or to reprimand you like some disapproving dowager or, worse yet, your father.'

He adjusted his grip on the reins. 'You could never sound like him.'

'Oh, I don't know. Theresa has given me many years of practice correcting behaviour.'

'But you speak with genuine concern and from the heart. Whatever heart he had died with my mother.' He rose up a little in the stirrups, remembering the things he'd told her about his father's death. The shame of it gnawed through him and he wanted to bolt off across the fields and leave the memories of his father in the dust of his horse's hooves. He settled back into his seat, determined to remain steady, refusing to let fear overwhelm him and turn him again into the snivelling boy he loathed, the one who'd driven Cecelia away.

'Are you all right, Randall?' Her voice broke through the grey surrounding him.

He studied her atop the horse, waiting for his answer. There was no reason to run. She knew his secret, but she'd never judged him because of it. She only judged the man he'd become since. She might apologise for chastising him, but he knew she was right. 'I'm better now that you're here.'

She looked down, but not before he caught the faint red creeping over her fine, straight nose. Then the uncertainty vanished and she faced him with a smile again. 'Then let's hope everything works out between Theresa and Mr Menton, so you may see a great deal more of me in the country.'

'I'd like that very much.'

She turned her attention back to the path, uncertainty replacing the mirth in her eyes, as though she struggled between believing him and maintaining her humour, and her distance.

The high afternoon sun caressed her face and played in the green and brown of her eyes. She rode with confidence, her back straight, her high breasts graced by the fitted fabric of her habit before it flowed down to cover her slender legs.

He tugged at one glove, wanting to reach out and stroke the graceful arm relaxed by her side, but he kept his hand on the reins. He didn't want to break the easy mood between them or send her galloping back to the manor because of his boldness.

He let his grip slacken on the reins. How different things would be if he hadn't pushed her away all those years ago. He could draw her from her horse, lay her down in the grass and savour her kisses, let her soft arms envelop him and make him forget all the filth and muck of town.

Their horses maintained a steady pace as they crossed the wood bridge spanning a clear stream as it poured down the rocks before emptying into the River Stour. Downstream, the mill sat on the bank beneath a thick grove of tall trees, the wooden waterwheel turning in a steady rhythm, creaking on its axle as it splashed and dripped water into the calm pond.

'What happened to the old mill?' she asked with disappointment. 'I was looking forward to seeing it.'

'The river overflowed its banks during a storm a few years ago. The mill was badly damaged and had to be rebuilt.'

'I suppose nothing stays the same.' She sighed.

'Some things have.'

'Such as your uncle's garden? I have yet to explore it.'

He ran his fingers along the edges of his lips, trying to hide his embarrassment. It was not an art collection he was proud of and, unlike the paintings, much more difficult to dispose of. 'I've made some changes, but the spirit is the same.'

'Yes, Lady Ellington told me about it. I'm going to have quite a time keeping Theresa from such scandalous figures.'

'Let her see them. Best she learn a few things now. It'll give her an advantage.'

'I know I shouldn't agree with you, but I do.'

'That's because you're sensible. Now come along and I'll show you the new building.'

They guided the horses to the flat area in front of the mill, stopping at the post. Randall dismounted and wrapped the reins of both horses around the knotted wood. He reached up to help her down and she held his shoulders as she slid from the saddle. Her stomach and breasts brushed against his chest and he closed his eyes, struggling not to groan at the pressure of her body against his. She continued to lean into him as her feet touched the ground and he opened his eyes, his hands lingering on her waist, just above the curve of her hips. The light falling through the trees played along the arches of her cheeks and his fingers tightened on her waist, matching the taut grip of his desire as he struggled to keep from pressing his lips to hers. Though her hands rested lightly on his shoulders, her hesitant expression made him step back and let go, fearing their fragile friendship might slip away like the water pouring under the bridge.

'This way.' He swung his hand at the wooden mill door.

She reached for the handle, but it didn't budge. 'It's locked.'

'Mr Robson must have gone to fetch something. Shall we wait?'

'Yes.' She stepped over to the small railing overlooking the waterwheel. Her fitted habit pulled tight over her round buttocks as she leaned over to look into the water. The simple material and lack of design enhanced her curves and he opened and closed his hands at the memory of her firm body between his palms. When she turned to him and pointed to the reeds, he caught a teasing glance of the smooth skin of her breasts beneath the open V of the bodice. He was so mesmerised by the sight of her, he almost didn't hear the question.

'Is that the boat?'

He pulled himself from his trance and looked to where she pointed. Deep in the tall reeds along the bank, almost hidden by the foxtails, the grey and weathered bow of the wooden boat stuck out just above the surface of the water, a perch for a fat green frog.

'It is.' Something inside him dropped. 'I guess it didn't survive the storm, either.'

'Pity. I was looking forward to rowing again.'

'It wouldn't be proper for a rake and widow to be alone on the water,' he teased, driving away the gloom settling between them.

She rewarded him with an agreeing smile. 'No, I don't suppose it would.'

They started down the dirt path to where it dipped close to the pond before rising up to the stone bridge spanning the wide waterfall. Reverend romped in the water along the shore as Randall and Cecelia crossed the bridge. They paused at the centre and leaned over the railing to watch the green moss dance in the current below. The slope of the land was longer here and the water didn't spill as fast or as loud over the rocks.

Across the pond, Randall noticed the boat again. The sight of it sunken and ruined dragged on him like the tumbling water pulling down leaves and twigs, reminding him of all their lost time together.

'Were you happy with Daniel?' he asked.

She straightened, looking more surprised than when he'd appeared at her house yesterday with Reverend. He expected her to chastise him for asking something so private, but she only folded her hands together and faced the pond. 'Yes. He was a kind and generous man.'

A knot of jealousy twisted his insides. If she'd told him the man was cruel, he'd have cursed him to Hades, but hearing her speak fondly of him did not ease Randall's mind. Few would remember him so kindly. 'Did you love him?'

She traced a groove in the capstone, the outline of her wedding band just visible beneath the fitted kidskin glove. 'I was fond of him at first. He was so sweet and kind. Only later, after we'd struggled with Belle View and so many other things, did the love come.'

The pain of realising again how completely he'd lost her rose up in him before he pushed it down. He wouldn't be jealous of a dead man, not when she was standing beside him. 'And there were no children?'

Her fingers curled on the edge of the stone, the answer evident.

Randall laid one hand over hers, squeezing it tight. 'I'm sorry, I shouldn't have asked.'

'No, it's all right.' She swallowed hard, her eyes fixed on the pond. 'There was a child our second year together. A beautiful little boy, but a fever took him. It almost took Daniel, too, but he recovered. After the illness, there were no more children. The midwife said it can happen when a man catches the fever so late in life.'

Her voice faded away, lost to the rushing water, and he wrapped his arms around her. She didn't cry, but clutched his coat as she buried her face in his chest. He rubbed her back, the gesture inadequate for the depth of her suffering and he wished there was something, anything he could do to free her of this loss. He closed his eyes and laid his cheek on her hair, tightening his arms around her and trying to shield her from a soul-wrenching grief he knew too well.

They stood together, the water flowing beneath their feet, the plunk of the frog jumping from the boat into the water joining the rustle of leaves in the breeze. He held her until she relaxed against him and her arms slid around his waist beneath his coat.

'I'm sorry if I upset you. I only want you to be happy while you're here,' Randall whispered, the pressure of her arms on his waist worth more than any embrace he'd ever known before.

'Don't be sorry. This isn't the first time we've been here and shared something so private.' Her thumb caressed the small scar on his back through his shirt, the faint movement tearing through him like a gale wind. There was a trust in her comfort, the same one he'd felt ten years ago in the boat when she'd touched his cheek.

'Do you still struggle?' he asked, testing the new bond between them, hoping she might share more of her secrets and troubles.

Instead her thumb stopped and she leaned back, sliding her arms out from around him. He caught her hands, refusing to let her completely pull away or to build higher the wall he was working so hard to scale. 'We all have difficulties to face.'

'Are yours behind you, or is there something more?' He watched, waiting for her to confide in him so he could help her and make some small amends for all his shortcomings.

Her hand tightened in his, as if accepting his touch, but still weighing his trustworthiness.

Then the crack of twigs and the fall of footsteps drew their attention up the path. Randall turned to see Mr Robson, the miller, returning from town with a sack slung over one shoulder. He opened his hand and hers slid out, the warmth and comfort gone.

Randall waved to the man. 'Good afternoon, Mr Robson.'

The miller stopped and laid down his sack. 'Lord Falconbridge, I didn't know you'd returned.'

'Just this afternoon.' He took Cecelia's elbow and drew her back up the path. 'This is Mrs Thompson—you might remember her as Miss Fields. She spent the summer here once.'

The miller's ruddy face beamed. 'How could I forget? I was always chasing after the boat when you two were done. How are you, Mrs Thompson?'

'Well. And how is your son?'

The miller's thick chest puffed out with pride. 'Peter's a doctor now with his own practice in York. I can't thank you enough, Lord Falconbridge, for everything you did for him. If it hadn't been for the money you gave him for school—'

'Of course, it was my pleasure,' Randall cut the man off, feeling Cecelia's wide eyes boring into him. To his shame, the London rake in him knew Mr Robson's slip was to his advantage. However, like his arrangement with Lord Westbrook, he preferred not to announce to everyone his generosity, not even to Cecelia. 'Mrs

Thompson is eager to see the inside of the new mill. Perhaps you might show her.'

'You're not joining us?' she asked.

'No, I have business with the estate manager and I must see to Reverend before he tracks mud inside the manor. Aunt Ella forgives a great many of my sins, but not ruined carpets. Until dinner.'

He tipped his hat to her, then headed for his horse, calling Reverend with a sharp whistle. A second whistle brought the dog running from the edge of the pond, his dark fur dripping with water.

Randall mounted his horse as Cecelia paused at the mill door, watching as he left. While he rode, he tried to think about what he needed to discuss with the estate manager, but he could think of nothing except the pain on Cecelia's face when she'd stared into the pond, unashamed to reveal her old grief. It touched him to know she could trust him with her sorrows, all except one.

Randall flexed his fingers, missing the feel of her small hand in his. In the soft caress of her thumb, in the slight pressure of her cheek against his chest, he'd felt the faint flicker of something more than friendship. He kicked the horse into a canter, refusing to name it, afraid to bring it into the light and see it wilt like a seedling planted too early.

Chapter Twelve

Cecelia pushed the cooked pheasant around her plate. Despite the tempting smell, she had no appetite tonight. Lady Ellington and Theresa sat across from her, deep in conversation and plans for the assembly tomorrow night. Every once in a while, Theresa tried to draw her into the conversation, but Cecelia offered only the slightest of responses, unable to share in her cousin's excitement.

After leaving the mill, Cecelia hadn't returned to the manor. She'd let the horse wander along a trail by the river, trying to recapture some of the peace she'd enjoyed before Randall had joined her, but it proved as elusive as the mist lying between the low rocks.

She'd struggled so hard not to cry when he'd held her, afraid of releasing even one tear for fear the heartache of the past two years would come tumbling out. He'd cared enough to comfort her, but still she wasn't ready to be so weak in front of him.

'Cecelia, Randall told me you saw the new mill,' Lady Ellington said from across the table, snapping Cecelia out of her musings.

'Yes, it's lovely and the miller says it's made quite a difference to the farmers and villagers.'

'It has. They're most grateful to Randall for rebuilding it.'

There it was again, Randall's kindness, always hidden from her. She glanced at his empty plate rimmed with gold, wondering why he kept such things a secret, or why it embarrassed him to be so generous and considerate.

'Cecelia, you didn't tell me Lord Falconbridge arrived this afternoon,' Theresa said, motioning for the footman to refill her wine.

'I'm not sure you would have heard me even if I had.' Cecelia laughed, waving the footman away from Theresa's glass.

'Oh, I wouldn't have missed something so important.'

'A gentleman returning to his own home is not important.'

'It is when you're one of the first people he sees,' Lady Ellington countered, sliding her full glass of wine to Theresa, one ring clinking against the crystal. Theresa snatched up the glass and took a sip, shooting Cecelia a smug look that had more to do with Randall than the forbidden drink.

Apparently, Theresa's and Mr Menton's match wasn't the only one occupying their minds. If Cecelia thought spending too much time with Randall was risky, she could only imagine the danger of spending so much time in this conniving couple's presence. Lady Ellington would have the modiste here again and it would be Cecelia standing on the stool and stuck with pins.

As if his ears burned from hearing himself talked about, Randall strode into the room, Reverend trotting along beside him, and what remained of Cecelia's appetite vanished. He wore a dark coat, the collar stiff against his angled jaw, the line of his hair curling just above it. As he approached the table, he didn't look at the others, but focused on her, moving with all the confidence of a sturdy ship cutting through still water. Cecelia's hands tightened on the silverware, desire gripping her like a tangled bedsheet and she took a deep breath, but it failed to calm the quiver deep inside her.

'I apologise for being late. What have I missed?' He took his place next to Cecelia, Reverend sitting on the floor between them, looking back and forth from one plate to another.

'Nothing, only women's talk,' Lady Ellington assured him. 'In fact, I'm afraid if it weren't for Cecelia's company, you might find your time here in the country incredibly dull.'

Lady Ellington shot Cecelia a telling look and Cecelia nearly dropped her fork.

If Randall noticed, he didn't reveal it, turning to Theresa. 'Miss Fields, you're looking lovely tonight. It appears being in love does wonders for you.'

Theresa blushed, dipping her head in a rare moment of embarrassment.

'Don't tease the girl, Randall,' Lady Ellington chided, laying her hand on the gold locket with her late husband's miniature pinned to her dress. 'Just because you picked up Edmund's habit of sneering at love doesn't mean the rest of us do.'

'I'm being quite serious.' Randall leaned back as the footman placed a plate of food in front of him. 'In fact, I'm late tonight because I was in the service of love.'

Cecelia touched the pendant hidden beneath her dress, thinking of the gelding in the stable and wondering if the woman who rode it was the same one who'd kept Randall from dinner, and her.

'I've just come from Hallington Hall,' he announced.

'Mr Menton's estate?' Theresa squeaked and Cecelia dropped her hand, relieved to know it was the Mentons who had made him late and not some country paramour.

'Sir Walter and I are on very good terms,' Randal explained, cutting into his meat. 'He told me about a garden party Lady Menton is hosting in a few days and I've secured us an invitation.'

Theresa let out a squeal to shatter the crystal while Lady Ellington clapped her hands, her rings clanking against each other. Cecelia could only stare at Randall, who took a bite of pheasant, watching with satisfaction as Theresa and Lady Ellington fell into a fit of rushed words over what Theresa should wear.

'You don't share their enthuslasm?' Randall asked, slicing through a stalk of asparagus.

'I'm stunned. I've wouldn't have taken you for an assistant to Cupid.'

He speared the asparagus with his fork. 'I can't lie to you. Securing the invitation wasn't difficult. Sir Walter was candid enough to tell me how Lady Menton would be beside herself to have a Marquess at her little gathering. Though he suspected it had more to do with bragging to her friends than a desire to be a good neighbour.'

'You still didn't have to do it.'

'Of course I did.' He bit the vegetable, his silver fork catching the candlelight before he lowered it.

Cecelia fingered the stem of her wineglass, noting the absence of one from his setting. 'It's a shame you don't let more people see this generous side of you.'

He sliced another asparagus, the knife grating across the china. 'I prefer to keep silent about my business.'

'The good business, you mean?'

'I'm not the one who spreads tales of my nefarious deeds. Madame de Badeau and others are quite content to do it for me.'

Cecelia answered his frown with a challenging smile. 'Then perhaps I'll counter their influence and spread more illustrious stories about you.'

'Such as my horticultural skills?' His eyes met hers, heavy with suggestion. 'You should see how I've laid out the beds in Uncle Edmund's garden, there isn't a flower in them unopened.'

She took up her knife and fork and carefully cut the end off a carrot. 'Unless the heat has wilted them.'

He dropped his head, his voice sliding to her in a whisper. 'The heat never wilts my stalk.'

'Even when it's wet?' she breathed.

'Especially when it's wet.'

She crossed her ankles beneath the table, the low tenor of his suggestion curling through her like a vine.

'Lord Falconbridge, you must tell me all about Mr Menton's parents and Hallington Hall,' Theresa begged, her voice like cold water on the fire building between them.

Over the quick tempo of her heart, Cecelia listened while Randall answered all of Theresa's questions about the Mentons, humouring and teasing her like a favourite uncle. She took up her wineglass, willing her arm to move slowly as she raised it to her lips, the tart liquid sliding through her and easing the tension low in her stomach. She set the wineglass back on the table, Randall's deep laugh beneath Theresa's giggles comforting like a bell on a foggy day. More than the wine, it eroded Cecelia's defences, the ones which had nearly come crashing down today beneath the weight of Randall's embrace. He made it so hard to maintain her distance, especially when he'd held her tight, drawing her into a deeper intimacy she feared. Watching Theresa turn red as Randall teased her again, Cecelia knew she must be more guarded in the future in order to better protect their secret and her heart.

The last course was barely finished when Lady Ellington hustled Theresa from the table, all decorum abandoned in their eagerness to select Theresa's gown for the garden party. Cecelia followed them to the dining-room door, then fell behind, forgotten and unnoticed as their excited chatter disappeared down the hall. Reverend trotted behind them, adding a loud yap to their discussion.

'Theresa is so fond of Mr Menton. I hope distance hasn't changed his feelings for her,' she said as Randall came to join her, leaning against the jamb.

'Mr Menton is a sensible man. If anything, the distance has only increased his affection.' Randall pushed away from the wood. 'Come with me to the library. I have something to show you.'

Without question, she moved with him down the hall, past Lady Ellington's prized Italian landscapes which now adorned the walls.

'You were very gracious with Theresa at dinner.'

'I enjoyed her conversation.'

'Liar.'

'I did. It's refreshing to see someone so innocent and in love. It's been a long time.'

She found it hard to believe Randall possessed any admiration for love, or even innocence, but she held her tongue, enjoying the easy familiarity between them.

They stepped through the wide library door, the tall

bookshelves stretching to the high ceiling exactly as Cecelia remembered. The only thing different were the paintings. A regal selection of relatives now hung where the Roman men and their lovers with arms painted too long used to frolic.

She stopped at a small table near the centre of the room, noticing a paper-wrapped parcel on the dark wood. 'Did you buy a new book?'

'No.' He picked it up and held it out to her. 'This is for you.'

She raised her hands, refusing to take it. 'Randall, you and your aunt have already been so generous. I can't keep accepting gifts.'

'Then make this the last. Please.'

She took it, surprised by the weight. Laying it back on the table, she undid the string, then pulled back the paper with a gasp. 'Daniel's hunting book.'

'I purchased it right after I saw you at the bookseller's.'

'But I told him, I told you I didn't need it,' she stammered, flustered by his generosity and her worry. 'Why did you buy it?'

'Because of how you looked when you sold it, as if you were giving away everything.' He laid his hand on hers. 'What's wrong, Cecelia? Please tell me and let me help you.'

Cecelia's composure nearly faltered under the pressure of his skin against hers. The words began to form in her mind, but the memory of his face in the conservatory so long ago kept her silent, the fear of how he might react when he realised he was paying attention to a pauper keeping her silent. Guilt racked her. He'd asked for her honesty and friendship, but she couldn't give it, not all of it, not until everything between Theresa and Mr Menton was settled.

She slid her hand out from beneath his and gripped the book, the sharp corner biting into her skin as she forced herself to look light and cheerful.

'Randall, you make it all seem so serious when I assure you, it's not. I told you, I mismanaged my funds, but more will arrive from Virginia shortly and everything will be right again. In the meantime, I want you to keep this, as a thank you for all you and your aunt are doing for Theresa.'

She held the book out to him and he shook his head.

'No, it's yours, it means something to you.'

'Please I want you to have it.' She slipped it into an empty space on a nearby shelf, the book matching the others as if they were all part of the same collection. She stepped back, thinking how lost it looked among all the other leather spines, yet giving it up tonight didn't wrench her heart like it had at the bookseller's. Perhaps it was because Randall would have it and not some stranger. She turned, surprised to find him still staring at the book. 'You look perplexed.'

'It fits.' He stepped up to the shelf and ran his fingers along the even row of spines. 'I couldn't find a place for it in London. Nowhere seemed right.'

A sense of discomfort laced the comment, of trouble whispered instead of proclaimed, as if he needed to unburden himself but couldn't, not without her drawing it from him. Tonight, she didn't possess the courage.

The clock on the large mahogany sideboard began to chime and Cecelia yawned, covering it with her hand, eager to avoid any more intimacies with Randall. 'I think it's time I retired. Tomorrow will be a busy day and the night a long one—Theresa's first encounter with Mr Menton since London.'

He glanced at the clock and she expected him to

chide her about keeping early hours, but he didn't. Instead he offered her his arm. 'Allow me to escort you.'

She hesitated. If he teased her upstairs as he had at dinner, there was nothing to stop them from indulging except her own will and she wasn't sure it was strong enough to resist temptation. Either way, she couldn't leave him standing like some footman waiting for an answer.

She took his offered arm, the hard muscle beneath his coat shifting as he led her from the room.

'How will you occupy yourself after your charge is married?' he asked as they turned the corner into the wide hall, the sound of their shoes echoing over the marble.

'I suppose I'll live with the happy couple. I'm not used to living on my own.'

'And what will you do all day while they moon about one another?'

'I don't know.' She'd given so little thought to anything but the present. 'Perhaps I'll take on the role of grandmama, help Theresa care for all the children which are sure to arrive.'

'You're too young to act like a grandmother and much too pretty.' His free hand covered hers, the heat of it nearly making her trip as they reached the top of the stairs.

'Then maybe I'll use my beauty to snare another husband.' She laughed, afraid to flirt with him in a dark and empty hallway so close to her bed.

She needn't have worried as his arm tightened beneath her fingers and his hand jerked away from hers to hang by his side. Apparently, the mere mention of marriage was enough to protect them both from an indiscretion. It seemed some things never changed.

'What about you?' she asked, her ego ruffled. 'Have

you a desire to take a wife and fill the nursery, or are
you willing to let Falconbridge Manor go to some distant cousin?'

'My distant cousin hasn't annoyed me enough to consider denying him the title, nor has he sufficiently impressed me enough to secure it.' He moved his free hand
behind his back, something of the imperious Randall
coming over him. 'If it weren't for Aunt Ella chiding
me to settle the matter one way or another, I wouldn't
even consider marriage.'

She stared straight ahead at the large painting of
some past Marquess hanging at the end of the hall, the
decision to keep her secrets justified. For all the tenderness he'd shown her at the bridge, for all his helping of
her and Theresa, it was clear he intended to offer nothing more than friendship. She might enjoy this brief
interlude of intimacy with him, but she couldn't allow
herself to expect more, nor should she. He owed her
nothing beyond an apology for the past, but even this
seemed too petty to expect in the face of his current
generosity.

'You're very quiet,' he observed as they approached
her room.

'I'm more tired than I realised.'

'Then you must make sure to rest.' He stopped at her
door, more the teasing London lord than the caring man
who'd held her at the mill today. 'I expect to be amused
and dazzled by your wit tomorrow.'

'I'll do my best.' She withdrew her hand. 'Thank you
again for everything.'

'It's my pleasure.' He leaned in and brushed a small
kiss over her cheek. Desire clashed with fear as she
inhaled the bergamot cologne on his skin. She moved
a touch closer, clasping the sides of her dress to keep

her hands from sliding along the angles of his face and bringing his lips down to hers. He lingered close to her and she closed her eyes, yearning for his mouth to cover hers, her heart drumming a steady rhythm as his breath whispered along her temple. The fine cotton beneath her fingers wrinkled as she waited, anxious for him to either take her in his arms or move away.

'Randall?' she whispered in frustration, opening her eyes to meet his, ashamed at how much she craved his embrace. What did he want from her? It seemed to change every minute, shifting like light through a stained glass window at the end of the day.

He straightened at the sound of his name and took one step back, his eyes burning with a want to match hers, but she caught the conflict beneath the flames—it echoed her own.

'Goodnight, Cecelia.' He walked off down the hall.

She released her dress, her hands going to the hidden pendant. There was more to this than calculated manoeuvring, something deeper she felt within her heart, but refused to put into words or believe. Men like Randall did not love.

Randall didn't remember the hallway to his room being so long. Behind him, he heard the click of Cecelia's bedroom door, but didn't look back. He couldn't and expect to maintain the self-control pushing him away. She wanted him and the answering need clawed at his insides, but he fought it, hating the strength of it, especially when all the while she held a part of herself back. He'd seen the mistrust flicker through her eyes in the library when he'd asked about her finances. It was brief, but as clear as the longing filling them just now, though he wondered if it was longing for him or his title.

He threw open his bedroom door and it banged against the iron doorstop behind it. Madame de Badeau and all her conniving be damned. He'd pursued Cecelia, he'd brought her here. If anyone was playing a game of conquest, it was him. Only it wasn't a game any more.

Randall took off his coat and tossed it over a chair.

'Good evening, my lord.' Blakely came in from the dressing room, unruffled by Randall's brusque entrance as he collected the coat.

Reverend lay on his chaise at the foot of the bed, his tail thumping against the pillows at the sight of Randall. He rubbed the dog between his ears, irked at Blakely's silence and missing Mr Joshua's easy conversation and humour. The valet was still in London, trying to learn something of Cecelia's secret, though Randall didn't hold out much hope of hearing any word from him. Not even he had been able to get at the truth of it yesterday. He'd spent the better part of an hour with Cecelia's solicitor, trying to cajole and then bribe the man into revealing what he knew. All the solicitor would say was her inheritance payment was not made and he'd referred her to the services of Mr Rathbone. Randall had then paid a visit to the moneylender, but it proved equally fruitless. The man was away from town on business and not expected back for at least a week. Waiting grated on him, but he had no choice. At least while she was here she was safe and a few more days without news would make no difference.

His hand paused over Reverend and the dog licked it until Randall resumed his steady strokes.

Why won't she trust me? Twice he'd asked her to confide in him and twice she'd lied, despite everything he'd done for Miss Fields, or the intimacies they'd shared today. It seemed even when he was at his most honest and forthright, she still held back.

From the dressing room, the sweep of the clothes brush over the wool coat scratched at Randall's nerves. He rubbed Reverend's head again, but not even this calmed him. 'That will be all for tonight, Blakely.'

'Yes, my lord,' the man answered, then left.

Randall pulled loose his cravat, unwinding the length of it from around his neck. He couldn't blame Cecelia for being cautious. His initial reasons for pursuing her were less than chivalrous and she knew it. She'd guessed it when he'd given her the pendant, the token he had yet to see her wear.

Randall dropped the cravat on the floor, the silence more irritating than the valet's scratching brush. He pulled open the French doors leading to the balcony and stepped outside, the cool air cutting through his silk shirt. A wide expanse of grass stretched out from the house and a herd of deer moved over the short grass, their breath clouding above their heads. Beyond them, at the far edge of the lawn, stood the large ash tree and beneath its wide branches rested Uncle Edmund and Randall's parents.

He plucked an ivy leaf off the wall and ran one thumb over the smooth surface. Perhaps in the end his father was right: he wasn't a man worthy enough for the affection of a woman like Cecelia.

Randall crushed the leaf and tossed it over the railing. No, his father wasn't right, he couldn't be. The old man didn't know him. Only Cecelia did and, despite his reputation and past mistakes, she was still willing to come here and be with him, to tell him her past sorrows and let him comfort her.

He glanced down the line of the house, noticing the slit of light through the heavy curtains of Cecelia's room.

She's still awake.

He gripped the railing, the rough stone digging into his palms and stopping him from returning to her door. Despite the need dancing in her eyes before they'd parted, and the faint disappointment sweeping across her face when he'd pulled away, the idea of going to her now felt too much like all the other halls he'd trod at various country houses. None of those women meant to Randall what Cecelia did and he wouldn't disgrace her by treating her like one of them. She might not trust him, but she hadn't pushed him away. As long as she was here, there existed the possibility of burying all her doubts and his.

Chapter Thirteen

Cecelia stepped outside, raising her hand to shield her eyes from the sharp morning sun breaking through the clouds and cutting between the back portico columns. The crunch of boots over gravel joined the chirping of birds and the short gusts of wind as Randall walked up the long path from the stables, Reverend bounding through the tall grass next to it. He stood straight, his shoulders relaxed. If he'd experienced even a small measure of the conflict which kept her from sound sleep, he hid it well.

Last night, the darkness had stretched out through the long hours as her mind ran in circles, working to tease out what Randall wanted from her. Every time he moved to cross the line of friendship, he drew back until she wanted to pull the pendant from her neck, hand it back to him and leave. Somewhere near midnight, all of Lord Strathmore's obvious ogling had almost seemed preferable to Randall's constant pursuing and retreating. At least the Earl was clear in his desire, unlike Randall.

Cecelia started down the stairs, moving slower with each step that brought her closer to him, reluctant to spend the morning guessing at his intentions. Somewhere inside, Theresa and Lady Ellington were lost in their preparations for the assembly. Cecelia should be with them, not here, pulled in more directions than a mule team hitched together.

Her foot touched the last step and she felt a pebble roll beneath her shoe. She lurched forward and Randall rushed to her. She fell against his chest, her hand clutching his coat. His arms clasped her, sturdy enough to balance her, but not the tripping in her heart.

'Steady now.' His voice rumbled through his chest and hers as he helped her regain her balance.

'One would think after three months on a rocking ship, I could walk a straight line on dry land.' She laughed nervously, aware of his heavy hands on her waist. She let go of his lapel and smoothed the wrinkled wool, her palm too firm against his coat, savouring the hard chest beneath. The memory of him as a young man emerging from the mill pond, fat drops of water sliding over the curve of his chest and catching in the sweep of hair in the centre, came rushing back to her.

'Did you enjoy sea travel?' His low voice drew her from the past to meet his eyes and an amused smirk.

'No, not at all.' She snatched back her hand, feeling a little too much like Lord Strathmore with all her pawing at Randall. 'In fact, I'll be happy to never set foot on a ship again.'

'Then you have no intention of returning to your lands in Virginia?' There was too much hope in his question, but not enough for her.

If only she could.

'Not at present. No. Perhaps some day. I don't know.' She stepped around him, making for the garden path, rattled by his innocent question, eager to escape it and the encroaching despair. Reverend trotted beside her, panting. 'I want to see your uncle's garden.'

He hurried to catch up to her as they reached the entrance to the statue garden at the end of the walk. An iron trellis marked the gateway, adorned with a full rose bush heavy with pink blooms.

'Are you sure a trip inside won't be too dangerous to your reputation?' Randall asked, teasing her happiness out from beneath her troubles. 'I've heard there are marbles of a most scandalous nature in there.'

She fingered a pink bud, unable to hold back a smile. 'I think I may risk my reputation just this once.'

'Then prepare to be stunned.'

Side by side they passed under the arch and into the garden, Reverend following at their heels. Among the deep green of ivy, white marble glistened in the sun. Where once the naked bodies stood proudly in the centre to scandalise a virtuous maiden, now they lay hidden behind roses and honeysuckle and peeked out from wooded grottos. Around them the hedges rattled with another gust, but the wind blew softer in here.

Reverend sniffed at the base of a half-naked goddess, the urn in her arms filled with cascading blue flowers which covered all but her bare shoulders. Then the dog found some unseen trail and followed it off through a tangle of high, feathery grass bending and rising with the wind.

'It's beautiful,' she exclaimed, trailing her fingers across the top of a row of yellow flowers.

'I told you I was quite the gardener.'

She threw him a disbelieving look. 'I can't imagine you mucking in the mud.'

'Well, my greensman and I. He did the work while I suggested what to plant and where.' He motioned to the statue of a large man holding up a sword, his stomach muscles rippled in white with veins of brown, his erect penis now draped with a tasteful kilt of honeysuckle.

'You've both done excellent work, I've never seen a garden like this.' She wandered along the path, her hem sweeping the flowers hanging over the gravel and collecting bits of dew and fine yellow pollen. She passed three dancing nymphs, admiring the tall hedge of purple flowers protecting their modesty. Just past them, where the paths merged in a wide circle in the centre of the garden, stood a willow tree. The arching branches draped over the marble bodies of Venus and Mars locked together in ecstasy, the sinewy screen swaying and shielding their full nakedness from everyone except each other.

It'd been so vulgar before, all of it, and something inside her caught at the beauty of it now. Randall might not believe in love, but, like his embrace on the bridge, all the carefully placed flowers and trees whispered of his caring and tenderness.

Randall trailed behind Cecelia, her breathy gasps of amazement and surprise worth more than all the impressed murmurings created by his art exhibit.

'Theresa will be very disappointed when she finally sees this. I've made it sound like some kind of statue Gomorrah, but you've transformed it into something wonderful.'

'As you can see, my talents extend beyond mere rumours and ruining people.'

'Yes, I know.' She touched something hidden beneath the dark pelisse. 'It's in everything you've created here and all your kindness to me and Theresa.'

Randall looked up to watch a small bird hopping between the branches. Despite what he'd done ten years ago, and all he'd done and become since, she was still willing to believe in him and it rattled him more than all his father's old curses.

'There aren't many who'd agree with your generous opinion of me.' He didn't deserve her belief, not when he'd worked so hard to gain it and to what end? What waited for them at the conclusion of all this, more broken figurines and Cecelia weeping on a chaise while he strode away? After comforting her at the mill, it sickened him to think they might become strangers again, avoiding each other across ballrooms.

'Your aunt thinks highly of you,' she offered optimistically, tucking a loose strand of hair behind her ear before the wind caught it again. 'She practically sings your praises and your uncle thought well of you, too.'

Without thinking, Randall reached out and tucked the hair behind her ear. She didn't flinch or pull away, but watched him with wide eyes, looking more like a porcelain statue than any of the solid marbles surrounding them. His hand hesitated by her ear, brushing the curve of it. He should stop this game, stop drawing her to him, but he couldn't.

He pulled back his hand. She deserved more than the little he could give her, the little he'd ever given anyone, including his father, who'd been right to call him selfish.

'My father didn't think so well of me.' He reached up and took one thin branch between his fingers, pulling it close to examine the leaves. 'Aunt Ella used to say he laughed more before my mother died. I never saw him laugh, or happy. I think that night I did him a favour. He wanted to die, to be with my mother, but couldn't because it's a sin.'

He tugged a handful of leaves from the branch and sent it bobbing back up over their heads. Death might have freed his father, but it'd trapped Randall with a torn past he could never mend.

She moved closer, the earthy scent of grass and

dew faint around her. 'You aren't to blame for what he thought of you or how he died.'

Randall opened his fingers and the leaves fluttered to the ground as he wrapped one arm around her waist, drawing her into the arc of his body. Her hands rested on his chest, light, easy, not tense or ready to push away. Temptation licked through him as her tongue swept over her lips, making them shine like her eyes. Old memories rose up before him, the dark hallway outside the manor dining room, Uncle Edmund's laughing inside, Cecelia pressed like this against him, free, willing, eager. Excitement shot through him as she tilted back her head, raising her mouth to meet his, offering herself to him as she had so long ago.

I've found you again.

He slid his other hand behind her neck and the small curls above her collar brushed against his fingers. His arm tightened around her waist, pressing her closer, her body warm against the chilly wind. With his tongue, he traced the line of her lips and she opened them, accepting his deeper caress. He drank her in, the taste of her like honey to a man used to vinegar.

Somewhere outside the garden, a far-off voice sounded before fading like the distant bleat of a sheep in the field. The voice called out again, closer now, and Randall clung to Cecelia, turning them away from the garden arch and everything beyond the trellis which sought to separate them. If he could kiss her deeper, hold her closer, she and all the comfort she offered might never vanish from his life again.

'Cecelia?' Theresa's voice rang clear from just beyond the hedges. Cecelia barely heard her cousin's calls or the soft rustle of half-boots on the grass, ignoring them in the hopes they might go away. She laced her fingers behind Randall's neck, holding him as if he were a large rock in the middle of a fast-moving stream. The current might rush around and over them, but it would not move them. If only the current could drown out the noise of the world beyond the garden.

'Cecelia?' Theresa's voice rang out again. It should have pulled her back, but instead she fell deeper into Randall, pressing her stomach into his, feeling the true depth of his need between them.

'Cecelia, where are you?' Theresa's voice insisted, much closer this time, the sharp tone startling Cecelia from this daydream.

She broke from Randall's kiss, all her forgotten caution rushing in to fill the small gap between their bodies. She widened it, looking around Randall, expecting to see Theresa at the garden arch. Instead, she could hear her moving through the leaves on the opposite side.

'Don't go,' he whispered, trailing his lips up the curve of her neck, his cheek soft against hers. Need and fear tugged her in opposite directions and she didn't know which urge to follow.

The sound of Theresa's footsteps near the garden entrance finally made her decision.

'I have to,' came her feeble protest.

Randall's arms eased around her and she stepped back. His thumb pressed hard against the palm of her hand as he led her away from the willow and to the arch where he finally let go.

'Here I am.' Cecelia stepped out of the garden, listening for the sound of Randall following behind her but there was nothing except the rustle of bushes in the wind. He remained hidden behind the hedges. Only

Reverend appeared, bounding up to Theresa, his tail wagging. 'What's wrong?'

'Nothing. Lady Ellington asked me to fetch you.' She patted the dog on the head. 'She's going to let us borrow some of her jewels tonight and she wants us to choose which ones we want to wear. Can I wear her diamonds? Please?'

'Diamonds aren't for unmarried ladies,' Cecelia chided with a laugh, her own nervousness bubbling up through her and heightened by her cousin's enthusiasm. 'Something more subtle like pearls will do.'

Theresa scrutinised Cecelia's face. 'You seem flushed. Are you feeling well?'

'Quite well, I only hurried up from the end of the garden when I heard your voice. Tell me more about the jewellery.'

Theresa took Cecelia's arm and together they walked back to the house, leaving Reverend to follow another trail across the lawn. Theresa continued to chatter, but Cecelia heard little of it. The soft urgency of Randall's kiss lingered on her lips, along with the relief of finally knowing where his intentions lay.

Movement in an upstairs window caught her attention and she noticed the Countess watching them, a wide smile on her face.

Cecelia stumbled, gripping Theresa's arm to steady herself. How long had Lady Ellington been standing there?

'Are you sure you're all right?' Theresa asked.

'Yes, my shoe slipped on the wet grass.'

'But the grass is dry.'

'Never mind. Come along. We can't keep the Countess waiting.'

Cecelia forced herself to focus on Theresa's lively

words as they entered the sitting room, the darkness unsettling after the bright light of the garden. They climbed the stairs and Cecelia looked out the large window at the top, but only the tips of distant trees were visible. She wanted to rush to it and know just how much of the garden one could see from here, but she couldn't, not with Theresa holding her arm.

They reached the end of the hallway and Lady Ellington came out of her room.

'Cecelia says I can't wear the diamonds. She wants me to wear the pearls, but I don't think they'll look right,' Theresa hurried forward to complain.

Cecelia lingered behind her, trying to ignore the way the Countess's eyes kept dancing over Theresa's shoulders to meet hers with a knowing gleam.

'Don't worry, I'm sure I have something which will suit you both,' Lady Ellington reassured her. 'Now go inside. My lady's maid has laid out the selection.'

Theresa practically skipped into the Countess's room, leaving them alone in the hallway.

'My dear, I'm so sorry we haven't had a chance to chat.' She clasped her hands together in front of her mouth, hiding the start of a smile behind her large rings. 'Though I think Randall has more than made up for my neglect.'

Cecelia didn't know whether to groan or worry. After years with the late Marquess, she doubted Lady Ellington would be scandalised by a stolen kiss, but if she saw them, it would only increase her matchmaking ideas. Cecelia barely knew her own feelings when alone in her room, much less under Lady Ellington's less-than-subtle scrutiny. 'Yes, Randall showed me the changes he made to the garden.'

'And were his improvements to your liking?' The smile peeked out again and this time Lady Ellington made no attempt to hide it.

Cecelia felt her own wicked smile escaping until it spread to match Lady Ellington's, not caring what she or any else thought. She was happy for the first time in two years and, even if it didn't last beyond their time here, she would enjoy it. 'Yes, the improvements are very much to my liking.'

Chapter Fourteen

Cecelia, Lady Ellington and Theresa entered the assembly room, the lively music increasing the anticipation building in Cecelia since the garden. The gentlemen stood in groups along the edge of the hall, laughing and exchanging news from London. Their wives, adorned in their country finest, chatted together around the dance floor while their sons and daughters spun though the vibrant quadrille. Everyone here seemed more at ease than at Lady Weatherly's ball and it reminded her of the many country balls she'd once attended in Virginia.

While Lady Ellington and Theresa searched the guests for Mr Menton, Cecelia looked for Randall, every tall man with dark hair making her heart stop until he turned and revealed himself to be a country gentleman.

Where is he?

She hadn't seen him since the garden. He'd disappeared, sending word to Lady Ellington to leave for the ball without him, intending to follow behind on his horse. She wondered what kept him away and whether it was regret at having laid himself so bare or qualms at having finally dropped all pretence of friendship.

'There he is,' Theresa gasped and Cecelia stiffened, relaxing only when she realised her cousin wasn't speaking of Randall.

Mr Menton wound his way through the crowd towards them, focused on Theresa, a smile as wide as hers lighting up his face. Cecelia breathed a bit easier. Randall was right, time had not changed his interest in Theresa.

'Miss Fields, you have no idea how wonderful it is to see you again. I hadn't expected it so soon,' he exclaimed, not bothering to hide his excitement.

His pleasure was not shared by all. Across the room, Cecelia noticed a thin woman watching the exchange with hawk-like eyes, her disapproval evident in the quick tap of her folded fan against her palm. Cecelia guessed by her scrutiny, and the narrow jaw she shared with the young man, that it must be Lady Menton.

The room burst into applause as the music and the dance came to an end.

'Miss Fields, may I have the pleasure of the next dance?'

Theresa accepted his invitation, allowing him to lead her to the dance floor, her new pink muslin gown with white embroidery floating around her as she walked. Theresa stood out in the dress, looking every inch the sophisticated London woman who possessed a fortune and lands. Paired with Mr Menton, they made a fine couple and more than one head turned to admire them.

'I think our plan is working.' Lady Ellington beamed as the young couple bounced and twirled through the lively steps.

'Indeed.' Cecelia tapped her foot in time with the music, her spirit buoyed by the festive atmosphere. 'It's been ages since I've seen her so happy.'

'She isn't the only one who deserves to be happy. Ah, here comes Randall now. I shall politely decamp to where the other ladies are standing.'

'No, you don't have to go,' Cecelia choked out, warmth spreading low and fast inside her at the sight of him. He moved through the crush with long strides, people stepping out of his way as he approached them.

'Of course I do.' Lady Ellington walked away to join her friends, leaving Cecelia to face Randall alone.

The candlelight glowing overhead deepened the darkness of his hair and sharpened the angles of his cheeks. She touched the pendant hanging above the low neckline of her gown. She'd chosen to wear her black-silk dress embroidered with gold flowers because the fine thread captured the glimmer of the pendant, making it stand out against her chest. His eyes dipped down to where her hand rested, a knowing smile drawing up the corners of his mouth.

He stopped in front of her, his eyes penetrating and shadowed, and she clutched her fan, waiting to know how to face him.

His fingers swept the swell of her breasts as he slid them beneath the gold chain to cup the pendant. Her skin pebbled at the light touch, the music and chatter fading into the background like a distant waterfall. She didn't care about the intimate exchange made in such a public place, nor what anyone who watched them might say. In this moment there was no one in the room but the two of them.

'You don't know how happy I am to see you wearing this,' he said.

'I have been for some time, only I kept it hidden.'

'Why?'

'I was embarrassed.'

He laid the gold gently on her chest, the heat of his hand tortuous above her skin. 'Of me or the gift?'

'Neither. I was afraid to show you how much it really meant to me.'

He brushed the curve of her cheek, pushing a small curl away from her face, tucking it behind her ear and making the diamond earring dance.

'Shall we go out to the balcony?' he tempted and she looked up at him through her lashes.

'I'm not sure I can court the dangers of such darkness.'

'Then let's stay here and see how your cousin fares.' He moved to stand beside her, his hand brushing the side of her dress, the faint touch thrilling against her thigh. 'There will be plenty of darkness for us to enjoy after the dance.'

If the afternoon without him had seemed long, the end of the assembly seemed an eternity to wait to be alone with him again.

'Lord Falconbridge, good to see you,' a male voice interrupted. Before them stood an older gentlemen and Lady Menton, her face pinched where her husband's was wide and friendly.

'Good evening, Sir Walter, Lady Menton,' Randall greeted. 'May I introduce Miss Fields's guardian, Mrs Cecelia Thompson.'

'It's a pleasure to meet you, Mrs Thompson.' Lady Melton's lacklustre tone indicated it was anything but.

'You don't know how glad I am to meet you.' Sir Walter bowed, an appraising twinkle in his eye. 'Lately, Adam has talked of nothing except Miss Fields, wouldn't you say so, dear?'

'Yes,' Lady Menton hissed with none of her husband's cheer.

'And it's a great pleasure to meet the parents of such an affable young man,' Cecelia flattered, but it did nothing to soften the woman's stony look.

'I'm hunting in the morning. Lord Falconbridge, care to join me?' Sir Walter offered, rubbing his large hands together.

'I'm afraid I can't. I have other matters to attend to. Perhaps another time.'

The baronet's eyes flicked to Cecelia before he shot Randall a knowing look. 'With such a lovely woman at your side, I don't blame you for not wanting to tromp through the forest at dawn.'

Beneath her tight brown curls, Lady Menton's forehead wrinkled in disapproval and Cecelia tried not to laugh. She took no offence at the comment, the baronet delivering it with as much affection as a weathered old grandfather. It was Randall's reaction which shattered her calm. He laced his fingers behind his back, the same stiffness she'd felt in him at the mention of marriage last night straightening his spine.

'Since I can't tempt you with pheasants, will you join me for a hand of cards?' the baronet invited.

'Yes, only allow me a moment with Mrs Thompson.'

'I'll save a chair for you. Mrs Thompson, it was a pleasure to meet you.' He bowed, escorting his wife away then leaving her with some friends and making for the gaming room.

'He seems like a pleasant gentleman,' Cecelia offered and Randall shifted on his feet, his gaze everywhere but on her. 'I can't say the same about his wife.'

'It's as much as I expected from her. She's ambitious for her son,' Randall stated, the superior man who regularly appraised others in London sounding in his words. 'When you see her at the garden party, be sure to mention the size of Theresa's dowry. It's sure to overcome any of her objections.'

On the dance floor, Mr Menton took Theresa's hand to execute a turn and Cecelia touched the pendant, more than one hope dimming inside her. If Theresa's happiness came down to money, then all was lost. She had no collateral to secure another loan from Mr Rathbone and no way to repay it even if he advanced her the funds.

'Perhaps I should speak with her again, try to charm her,' Cecelia suggested and Randall shook his head.

'Wait until the party. Lady Menton will seek you out if only to curry favour with me and my aunt, which is exactly what you want.'

'You're very good at this game,' Cecelia stated flatly.

'I've been playing a different version of it for longer than I care to recall.'

'Yes, it's always about the game, whether here or in London,' she snapped.

His jaw tightened. 'If you wish to cease playing, you have only to say so, but I think you'll find it isn't an easy one to give up.'

She didn't answer, knowing she was caught in her own game, one she'd been playing since the day she'd arrived in London. Now she played another with Randall and the Mentons. How long before she, too, forgot what it was like to live without all the manoeuvring and lies?

She looked at Randall. He watched the dancers with sharp eyes, his demeanour stiff with all the airs of his title and position. It was so different from the man who'd greeted her a few moments ago, or the one who'd kissed her in the garden. She pressed her lips together, remembering the urgency of his touch near the willow tree. Would he help her with Theresa's dowry if she asked him? She wasn't sure. Mr Robson might boast of Randall's generosity, but he was a poor miller deserving of the rich lord's charity. She was a woman perpetuating a lie and she couldn't take advantage of Randall's affection for her. If she did, then she was just as duplicitous as she had once accused him of being.

'If you'll excuse me, now is my chance to exert more of my influence on Mr Menton.' Randall bowed and walked away.

Her heart dropped, sensing he left more to get away from her than to further Theresa's cause. In private he might hold her as if afraid she would flee, but she saw how the passionate man faltered under the good-natured jibe of a country baronet. A heaviness settled over her and she sought out a small bench along the wall, hidden as much by the backs of the crowd as the shadows. In the privacy of the estate they could enjoy a certain intimacy, but in London she sensed people like Madame de Badeau would kill it faster than a new shoot in a hard frost.

Over the rising music, she barely heard the rustle of muslin as a young lady stepped in front of her.

'Mrs Thompson?'

Cecelia looked up at a round-faced girl not much older than Theresa. 'Yes?'

'I'm Miss Caufield. I know you must think me impertinent, but you being so close to Lord Falconbridge and his family, I must speak with you.'

'I don't think you impertinent at all.' Cecelia motioned to the bench and the girl took the empty seat beside her.

'I'm Lord Westbrook's fiancée.' The girl fingered a bow on the skirt of her dress. 'You know what transpired between Lord Falconbridge and Lord Westbrook?'

'Yes. Do you wish me to speak to Lord Falconbridge about restoring Lord Westbrook's property so you might wed?'

The girl's face scrunched with confusion, then she

shook her head. 'No, not at all, for Lord Falconbridge has already forgiven the debt.'

It was Cecelia's turn to be confused. 'He did? When?'

'In London.'

'On what terms?'

'None, except Lord Westbrook is not to visit London for three years until people have forgotten the incident.'

'Lord Falconbridge returned Lord Westbrook's fortune.' It seemed beyond belief for Randall to show compassion to someone in society and ask nothing but their silence in return, but the girl said it with enough heartfelt gratitude for her to know it was true.

'He even suggested a stock to invest in. Because it promises to turn quite a profit, my parents have allowed us to marry, though for the moment I must keep silent, in accordance with Lord Falconbridge's wishes. I can't tell you what his generosity has meant to us.'

'I can well imagine.'

'Please don't tell him I told you, but if you could find a way to thank him for me, I would very much appreciate it. We both would.'

'I will. Of course.'

An older woman with the same brown eyes and round face as the young lady waved to Miss Caufield. 'That is my mother. I must go. Thank you, Mrs Thompson.'

Cecelia nodded, not sure how else to respond or what to think about Randall.

The large clock in the hall chimed the late hour as Randall strode in from the stables, pulled off his riding gloves and tossed them on a table. Sir Walter's comment about Cecelia still nagged at him and riding behind the carriage from the assembly had done nothing to settle his annoyance at the baronet or himself. He should have ignored Sir Walter's ill-conceived joke, trusted his better judgement and not allowed London ways to rule him, but the familiar habit proved difficult to break.

He slapped the dust from his breeches, the dirt of a horse preferable to riding with the ladies and enduring another round of Cecelia's disapproving looks. In the assembly, when he'd seen the pendant hanging around her neck, he'd thought they'd put an end to such nonsense. He should have known better.

Upstairs, the ladies' voices drifted down from the hall. He started up, then paused, tempted to wait for silence. No, he wasn't about to hide down here in the dark. He grabbed the thick railing and took the stairs two at a time. If Cecelia was still in the hallway when he reached it, then so be it.

Light flickered in the centre of the hallway as Randall reached the last step. Cecelia stood by her open bedroom door, arms crossed. She was only a short distance from him, but the gap felt wider.

He strode towards her, expecting to be reprimanded like some schoolboy and determined to ignore it.

'You gave Lord Westbrook his lands back,' she said, her soft voice breaking the tense quiet.

He jerked to a stop before her. He hadn't expected this. 'How do you know?'

'His very grateful intended approached me at the assembly.'

He clasped his hands behind his back. 'She wasn't supposed to speak of it.'

'She asked me to find a way to thank you.'

'Then she has succeeded.'

Cecelia studied him, the warm light dancing in the diamonds dangling from her ears. 'Every time I think

I know you, you change. It seems I can never be sure of who I'll be with whenever we're together.'

Her steady voice harried him more than all the anticipated chastisements, but he held his stance, refusing to be brought to heel. 'I'm the man you spent today with, just as I've always been.'

'No, not tonight, you weren't. I saw your face when Sir Walter commented on our connection. It troubled you.'

'Sir Walter is an affable man, but not all his jokes are welcome, especially when made at your expense.'

'You mean at your expense. I have no doubt Sir Walter is good-natured, but not even he is allowed to tease the imperious Lord Falconbridge.'

Randall stiffened. 'I didn't appreciate him making light of our acquaintance.'

She crossed her arms. 'Acquaintance?'

'Our friendship.' Damn, she was rattling him.

'I see.'

'And what exactly is it you think you see?' he challenged, his frustration with the baronet, her, himself rising to break his restraint. 'A man who's nothing but a scoundrel waiting to ruin everyone he meets?'

'It's your past, not mine, which leads me to such conclusions.'

'And you draw them again and again. No matter what I do or whom I help,' he snarled.

Her ire rose to meet his. 'How am I to know your good deeds when you hide them like something to be ashamed of?'

'Even if I told you, it wouldn't make a difference.' She opened her mouth to speak, but he kept going, a hurt deeper and older than she knew driving him on. 'You curse me for hanging on to my London ways, yet you cling to my past, constantly conjuring it up to keep me at a distance. You're determined to see me as a rake unworthy of you.'

'And you're determined to keep me dangling between friend and something more.' Her hands balled at her sides. 'What is it you want from me, or do you even know?'

Love. The word almost escaped before he bit it back. Not even he would believe it once uttered, yet there it sat in his mind, as clear as the mill pond on a calm day.

He raked one hand through his hair. 'You keep urging me to be a better man, but I can't change in a matter of days, not even for you.'

She crossed her arms beneath her breasts, the gold pendant glowing against her fair skin in the low light. She was so beautiful and he hated the feel of her drawing away.

'It's more than recent days, Randall.'

'I know and I'm sorry,' he roared, frustration tearing the truth from the dark place inside him. 'I'm sorry for the way I treated you. I'm sorry today and I was sorry then, for weeks, months, years afterwards. I was sorry every time Aunt Ella read me one of your letters and I knew every chance I ever had to win you back was gone.'

He took a deep breath and waited for her to laugh in triumph, to wound him the way he'd once so callously wounded her.

She raised her hand and he braced himself for the slap. He deserved it for everything he'd ever done to her, his father and so many others.

'No, Randall.' She laid her warm palm against his cheek. 'Not gone. Not any more.'

Forgiveness followed the light sweep of her fingers

across his face and he took her in his arms, pressing her hard against him. Relief slid through him, every wrenching ache their separation had caused soothed by the warmth of her body against his. She rose up on her toes, meeting his lips as he brought his down to cover hers, the taste of her sweeter than any delicacy he'd ever known.

She tangled her hands in his hair and he inhaled the magnolia perfume lingering on her wrists. Slowly he drew her back into her room and kicked the door closed, unwilling to let go or break the kiss for fear she might slip away.

His tongue slid between her teeth, caressing hers as his fingers worked open the tiny dress buttons following the arch of her spine. She didn't pull away, but matched his movements, opening the buttons of his coat and then his waistcoat. With reluctance he let go of her waist and broke free of her lips, lowering his hands to his sides as she slid the wool down over his arms to fall to the floor. Her hands slipped beneath his waistcoat, her touch hot through his shirt as they swept across his chest and pushed the silk over his shoulders. He shrugged free of the garment, dropping it on the floor with the coat.

Reaching out, he caressed the silken skin of her shoulders, pushing the dress from her body until it slid free of her arms, catching on the roundness of her hips. He laid his hands above the draping fabric and brushed the curve of her until the silk pooled around her feet.

Turning her with a light pressure, his fingers traced the line of her back to the neat bow of her stays and he pulled the long ties until the bow came loose. His manhood stiffened with each slip of the ribbon through the small holes until the stays opened and he tossed them aside. He laid a gentle kiss on first one shoulder and then the other before grasping the sides of the chemise and drawing it up over her head.

Reaching around in front of her, he looked down at her naked body and the pendant hanging between her full breasts, glittering in the candlelight. He cupped the mounds, the heaviness in his hands worth more than any jewellery he could ever purchase for her. With his thumb, he stroked the pink nipples and she sighed, the quiet noise tightening his manhood to the point of pain. She laid her head back against his chest, her eyes closed and trusting, surrendering to him in a way no woman ever had before. Laying a kiss on her temple, he pressed his hardness against her soft buttocks, eager to be free of his breeches and know the pleasure of her full embrace.

She turned in his arms, no shame gracing her face as her ample breasts rose and fell with each short breath. Instead her heated eyes met his, travelling quickly over his bare chest before she reached for the front of his breeches. His whole body tightened as her fingers moved so close to his hardness, the air cool against him when the buttons were undone and the wool fell to the floor. Through her lashes she pinned him with a hungry look, her desire free of all greed of what this pleasure might gain her.

Clasping her wrists, he drew them up and around his neck, then slid his arms beneath her back and legs and lifted her up and carried her to the bed.

She lay back against the fine sheets, watching him like the beautiful goddess she'd portrayed in Sir Thomas's studio. Only tonight there were no stern looks or chiding remarks, only acceptance and want.

He stretched out above her, dipping down over her body to nip and suck at the firm flesh of her breasts, taking one tender bud in his mouth and circling it with his tongue. She clung to him as he continued to tease her, his fingers tracing the length of her flat stomach to the sable curls between her thighs. She gasped when he found the tender pebble of her pleasure, her breath fast in his ear as he teased and stroked, sliding one finger, then another into her need. The feel of her around him, vulnerable and wanting, asking nothing of him but this coming together made his being ache.

Sensing the crest of her pleasure rising in the firm embrace of her body, he withdrew, wanting to feel the first waves of her release caress his member. She sighed in frustration, then reached up and drew him down to cover her. The soft curls of her womanhood teased his aching rod as he settled between her sweet thighs, the tip of his member resting light against her centre.

The gentle pressure of her hands on his buttocks urged him forward and he slid into her warmth. Taking her mouth with his, he forced himself still for a moment, as much to savour her as to regain control. Then her hips began to move against him and he met her steady pace. Deeper and deeper he led her into pleasure, one with her, his thrusts building as she tightened around him, their bodies moving together until his groans matched her cries and release tore through them both. He shuddered within her, arms hard around her as he pressed his forehead to hers and she trembled beneath him.

When their bodies stilled and their hard breaths softened, he rolled to one side and pulled her into the crook of his arm. Her cheek rested against his collar as her fingers brushed his chest. The candles burned low, the wax sputtering until one by one the flames died out.

'I love you,' he whispered, waiting in the darkness for her answer.

'I love you, too, Randall.'

He dropped a light kiss on her forehead, holding her close until her hand rested on his chest and her body grew heavy against his. Then he closed his eyes and joined her in sleep.

Chapter Fifteen

The sharp explosion of a pistol split the morning still and acrid gunsmoke filled the air. A neat hole near the centre marred the target on a bale of hay a few yards away.

'Well done.' Cecelia clapped as Randall handed his pistol to a footman and then accepted another.

'I can do better.' He took aim at the red circle and pulled the trigger. The gun kicked back in his hand, the smoke hovering and blocking their view before it cleared, revealing a clean hole in the centre of the target.

'Very good.' Cecelia came forward from the edge of the range. 'Now let me try.'

He moved aside, allowing her to take a smaller pistol from the footman.

She stepped up to the line and levelled the barrel at the target. Despite the pleasures of last night and the early hour she'd awoken to watch him leave before the maid arrived to light the fire, she felt no exhaustion. Her body hummed with energy, excitement and anticipation. The apology she'd waited so long to hear had finally come and with it a new belief in Randall and their future. He loved her and everything would be all right.

'Would you like some pointers?' he asked, mistaking her silence for difficulty with her aim.

'No, thank you.' She pulled the trigger, the small explosion reverberating up through her arm.

They stared down the range at the target. It was a respectable shot, hitting the outermost edge of the rings.

'Quite commendable for a lady.'

'A skill I learned, but did not master, in Virginia.'

'Then allow me to continue your education.' He took her gun, exchanging it with the footman for a new one and handing it to her.

'Now, ready yourself.' He laid his hands on her shoulders, turning her to face the hay. 'Hold up the pistol.'

She obeyed and he slid one hand around her waist to rest on her stomach. Closing her eyes, she inhaled his heat mixed with the earthy scent of the hay. She opened her eyes, struggling to keep her hand steady and not set off the gun.

'To fire correctly, you must know your weapon.' He pressed his desire against her back as he wrapped his hand over hers to help hold the pistol. 'This one errs to the left, therefore, if you wish to strike the middle, you must aim further to the right.'

He brought his face down next to hers as he moved her arm ever so slightly to the right. She struggled against the rapid beat of her heart to hold the gun steady, then closed one eye and looked down the barrel until the bright red circle came into view.

'Exactly,' he whispered, his breath spreading over her neck. 'Keep your fingers light but firm and your arm tight. When you're ready, pull the trigger.'

She slid one finger out from beneath his and curled it around the metal trigger. She pulled it back and the gun fired, Randall's strong hand keeping it from recoiling hard against her palm. They waited a breath for the smoke to clear before the hole, so close to Randall's in the centre, came into view.

Cecelia turned, snuggling into his neck. 'You're right, I have so much more to learn.'

He lowered their arms, his hand tightening over hers. 'It will be my pleasure to complete your education.'

'You'll find me a most willing student,' she purred.

His lips covered hers and she opened her mouth to accept his teasing tongue, oblivious to the footman or how visible they were to anyone who might pass by.

'Shall we go inside, or would you like me to continue your education here?' Randall's teeth nipped her earlobe and she shivered.

She glanced at the footman, who wiped black powder from the spent pistol, his back politely to them. 'What about your aunt?'

'She took your cousin to the village to purchase a new parasol for tomorrow's garden party,' he whispered, the heat of his breath catching hold deep inside her. 'They will not be back for some time.'

'It sounds so sinful.'

'It is.'

She offered no resistance when he took her hand and led her up the lawn toward Uncle Edmund's garden. At the entrance, Randall jogged through the arch, pulling her behind the boxwoods. They were not two steps in when he pressed her against a slender beech tree near the start of the path. The bark scratched through the thin wool of her dress, but she barely noticed as Randall leaned against her, kneading her breast until the tip pressed firm against her stays.

She buried her fingers in his hair, revelling in his kiss as his hand slipped along the length of her side to rest against one thigh. He raised the hem of her skirt until the cool breeze brushed against her legs, the soft sweep of the air intensified by the heat of Randall's caress. Her hands moved down his chest, eager to free him from his breeches, to feel again the fullness of him within her when the memory of Lady Ellington at the upstairs windows made her freeze.

She broke from his kiss, pushing down his hand and the dress. 'Not here.'

'Why not?' His hand slipped back beneath the wool, tracing a line up to her buttocks and making her shiver.

'I'm not so adventurous.' She struggled to speak as he drew circles on her inner thigh, each one bringing him closer and closer to the curls between them.

'Yes, you are.' One finger slid into her and she rose up on her toes, biting her lip as his thumb teased the tender bud. She tilted her face to the sun, lost to everything but the steady motion of his touch. His tongue traced the line of her throat, sliding between the V of her dress to taste the space between her breasts.

She held tight to Randall's neck as the rising wave of her release began to build, threatening to break her beneath the pressure when he pulled back.

'You're too wicked,' she panted, grasping his upper arms to steady herself.

'Not wicked enough,' he growled, undoing the buttons on his breeches.

He grasped her raised leg, his mouth muffling her cry as his member filled her, his demanding strokes claiming her. They rocked together, each move matched by the other as if they'd spent every night of the last ten years together, not separated by an ocean.

She opened wider, clinging to him, willingly embracing each powerful thrust. They pushed her higher and higher until she cried out as the spasms of pleasure tore through them both.

He withdrew from her, his face moist against hers as their racing hearts slowed and the birds in the tree above them resumed their songs.

'How easily you make me forget everything.' She sighed, lowering her leg and leaning against the tree, wishing she could lie down in the grass with him and watch the clouds pass overhead.

He buttoned his breeches, then propped one arm against the trunk near her ear, a devilish smile playing on his lips. 'The day is not over yet.'

He trailed his fingers along the length of her arm, clasping her hand tightly as he drew her from the garden, along the path and up the stone stairs into the house.

Passing through the sitting room, they hurried down the hallway and up the stairs. At the top, Randall jerked to a stop before colliding with the butler.

'A letter arrived for Mrs Thompson,' the butler announced, holding out a tray to Cecelia.

The looped handwriting on the letter cooled some of her former heat as she picked it up. 'Thank you.'

The butler nodded, then descended the stairs.

Randall studied her as she opened the letter. 'Who's it from?'

'Madame de Badeau.' She read the short note to herself, aware of Randall watching her.

As your friend, I must warn you that your absence and Randall's has been noted among society. Lord Strathmore is particularly troubled to hear you are at Falconbridge Manor. I've told him it is only to forward the interests of your cousin,

*but I do not think he believes me. I suggest you
write to him at once and confirm your cousin's
situation and put his mind at ease. I should hate
for you to lose the esteem of such a worthy gentleman, especially for one who is quite determined
to avoid springing the parson's mousetrap. I also
suggest you not stay away from London for too
long. I should hate to see people draw the wrong
conclusion about your friendship with Lord Falconbridge.*

Your Dearest Friend,
Madame de Badeau

Despite the friendly tone, Cecelia heard the warning and her briefly forgotten worries began to rise up
around her again.

Randall's eyes narrowed. 'What does she say?'

She handed it to him. 'It seems our presence in London is missed.'

'Ignore it.' Without reading it, he tore it into pieces
and dropped them on the floor. 'She means nothing
to us.'

The paper rustled beneath their feet as he cupped
her face and met her worry with a lingering kiss. This
was the Randall she'd waited so long for, the one who
loved and wanted her. Let Madame de Badeau and Lord
Strathmore wonder at their absence. Her fate would no
longer be decided by necessity or lecherous men.

Pulling her down the hallway, Randall led her into
his room and the semi-darkness of the half-drawn curtains. The door clicked shut behind them and they tore
at each other's clothes, cursing all the buttons and knots
until the garments lay tossed over silk-covered chairs

and strewn across the fine woven carpets. They toppled naked into his massive carved bed, legs intertwined, the heat of his hardness searing Cecelia's stomach and making her centre burn.

'Tell me what you want, how I can please you,' Randall demanded, caressing one breast until the nipple grew taught.

'Keep your fingers light but firm,' she breathed, mimicking his words.

With a wicked grin, he slid his hand down the line of her stomach and cupped her mound. His fingertips found the nub of her pleasure and began to work the sensitive flesh. 'Like this?'

'Yes,' she moaned, the unyielding play of his thumb against her pearl making her hips writhe. He took one nipple in his mouth and she arched her back, balling the sheets in her hands, eager for him to enter her again.

His steady caress eased as his lips swept the side of her breast, pressing against the space between them before finding her other nipple. His fingers moved lower, sliding into her, their motion as constant as the firm circles made by his tongue.

Then he raised his head and kissed her neck, tracing the line of her jaw until his heavy breath brushed her ear. 'To fire correctly, you must know your weapon.'

He withdrew from her and, easing her hand from the sheet, guided it to his member.

It throbbed when her fingers tightened around it, the firmness making her insides quiver. He closed his eyes as she stroked the length of him, her pace matching the quick rise and fall of his chest. Resting on one elbow, she slid her tongue over the hard muscle of his stomach, following the firm length of his torso up to the base of his neck, tasting the salt and sweat of him until his eyes snapped open and he pulled her hand away.

'Enough play.' He smirked, settling between her thighs, his staff hot against her skin. 'Now we must hit the target.'

He plunged into her and she dug her fingernails into his back, the fullness of him threatening to shatter her. The worries of the letter and London faded beneath the groans of his arousal and she wrapped her legs around his waist, drawing him in deeper, meeting each thrust until they shuddered together, panting in their release.

'You are a quick study,' he whispered, grazing her earlobe with his teeth.

'I told you I'm a most willing student.' She nestled into the curve of his body and he settled on his side next to her, his arm over her stomach, caressing her hip. She held his bicep, trailing her fingernails down the line of it, revelling in the warmth of him beside her. Outside, a footman's sharp whistle followed by Reverend's bark carried into the room. She looked towards the window, catching a small slip of paper on the floor next to a discarded shoe.

The letter.

Her fingers stopped.

On the pillow beside her, Randall opened his eyes. 'What's wrong?'

She rolled to face him, tracing the line of his jaw with one finger, the woman who'd spent weeks carefully guarding herself from hurt briefly returning. She wanted to ask him about their future and what would happen when they returned to London, but she held her tongue. He loved her and it was foolish to doubt him or think he might retreat again in the face of society's judgement.

'Nothing.' She laid her head on his chest, letting the steady rhythm of his heartbeat soothe her concerns.

Outside, the faint grinding of carriage wheels over gravel and the driver calling the horses to stop joined Reverend's barks.

'They've returned,' Randall murmured as the entreaties of Lady Ellington for Reverend to stop barking drifted up to them.

'Yes, they have.' She sighed, not wanting to leave the sanctuary of this room and Randall's embrace.

'Shall we go down?'

She propped herself up on his chest, her breasts flattening against the hardness of it. 'No, instruct the footman to tell your aunt we're both indisposed. No doubt she'll understand and keep Theresa occupied.'

'And you told me you weren't adventurous.'

He rolled over, pressing her into the sheets, and she opened to him, ready to enjoy him as many times as this day would allow.

Chapter Sixteen

The day bloomed bright and warm for Lady Menton's garden party. Cecelia sat with a small circle of country matrons under the large white canopy, tired but happy after a night spent in Randall's arms. His throaty laugh carried over the party from where he stood with Sir Walter on the far side of the patio and she watched him, his manner free of the arrogance and conceit she'd seen at the assembly. She wanted to go to him, to stand beside his lithe body and savour the sound of his deep voice, but decorum demanded they maintain their distance.

The matrons laughed and Cecelia realised once again she'd lost the thread of the conversation. Tired of pretending to possess an interest in the discussion of flower beds, she rose, taking up her empty glass. 'I think I'm in need of more lemonade.'

Walking out of the shade of the canopy, she moved to the table of refreshments on the patio, trying not to stare at Randall, but unable to keep from throwing looks in his direction. More than once he met her gaze with a wink, just as he had this morning over breakfast and again in the carriage. She struggled to hide her bright smile as she looked over the selection of food and he returned to his conversation.

'They're making excellent progress,' Lady Ellington remarked, coming to stand next to Cecelia, the lace edge of her parasol swaying.

The clatter of bowling pins drew her attention across the grass to where Mr Menton and a group of other young people applauded Theresa's efforts. Like a dutiful suitor, Mr Menton hurried across the lawn to retrieve the ball, his eyes never leaving hers as he strolled back and held it out to her. Theresa took it, their hands lingering a minute before she moved to try again.

Across the patio, Lady Menton watched them with pinched eyes.

'I don't think Lady Menton shares our enthusiasm,' Cecelia observed.

'Come, then, we'll have a chat with her. I know something of what makes the woman tick and can mention enough titled friends and connections to have her grovelling at our feet.' Lady Ellington led the way across the portico to Lady Menton, something of Randall's confidence in her comment and her walk.

The baronet's wife watched their approach with a mixture of forced gaiety and stern disapproval, her eyes travelling up and down Cecelia, inspecting her deepred dress as if assessing whether a horse were fit to purchase.

'Good day, Lady Menton,' Lady Ellington greeted. 'You've been blessed with beautiful weather for the party.'

'Indeed.' Lady Menton struggled to smile as she stood, looking torn between acknowledging an inferior connection and impressing her better.

'And doesn't your son look happy.' Across the lawn,

Mr Menton and Theresa laughed as his ball rolled wide of the pins. 'Oh, did you hear about Lady Tollcroft and Lord Vernon? I received a letter from the Duchess of Cliffstone about it just the other day.'

Cecelia covered a smile with her hand, noticing how many titled people Lady Ellington had managed to squeeze into the one sentence, but it achieved the desired effect. Lady Menton perked up, looking a little too eager to know the stories.

Cecelia barely heard the gossip as Lady Ellington related it with her usual flourish. She could only focus on Randall as he laughed with the baronet, more at ease today than she'd ever seen him in London. As if feeling her watching him, he tossed her a wide smile. Touching the pendant lying outside her dress, she knew, despite all her previous denials and refusals, and all the tiny fears still pestering her late at night, that she loved him as much today as she had ten years ago.

Then Randall scowled, focusing on something behind her. She turned to see a gentleman and his tall wife step out from the house, accompanied by another young man Cecelia didn't recognise.

'Ah, there is Lord and Lady Hartley and Lord Malvern,' Lady Menton announced. 'If you'll excuse me, I must welcome them.'

Lady Menton swept past them to greet the new guests.

'No wonder she enjoys such little success in town.' Lady Ellington shook her head. 'She has the conversational skills of a parrot.'

'Shall we see what the gentlemen are discussing?' Cecelia suggested, eager to be by Randall's side and to know what about the Hartleys and Lord Malvern bothered him.

'You go ahead. I don't wish to interfere in your and Randall's enjoyment.' With a conspiratorial wink, Lady Ellington made for the bowlers.

Smiling in spite of her concern, Cecelia walked to where the gentlemen stood listening to Sir Walter describe his new horse.

'She's a fine mare and I expect a long line of winners from her,' Sir Walter bragged. 'Are you a horse-woman, Mrs Thompson?'

'I am.'

'Then you must have Lord Falconbridge bring you to see her once she arrives.'

A footman stepped up next to Sir Walter. 'Lady Menton requests your presence inside.'

Sir Walter patted his generous stomach. 'If I must, I must. If you'll excuse me.' He walked off with the footman just as Lord Hartley came to join them.

'Lord Falconbridge, I'm glad to see you here today. Good to know I'm not the only exile from London.'

'I wouldn't call it an exile.' Randall moved a touch closer to Cecelia, his arm brushing hers. 'Why aren't you in London?'

'I wish I was, but as you predicted, Morton's tongue forced him back to the country.'

'You shouldn't have accompanied him.'

'I didn't have a choice. Seems all my wife's relations are determined to trouble me this Season. Morton's cousin decided to elope with a veteran from Waterloo, some captain covered with medals. Created something of a scandal. Thankfully, she sneaked off before I had to pay for the dresses she ordered from the local modiste. Now, if only Morton would decamp to Gretna Green and save me the pain of his company.'

Randall and Cecelia exchanged a knowing look, the full scandal behind Theresa's new wardrobe revealed.

'Where is your *illustrious* nephew now?' Randall asked.

He looked around, then shrugged. 'I don't know, probably into the port in the dining room. Don't worry, I expect to be thoroughly embarrassed by him before the day is through.'

'In that case, it's time for me and Mrs Thompson to explore Lady Menton's excellent grounds. I don't think I can tolerate Malvern's wit.'

'You aren't the only one.' With a roll of his eyes, Lord Hartley took his leave.

'Mrs Thompson, there's an excellent Greek temple by the lake full of pagan gods waiting for worshippers.' Randall held out his arm, his eyes hot and inviting. 'Shall we become heathens?'

'I'd love nothing better.' She laid her hand on his coat, eager to worship with him.

They started off but only made it a few steps before Cecelia's shoe caught the hem of her dress. The gown pulled and she heard it rip before she stopped, looking down to where the hem hung ragged.

'I'm afraid the gods will have to wait.' She frowned, annoyed at their time alone together being delayed. 'I'm sure one of the maids can help me with this.'

'Then I'll wait here for my nymph to return.' He flicked his teeth with his tongue and Cecelia nearly forgot the hem. As much as she wanted to follow him, she couldn't risk ruining the dress. She didn't have the money to replace it.

Lifting the skirt a little to keep it from dragging on the grass, she ventured inside in search of a maid. Her eyes struggled to adjust to the darker room as she moved through it and into the Gothic hallway just beyond. She looked back and forth, thinking to go right when a woman's voice caught her attention. She followed the sound, hoping it might be a maid when a snippet of conversation made her freeze.

'Mrs Thompson is a nobody,' came Lady Menton's high voice, 'and she's trying to foist off her cousin on our son.'

Cecelia crept closer to the door of the room where the voices emanated. It stood slightly ajar and she leaned against the wall, out of sight to listen.

'She's a close friend of the Marquess and his family,' Sir Walter responded. 'A man like Lord Falconbridge could do a great deal for Adam. You want him in Parliament. The Marquess could get him there.'

'If Lord Falconbridge were married to her, it would be different. I spoke with Lord Malvern and he told me about the rumours circling her. I won't throw Adam away on the cousin of Lord Falconbridge's whore, not when there are other wealthy young ladies with more reputable connections.'

Cecelia didn't wait for Sir Walter's response, but stole away from the door, fear following her as she struggled to find her way back out of the house. This was how it had begun in Virginia, people whispering in corners, repeating General LaFette's awful lies. She struggled to breathe as she tried first one room and then another, not finding the sitting room she'd come in through. If it happened again, if everyone turned against them, where would they go, how would they survive?

She finally turned into the empty sitting room overlooking the back portico and pressed herself into the shadows next to the door. Rubbing her trembling fingers over the gold pendant, she fought to steady herself against a barrage of anger, shame and discouragement.

Outside, Randall's deep voice cut through the muffled murmur of the guests. She hurried out of the room and down the steps to him, not caring who saw her or what they thought. Randall loved her and he'd protect her. She only needed to speak with him and settle all the worries making her chest tighten.

Seeing her, he hurried across the grass to meet her. 'What's wrong?'

'I can't speak of it here. Let's walk down to the lake.'

They turned, ready to leave, when a man's slurred voice rang out over the party.

'Lord Falconbridge, I see you're enjoying the delights of the country.'

Cecelia's back stiffened and she turned with Randall to find the young man who'd entered with the Hartleys staggering towards them.

'Who is that?' she asked, gripping his arm.

'Malvern,' he growled, lacing his hands behind his back.

'You've been missed in London,' Lord Malvern announced in a loud voice, glancing back and forth between her and Randall. Far behind him, Lord Hartley nearly dropped his plate on the bowling green before shoving it at his wife and rushing towards them.

'Mrs Thompson, I presume.' Lord Malvern offered a wobbly bow, then struggled to straighten. 'You've made quite a name for yourself this Season as Lord Falconbridge's light o' love. Had I known your name sooner, I might have won a tidy sum at White's.'

Randall rushed at the man, who stumbled back, nearly banging into his uncle. 'You will apologise to the lady at once, or I will demand satisfaction.'

Lord Malvern's mouth opened and closed as though struggling to form some witty response which might spare him the apology and the meeting at dawn. It never came and his uncle slapped him hard on the back. 'Apologise or I'll blow your stupid head off myself.'

Lord Malvern's bravado wilted and with a childish pout he turned to Cecelia. 'I'm sorry if I've caused offence, Mrs Thompson.'

She didn't reply, shaking too hard with anger and embarrassment to trust her voice.

'And the Marquess,' his uncle insisted.

'My apologies to you as well, Lord Falconbridge.'

Lord Hartley grabbed Lord Malvern by the arm and dragged him away.

It was then Cecelia noticed everyone watching them, including Lady Menton, who bit her nails as if a flock of sheep had just tromped though her party. Cecelia could practically hear the word *whore* whispering through her mind and everyone else's.

She swallowed hard, searching for Lady Ellington, but she didn't see her or any other kind faces in the crowd, only hard stares and disapproving looks. Whatever they thought of her and Randall, it had found an outlet in Lord Malvern's insolence and not even decorum or respect for Randall's rank could keep their thoughts from showing on their faces.

'Come with me,' Randall said, taking her by the arm and drawing her back towards the path.

She followed him into the shade of the trees, leaving the party behind, but not her shame. Not even Randall's firm grip could shield her from the sting. She'd spent so much time in London maintaining her reputation, only to watch it slip away in one nasty remark. Unlike General LaFette's lies, nothing Lady Menton and Lord

Malvern had said was untrue. Cecelia and Randall were lovers and now everyone knew.

She glanced up at Randall, the tight set of his jaw and his hard eyes frightening her more than Lady Menton's comments.

The path opened on to the shore of a small lake with a Greek temple perched on the opposite side. They could see nothing of the house from here, but through the trees, the occasional high voice from the party drifted down to them. Randall let go of her and marched to the edge of the water, his body stiff, and she felt him pulling away.

A breeze rippled across the water's surface, pushing small waves over the pebbled shore to nip at Randall's boots. His hands moved to his back, but he caught himself and forced them to hang at his sides. His fingers tightened into fists until they shook with the pressure, the tension rising to his elbows before Cecelia's hand slid over his knuckles.

'Randall?'

He eased open his fingers.

'Malvern will regret what he said today.' He stroked her cheek, her stricken face making his blood boil. 'How dare he try to humiliate me. I'll rip him to shreds in every gaming room and club until he's driven from London.'

'Why? He only said what many were thinking, including Lady Menton. In the house, I heard her tell Sir Walter I was your whore.'

'Who is she to judge us?' he sneered. 'The daughter of a merchant with nothing to recommend her except a willingness to bow and scrape before her betters and weasel her way into society.'

She let go of his hand. 'She's only doing it to help her son, the same way I've helped Theresa.'

'She'll ruin him with all her grasping. Insulting you is like insulting me. Doesn't she know I could raise or lower her son with a few words?'

'She doesn't just want standing, but a respectable match for him. At the moment, Theresa and I can offer neither.'

'Of course you can. Increase Miss Fields's dowry.' Randall began to pace, the small stones shifting beneath his boots. 'If Lady Menton is foolish enough to toss it away, then I'll see to it your cousin has a hundred other suitors clamouring for her hand.'

'There's no dowry, no money and none is coming from Virginia.'

He came to a halt. 'What?'

She stood alone against the water, her face as desolate as the dark surface of the lake. 'I'm poor, Randall, painfully so. Paul stole everything and what little I have was advanced by a moneylender with no hope of repayment. Until today, all I had was my good name now even that's gone. I must know, will you make me respectable again? Can I give Theresa at least that?'

He stared at her, everything falling into place— Mr Rathbone, her town house, her worry over her reputation and the refusal to trust him or tell him the truth. Yet none stunned him as much as Madame de Badeau's words ringing through his mind.

She's subtle and you won't see her plan until she has you before the vicar.

No, it wasn't true. It couldn't be. 'Why didn't you tell me before?'

'I thought if you knew the truth, you'd push me away like you did in the conservatory.'

He grunted as if she'd slammed him in the chest. 'And I thought you'd forgiven me.'

'I have forgiven you, that's why I'm telling you now.'

'But not before, not when I asked you so many times to trust me.' He clasped his hands behind his back, a crushing emptiness seizing him and threatening to shatter his control. 'You've played a good game, madam, all the while chiding me for doing the same. No wonder I didn't see it.'

'It wasn't a game, not with you.'

'With who, then? Strathmore?' he bellowed. 'Was that why you never rebuffed him? You intended to keep us both dangling, so if one didn't come through the other might?'

'No, it wasn't like that, at least not now.'

'But it was at first, until I became the better candidate.' A humiliation more piercing than any he'd suffered at his father's hands flooded through him, made sharper by the memories of Malvern's words and the judging eyes at the garden party.

'No. You pursued me for weeks despite my refusals, chipping away at them until I finally succumbed, and you accuse me of playing a game?'

'Because I see it now, how you led me on with false kindness when all the while you wanted me for your own ends.'

She marched up to him, her chin set in defiance. 'I did no such thing.'

He leaned in close, his face inches from hers. 'I thought you were the only person not interested in my title and station, the only one to see beyond it and everything else and to love me for who I am. I see now you coveted it far more and schemed to get it with far more skill than all the others.'

Her mouth softened. 'No, I love you, I always have.'

She reached up to touch his cheek, but he jerked away.

'I won't stand here and listen to any more of your lies.'

He stormed off, following the curve of the shore.

She didn't love him, she'd never loved him, she'd only used him, playing on his deepest fears to try to bend him to her will.

He came to a stop and squeezed his eyes shut, the pain rippling out from his centre like waves from a large stone thrown in the lake. He struggled to remain standing under the force of it, feeling himself eighteen again, guilty, lonely and grieving, his father's death fresh on his hands.

Opening his eyes, he climbed the steps of the Greek temple, hurrying to the far side, away from the lake, Cecelia and anyone who might happen by to laugh at his humiliation. She'd made a fool of him and he'd been too blinded by desire to realise it. How Madame de Badeau and so many others would delight to see him now, brought low by the one person he'd believed in the most, the one he'd thought would always believe in him.

Resting his forehead against the cold marble, he drew in ragged breaths, trying to silence the faint words echoing from his past. *You aren't worthy.*

Cecelia sat on a stone bench beneath the trees, staring out over the flat surface of the lake, waiting the way she had for so many days after word reached them of her father's ship, hoping all was not lost and he might return.

Her father had never come back and neither would Randall.

Her fingers tightened on the edge of the stone bench, anger and pain rising behind her eyes. She'd trusted Randall with her heart and the future and, like almost everyone in her life, he'd let her down.

A fish broke the surface of the lake, then fell back into the empty expanse and she understood for the first time ever her mother's desolation after Cecelia's father had died. Digging the heel of her hand into her forehead, she tried to push back the hopelessness and the temptation to dive beneath the surface and never come up.

Rustling on the path made her jump and she twisted to see Lady Ellington approaching.

'Cecelia, are you all right?' She looked around the clearing. 'Where's Randall?'

Summoning the last of her dignity, Cecelia rose, fighting to keep the stinging tears from falling. 'I'm fine. Randall is… Well, he's…he's gone.'

She crumbled beneath the soft concern etching the Countess's face and tears spilled down her cheeks. She buried her face in her hands, dropping down on to the bench. 'How could he have done it? How can this all be happening again?'

'Oh, my dear.' Lady Ellington wrapped her plump arms around her, the motherly gesture making the tears come harder.

Everything from the past year drained from Cecelia as she clung to Lady Ellington, the truth pouring out with her choking sobs. The Countess listened in silence, rubbing Cecelia's back while she spoke. Then at last, wrung out and unable to say more, Cecelia sighed, her body as limp as the damp handkerchief in her lap.

'You've been very brave for keeping your chin up under so much.' Lady Ellington squeezed Cecelia's hands. 'I don't know if I could've done the same.'

'What good has it done me?' Cecelia sat back. 'I still have nothing.'

'No, dear, not nothing. For all his silly faults, I know Randall loves you, he always has.'

'No, or he wouldn't have been so quick to believe the worst of me.'

'He did it because he believes the worst of himself. It's why he gets up to all sorts of things in London.' Lady Ellington shook her head. 'He thinks if he can make the world adore him, it will fill the emptiness inside him. You're the only one who's ever been able to do that. He knows it, but he hates being so vulnerable. That's why he did what he did today.'

'I know you're right.' Cecelia held up the pendant, sliding her thumb over the bricks before she dropped it to thump against her chest. 'But I don't care any more. He's never been willing to lower himself to truly love me.'

'Don't close your heart yet, my dear. Randall is stubborn, painfully so at times, but he's no fool.' Lady Ellington levelled a jewelled finger at her. 'You wait and see. He'll find a way to deserve you.'

'Even if there was a way, he wouldn't try it. His ego would never allow him to admit he's wrong.' She twisted the handkerchief. 'No, there's nothing he can say or do to make me trust him again, or give him another chance to belittle and humiliate me.'

The Countess rose, taking Cecelia by the elbow and drawing her up from the bench. 'Come with me.'

'Where are we going?'

'Home.' Lady Ellington guided her up a small path cutting through the trees along the far edge of the lawn. 'This leads up to the driveway without being seen by the house. I've already called the carriage. No doubt

Theresa is in it and in a state because I've been gone so long. She's so worried about you.'

Cecelia came to a halt, new tears blurring her vision. 'I've ruined her chances with Mr Menton.'

'Nothing is lost yet.' Lady Ellington patted her hand. 'You leave everything to me. I'll make sure Lady Menton approves of Theresa.'

'But what about her dowry and my debts?'

'That may be trickier,' she conceded, tapping one finger against her chin. 'Randall manages my inheritance from both Edmund and my late husband. I can't draw a large amount without him noticing.'

'I won't take money from you. I can't.' There was no way she could ever repay it.

Lady Ellington laid her hands on Cecelia's shoulders. 'If everything works out the way I think it will, you won't have to.'

Cecelia wiped her eyes with the back of her hand, wishing she shared the Countess's optimism. Lady Ellington might believe in the strength of Randall's love, but Cecelia didn't. Nor did she believe in Mr Menton's ardour overcoming his mother's objections.

'And if it doesn't work out?' she asked.

Lady Ellington frowned. 'Then Randall doesn't deserve you.'

Randall walked up the lawn from the stables, Falconbridge Manor little more than a silhouette in the large moon rising behind it. He'd spent a long time standing in the shadows of the Greek temple, unwilling to rejoin the party, unwilling to face Cecelia. Then at last he'd made for the house, only to be greeted by an apologetic Lady Menton and the news the ladies had returned to Falconbridge without him. He'd borrowed a horse from

Sir Walter, wandering for hours over the countryside, trying to clear his mind, but calm never came.

He looked up at the window a few down from his. Cecelia's room. It was dark and he imagined her inside, eyes red from crying. He stopped, the urge to go to her, comfort her and beg for her forgiveness startling him with its strength. More than once during the long ride back from Hallington Hall he'd wondered if he'd been wrong about her and her intentions.

'I wasn't wrong,' he snarled, continuing up the lawn until the warm light in the drawing room greeted him. It had never been about love for Cecelia, and the knowledge she'd so easily twisted his affection for her own ends roiled his gut.

He marched through the drawing room, down the hall and up the stairs, determined to bring this farce to an end. He didn't care if she was awake or asleep, if she wept or insulted him, it was time for her and the cousin to go and for him to be free of all the torment he'd experienced since first seeing her in London.

At Cecelia's room, he threw open the door, stopping short at the threshold. The bed stood untouched, the coverlet stretched smooth over it.

No doubt she was crying her heart out to Aunt Ella, winning the woman to her side with all her false grace and charm. He stormed down the hall, determined to thwart her conniving.

He threw open Aunt Ella's door without knocking and the candlelight danced wildly over the shining brocade. 'Where is she? Where's Cecelia?'

Aunt Ella laid aside her book, as steady in the face of his outburst as when Uncle Edmund used to shout down the house. 'She's gone back to London.'

Desperation seized him before anger beat it back. 'Running to Lord Strathmore already?'

'I wouldn't blame her if she did, not after the way you've behaved.'

He rolled his shoulders, shrugging off the strike. 'I assume she took the cousin with her.'

'No, Miss Fields is staying here under my care until things with Mr Menton are settled.'

'You will send her back to London first thing in the morning,' he demanded. 'Neither she nor Cecelia are to receive any more of our help.'

'Do not command me as if I were a servant.' Aunt Ella rose, drawing up all her diminutive height. 'Whom I have as a guest is no more your concern than whom you fritter away your nights with in London is mine, except where Cecelia is concerned.'

Randall ground his teeth. This was only the second time she'd ever taken such a tone with him. 'I see she's fooled you, as well.'

'She's fooled no one. She loves you, she always has and she's never wanted anything more from you than your love in return.' Her composure softened, the motherly woman returning. 'When you first told me she was back and I saw the way your whole face changed whenever you mentioned her, I was so happy for you. It's the rare instance when we get a second chance at love.' She touched the small locket pinned to her dress, the one with her late husband's portrait inside. 'I didn't, and neither did your father nor Edmund.'

'Uncle Edmund was never in love,' he scoffed.

'He was once, long before you were born, but our father forbade the match. She married another and died in childbirth. Edmund regretted losing her all his life. It's why he never spoke of it. It seems my brothers and I were all doomed to love and lose.' Aunt Ella approached him, laying one hand on his arm. 'There's still time, Randall. Don't let Cecelia slip away from you again and deny yourself this chance at happiness.'

He turned away from her soft entreaty and moved to the window overlooking the lawn. At the far end, the faint glow of moonlight against his parents' headstones stood out like a phantom in the darkness beneath the large ash.

A decanter of Aunt Ella's plum wine sat on the table in front of him. Randall laid his palm on the smooth stopper, his fingers closing over it one by one. It didn't matter if Cecelia was gone. He didn't need her any more than he'd needed all the other grasping women who'd clawed at him over the years, hungering after his rank and status, but never him, never the man beneath the reputation.

He pulled out the stopper, snatched up a glass and filled it. The sweet, sharp scent curled his stomach, but he held it up, swirling the wine in the crystal, eager to slide into the warm oblivion waiting at the bottom. Then the candlelight flickered with a draught and the light danced in the wine the way it had in the raindrops on the vicarage window the night his father died, the night everything inside him shattered.

He lowered the glass and with it the shallow promise of peace. There was no comfort in the liquor, no more than in any of the arms of the numerous women he'd bedded or in any of the scandals he'd created. In all of it there was only the numbing cold of the long walk back to Falconbridge Manor with the icy rain pouring over his neck, the chill of it cutting as deep as the loneliness and despair, the self-loathing and hate which had consumed him until the moment he'd met Cecelia.

Out the window, the headstones faded as a cloud passed in front of the moon. His father was gone, buried along with all chances of forgiveness, but Cecelia was still here.

The door squeaked open and Reverend ambled into the room. He sat down next to Randall and leaned against his leg. Randall dropped his hand on the dog's head, stroking the soft fur.

He was worthy of Cecelia's love, just as she was worthy of his, and he'd prove it to them both.

He poured the wine back into the decanter, replaced the stopper and turned to face his aunt.

'I'd like you to pay a call on Lady Menton tomorrow,' he began, respectful to the woman who'd been like a mother to him. 'Make it clear to her, in blunt terms if you must, that if she doesn't oppose the match, Theresa will have five thousand pounds for a dowry and Mr Menton will have my full support on either a bid for Parliament or whatever business venture he wishes to pursue.'

'And Cecelia?'

He looked at the small portraits of Aunt Ella, his father and Uncle Edmund painted in their youth and hanging above the dressing table. He would not lose Cecelia, he would not let his mistake drive her into the arms of another man, not if he had to stand outside her house every night for the rest of his life until she finally granted him entrance.

'I'll leave for London as soon as the carriage is ready and call on Mr Rathbone to settle her debts. Then I'll see her.'

Aunt Ella twisted the largest diamond ring off her finger and held it out to him. 'Here, take this.'

'Your engagement ring?'

'You need it more than I do and I'd be proud to see Cecelia wear it.'

'Thank you.' He moved to leave, then stopped. 'You were a bright spot during a terrible time.'

'I did my best.' She smiled with all the love he used to take for granted. 'Now it's time to do yours.'

Chapter Seventeen

Randall rapped on the Fleet Street town-house door, impatience making his fist heavy. A blinding evening sun cut in between the buildings, a stark reminder of the time he'd lost on the road to London. First a cracked carriage wheel, then a lazy carpenter had delayed them for hours at a coaching inn. He'd have hired a horse and finished the journey but the shamble of a place hadn't possessed one suitable nag. Near daybreak, he'd given up any hope of reaching London by morning and rented a room, catching a few hours of fitful sleep before his driver roused him to continue the journey. Muddy roads crammed with carts and carriages had further slowed their progress until the spires of London had finally come into view, the afternoon sun low behind them.

At last a butler pulled open the door, the servant as well poised as any in Mayfair. 'Yes, sir?'

'Lord Falconbridge to see Mr Rathbone.' Randall stepped into a clean entrance hall furnished with fine paintings and furniture, all of it probably seized from one of Mr Rathbone's poor clients. Randall's hand tightened on his walking stick as he wondered how close Cecelia's things had come to ending up in this horde.

A door on the opposite wall creaked open and a tall, young man approached, his clothes simple but of fine material and superbly tailored.

'Lord Falconbridge,' he greeted, as stiff and formal as the butler, but not overawed at having a Marquess in his presence. No doubt it wasn't the first time a titled man had graced his entryway. Mr Rathbone motioned to the office. 'If you please.'

The office was as neat as the hall, if not more so, the desk clean except for the short stacks of papers resting on one corner. Mr Rathbone took a seat behind the polished desk and Randall perched on one of the chairs in front of it.

'To what do I owe the pleasure of your visit, my lord?' Mr Rathbone asked.

'I'm here to settle Mrs Thompson's debt.'

A faint trace of surprise crossed his face, so subtle it might have been missed if Randall were not facing the man. 'The debt has already been settled.'

'By whom?'

'Madame de Badeau. She purchased it yesterday.'

Randall's stomach tightened. What the devil was she doing involved in all this? 'Why?'

'It's not my habit to enquire into the nature of my clients' affairs except where collateral and the ability to repay are concerned.'

'Yes, I'm sure it was only Mrs Thompson's collateral you were interested in, not whether her dealings with you would ruin her.'

If he hoped to raise the man's ire, he was sorely mistaken, for Mr Rathbone continued to face him, as calm as if they were discussing the weather. 'Mrs Thompson came to me, Lord Falconbridge, and asked for my assistance. I did not seek her out.'

'Yet you advanced her funds, knowing she must be in trouble and that her debt might ruin her.'

Again Mr Rathbone failed to take umbrage or meet the challenge. He only rested his elbows on the desk and laced his fingers over the leather blotter. 'Based on Mrs Thompson's limited collateral, I provided much less than the amount she requested. It does neither me nor my clients any good to advance sums on which they will default.'

'No, of course not.' Randall's anger in the face of Mr Rathbone's calm faded. He wanted to blame the man for Cecelia's troubles, but he couldn't. The money-lender had been fair in his dealings with her, more so than Randall. Again he kicked himself for not visiting the man sooner. This whole situation might have been avoided if he'd taken a chance and risked his once-precious ego and reputation. He rose to leave. 'Thank you for your time.'

Outside, Randall took a deep breath. He hadn't expected this complication, but he should have known coming back to London would not be as easy as waltzing into Cecelia's and solving all her problems. He'd approached Mr Rathbone first in the hopes of arriving on Cecelia's doorstep with the debt and tearing it up in front of her in an effort to prove his sincerity before he begged for her forgiveness. Now there was Madame de Badeau to contend with. She hadn't purchased the debt to help her friend. No, there was a much more sinister reason behind it.

Miss Domville's words in Madame de Badeau's hall came rushing back to him along with the sickening sense he'd brought the vile woman's wrath down on Cecelia. He didn't know what she was planning, but if she threatened or hurt Cecelia, he would see her crushed.

* * *

A distant knock pulled Cecelia out of a deep sleep. She opened her eyes and struggled to focus in the dim evening light turning the bedroom grey. She'd come upstairs a few hours ago to rest after a long night on the road and a difficult day pacing the house, trying to work out what to do next. She hadn't expected to fall so soundly asleep.

She sat up and the pendant slid over her dress, bringing back all the loneliness of the carriage ride to London and the memory of Randall storming away from her at the lake.

At least he left me something to pawn.

Her eyes stung with new tears and she gripped the edge of the mattress, determined not to lie down and curl into a crying ball. There were decisions to be made about her and Theresa's future. In spite of Lady Ellington's confidence, Cecelia expected to see her cousin back in London at any moment, banished by Randall in a bid to wash his hands of both of them.

Mary's steady footsteps sounded on the stairs and she suspected the maid was coming to announce Theresa's arrival.

With a sigh, she rose and poured water from a pitcher into the chipped porcelain basin on the dressing table. She dipped her hands in the water and splashed her face, trying to shore up the strength she needed to comfort the broken-hearted girl.

Mary opened the door. 'Mrs Thompson, Madame de Badeau is waiting for you downstairs.'

Cecelia snatched up a towel, in no mood to see the Frenchwoman. 'Tell her I'm sick and I'll call on her in a few days.'

'I already told her, but she said it's a matter of urgency and she won't leave until she's seen you.'

Cecelia rubbed her damp and raw cheeks, knowing exactly what the woman would see. She debated sending Mary downstairs with a more curt dismissal, but Cecelia wouldn't put it past Madame de Badeau to march upstairs anyway. 'I'll see her.'

She slid her feet into her shoes and made her way downstairs, hoping Madame de Badeau would mistake her worn appearance for proof of illness and keep the meeting brief.

'Madame de Badeau, what an unexpected surprise.' She nearly choked on the polite words as she walked into the morning room. The woman stood by the fireplace, dressed in a deep blue silk gown, her wide bosom covered in diamonds. 'I'm sorry I didn't send word to you sooner, but I haven't been well today.'

'Yes, travel can make one so very ill.' She sounded less than sympathetic and the way she eyed Cecelia like a goose about to pounce on a June bug made her wary. 'Tell me, is everything settled between your cousin and Mr Menton?'

'No, but it will be shortly.'

'Whatever objections can there be?' Madame de Badeau clasped one surprised hand to her chest, her diamonds sparkling.

'Lady Menton is a proud woman.'

Madame de Badeau's lips curled into a wicked smile. 'Or perhaps she doesn't want her son tricked into marrying a poor young lady in search of a rich husband.'

'What do you mean?' Cecelia rubbed the pendant between her fingers, trying to soothe her rising worry.

'I know all about what your stepson did, and General LaFette, and how the two of them drove you back to England without a penny to your name.'

Cecelia gripped the back of a chair, the floor shifting beneath her. 'How?'

'Many years ago in France, I knew General LaFette and we've enjoyed a lively correspondence ever since. In his last letter, which I received shortly before your first visit, he told me everything about you. You see, despite all your pretences to wealth, I've known all along you're nothing but a beggar.'

Cecelia's fingers tightened on the chair, one fingernail finding a small hole in the fabric. 'If you knew, then why did you trouble with me?'

'Revenge.' The word slid out, low and icy, the destruction of her life by Paul's selfishness and General LaFette's lies all echoing in the simple declaration.

'What have I ever done to you?'

'Not you, your mother.'

She stared at the Frenchwoman in disbelief. 'What could she have done to hurt you?'

'That conniving whore stole your father from me,' she seethed, her composure slipping. 'Do you know what I suffered under Chevalier de Badeau before Madame Guillotine killed him and left me with nothing? I had to crawl and scrape my way back from the gutters. Then you returned to London and, like your mother, tried to steal the man I love. Randall is mine and I won't lose him to someone like you.'

Cecelia wanted to laugh at the absurdity of Madame de Badeau loving anyone, but she bit it back, striking instead with the only barb she still possessed. 'You can't lose what you never had.'

'And you think he loves you?' Madame de Badeau sneered. 'When I first heard you'd gone to Falconbridge

Manor, I thought you'd won, but now you're back without him and without the happy look of love on your face. He's thrown you over, had his way with you and forgotten you, just like all the others. Except me. I've maintained the one thing none of them could—his friendship. When he returns to London, I'll tell him how you hid your poverty and tried to trap him.'

'He already knows I'm poor.'

'Good. Then he'll see once again how I was right and how I'm the only person who's ever cared about him.'

Cecelia's heart dropped, hearing too much truth in Madame de Badeau's nasty words.

'Don't look so cheerless, my dear. After all, there is still Lord Strathmore to consider. When I heard you'd returned without Randall, I told him at once. Not only was he delighted, but he informed me of his plan to ask you to marry him tonight at the theatre.'

'I'm not going to the theatre, nor am I about to let you humiliate me in front of all London.'

'Oh, I think you will. You see, I've purchased your debt from Mr Rathbone.' Madame de Badeau withdrew a piece of paper from her reticule, unfolded it and held it up. From across the room, Cecelia could see her signature at the bottom of the paper and with it her happiness and future signed away. 'If you don't accept Lord Strathmore's proposal and agree to his plan to expedite your happy union, I'll reveal to everyone that you and your cousin are penniless. I'll deliver the proof to Lady Menton myself and then insist you repay your debt to me. If you don't, I'll send the bailiffs to secure it and your place in the Fleet. Then I'll watch as you and your cousin sink from good society for ever.'

Madame de Badeau took a menacing step closer,

but Cecelia stood her ground, meeting the woman's icy stare, refusing to be cowed.

'I know what it is to suffer poverty and the humiliating depths which one must sink to survive,' Madame de Badeau hissed. 'Imagine your sweet little cousin suffering at the hands of sailors, or the depraved young lords who frequent the bawdy houses.'

Cecelia stared at the debt clutched in the woman's hand, the horror in Madame de Badeau's words made more terrifying by their truth. The Fleet or worse had been her greatest fear since arriving in London and starting this risky game. It was the fate she and Theresa might suffer if she refused Madame de Badeau. Unless Lady Ellington could help them.

'I know what you're thinking. You're wondering if Randall still has enough feelings left for you to save you,' Madame de Badeau jeered. 'I assure you, he doesn't. Once he's finished with a dalliance, he doesn't look back. In fact, he'll welcome your marriage to Lord Strathmore as an easy end to this whole affair.'

Randall possessed the power to stop Lady Ellington from helping her and, after yesterday, Cecelia knew he would.

An isolation stronger than the one she'd known the morning her mother packed her into the post chaise for Falconbridge Manor gripped her. At least then there'd existed the promise of a future. What future did she have now?

Lord Strathmore.

'What about my debts? Will you return them to me or continue to hold them over my head?'

'I have no intention of forgiving them. I've laid out a tidy sum to Mr Rathbone and I expect to see it all returned to me in full.'

'You know I have no money.'

'Once you're married to Lord Strathmore and he realises you aren't the saviour he's been waiting for, he'll have to part with the many items he's spent countless hours boring me about. When his creditors demand those things be sold, I'll be there with my note to collect. I'm a patient woman and willing to wait for what I'm due.'

Cecelia shuddered, seeing no other option and knowing even in marriage her torment would not end. 'You've dallied long enough and we're losing needed time to get you ready for the theatre.' Madame de Badeau flapped the paper in front of her. 'Will you or will you not agree to my terms?'

Cecelia stared at the paper, the fight in her fading. Weeks of worrying, of scraping by and selling her precious things had all come to nothing. She'd been doomed from the beginning. If she agreed to Madame de Badeau's terms, Lord Strathmore's title would protect them from the Fleet. Perhaps the title of Countess and whatever money she could secure from Mr Rathbone would be enough to gain Theresa a husband and a better future than the one facing Cecelia. 'I will.'

Randall slammed the knocker against Madame de Badeau's door, irritated at being made to wait. The daylight was long gone from the sky and the stars were difficult to see in the light of the rising moon. After leaving Mr Rathbone's, he'd gone straight to Cecelia's, determined to put things right, but the house was dark and empty and no answer met his persistent knock.

He'd made for Madame de Badeau's, determined to face the woman. He didn't know what game she was up to, but he'd be damned if he'd allow her to hurt Cecelia.

He balled his fist and slammed it against the door. If breaking it down would bring anyone in the house to greet him, he'd shatter it into splinters, but it wouldn't. All he could do was stand in the dark, cursing the silence and considering where to go next.

Movement along the far side of the house caught his attention. He stilled, watching as a woman with a plain bonnet pulled low over her head passed through the wrought-iron servants' gate, the metal clanging as her travelling case knocked against it. The woman was too small to be Madame de Badeau and, when she turned to survey the still street, Randall caught a faint blonde curl against the dark pelisse.

'Miss Domville. What are you doing?' Randall demanded, storming to her.

The girl dropped the case, whirling to face him. 'Nothing.'

'Does nothing carry a portmanteau out of the servants' gate without a chaperon at night?'

Her initial surprise changed to defiance and she stuck her chin in the air. 'I won't go back in there. I won't live with her any longer.'

'I'm not suggesting you do, nor am I about to let you roam London in the dark.' He picked up the case. 'I need your help.'

She grabbed the handle, trying to tug it away. 'Why should I help you?'

'Because if you do, I'll see you get wherever it is you're trying to go, assuming it's respectable.'

She let go of the handle. 'I'm going to Nottinghamshire, to the Smiths who raised me. Is that respectable enough for you?'

'They've agreed to take you back?'

'I wrote to them.' She shifted on her feet, her confidence faltering. 'I haven't received a response, but I'm not staying here another night.'

'You won't have to if you help me.'

'What makes you think I can?'

'Because I know you listen at keyholes. Now come along.' He took her by the elbow and led her to the carriage. 'Why isn't Dalton answering the door?'

'Helene told him not to. She's not in the house anyway.'

'Where is she?'

'With Mrs Thompson.'

'I've just come from her house and they aren't there.'

'Then I don't know where they've gone.'

Mr Joshua stood next to the open carriage door as Randall handed Miss Domville inside and gave the portmanteau to the groom.

'Mr Joshua, check the theatre, Lady Weatherly's, anywhere Madame de Badeau may have taken Cecelia for the evening. Come back to me when you find them.'

'Yes, my lord.' The valet ran off in the direction of Drury Lane as Randall stepped into the carriage.

He sat across from Miss Domville and the vehicle rocked into motion. 'Why did your sister purchase Mrs Thompson's debt?'

Miss Domville twisted her hands in her lap. 'She wants to force Mrs Thompson to marry Lord Strathmore. He's on the verge of bankruptcy and Helene has convinced him Mrs Thompson is rich. He won't find out the truth until after they're married. It's part of her revenge for the way he left her for that actress two years ago.'

Randall's hand tightened on the squabs. The Frenchwoman must have lain in wait for Cecelia to return so she could pounce. Madame de Badeau couldn't touch her when Cecelia was with him in the country and if he hadn't acted like such a fool, they might still be there, Cecelia safe instead of who knew where with the conniving woman. 'What about Mrs Thompson?'

'If Mrs Thompsons refuses him, Helene will reveal her debts and ruin Theresa's prospects with Mr Menton. I tried to warn Theresa and Mrs Thompson, but Helene caught me writing to them. She hit me, forbade me to see anyone or leave the house, but I'm not about to obey. My *sister* will pay for striking me,' she hissed, the word *sister* laced with venom. 'While Dalton was at the brandy again today, I went through her desk to see if I could find any money and I found these.'

She withdrew a small packet of old letters from the pocket of her pelisse. They were yellowed and torn along the edges, the pink ribbon tying them together frayed at each end. She pulled the top one from the stack, opened it and held it out to him. 'You won't believe the things she's done.'

Madame de Badeau's looped handwriting filled the page and Randall held it up to the carriage lantern to read the faded words. Not even Randall, who knew a number of Madame de Badeau's secrets, was prepared for this. He lowered the letter, unable to fathom how he'd tolerated the vile woman's company for so many years. No wonder Cecelia was hesitant to trust him. That she gave him a chance at all spoke of her love and belief in him, one he'd make sure to deserve. 'Madame de Badeau is your mother?'

Tears welled up in Miss Domville's eyes and she wiped them away with the back of her hand, a dark bruise around her wrist revealed when her sleeve pulled back. 'When she moved to London from Paris, Chevalier de Badeau was long dead and she didn't want to be disgraced by having me.'

Randall handed her his handkerchief. 'So she placed you with the family in Nottinghamshire.'

'Everyone told me we were sisters, but we weren't. I was her daughter and this is how she treated me.' Fresh tears streamed down Miss Domville's face. 'I don't even know which one of her lovers is my father.'

'I'm very sorry, Miss Domville. When we reach my house, you'll go to my aunt at Falconbridge until you hear something from the Smiths.' Aunt Ella would know how to comfort the poor girl. 'Now, let me see the other letters.'

She passed them to him and he skimmed each one. They were copies of the originals paired with those received in response. They detailed her time as a courtesan and the kept woman of not one, but many wealthy Frenchmen, including a General LaFette.

Randall shifted in his seat as he read the last one describing her friendship with him and the ruined reputations they'd left in their wake. She painted a poor picture of him, but when he turned the letter over to read the back, his discomfort turned to blazing anger. There Madame de Badeau laid out her joy at the prospect of watching Cecelia suffer under Lord Strathmore's depravity.

Randall crushed the letter in his hands, about to rip it to shreds before he stopped. It was worth more to him wrinkled than torn and was the key to banishing Madame de Badeau from their lives for good.

Chapter Eighteen

Madame de Badeau glowed like a lantern as she escorted Cecelia into the theatre.

'Smile, my dear. After all the effort I took to make you lovely, I don't want your frown ruining it,' Madame de Badeau snapped, her nails biting into Cecelia's skin as she hustled her through the crowd.

Cecelia tried not to stumble on the hem of her gown as the woman dragged her upstairs. The ribbon Madame de Badeau had wound through her hair cut into the back of her neck and the curls scrapped into a tight coiffure pulled at her temples, adding to her discomfort.

At the entrance to her private box, Madame de Badeau tugged aside the curtain, huffing at the empty chairs. 'Where can he be?'

She pushed Cecelia into a seat, then brushed past her to stand at the front and look over the crowd, tapping her fan against the railing.

Hope flared in Cecelia as she tried to tug the hair ribbon loose. Maybe Lord Strathmore was smarter than she believed and refused to be a pawn in the wicked lady's game.

Then the curtain behind her rustled and she tensed as Lord Strathmore entered the box.

Madame de Badeau whirled to face him, all beaming smiles and charm. 'Lord Strathmore, do join us.'

She waved to the chair next to Cecelia and he was quick to slide into it.

'You look beautiful tonight, Mrs Thompson.' His gaze raked her chest and he ran his tongue over his lips, greedy lust filling his eyes. 'This is very striking—is it new?'

He lifted the pendant, his dry fingers scraping along the tops of her breasts.

She leaned away from him, wondering which he coveted more, the gold or her. 'No, it was a gift.'

He dropped the pendant like a hot stone, his languid eyes hardening. 'From Lord Falconbridge?'

She didn't answer and the Earl tugged at his cravat, his skin red above the white linen. He turned his attention to the play, a slight wheeze marking each exhale and making Cecelia's skin crawl.

Madame de Badeau sat in the single chair in front of them, pretending to watch the performance, but Cecelia knew she was listening and waiting.

An actor on stage launched into a long-winded monologue until the boos from the pit brought it to an end.

'You don't know how happy I am to see you tonight,' the Earl finally spoke, taking Cecelia's hand, her satin glove keeping the full chill of his skin from hers. 'London was lifeless without you.'

She focused on the stage and the young actress waving to Lord Weatherly. 'I can't believe you missed me so much.'

'Yes, so much that I've decided not to let you slip away from me again. Mrs Thompson, will you marry me?'

Madame de Badeau shifted in her chair, waiting for Cecelia to deliver her own lines without fail.

Cecelia's throat tightened. She could rise, march out of the box and face whatever wrath her defiance brought down on her, but she couldn't, not with Theresa's future in danger, too.

'Yes,' she whispered, the word lost in the audience's laughter.

'Pardon?' He leaned in closer, stale port heavy on his breath.

'Yes,' Cecelia choked out as the audience quieted, the word seeming to echo through the box. Across the theatre, Lady Weatherly watched them before directing the woman beside her to do the same.

'Splendid, splendid.' Lord Strathmore's beady eyes bored into her as his fingers rubbed the back of her hand, almost to the point of pain. 'My carriage is outside. Let's be off.'

'And go where?' She tried to withdraw her hand, but he held it tight.

'My house, of course. We'll leave for Gretna Green in the morning. It will spare us having to wait for the banns.'

She pulled back her hand, nearly losing the glove. 'I'm flattered by your eagerness, but it isn't proper for me to spend the night at your house alone before we're married.'

'Not to worry. Madame de Badeau will stay with us tonight so your reputation remains intact. I can't have people thinking ill of my future Countess.'

'Shall we be off, then?' Madame de Badeau stood, Lord Strathmore moving to join her.

They hovered over Cecelia like a menacing wall about to tumble down and crush her. She could do nothing except rise and follow them into the hallway. Lord Strathmore wrapped her hand around his arm, his beaming smile increasing her disgust.

Outside the box, Madame de Badeau stopped. 'I must speak with Lady Weatherly and share the good news. Don't wait for me. I'll follow behind in my own carriage.'

Madame de Badeau pinned her with a triumphant smile before sweeping off down the hall, ending all pretence of safeguarding Cecelia's reputation or sanctity.

'Come along.' Lord Strathmore pulled her towards the stairs and the theatre entrance.

Panic swept through her at being alone with Lord Strathmore. However, without Madame de Badeau standing guard, maybe she could convince him to see the folly of the union and abandon his pursuit.

Hope faded as fast as it rose. Even if she persuaded him to break the engagement, Madame de Badeau still held the power to ruin her. The dreaded letter to Lady Menton had probably already been sent and, with Lady Weatherly learning of the engagement, it wouldn't be long before Randall heard of it, too. He'd probably rejoice at being so easily rid of her.

Outside, Lord Strathmore paused, looking up and down the long line of carriages pressed together in the street, their drivers huddled in groups chatting and laughing.

She envied the men, wishing she possessed their freedom, when one face among them stood out.

Mr Joshua.

Was Randall here? She searched the carriages for his, but didn't see it.

'Ah, there is my carriage,' Lord Strathmore exclaimed, pulling her down the steps.

She watched her feet to keep from falling. When she looked up again, the valet was gone, probably home to tell Randall what he'd seen.

At the bottom of the stairs, three men approached Lord Strathmore. She didn't recognise them, but the poor quality of the middle one's coat and the ill-fitting breeches of the two burly men flanking him whispered of disreputable dealings.

'Wait here while I deal with these men.' Lord Strathmore stepped off to one side to speak with the strangers and she heard snippets of the conversation over the horses and laughing drivers.

'…you owe quite a sum…'

'…the lady is wealthy. If you'll be patient, I'll have the money soon…'

Their conversation continued, muffled by the sound of approaching footsteps. Cecelia thought of running, making for her house, but what good would it do? Madame de Badeau and Lord Strathmore would only follow.

'Mrs Thompson,' came a male voice from beside her and she turned to find Mr Joshua next to her. 'Are you all right?'

The concern on his face touched her and she wondered if it was his regard or Randall's which led him to ask. She hesitated, unsure what to tell him, and wondering if anything she said would make a difference.

'What are you doing talking to him?' Lord Strathmore demanded, grabbing her by the arm and tugging her back.

'I was giving him a message for Ran— I mean, Lord Falconbridge,' she protested, her body tense with fear.

'Here's a message for him.' He snatched the pendant from her neck and flung it at Mr Joshua. 'The lady and

I are to be married tomorrow. Tell Lord Falconbridge he may send his regards to my house. Now be gone.'

He jerked her away, her neck stinging from where the chain had scratched it.

'Let go of me,' she demanded, looking back to watch the valet disappear around the building. 'You had no right to give away my necklace.'

He stopped and pulled her close, his fingers digging into her upper arms. 'You're mine, do you understand? You agreed to marry me and be my wife and you will treat me with the respect I deserve.'

'And what of my respect?' she challenged, trying to twist out of his grasp.

'What respect do you deserve, whoring with the likes of Falconbridge? Well, no more. Now come along.'

He pulled her down the line of carriages, stopping more than once to search for his. He finally spied it, wedged between two town coaches, the red lacquered side and the gold trim along the top standing out in the dark.

He pulled open the door and shoved her inside.

'To my town house, at once,' he called to the driver.

'But sir, the other carriages will have to move. It'll take time to find the drivers.'

'Then get to it.'

Randall's carriage turned into Grosvenor Square. As it approached his town house, he saw Mr Joshua standing with a horse by the mounting block. Randall jumped from the carriage before it came to a full stop and rushed to the valet. 'You've found her?'

'She's in trouble, sir.' He held out the pendant by its broken chain.

Randall took it, his fury rising as his fingers closed over the gold. 'Where is she?'

'Leaving Drury Lane with Lord Strathmore. I think he's taking her to his town house. I don't trust her alone with him, my lord. He was rough with her.'

Randall shoved the pendant in his pocket. If Strathmore hurt her, he'd kill the man.

'I readied the horse for you, my lord. It'll be faster.'

'Well done.' Randall snatched up the reins and mounted, sure he could spot Strathmore's ostentatious coach along the main streets. 'Miss Domville is in the carriage. See to her until I return.'

He kicked the horse into a gallop, making for Drury Lane.

The tense minutes stretched on as Cecelia sat in the dark carriage with Lord Strathmore, rubbing her sore arms. The Earl hung out the window, shouting along with his driver for the other carriages to move. She eyed the opposite door, the brass handle temptingly close. She could leap out while he was distracted, but not without tripping over his thick legs and risking more bruises from him.

At last, after more screaming and the crack of a whip, the carriage broke free of the crush and Lord Strathmore resumed his seat, his eyes fixed on her breasts. 'At last, we're alone.'

She covered her chest with her hand. 'Lord Strathmore, we cannot wed.'

His piggish eyes snapped to hers. 'You've already agreed to the marriage and, if Madame de Badeau has told Lady Weatherly, all society will learn of it before the third act.'

'I only agreed because Madame de Badeau threatened me.'

'Threatened you?' he scoffed. 'What is she, some kind of highway robber?'

'No, but she failed to tell you the true state of my finances. I'm penniless and in debt.'

She expected the news to send him into a stuttering panic. Instead, his eyes sharpened into two hard points. 'Are you trying to make a fool of me?'

'No, Madame de Badeau is trying to make fools of us both.'

'You're the only one making a fool of me,' he shouted and Cecelia pushed back against the squabs. 'All the attention I paid to you, the loan of my horse, the painting, everything, and you run off to Falconbridge Manor like a common Cyprian. Well, you won't embarrass me again, you'll be mine.'

He flew across the carriage, his weight pressing down on her until she could barely breathe. 'Get off me.'

'I won't hear any of your lies. You owe me.'

He clawed at her dress and a seam ripped. She pushed her hands against his chest, struggling to free herself, but he grabbed her arms, forcing them above her head and pinning them in one large hand. His legs straddled hers as he struggled to raise her skirt and, with all her might, she rammed her knee into his groin. He gasped, his grip on her loosening, and she wrenched herself free, shoving him back. She lunged for the door, ready to break an arm to reach safety, but he snatched her around the waist. She gripped the frame of the open window, struggling to keep him from pulling her back, but her fingers slipped from the lacquered wood. He threw her down on the squabs, his bulk pinning her as she fought against his pawing hands.

'Now you'll know the humiliation you've subjected me to. All London was laughing at me and I won't have it, do you hear me? I won't.'

His hot mouth covered hers, his teeth grating against her lips as he gripped her wrists, pulling her clawing hands from his face.

Outside the carriage, the faint sound of someone calling out carried above the horses and Lord Strathmore's laboured breathing. The horses whinnied and the carriage came to a hard stop, sending her and the Earl tumbling to the floor.

Lord Strathmore's head jerked up. 'We've stopped, why have we stopped?'

The carriage door swung open and Randall stood there, eyes blazing.

Randall hauled Strathmore from the carriage and slammed him against the side.

'It isn't what you think,' Strathmore squealed.

Randall banged him against the carriage again. 'Then explain to me what it is.'

From the high seat, the driver clutched the whip, ready to climb down. With a shake of his head, Randall warned him not to interfere.

'She's mine. She's going to marry me,' Strathmore rushed in a shaky voice.

'No, never,' Cecelia called out, slipping from the carriage and coming to stand behind Randall.

'You promised me, you little whore,' the Earl spat.

Randall pulled back his arm and slammed his fist into Strathmore's cheek, the pain in his knuckles unequal to the anger tearing through him. 'Speak to the future Marchioness of Falconbridge like that ever again and I'll tear you apart.'

Behind him Cecelia gasped, the delicate sound cutting through Randall's fury and giving him the calm he needed to not beat the life out of the earl. Instead he opened his hand and Strathmore slumped to the ground, clutching his bruised face and whimpering.

Randall stood over him, disgusted. 'She's poor, Strathmore, penniless, living off pawned silver and credit.'

'Then why did Madame de Badeau encourage the match?'

'Because she hates you for humiliating her two years ago. This was her revenge and you fell for it.'

Randall watched as the truth sank into the man's thick skull.

'I'm ruined.' Strathmore sobbed. 'Ruined.'

Randal stepped back and held out his arms to Cecelia. She rushed to him, clinging to his chest, trembling as he held her tight.

'I'm sorry, Cecelia.'

'I know, and I am, too.' She slid her hands around his waist, meeting the tightness of his embrace. Relief slowed his pounding heart, and he kissed her forehead. In the pressure of her hands against his back, the soft weight of her cheek against his chest, he felt his forgiveness and a warmth no wine or reputation could ever provide.

'You came back,' she whispered and he slid his fingers beneath her chin, lifting her face to his. 'Your aunt said you'd come back, but I didn't believe her. I was wrong.'

'No, I was wrong, about so many things.' Reaching into his pocket, he withdrew the pendant, dangling it between them on its broken chain. 'I came to make you respectable again. I want to give you that and more. Cecelia, will you marry me?'

She laid her hand on his cheek, the love in her eyes touching his soul as she drew him down to her, the answer in the sweet taste of her kiss.

* * *

Cecelia leaned into Randall's body, his heart beating beneath her hand. In his firm kiss lay the fulfilment of every promise all the others in her life had ever broken. His tongue caressed hers and her fingers tightened on the back of his neck. She would never be lonely again and she and Theresa would be safe, free from uncertainty and ruin, and protected by Randall's love.

At their feet, Strathmore snivelled.

'What about Madame de Badeau?' She stiffened, one last threat to her happiness lingering. 'She won't leave us in peace after this.'

'Yes, she will.' He swept her lips with a comforting kiss and her fear faded.

He let go of her and knelt down next to the earl, who backed up as far as he could against the carriage wheel.

'Don't hurt me, please,' the pathetic man whimpered like an injured rat.

'Unfortunately, I need you too much to hurt you.'

'But I have nothing, nothing,' he gasped, about to sink into a fresh fit of blubbering when Randall grabbed him by the collar and gave him a sobering shake.

'Shut up and listen to me. If you do everything I tell you, you may just save yourself from complete ruin.'

Chapter Nineteen

'The Marquess of Falconbridge,' the footman announced and Randall strode into Lady Weatherly's salon.

Conversation hushed and the rustle of people stilled as he walked the length of the long room. A few were brave enough to watch him, but their eyes dropped the moment he noticed them.

He stopped by the open terrace doors, his position offering an excellent view of everything.

In a short time, everyone fell back to their conversations or card games. Even the young lady at the pianoforte resumed her playing and the dancers returned to their turns and twirls. No one approached Randall and he ignored the many curious looks thrown at him, his attention fixed on the doorway.

He didn't have to wait long before Madame de Badeau appeared, announced by the footman. If she noticed the furious whispering spreading through the room, it didn't show in the wide smile she wore as she crossed the room to join him. Her fine dress fluttered about her legs as her misjudged triumph emphasised her swinging gait.

'Randall, I see you've returned from your little folly in the country.'

'I have.' He looked around the room. 'Tell me, where is Miss Domville tonight?'

'I don't know where she's gone.' Madame de Badeau frowned. 'I'd like to believe she eloped, but the girl's too stupid for such a rational step. No doubt her current escapade is only another of her many attempts to spite me, despite everything I've done for her.'

Randall laced his fingers behind his back, struggling against his disgust to maintain the detached London facade which used to come so easily to him.

'Of course, she isn't the only one who's acted like a fool,' Madame de Badeau continued, her sister forgotten. 'People are whispering about how a little-known widow humiliated the notorious Marquess of Falconbridge. It's all I seem to hear about of late. No doubt this whole room is filled with people laughing about it.'

'If they are, it makes no difference to me.' And for the first time in ten years he knew it was true. They were whispering about him and who knew what they really said, but he didn't care. They could all go to Hades and take Madame de Badeau with them.

'I see your pretty little widow has not arrived,' she purred, following the line of his gaze to the door.

'Yet.'

She slapped her fan against her hand. 'No, she's not coming, not tonight or ever again.'

'You seem so sure.'

'Oh, I am. You see, I received a letter this morning from Lord Strathmore. It contained the most delightful account of his trip to Gretna Greene with your precious Cecelia.' She reached into the small gap of her bodice and withdrew the missive, then held it out to Randall. 'You may read it if you like.'

'No, I already know what it says.'

The steady rise and fall of her chest paused before she took a deep breath. 'Did your precious widow already write to you of her happy news?'

'No. I drafted that letter and gave it to Strathmore to copy and send to you.'

The paper crinkled in her hands as her fingers curled into a tight fist. 'But I saw them leave together.'

'You did, but you didn't see me intercept them, nor pay Strathmore in kind for what he tried to do to Cecelia. It's the reason you haven't seen him. He's at his estate, recovering from a nasty black eye.'

'I don't believe you.' Her confident tone wavered.

'Then you won't believe this, either. The price he paid to avoid my calling him out was to write the letter you're holding and another to Lady Weatherly outlining your plot to ruin him and Cecelia.'

Horror flashed across Madame de Badeau's face, followed by searing anger. 'You're trying to get the better of me, but you won't, and neither will that little whore.'

'Mind how you speak of her,' he warned, fingers laced tight together behind him.

'Don't tell me what to do. Do you really think I'll allow you or her to make me a laughingstock, to let her do to me what her mother did before?'

'You've brought this and more on yourself.'

'More?' Her voice cracked.

'I know where Miss Domville is. She's with my aunt at Falconbridge Manor. Before she left, she entrusted a packet of letters to me describing your life in France, your plans to destroy Cecelia and Lord Strathmore and how you tried to pass off your daughter as your sister.'

Madame de Badeau covered her mouth with a shaking hand, her horror the most genuine emotion he'd ever seen cross her face.

Before she could answer, another flurry of whispers wicked through the room and all eyes turned to the door.

Cecelia stood at the threshold, dressed in her black silk dress with gold embroidery, diamond earrings dangling from her ears, the pendant warm against the smooth skin of her chest. She met the curious stares of the guests and he sensed the ripple of nerves spreading beneath her confidence. She touched the pendant and then her eyes met his. He winked at her and a sweet smile spread across her lips, matched by his own. He saw her stand a little straighter, his silent encouragement bolstering her courage.

Conversation ceased as everyone waited while Cecelia whispered to the footman.

'The Marchioness of Falconbridge,' the footman announced.

The collective gasp nearly shattered the plaster ceiling, but none was as loud as Madame de Badeau's.

With the delightful sound ringing in his ears, Randall strode across the room to stand beside his wife. He would crawl over the shards of his own reputation, cross a hundred ballrooms on his knees with all London laughing at him to be by her side.

Cecelia slipped her hand around his arm, Aunt Ella's diamond sparkling on her finger as he escorted her into the centre of the room.

Lady Weatherly approached, greeting them with a regal curtsy. 'Lord Falconbridge, you've outdone yourself.'

He squeezed Cecelia's hand. 'It will be the last time.'

'Oh, I think we'll shock a great many people with your newfound respectability before we're through.' Cecelia laughed. 'Imagine what they'll say when there is a little one in the nursery?'

'Are you increasing?' Lady Weatherly asked, almost hyperventilating with the excitement of new gossip.

'No, but I'm sure it will happen in time.' She shot Randall a sinful glance, her hope for the future as strong in the look as her desire for him.

'I'm sure it will.' He raised her hand to his lips, wanting to give her this gift and ease the last of her past heartaches.

'No, this can't be,' Madame de Badeau screeched, rushing at them. 'How dare you, how dare you?'

Cecelia's hand tightened on his arm, but she didn't draw back, steady as ever by his side.

'Madame de Badeau, remember yourself,' Randall commanded and for a moment the woman was stunned silent.

'Perhaps it would be best if you left,' Lady Weatherly suggested.

'Don't you dare chastise me, you whore,' Madame de Badeau spat. 'I know your secrets, all of them.'

With her head held high, Lady Weatherly turned on one heel and walked off, leaving Madame de Badeau to stand by herself, a spectacle to amuse the room.

'How dare you cut me?' Madame de Badeau screamed after her before she noticed the others watching. 'How dare any of you look down on me? I know all your secrets, yours and yours, and yours.'

She jabbed a finger at first one lady and then another. As she did, they rose and followed Lady Weatherly into an adjoining sitting room until one by one the salon drained of people and only Randall and Cecelia remained.

Madame de Badeau whirled on them, her face creased with rage. 'You think you've won, but you haven't. You think you'll be able to walk through society with your heads held high, but you won't.'

'There's nothing you can do to make us feel ashamed,' Cecelia shot back.

Madame de Badeau's eyes hardened on Cecelia, ready to attack like some rabid dog.

Randall stepped forward, dropping his voice to a tone as red as hot iron. 'Say one word against us, breathe even one insult, and I'll reveal to all of London the truth about your time in Paris and about Miss Domville.'

'No, Randall. You see, I have letters, too, and I'll write more if you dare share my secrets. Imagine how all of London and everyone you've ever humiliated will salivate to see you brought low.'

He leaned in so close he could see the grains of face powder covering her skin. 'Let them. I'll gladly accept their ridicule if it means never having you in our lives again.'

Her jaw dropped open, her bravery vanishing under the force of his words.

He straightened and took Cecelia's hand, leading her towards the terrace.

'Might I suggest Italy?' he said carelessly. 'It can be quite a haven for those who've been disgraced.'

The quick click of Madame de Badeau's shoes as she fled the room was the only response.

Outside, the darkness of the sky melded with the faint lights illuminating the windows of the city. He took Cecelia in his arms and she glowed like the diamonds gracing her ears.

'You were bold to tell Lady Weatherly of our intimate relations.' He touched her cheek, revelling in the love making her eyes sparkle.

She wound her hands around his neck, falling into him with a sigh. 'I very much enjoy our intimate relations.'

'Careful, my dear…' he grazed her throat with his teeth '…or you'll earn yourself a scandalous reputation.'

'Let everyone be scandalised by our love,' she murmured in his ear, pressing her hips against his. 'I intend to flaunt it through town.'

'Good, because I intend to create quite a scandal with my ardent passion for my wife.'

He covered her lips, kissing her with all the strength of his love and she fell against him, her embrace full of the promise of this night and every night to come.

* * * * *

MISS MARIANNE'S
DISGRACE

To all the writers who struggle through
challenges to achieve their goals.

Chapter One

England, September 1820

The crack of shattering porcelain cut through the quiet. Miss Marianne Domville whirled around to see Lady Ellington, Dowager Countess of Merrell, on the floor amid shards of a large *chinoiserie* bowl. Moments ago the bowl had been resting on the edge of a table while Lady Ellington had walked about the room, admiring the Italian landscapes adorning the panelling.

'Lady Ellington!' Marianne rushed to her companion. 'Are you all right?'

Mrs Stevens, their new friend, knelt on the Dowager's other side. Together, they helped Lady Ellington to sit up. Next to her lay a large sliver of the broken bowl, the razor-sharp edge rimmed with red from where it had sliced Lady Ellington's upper arm.

'I—I don't know,' Lady Ellington stammered. She clasped the wound as blood seeped through her fingers and ran down over the elbow to stain the top of her satin gloves. 'I tripped on something and somehow knocked the bowl to the floor when I fell.'

'Let me see.' Marianne tried to look at the injury, but Lady Ellington twisted away.

'You needn't fuss so much,' she chided in a shaky voice. 'It's just a scratch, nothing more.'

'Then allow us to examine it.' Mrs Stevens reached over and gently peeled Lady Ellington's fingers away from the wound. Her lips tightened as she studied the wide and bleeding cut.

'This needs immediate attention.' She pressed her handkerchief over it.

Lady Ellington winced and a fine perspiration spread out beneath the line of her light-blonde hair streaked with grey.

'Will she be all right?' Marianne asked as the embroidery on the linen blurred with red. One of her schoolmates at the Protestant School in France had cut herself this deeply. It had become inflamed and she'd gone from a lively child to resting in the churchyard in the space of two weeks. For all Marianne's misfortunes, none would equal losing Lady Ellington.

'Of course,' Mrs Stevens reassured in a motherly tone. 'But the wound must be closed. Fetch my son. He used to be a naval surgeon. He'll see to it.'

'But he wasn't at dinner.'

'He came in after we withdrew and is probably with the men. Go quickly. I'll stay with Lady Ellington.'

Marianne rose on shaky legs and walked in a fog of worry out of the study. She turned down one hall, then paused. The heavy sauce from the fish course twisted in her stomach. This wasn't the way. As she doubled back, the sweep of her footsteps on the carpet dulled the panicked thud of her pulse in her ears. She hadn't paid much attention when she'd followed the ladies to the study after leaving the sitting room. She'd been too busy fuming over Miss Cartwright's snide comments to concentrate on what turns they'd made to reach the distant room.

'Where's a footman when you need one?' They'd been as thick as fleas along the wall at dinner and in the sitting room afterwards. Now there wasn't even a lowly maid scraping out ashes in any of the empty rooms flanking the hall. Lady Ellington might bleed to death before Marianne found her way back to the other guests.

No, she'll be fine. All I need to do is find Mr Stevens.

She turned a corner and the door to the wide front sitting room came into view. She exhaled with relief and rushed towards it, careful not to run. She didn't want to fly into a fit of worry, not with Lady Ellington relying on her to keep a level head. Hopefully, the men hadn't lingered in the dining room.

No such luck.

The women looked up from around the card table as Marianne stepped into the doorway. Their faces were no warmer or more welcoming then when she'd left them fifteen minutes ago.

'Can we help you, Miss Domville?' Lady Cartwright drawled, as if it hurt her to be polite.

'Lady Ellington has injured herself and is in need of help. I must find Mr Stevens.'

'*Sir Warren,*' Miss Cartwright corrected, her lips pulling back over one crooked front tooth as she laid a card on the pile in the centre, 'is in the dining room with the men.'

'I'll call a footman to summon him. After all, it can't be too serious,' Lady Cartwright sneered under her breath to Lady Astley and Lady Preston who sat with her at the card table.

'No, thank you, I'll fetch him myself.' Marianne made for the dining room, not about to lose time waiting for these hard women to decide whether it was more important to put Marianne in her place or to help Lady Ellington.

She didn't remember the hallway being so long when Lady Ellington had walked beside her, chatting gaily with Mrs Stevens about the new Italian landscape paintings they were about to view. Marianne quickened her pace, stumbling a little over a wrinkle in a rug before righting herself.

The deep laugh of men muffled by the double oak doors punctuated the growing whispers of the ladies congregating in the sitting-room doorway behind Marianne. They gasped in shock, practically sucking the air from the hallway as Marianne pushed open the doors and stepped inside.

They weren't the only ones who were stunned. The footman jumped in front of her so fast, he almost lost his wig.

'Miss, you shouldn't be here.' He shifted back and forth to block her view, as if she'd walked in on the men dancing naked in front of the buffet.

'Move aside, I must see Sir Warren.' She slipped around the ridiculous footman and headed for the table.

The men were too lost in a weedy fog of tobacco and fine port to notice her. All the candles but those at the far end of the long table of Lady Cartwright's ridiculously long dining room had been extinguished, deepening the smoky shadows outside the circle of light.

'I tell you, Warren, it's an investment you can't miss.' Mr Hirst thumped the table in front of him. His words were thicker and more slurred than when he'd rattled on to her at dinner about his intention to import a new type of tobacco from North Carolina. He'd pleaded with her to speak to Lord Falconbridge about investing in his venture, addressing her breasts more than her during the discussion. *The noxious little man.* His lust was all she'd come to expect from most gentlemen. Carnal pleasure was the only thing the men who'd streamed through Madame de Badeau's entrance hall had ever wanted from her and they'd despised her for not giving it to them.

The men on either side of Mr Hirst nodded in agreement, except for Lord Cartwright who slumped forward on the high polished table, snoring beside an empty wine glass.

'You could make a fortune,' Mr Hirst insisted.

'Rupert, I've already made a fortune with my novels,' the man who must be Sir Warren replied. He sat with his back to Marianne, a glass of port held at a languid angle to his body.

'Sir Warren,' Marianne called out, interrupting his leisure.

Chairs scraped and men coughed and sputtered as they hurried to stand. Even Lord Cartwright was hauled to his feet by Lord Astley. Lord Cartwright's bleary eyes fixed on her.

'What in heaven's name are you doing in here?' he sputtered, wavering and nearly falling back into his seat before Lord Astley steadied him.

'I need Sir Warren. It's urgent.'

'I'm Sir Warren.' The man with his back to her set his drink on the table and turned.

She braced herself, ready to receive from him another chastising look like the others had flung at her, but it wasn't there. Instead, his deep-green eyes were wide with the same surprise filling her and it dissolved all of Marianne's sense of urgency. He was tall, with a broad chest she could lay her head on, if she was inclined to embrace people, which she wasn't. His long, sturdy arms ended in wide hands with slender fingers tinged a slight black at the tips. He was taller than the other gentlemen with long legs and narrow hips. The softness of the country hadn't set in about his flat stomach beneath his waistcoat or along the line of his jaw shadowed by the first hint of light stubble. He wore his blond hair a touch longer than the other men with a few strands falling forward over his forehead. There seemed something more professional man than gentleman in his bearing. Although his clothes were fine, they weren't as tidy or well pressed as the other gentlemen's and his cravat was tied, but the knot was loose.

Unlike his companions, he didn't appraise her large breasts, which she did her best to hide beneath the chemisette and high bodice. Instead he waited patiently for her to explain herself, like Mr Nichols, the old vicar at the Protestant School in France used to do whenever he'd caught her being naughty. Where had this man been at dinner? With him by her side instead of old Lord Preston, she might have actually enjoyed the overcooked lamb.

The rest of the men weren't so kind, brushing her with their silent disapproval and more lurid thoughts.

'How can I be of assistance?' Sir Warren prodded, snapping her out of her surprise.

'You must come at once. Lady Ellington has cut herself badly and needs your help.' She reached out, ready to pull him along to the study before she dropped her hand. To touch a man, even innocently, was to encourage him and she needed his assistance, not his ardour.

His smile faded like the last flame licking at a coal in a fireplace. He slid a glance to Mr Hirst. It was a wary, troubled look like the ones Mr and Mrs Smith used to exchange during Marianne's first month at their house when they'd been forced to tell her Madame de Badeau still hadn't written.

Hollow disappointment crept into her already knotted stomach. Sir Warren wasn't going to help her. Like every other reputable gentleman, he'd swiftly but politely decline any involvement with her before rushing across the room to avoid the taint of her and her reputation.

How petty.

She opened her mouth to shout him down for not

having the decency to rouse himself from propriety long enough to help an ailing woman, but he spoke first.

'I'll see to her at once.' Sir Warren motioned to the door. 'Please, lead the way.'

She clamped her mouth shut, near dizzy with relief as she hurried back across the dining room, keenly aware of his steady steps behind her.

'You there, lead us to the study.' She snapped her fingers at the footman, afraid she wouldn't remember the way and waste more time heading down pointless hallways.

The footman jumped at the command, walking briskly in front of them as Marianne and Sir Warren followed him out of the dining room.

'What happened?' Sir Warren asked in a voice as rich as the low A note held down on the pianoforte.

Marianne twisted her hands in front of her, noting the hard faces of the women watching them from the sitting-room doorway. 'She cut herself on a broken porcelain bowl.'

Sir Warren jerked to a halt in the hallway as if he were about to change his mind.

'Your mother said you could help,' Marianne encouraged, afraid to lose him now and in front of the sneering women.

'Yes, of course.' He lost his hesitation and they resumed their steady pace.

They approached the ladies clustered behind Lady Cartwright and her imperious scowl. Their whispers ceased as Marianne and Sir Warren passed, and

Marianne could practically hear the scandal wicking through the countryside. She could stop and explain, but there was no point in wasting the breath or time. Some might understand and forgive her. The rest wouldn't be so charitable even if she were summoning help for the Archbishop of Canterbury.

'It's just the type of inappropriate behaviour I'd expect from someone related to Madame de Badeau,' Lady Cartwright's barely concealed voice carried down the hall behind them.

'She should be ashamed of herself,' Lady Astley whispered.

Marianne winced, expecting their censure to make Sir Warren change his mind about assisting her. To her astonishment, he turned and strode back to their hostess.

'Lady Cartwright, would you be so kind as to fetch a sewing kit, a roll of linen, a few towels and vinegar and see them delivered to the study. Lady Ellington has been seriously injured and I need the items.'

Lady Cartwright's long face dropped as the crow finally grasped the urgency of the situation. 'Of course, I'll have the housekeeper see to it at once.'

She grabbed the skirt of her dress and fluttered off in the opposite direction, leaving her daughter and the rest of the ladies to huddle and whisper.

Sir Warren returned to Marianne. 'Shall we?'

'Yes, of course.' Marianne started off again, amazed at his command of Lady Cartwright and the alacrity with which he'd defended her. She wished she possessed the power to wipe the nasty sneers from the women's faces. After four years, most of the country families still believed she was as bad as the late Madame de Badeau. They couldn't see past all of the dead woman's scandals to realise Marianne, despite having the woman's blood in her veins, wasn't a brazen tart like her.

'Does Lady Ellington have a strong constitution?' Sir Warren asked as they turned the corner.

'The strongest.'

'You're sure? It'll matter a great deal to her recovery if the wound is deep.'

'I'm quite sure. I reside with her. She's my friend.' And almost the only person who'd accepted her once the scandal with Madame de Badeau had spread. Her support, and the influence of her nephew and his wife, the Marquess and Marchioness of Falconbridge, stood between Marianne and complete isolation from society.

As they continued on to the study, Sir Warren's presence played on her like a fine piano sonata. She'd never been so conscious of a man before, at least not one who wasn't ogling her from across a room. He didn't glance at her once as they crossed the hallway and he hadn't been inappropriate in his regard, not even when she'd first faced him in the dining room. She wondered at the strange awareness of him and if it meant the penchant for ruin did linger inside her, waiting for the right man to bring it out. After all, Madame de Badeau had been in control of herself for many years, until the thought of losing Lord Falconbridge had pushed her to near madness. If it did exist in Marianne, she'd stand strong against it, as she had all Madame de Badeau's wickedness, and make sure it never ruled her.

At last, the study door came into sight and she forgot Sir Warren as she focused on her friend.

'Stay here in case we need you,' Sir Warren instructed the footman and the man took up his place along the wall.

Marianne hurried forward, eager to know if Lady Ellington was any better or worse, but Sir Warren's hand on her upper arm brought her to a halt. He gripped her lightly, drawing her back to him. She whirled to face him, fingers curling into a fist, ready to strike him like she used to the lecherous men at Madame de Badeau's, but the melancholy shadow covering his expression made her hand relax.

'Miss?' he asked, the question as soft as his pulse flickering against her skin.

'Domville.' She braced herself, expecting recognition to ripple through his eyes and make him recoil from her.

It never came.

'Miss Domville, I'll do all I can for Lady Ellington, but you must understand how small an arsenal I possess against the chance of inflammation.'

Marianne began to tremble. 'Are you saying this to scare me? Because I assure you, I'm already frightened.'

He slid his thumb along her skin, the gesture subtle but comforting, soothing her in a way she'd craved so many times during her childhood at the Protestant

School and in the face of Madame de Badeau's callousness. Deep in the back of her mind, the raspy voice of experience urged her to pull away. She'd learned years ago not to seek solace in others or to accept so familiar a touch from a man. Both were the quickest paths to disappointment. For the first time, for no logical reason she could discern, she ignored the voice and experience.

'I'm saying this because I have no desire to deceive you about the strength of my skills, or those of any man of my former profession,' he explained. 'We're helpless against everything but the most minor of ailments. Even those outdo us from time to time. It's a truth many medical men are loath to admit.'

There seemed more to his admission than a need to discredit himself. Something about his past in medicine drove him to speak when most physicians would be pushing expensive and useless treatments on her. She caught it in the tight lines around his mouth. Was it a failure or a lost patient? Whatever it was, the silent plea wasn't just for understanding, but for forgiveness. She covered his hand, her chest catching as he tightened his fingers around hers. Despite the inappropriateness of this exchange, she knew too much about pain to leave someone else to suffer.

'Sir Warren, Lady Ellington means more to me and has done more for me than anyone else and has never expected anything in return except my friendship. I understand the shortcomings of your profession and appreciate your honesty and willingness to help. Whatever happens, I won't blame you. I only ask you to do your best.'

He squeezed her hand. 'I will.'

Warren's palm went cold the instant he let go of Miss Domville. A trickle of perspiration slid down the arch of his back. He swiped at it, leaving his shirt sticking to his skin beneath his coat. If he didn't detest the feeling so much, he'd call it fear.

The candles in the candelabrum near the door wavered with the draught as he entered the study. Lady Ellington sat grimacing on the floor, pillows propped behind her. Faint streaks of drying blood ran the length of her arm beneath the soiled handkerchief. Darker drops littered the floor and stained her mauve skirt and the carpet.

Warren paused on the threshold, the brackish taste of mouldy cask water burning his tongue. He took a deep breath, coughing slightly as the scent of burning wood and gunpowder filled his nostrils.

His mother looked up, apology as heavy as concern for the patient in her expression. 'Warren, thank goodness you're here.'

Warren pushed forward, forcing his feet to move one in front of the other. He carefully brushed aside the broken porcelain pieces so he could kneel next to the regal lady and better view the laceration. He removed the blood-soaked handkerchief and steadied himself as he examined the gaping wound.

'How are you tonight, Lady Ellington?' He tried to sound cordial but the words came out tight.

'I've certainly been better.' She offered him a weak smile, her wide chest covered in diamonds struggling to reflect the low light.

'Miss Domville, please bring the candles closer.'

Miss Domville's dress fluttered behind her as she took the candelabrum from near the door and set it on the table above Lady Ellington. The memory of his assistant surgeon holding a candle over Warren's head while Warren dug splinters out of a seaman's neck flashed in the facets of Lady Ellington's diamonds. Some of the sailors had survived thanks to his skill. Many more hadn't, no matter how much he'd done for them.

Miss Domville knelt beside Warren. The whisper of silk and her fresh peony scent pushed back the old stench of seared flesh. He offered her an encouraging smile, wishing he could wallow in her faint answering one. He couldn't and focused on the patient.

'I'm sorry, Lady Ellington, but the cut is deep and will require sutures.'

Lady Ellington's pale face went almost transparent. 'It will hurt, won't it?'

'It will, but without them I can't stop the bleeding.'

'Don't worry, Lady Ellington, you've faced worse,' Miss Domville encouraged. The worry he'd caught in her voice in the hallway when he'd cautioned her about believing too much in medical men was masked by her reassuring words.

'You're quite right, my dear. We must soldier on tonight as we always do, mustn't we?' Lady Ellington reached out with her good arm and patted Miss Domville's knee. The young lady didn't stiffen beneath the older woman's touch as she had with Warren's, nor did the tenderness of her smile fade.

'Sir Warren, I brought the items you requested.' Lady Cartwright's voice ended the sweet comfort of the ladies' exchange.

At the door, Lady Cartwright covered her mouth in shock. Warren wasn't certain if it was for Lady Ellington or the now-stained carpet. He suspected the latter as he took the sewing box and bottle of vinegar from the stalwart housekeeper and set them next to him.

'Come away from there at once, Miss Domville.' Lady Cartwright flapped her hand at her guest. 'Next to a surgeon is no place for a young lady. You'll only get in Sir Warren's way.'

'No, I need her help and her friend needs her comfort,' Warren countered as he took up the needle and began to thread it with sturdy white silk. His hands were solid on the slender metal, but he felt the tremor rising up through his body. He was determined to finish the task before it swept over him and made him appear weak and incompetent. He took a deep breath, inhaling Miss Domville's sweet scent. It calmed him more than any drought of laudanum or dram of rum ever had.

When the needle was ready, he handed it to Miss Domville. 'Hold this, please.'

Their fingers met and she pulled away as if he'd pricked her, the tension he'd sensed when he'd touched in her in the hallway returning. He wished he could

soothe whatever worries made her flinch, but it was
the patient who needed him now.

He took up the bottle of vinegar, splashed some on
to the clean cloth and pressed it to the wound. Lady
Ellington winced.

'You might have warned me.' She scowled, a touch
of humour behind the reprimand.

'It would have hurt more if I had,' Warren countered with a half-smile. He set the cloth and vinegar
aside and took the needle from Miss Domville. He
pinched the top of it, careful not to touch her this time.
'Put your hands on either side of the skin and push it
closed.'

Without question or hesitation, Miss Domville did
as she was told. A trickle of blood seeped over her long
fingers, but she didn't flinch or blanch. He admired
the girl's pluck. Most genteel young ladies would be
swooning on the sofa by now.

Not to be outdone by a young woman, Warren drew
in a bracing breath and set to work.

Lady Ellington whimpered with each pierce of the
needle and draw of the thread, but she didn't scream
or jerk away. Warren worked fast, eager to cause her
as little pain as necessary.

Over his shoulders, an occasional whisper broke
through his concentration. To Lady Cartwright's credit,
she kept the other ladies from crowding into the room
and interfering. To her detriment, she didn't staunch
the steady stream of derision aimed at Miss Domville.

'She'll ruin her dress,' Lady Preston sneered.

'She's acting like a common camp follower,' Miss Cartwright hissed.

Warren made the final suture, tied it off with a neat knot and used the scissors in the sewing kit to snip the needle free of the thread. 'You'd make quite a surgeon's assistant, Miss Domville. You have the steady nerves for it.'

She frowned and glanced past him to the door. 'Not everyone agrees with you.'

'Ignore them.' He handed her a clean towel, eager to see her lovely white fingers free of the red taint.

'I spend my days ignoring them.' She roughly scrubbed her skin.

He wondered what had happened to turn the others against her. Perhaps it was jealousy. She was sensuous like a Greek sculpture with shapely arms ending in elegant hands. When her fingers were clean and white again, she handed him the stained towel, avoiding his touch. Then she adjusted the lace chemisette covering her very generous décolletage. The brush of her fingertips across her breasts proved as teasing as it was modest. It made him forget the dirty linen in his palm as he watched her straighten a pin in her golden hair with its faint hints of amber circling her face. It was arranged in small twists which were drawn together at the back of her head, emphasising her curving neck and the small curls gracing it. While he watched her, he was no longer irritated at being drawn back to the sickroom he despised. If he'd known this beautiful woman was waiting in the sitting room for the men to finish their port, he'd have insisted they leave the dining room at once.

'Warren, perhaps you should see to the bandage,' his mother encouraged, interrupting his admiration of Miss Domville.

'Of course.' Warren took up the roll of linen and wound it over the wound, attempting to ignore the blood covering his fingers and to focus on Miss Domville's steady presence beside him. As he tied the bandage, a small spot of red darkened the centre, but it spread out only to the size of a thruppence before stopping. 'There now, Lady Ellington, all is well again.'

Lady Ellington looked at her arm and the dried streaks running down it. 'To imagine, all this trouble because I tripped.'

'It was no trouble at all. I'm glad you summoned me.' He patted her good shoulder, hoping his smile hid the lie. It didn't and his mother caught it, offering him a silent apology, but he ignored it. The old fear humbled him enough without anyone noticing it. 'Let's help her up to the sofa so she can rest.'

The moment Lady Ellington was settled against the cushions, the invisible dam holding the ladies back burst. They flooded into room, surrounding the Dowager Countess in a flurry of chirping and silk. Warren moved back, surprised to find Miss Domville next to him.

'She really will be all right, won't she?' she asked, her fear palpable. She wasn't the first person to seek his reassurance about a patient.

'There was no cloth pushed into the wound to fester and, given her robust health, I think she'll recover well.' It was the best he could offer.

Pink replaced the pale worry on the apples of her cheeks. He'd experienced the same reprieve the day he'd returned to Portsmouth and resigned his commission. He'd vowed that day never to climb aboard another Navy frigate again, and heaven help him, he wouldn't.

'I'll write out instructions for properly seeing to the wound while it heals and a recipe for a laudanum tonic to help ease any pain.' He walked to the escritoire, the activity relieving some of the tension of having attended to a patient for the first time since his sister's death over a year ago. He pulled out the chair, making it scrape against the wood floor, irked that a simple cut could affect him or dredge up so many awful memories. His reaction was as shocking as when he'd turned to find Miss Domville in the dining room asking him to help the same way his mother had asked him to intervene during Leticia's travails.

Seating himself, he selected a piece of paper from the stack on the blotter. He paused as he laid the clean sheet over the leather. Blood darkened the tips of his finger and the side of his hand. He rubbed at the stains with the linen towel, but the red clung to his skin as it used to during a battle. He tightened his hand into a fist, desperate for water and soap to rid himself of the filth.

He looked up, ready to bolt from the room in search of cleansing when his eyes caught Miss Domville's. She glanced at his clenched hands, then back to his face. It wasn't his mother's pity in the stunning blue depths of her eyes, but the same bracing strength she'd offered Lady Ellington before he'd begun his work.

He snatched up the pen, his fingertips pressing hard on the wood as he scratched out in shaky letters the directions for mixing the laudanum and alcohol. He pushed back the haunting memories of his cramped cabin below the waterline and focused on the proportions, determined not to get the dosage wrong and leave poor Miss Domville at fault for easing her friend's pain for good.

'My, it's cold in here,' Lady Astley's voice rang out above the noise.

A poker clanged in the grate and Warren flinched, running a streak of ink across the paper. The scrape of rods shoved down cannon barrels echoed in the sound, the balls buried deep inside and ready to wreak a destruction his surgical skills could never hope to undo.

'Ladies, I think Lady Ellington should be left alone to rest until the carriage is called.' Miss Domville's firm suggestion sounded above the clatter, silencing it.

Warren, pulled from the past by the steady voice, was surprised by the young lady's ability to remain composed in the face of so many hostile stares. She reminded him of a seasoned seaman calmly watching the coming battle while the new recruits wet themselves.

Lady Cartwright huffed up to Miss Domville, not content with a silent rebuke. 'I don't think *you* should instruct us on how to behave. You didn't even have the decency to tell us what was wrong, bursting in on the men and leaving us to think who knows what.'

'It was an emergency. There wasn't time for pleasantries.' The twitch of small muscles around the young woman's lips undermined her stoicism.

Lady Cartwright opened her mouth to unleash another blow.

'She was right to summon me as she did.' Warren rose to defend Miss Domville, tired of the imperious woman. Miss Domville had endured enough tonight worrying over her friend. She didn't need some puffed-up matron rattling the sabre of propriety over her blonde head. 'And she's correct. Lady Ellington needs space and rest. Lady Cartwright, would you call for her carriage? Mother, would you escort her and Miss Domville home? I'll send my carriage for you.'

'Of course.' His mother arched one interested eyebrow at Lady Ellington, who offered a similar look in return before her face scrunched up with a fresh wave of pain.

Lady Cartwright's nostrils flared with indignation, not nearly as amused as the two ladies on the sofa. 'I'll summon Lady Ellington's carriage. After all, we wouldn't want to detain Lady Ellington or *Miss Domville* any longer.'

She struck Miss Domville with a nasty look before striding off in a huff.

The long breath Miss Domville exhaled after Lady Cartwright left whispered of tired resignation. It was as if she'd waged too many similar battles, but had to keep fighting. He understood her weariness. Aboard ship, he'd faced approaching enemy vessels with the same reluctant acceptance.

Her gaze caught his and he dropped his to the paper as if he'd stumbled upon her at her bath, not in the middle of these chattering biddies. Unable to stand the noise any longer, Warren snatched up the instructions and quit the room. In the quiet of the hallway, he spat into his palm and rubbed the handkerchief hard against his skin. It smeared the red across his hand, dirtying the linen as it had stained the rags aboard ship. There'd never been enough buckets of seawater to clean the grime from beneath his fingernails.

He screwed his eyes shut.

This is nothing like then. Nothing like it. Those days are gone.

The war against Napoleon was over, his commission resigned. He was no longer Lieutenant Stevens, surgeon aboard HMS *Bastion*. He was Sir Warren Stevens, master of Priorton Abbey and a fêted novelist.

A fêted novelist who'd be destitute and a disappointment to his family like his father had been if he didn't finish writing his next book.

He opened his eyes and scrubbed harder until at last the red began to fade, cursing the troubles piling on him tonight.

'Sir Warren, are you all right?'

Miss Domville approached him, the flowing silk of her dress brushing against each slender leg. Beneath her high breasts, it draped her flat stomach and followed the curve of her hips. She stopped in front of him, her eyes as clear and patient as when they'd faced each other before.

Humiliation flooded through him. He wouldn't be

brought low by memories. He clutched his lapels and jerked back his shoulders, fixing her with the same glib smile he flashed adoring readers whenever he signed their books. 'Yes, why shouldn't I be?'

'I don't know. You seem troubled.' She studied him the way his sister, Leticia, used to, head tilted to one side, her chestnut curls brushing her smooth cheeks. It had looked so dark, matted against her forehead with sweat, her hazel eyes clouding as the life had faded from them. Hopelessness hit him like a jab to the gut.

'I'm fine.' He handed her the now-wrinkled and sweat-dampened paper, ashamed by this bout of weakness. It had been a long time since the memories of his time at sea had overwhelmed him like this. He'd thought he'd overcome them in the ten years since he'd left the Navy. Apparently, he hadn't. 'Follow the directions precisely, otherwise you may do more harm than good.'

'I will, and thank you again for your help.' Miss Domville folded the paper, pausing to straighten out a crease in one corner as she glanced past him to the fluttering women. 'All of it.'

'It was the least I could do. Now, if you'll excuse me.' He turned and left, ignoring the confused crease of her smooth forehead as he all but sprinted away from her and the study. He regretted the abrupt departure, but he'd embarrassed himself enough in front of her already. Despite the draw of Miss Domville's presence, the faint desire to linger in her sweet smile and vivid blue eyes, he needed the solitude of home and his writing to calm the demons stirred up by tonight.

Chapter Two

'You entered the dining room where the gentlemen were?' Lady Ellington's cousin, Rosemary, Dowager Baroness of St Onge, gasped, clutching the long strand of pearls draped around her thin neck. 'By yourself?'

Marianne gritted her teeth as she poured Lady Ellington's tea. 'It was a matter of some urgency.'

'But, my dear, you'll be the talk of the countryside for being so bold.'

Marianne tipped a teaspoon of sugar in the cup. 'I'm already the talk of the countryside, whether I storm in on the men at their port or spend all my days practising the pianoforte.'

'But to interrupt gentlemen in the dining room.' Lady St Onge pushed herself to her feet. 'It just isn't how young ladies behave.'

'Now, now, Cousin Rosemary.' With a look of sympathy and a small measure of amusement, Lady Ellington took the tea from Marianne. The rings on every finger sparkled in the afternoon sunlight as she leaned

back against her *chaise.* 'I'm sure everyone under-
stands Marianne was acting on my behalf and not because she wanted to create a scandal.'

'You give them too much credit, Ella. I can almost
hear the country ladies' tongues wagging from here.'
Lady St Onge shuffled out of Lady Ellington's dressing room, a long string of muttered concerns trailing
behind her.

Marianne frowned. 'Why can't she stay at your London town house while the roof of her dower house is
being repaired? Why must she be here?'

'Patience, Marianne,' Lady Ellington urged, prop-
ping her injured arm up on the pillows beside her. After
a restless night, Lady Ellington had regained her spirits, but not her usual vigour. 'You more than anyone
know what it is to need a safe haven from the small
troubles of life.'

'If only they were small.' She splashed tea into her
cup and a hail of drops splattered over the edge and
on to the saucer. Her undeserved reputation kept good
men away while attracting scoundrels and gossip. Sir
Warren had been proof of it last night. Despite his defending her against Lady Cartwright, he'd bolted from
her the moment his services were no longer needed.
Typical gentleman.

'Your problems aren't so very large they can't be
overcome,' Lady Ellington insisted, ever the optimist.

Marianne peered out the window at the tall trees
swaying over the front lawn. Welton Place, Lady
Ellington's dowager house on the grounds of Falconbridge Manor, had proven a refuge for Marianne.

However, the sturdy brick walls and Lady Ellington's solid reputation couldn't keep all the scandals and troubles from touching her. 'Lady St Onge is right, the gossips will talk. Even with your influence, they refuse to believe that I am nothing like Madame de Badeau.'

'They are stubborn in their views of you, which is surprising since Lady Preston has all but fallen on top of half the eligible gentlemen in the countryside and no one is cutting her. I think her old husband must not mind since it saves him the bother.'

Marianne laughed, nearly choking on her tea.

'Now there's a smile.' Lady Ellington offered her a napkin.

Marianne dabbed at the moisture on her chin.

'You're so pretty when you smile. You should do it more often.'

Marianne tossed the linen down beside the china. 'If I had more to smile about, I would.'

'Nonsense. You're too young to hold such a dim view of life.' She raised one ring-clad hand to stop Marianne from protesting. 'Yes, I know you've seen a greater share of trouble than most young ladies. But it does you no good to be morose. You'll only end up like poor Rosemary.'

'Now, that's unfair.'

'True, but we can't have you languishing here and becoming a spinster, not with your enviable figure and your money. We'll go to London next Season and find you someone.'

'No. I won't go back there.' She could manage the

scrutiny of a few country families, but not the derision of all society. Besides, whatever hopes Lady Ellington harboured about Marianne's wealth and looks landing her a good husband, she didn't share them. Marianne brushed at the lace over her breasts, wishing she didn't possess so much figure, but it was what it was. As for the money, leaving her well settled had been the one and only thing the vile Madame de Badeau had ever done for her. Marianne shuddered to think how the woman must have earned it. 'The only gentleman attracted to me is the broke Lord Bolton. Hardly a suitable pool of suitors.'

'Then we'll increase it. After all you can't spend your entire life composing pianoforte pieces.'

What else is there for me to do?

The other young ladies in the country were planning amusements for the autumn while the experiences of their last Season in London were still fresh. Those not dreaming of winter balls and house parties were at home with the husbands they'd landed in the spring, or tending to their new babies. There was little for Marianne to look forward to, or to keep the days from passing, one dreary, empty one after another.

She dipped her teaspoon into her tea and listlessly swirled the dark brown water. She should be thankful for the tedium. She didn't want to flirt with temptation and discover she really was no better than the gossips believed.

'Speaking of things to do.' Lady Ellington took up a letter from the table beside her, eyeing Marianne with a whiff of mischief. 'Mrs Stevens sent a note asking

after me. Tomorrow, we'll pay her a call and thank her
and her son for their help.'

Marianne paused over her teacup, the steam rising
to sweep her nose. 'So soon?'

'I'm not sick enough to lie about all week and I want
to see how the repairs to Priorton Abbey are coming.
Be a dear and bring me my writing box. I'll send a
note to Mrs Stevens right away.'

With some reluctance, Marianne set down her cup
and made for the writing desk. There was no good
excuse she could contrive for why they shouldn't go.
After all, they did owe them thanks for their help. She
liked Mrs Stevens. She couldn't say the same about
Sir Warren. Despite his assistance, in the end, his response to her had been no different from anyone else's
outside the Falconbridge family. His all but running
from her still grated. Who was he to cast judgement?
He was no hereditary baronet, only a writer with the
Prince Regent for an admirer.

Then again, who was she? The only relation of London's most notorious lady scoundrel.

She paused over the lacquer writing box, the Falconbridge family crest gold and red against a three-pointed
shield. The loneliness which had haunted Marianne
since childhood filled her again. It was the same aching pain she used to experience each Christmas at the
Protestant School in France when all the other girls
had received packages from their families while she'd
received nothing. Madame de Badeau had never sent
Marianne so much as a letter during all the time she'd
spent at the school. The only thing she'd done was ar-

rive on Marianne's tenth birthday and take her from the only family she'd ever known and carry her off to England before the Peace of Amiens had failed. On her way to London, Madame de Badeau had dumped her with the Smith family, all but forgetting about her for another six years until she'd thought it time for Marianne to marry. Then she'd dragged her to London to try and pawn her off on any dissolute lord who took an interest in her, no matter how old. Only Marianne's stubbornness had kept her from the altar.

A proud, wicked smile curled Marianne's lips. Madame de Badeau's face had practically turned purple when Marianne had tossed Lord Bolton's roses back at him when he'd knelt to propose. It had been worth the beating to defy the nasty woman.

Marianne's smile faded and with it her determined spirit. In the end, Madame de Badeau had got her revenge and ruined Marianne's life.

She grasped the cold metal handles on either side of the box. It didn't matter. There was nothing she could do except bear it as she had all the other disappointments and insults the woman had heaped on her. She started to heave the box from the table when the door swung open, stopping her.

'Lady Ellington, how are you?' Cecelia, Marchioness of Falconbridge, moved as fast as a lady so heavy with her second child could to hug Lady Ellington. Her husband, the Marquess of Falconbridge, followed behind. Lord Falconbridge was tall with a square jaw and straight nose, his blue eyes made more stunning by his dark hair. 'I was so worried when I heard about your accident.'

'You needn't fuss over a little scratch, not in your condition,' Lady Ellington chided. 'Randall, how could you let her scurry about the country when she should be at home resting?'

'I couldn't stop her.' Lord Falconbridge dropped a kiss on his aunt's cheek. 'Besides the two miles from Falconbridge Manor to Welton Place is hardly scurrying about the country.'

'It's the furthest I've been from the house in ages.' The Marchioness rubbed her round belly then shifted in the chair to turn her tender smile on Marianne. Her brown hair was rich in its arrangement of curls and her hazel eyes flecked with green glowed with her good mood. 'Thank you so much for looking after Lady Ellington. It means so much to us to have you here with her.'

With Lord Falconbridge's help, Lady Falconbridge struggled to her feet, then embraced Marianne. Marianne accepted the hug, her arms stiff at her sides. She should return the gesture like Theresa, her friend and Lady Falconbridge's cousin, always did, but she remained frozen. The Marchioness had always been kind to her, even before she'd risen from an unknown colonial widow to become Lady Falconbridge. It was the motherly tenderness in the touch Marianne found more unsettling than comforting. She wasn't used to it.

At last Lady Falconbridge released her and Marianne's tight arms loosened at her sides. Unruffled by Marianne's stiff greeting, the Marchioness stroked

Marianne's cheek, offering a sympathetic smile before returning to the chair beside Lady Ellington.

Despite her discomfort, Marianne appreciated the gesture. The Smiths had been kind, but she'd never really been one of their family, as she'd discovered when the scandal of Madame de Badeau had broken. Afterwards, despite the years Marianne had spent with them, they'd been too afraid of her tainting their own daughters to welcome her back.

Marianne swallowed hard. Of all the past rejections, theirs had hurt the most.

'Oh, Cecelia, how you carry on.' Lady Ellington batted a glittery, dismissive hand at the Marchioness. 'You'd think I was some sort of invalid.'

'We know you're not, but we're grateful to Miss Domville all the same.' Lord Falconbridge nodded to Marianne as he stood behind his wife, his hands on her shoulders. Four years ago, Marianne had discovered Madame de Badeau's letter detailing her revenge for Lord Falconbridge's rejection of her by seeing Lady Falconbridge assaulted by Lord Strathmore. Marianne had given him the letter from Madame de Badeau outlining her plans and with it the chance he needed to save Lady Falconbridge. The revealing of Madame de Badeau's plot had led to her ultimate disgrace and gained for Marianne the Falconbridge family's appreciation and undying dedication.

Marianne shifted on her feet. Lord Falconbridge's gratitude made her as uncomfortable as the hug. A notorious rake she'd once thought as hard as Madame de Badeau, love had changed Lord Falconbridge. What might it do for her? She wasn't likely to find out. No man worth his salt was going to push past the rumours and gossip to ever get to know her.

'Marianne, guess what? Theresa is expecting again. Some time in the spring,' Lady Falconbridge announced.

'How marvellous.' Despite Theresa being one of Marianne's only friends, the good news stung. It illustrated once again the love and happiness Marianne would never enjoy. 'I'll write to her at once with my congratulations.'

She fled the room before the envy and heartache found its way to the surface. She made for the sitting room downstairs near the back of the house, eager to reach the pianoforte and the smooth black-and-white keys. Once inside the room, the view of Lady Ellington's prized rose garden through the far window didn't calm her as it usually did. She withdrew a red-brocade composition book from the piano bench. The spine creaked when she opened it. She flipped through the pages and the notes bounced up and down on the staffs, punctuated every few lines by a smudge of ink or her fingerprint. It was her music. It had comforted her during the long, lonely hours at Madame de Badeau's, and afterwards, before her life had settled into the even cadence of Lady Ellington's dower house.

Selecting her most recent composition, she propped the book up on the music stand and lifted the cover over the keys. Wiggling her fingers, she rested them on the ivory until it warmed. Then she pressed down and began the first chords, wincing at each wrong note until she settled into the sweet and mournful piece. Through the adagio, she concentrated on the shift of the foot pedal and the strength with which she struck each key and how long she held it until sweeping on to the next. The black notes tripped along in her mind, memorised from hours of practice.

Finally, the piece reached its slow, wailing end and she raised her hands. The last notes vibrated along the wires until they faded away. Blinking through wet lashes, her cheeks and neck cold with moisture, she studied her hands. They were smooth and limber now, but some day they'd be wrinkled and stiff and here she'd be, with any luck, living under the protection of the Falconbridge family, the scandals as forgotten as she.

She wiped the tears from beneath her chin and turned the page to one of her slightly less sombre compositions. Crying wouldn't do any good. If Lady Ellington didn't think it was hopeless, then perhaps it wasn't. If nothing else, there was always Lord Bolton.

'There's a fortune to be made here, Warren, can't you see it?' Rupert Hirst, Warren's brother-in-law, paced back and forth across the rug in front of Warren's desk. A little wrinkle rose up in the patterned carpet where his heel dug in to make the turn.

Warren frowned. If Rupert paced long enough, he'd wear a hole in the thing and then it would be another repair for Warren to pay for. The workers were behind enough already, despite the rush to finish before the good weather ended, and the costs were increasing by the day. If Warren didn't write this book and get it to William Berkshire, his publisher, and collect the remainder of his advance, there'd still be holes in the roof come the first snow.

Lancelot, Warren's red Irish setter who chased sleep more than he did birds, watched from where he lay on the hearthrug, not bothering to rise.

'I can see the potential. I can also see myself losing a great deal of money if your optimism proves unfounded.' *Which wouldn't be the first time.* Despite his brother-in-law's best efforts, Rupert hadn't made a go of his last venture and it had faltered. Even his love for Leticia had proved destructive in the end.

Warren twirled his pen in his fingers. It wasn't fair to blame Rupert. He'd loved Warren's sister. If only Mother Nature had been so enamoured. The cruel witch had turned her back on Leticia and her poor little babe, failing to answer even Warren's entreaties for help as he'd struggled to save them both.

'I'm committing most of my small inheritance to hiring the best captains and ships to import the tobacco, and securing the crops of numerous farmers, so it can't fail. I won't let it,' Rupert protested, frustration and desperation giving his voice an unappealing lilt. 'I need your backing, not just financially, but your name. It will attract others and once they've invested or become buyers, the risk to you will be minimal.'

'But not non-existent.' Warren gathered up a small stack of books from the corner of the desk and carried them to the dark wood bookshelves lining the lower floor of the study. He examined the spines in the bright daylight filling the room from the row of leaded glass windows behind his desk. At least the sun saved him the expense of lighting candles. 'The repairs to Priorton are proving expensive. I can't afford to risk money on a business venture.'

Warren climbed the curving staircase to the balcony and opened a glass case and deposited a thick medieval text inside. If he could write the next damned book he might be able to take a chance. The manuscript was already months overdue. Mr Berkshire was a friend and a patient man, willing to wait for the next great sensation from Sir Warren Stevens, but he wouldn't wait for ever. Neither would Warren's readers. They'd move on to another emerging novelist if he didn't produce something soon.

'If my plan to import the new tobacco succeeds, you'll have plenty of money,' Rupert persisted.

'And if it doesn't, it will ruin my financial standing and my reputation.' Warren looked over the polished wood banister at Rupert. His company was tolerable enough and his vices non-existent, but there was nothing special about him. He still couldn't understand what Leticia had seen in him. 'I have no wish to go from celebrated author to hated hawker of bad investments.'

'But I need your support. I think it's the least you can do, considering.' The words came out low with the edge of a growl. Even Lancelot raised his head at the sound.

'Careful, Rupert.' Warren gripped the banister, setting hard on his arms as he leaned forward, staring the man down. 'She was as much my sister as she was your wife.'

'I'm sorry. I didn't mean to imply anything or to sound desperate, but some days I feel so lost without her.' He hung his head, raking one hand through his thinning dark hair, the simple gold wedding band glowing on his finger. 'If she were here, I'd have her support and it would make it easier to deal with the setbacks and disappointments.'

Warren eased his grip on the banister at the anguish in Rupert's words. Warren had lost his greatest supporter, too, when Leticia had died. She'd edited and read all of his manuscripts, telling him where they were best and what could be improved, and she'd believed in them, and him, even when he hadn't. Not even Mr Berkshire had matched her enthusiasm for his work and now she was gone.

He slid his hand over the banister, then took the spiral staircase step by slow step. He could almost hear Leticia begging him to help Rupert. She'd begged Warren to invest in Rupert's first business after they were engaged so he could make enough to allow them to marry. Warren had been as wary of that venture as he was this one, but Leticia had stood in front of his desk, like Rupert did now, pleading with him to change his mind, to help Rupert and to make her happy.

He approached his brother-in-law, the differences in their height making Warren look down on the slender man. Whatever Rupert's shortcomings, Warren had taken him on when he'd given his consent for the marriage. If Rupert did manage to make a go of things,

Warren could make a great deal. He'd need it, especially if he failed to deliver this next book or it didn't sell as well as the previous one. Without Leticia here to edit it, it might not. Since her death, his stories had all but deserted him.

'All right, tell me how much you need and I'll discuss it with my man of affairs. I can't give you everything you're asking for, but perhaps I can do something.' The key was not to risk too much.

Rupert snatched up Warren's hand and shook it. 'Thank you, Warren, you don't know how much this means to me.'

He did. Mr Berkshire had taken a chance on Warren's first manuscript ten years ago, paving the way to Priorton and Warren's title. He hoped Rupert enjoyed the same success. If not, it would be the last time Warren helped him.

'Warren?' His mother appeared at the door, a letter in her hand. Lancelot roused himself and trotted to her, his jingling collar joining the faint echo of hammers and saws trickling down from the upper floors. 'Lady Ellington and Miss Domville are coming to tea tomorrow. I'd like you to join us.'

Miss Domville.

Warren undid his loose cravat and twisted the ends back into an uncooperative knot. To say he was startled when he'd turned to find her in the dining room last night was putting it mildly. He couldn't have been more stunned if she'd marched in claiming he'd fathered a child. Since then, to his ire, he'd thought more about her than the heroine of his latest manuscript.

Her sharp cheeks highlighted by the fair hair pulled into tight ringlets at the back of her head, the blush of youth across the sweep of her skin and the azure eyes watching him with suspicion, had proved fascinating. She'd dressed modestly, with a higher bodice than even a vicar's daughter, but the raw appeal of her curving body had been jarring—just like her request for his help.

Shame made his cravat tighter and he pulled loose the knot again. Not even the other gentlemen's disapproving and less polite scrutiny had been enough to shake her determination, but his near refusal had. When he'd hesitated, it had sent a whisper of fear through her clear blue eyes before her determination had overcome it. She'd been like the most stalwart of captains, unwilling to let anything stop her from achieving her goal, not even a ridiculous sense of propriety. If only all people possessed the same judgement and resilience. The Admiralty certainly didn't, heaping pay and praise on physicians who did nothing but hide from illness onshore while the underpaid surgeons choked below deck treating the wounded men.

Warren gave up on the cravat and allowed the loose linen to dangle around his neck. He shouldn't have been so quick to leave Miss Domville last night. She'd caught his struggle with the past and despite her own concerns she'd reached out to him. Instead of thanking her for her sympathy, one people rarely offered him, he'd shoved her away. Despite his misstep, it was probably for the best given his inability to stop thinking about her. He didn't have the time or money for anything as expensive as a wife and family, even if the woman possessed means. He wasn't about to make his fortune by marrying it. He'd earn it as he always had, and as a man should, through his own industry.

'Warren, you can't be rude to Lady Ellington.' His mother shook her head at him, her lace cap fluttering over her dark hair which was more grey than chestnut now. 'Her nephew is a marquess who could do a great a deal for you and your career.'

'I have the Prince for a patron. I hardly need a lowly peer,' he teased with a grin she matched with a slightly more serious one as she patted Lancelot on the head. 'I have too much work to do. I'll rely on you to speak glowingly of me and cultivate her support.'

'So you won't come for Lady Ellington, I understand. But I thought for sure you'd want to see Miss Domville.' His mother was far more tenacious than Rupert, who'd watched the conversation with interest, but her company much more pleasurable

'Not if you want to maintain your good reputation,' Rupert snorted now.

'She's a very charming young lady,' Warren's mother corrected, silencing Rupert's chortles.

He didn't respond and Warren didn't press for the story behind his snide remark. Gossip didn't interest him and he hated encouraging the spread of it by asking for whatever tale Rupert had heard.

'Now, if you'll both excuse me, I have chapters to write.' He opened his arms and caught his mother by the shoulders and gently guided her to the hallway. He waved Rupert over and Rupert jogged forward to join them like a summoned spaniel.

'Perhaps you could discuss my business venture with Lady Ellington,' Rupert near panted. 'If she or the Marquess could be convinced to invest—'

'One thing at a time, Rupert.' He clapped him on the back, unwilling to solicit the county on his behalf, not when he could devote the same time and energy to selling his next book. Assuming he could write it.

'Come, Rupert, I'll show you the new plasterwork in the sitting room before you return to London.' His mother took Rupert's arm and led him into the hallway as Warren slid the study door closed.

He sagged against the heavy oak. Lancelot's eyebrows shifted as he watched his master.

Chapters. Warren had barely written a page today, much a less a whole chapter. It wasn't for lack of trying. His desk and the floor around it were littered with discarded papers full of useless words for pointless stories of boring characters that went nowhere and would make him no money.

Warren dropped into his chair and stared at the silent and cold collection of books and medieval manuscripts surrounding him. In the midst of it all, he felt as lonely and isolated as he had aboard ship when no one had understood his struggles or his dreams for a different future, except Leticia. And then he'd killed her.

He snatched up his pen and held it over the paper, determined, as then, to forge on. He wouldn't allow his doubts or guilt to hinder him, not with so much depending on his continued success and the money it would make him. The half-filled page taunted him from the blotter, along with the incessant banging of hammers from somewhere overhead. Pressing the nib to the paper, he wrote one word, then another, determined to push through. He had no choice, there was no one else who could do it or save him.

could see the vil... ... as that smelled faint
at Lady Carswright's. It suddenly ... the conf... dance ...

Chapter Three

Sir Warren still hadn't made an appearance by the time the butler removed the tea service. Mrs Stevens said he was busy at work and couldn't be disturbed. More than likely he was avoiding Marianne and her damaged reputation like every other gentleman of quality. The same couldn't be said of the large portrait of him hanging over the fireplace. It was of Sir Warren at his desk, an open book balanced on his knee, the pen in his hand poised over what must be his next great creation. Mr Smith used to devour Sir Warren's novels of medieval knights and ladies. Once, during a snow storm, when the family had been stuck inside for three days, he'd read a novel aloud. Marianne had only half-listened. Historical novels were not to her taste.

It wasn't the open book balanced on his knee or the manuscript which kept bringing her back to the portrait. It was Sir Warren's posture, the subtle way his body turned, his attention focused on the distance instead of the viewer. His brow shaded his green eyes, stealing their light. The haunted expression hinted at some threat just beyond the frame, something only he could see, like whatever it was that had troubled him at Lady Cartwright's. It undermined the confidence in his firm grip on the book and reminded her of his pained expression when he'd written out the laudanum recipe after helping Lady Ellington, before he'd darted away from her.

Irritation more than the warm autumn day made her tug at her high collar.

'How we must be boring you with all our talk of Italian landscapes,' Mrs Stevens apologised from across the round tea table.

Marianne jerked her attention to Mrs Stevens's kind round eyes, her son's eyes, and shook her head. 'No, not at all.'

'Liar,' Mrs Stevens teased. 'When I was young I used to hate sitting with old ladies and listening to them talk. Lady Ellington tells me you play the pianoforte. We have a lovely Érard in the music room. The man who sold us the house said it was once in the Palace of Versailles, but I'm not sure I believe him.'

'A French-made Érard!' Excitement filled Marianne more than when the carriage had approached the house, before it had become obvious Sir Warren had no intention of joining them. 'I used to play one at the Protestant School in France. Do you play?'

'Oh, heavens, no.' She laid a thin hand on her chest. 'I hate to think of a fine instrument going to waste. If you'd like to try it, you may. It's just down the hall in the music room. Third door on the left.'

'May I?' Marianne asked Lady Ellington, as eager to see the instrument as to escape the staring portrait.

Lady Ellington slid a sly glance at Mrs Stevens whose eyebrow arched a touch. 'I don't see why not.'

Marianne threw her companion a questioning look, wondering what she was up to. Lady Ellington ignored it in favour of adjusting the clasp on her diamond bracelet. The ladies must be eager to discuss something more salacious than Italian landscapes out of her hearing. Whatever it was, Lady Ellington would tell her about it later. Her companion didn't see the need to shield her from reality, not after Marianne had learned so much at Madame de Badeau's.

Marianne rose and shook out the skirt of her dress. 'Then I'd be delighted to play.'

'Wonderful.' Mrs Stevens beamed as Marianne made for the hallway. 'Leave the door open so we may hear your beautiful playing.'

Marianne stepped into the long main hall running the length of the front of the house. The faint dragging of a saw across wood and the thud of hammers carried down from somewhere upstairs. She headed left, past the large marble fireplace situated across from the main door, a medieval relic left over from the house's days as a priory. Mrs Stevens had told them something of the house's history over tea. Old swords and helmets dotted the panelled walls, creating a more menacing than welcoming effect in the low-ceilinged entrance hall with its thick exposed beams.

She followed the neat line of black-marble diamonds inlaid in the slightly uneven floor, counting the solidly spaced doors with their rounded tops and thick iron handles.

When she reached the third door on the left, she slid one of the wide panels aside, stopping as Sir Warren's eyes snapped up from his desk to hers. The troubled eyes from the portrait. They widened with shock before crinkling with annoyance, then embarrassment. In front for him were books arranged in an elaborate set of triangles and balanced against one another like a house of cards.

'You should have knocked.' Sir Warren jumped to his feet and rounded the desk. The large red dog sitting beside him raised its hindquarters in a stretch before trotting past his owner and up to Marianne. 'I was working.'

'Yes, it's quite a labour.' She leaned to one side to peer around his solid chest at his creation, ignoring the flutter in her stomach at this unexpected meeting and the cutting realisation he had been avoiding her. 'Is it a castle or a barn? I can't tell.'

'It's a castle.' Amusement replaced the flush of anger. 'I'll have you know, half of all writing is procrastination.'

'Then it appears you're making great progress.' Marianne tapped the dog lightly on the head with her fingers, then waved him away. He obliged, wandering over to the hearth rug and settling down on the spiral weave.

'If only I were.' He dismantled his castle and stacked the books in two neat piles. Then he faced her, leaning back against the desk and admiring her with more amusement than censure. His coat was missing and the wide sleeves of his shirt were flecked with small dots of ink. Dull black boots that wouldn't pass muster in London covered his calves and feet, and around his neck his cravat sat loose and crooked. 'Rather bold for a young lady to be wandering alone in a gentleman's house.'

'It isn't the first time I've been bold in the presence of a gentleman.' She approached him, determined to appear confident and collected and reveal nothing of the thrill racing through her at his unguarded humour. It would end soon when he decided it was best to not be alone with her and bolt off to see to some other matter in another part of the house.

'Nor do I suspect it will be the last.' Not a speck of derision marred his smile as he stroked his strong jaw. The play of his fingers along his chiselled chin, his sure stance and the curious way he regarded her proved as captivating as the time she'd watched the workers in the Falconbridge Manor fields in the evening, their shirts discarded as they'd swung their scythes. She could picture him among them, the gold sun across his back, his thick arms swinging the blade, the honey skin glistening in the low light. Marianne adjusted her collar, stunned by her suddenly lurid imagination. This wasn't the way she normally regarded men. It was dangerous.

'I'll have you know I wasn't wandering, but searching for the Érard. Mrs Stevens told me it was in the music room, the third door on the left.' She couldn't have counted wrong. Three was not a difficult number.

'The music room is the second door on the left.' He cocked his thumb at the wall and the arched door set snug between two bookcases. 'There's another entrance through there, if you'd like.'

'My apologies then. I'll leave you to your work.' And make sure it was she and not he who did the quick leave taking this time.

'No, please, stay.' He moved to place himself between her and the library door. The dry tang of dusting powder clung to him, punctuated by the faint richness of cedar. It struck her as strongly as his state of undress. It was too intimate for a woman of Marianne's undeserved reputation.

'No, I must go.' She tried to step around him, but he moved first, agile for a man of his robust build. The dog watched them as though he were bored.

'Please, I'd like it if you'd stay.'

'Why?' He wasn't the first gentleman to try and corner her alone in a room. If he dared to touch her, he also wouldn't be the first to feel her knee hitting his unmentionables. She'd learned fast how to defend herself against the lecherous gentlemen who used to haunt Madame de Badeau's. She'd had no choice. The awful woman hadn't lifted a finger to protect her.

'I wish to apologise for leaving you so abruptly at Lady Cartwright's. You were concerned about me and instead of thanking you, I was rude. Please, forgive me?'

She blinked, stunned. No one, not even Madame de Badeau when she'd been dying of fever in Italy, had ever asked for Marianne's forgiveness. To Hades

with his state of undress, she'd stay for this and savour the moment. It would probably be the last time
she'd receive an apology from anyone outside Lady
Ellington's house.

'It's been quite some time since I've attended to a
patient,' he continued in the face of her silence, something of the shadow from the portrait darkening his
expression. 'It brought back a number of painful memories and made me forget my manners.'

'What memories?' She didn't usually pry. People
were all too eager to tell her their business and everyone else's without any entreaty, but she couldn't stop
herself from asking. He hadn't rushed to condemn or
insult her like so many others did. It made her curious
and less wary about him than she should have been.

The bang of a dropped board echoed on the floor
above them. She thought he wouldn't answer, but to
her surprise, he did.

'During my time as a surgeon in the Navy, I saw
horrors so awful, if I wrote them into my novels, readers would think I'd exaggerated for titillating effect.'
He snapped his fingers and the dog strolled to his side.
He dropped his hand on the dog's head and ruffled the
silky fur. 'For a year or two after I left the Navy, the
memories used to trouble me. Usually it would happen
at night, but once in a while a familiar smell or something equally trivial would bring them back during the
day. Eventually, it stopped and I thought myself past
such episodes, but it happened again when I attended
to your friend. It's why I left so quickly. I didn't wish
to explain it to you, or anyone else. It's not something

people outside my family are aware of, or something I'm proud of.'

'Then why tell me about it?' It was insults people usually heaped on her, not confidences.

'You remind me of my sister, someone who might understand and not mock me for it.'

The faint connection they'd shared outside the study at Lady Cartwright's whispered between them once more. Sir Warren was offering her honesty and respect, treating her like a real person, not a tart to be pawed or derided. It was how she'd always longed to be viewed by strangers, especially gentlemen.

'No, I couldn't.' She fingered a small embroidered flower on her dress. 'It makes me a little ashamed of how much I pore over my own troubles. They're nothing compared to yours.'

'What troubles you, Miss Domville?' His voice was low and strong, like a physician trying to sooth an anxious patient.

'Don't tell me you haven't heard about me?' She flicked her hand at the study. 'I'm sure the neighbours rushed over to tell your mother the stories the moment the removers left.'

'We weren't here when the removers left and they didn't remove much. I bought the property lock, stock and barrel.'

'And no one informed you at Lady Cartwright's?' At times, it seemed as if the only topic anyone could discuss.

'I was delayed and missed the dinner. I left the party as soon as I finished with Lady Ellington. Why don't you tell me the real story, then I'll know the truth when Lady Cartwright gives me the exaggerated version.'

Honesty. He was holding it out to her again except this time it would be her sharing instead of him. She shouldn't, but she was tired of dragging the past and the secret of her lineage around like a heavy chain. Perhaps with this gentleman who treated her like an old friend instead of a pariah, his concern for her as genuine as Lady Ellington's, she could take the first step to being free of it. 'You've heard of Madame de Badeau?'

'She was the French courtesan who tried to ruin the Marquess of Falconbridge.'

She nodded as she twisted the slender gold band encircling her little finger. She should leave him as ignorant as everyone else of the truth about her relationship to the woman. She didn't know him, or have any reason to trust him, except for the strange calm his presence created in her. It reminded her of the first day she'd arrived at Lady Ellington's after Lord Falconbridge had stumbled on her trying to run away from Madame de Badeau's. The gracious woman had taken Marianne in her arms as if she were a long-lost daughter. Not even Mrs Nichols or Mrs Smith had ever hugged her so close. Marianne had earned Lady Ellington's affection by helping her nephew and his wife avoid ruin. Sir Warren owed Marianne nothing, yet he still looked at her as Lady Ellington had that first morning, as if she was as deserving of care and respect as anyone else. She should stay silent, but under the influence of his sincerity, she couldn't hold back the story any more than she could have held back the tears of relief in Lady Ellington's embrace.

'All my life, I and everyone else thought she was my sister. What few people really know is she was my mother. She had me long after her husband, the Chevalier de Badeau, died. She passed me off as her sister to hide her shame. I don't even know which of her many lovers was my father.' Her stomach clenched and she thought Mrs Steven's lemon cakes might come up. She shouldn't have told him. No one outside the Falconbridge family knew and there was no reason to expect his discretion. If he repeated the story, then the faint acceptance Lady Ellington provided would disappear as everyone recoiled further from the illegitimate daughter of a whore.

She waited for his reaction, expecting him to curl his lip at her in disgust or march into the sitting room and demand his mother have no further dealings with her. Instead, he nodded sagely as if she'd told him her throat hurt, not the secret which had gnawed at her since she'd riffled through Madame de Badeau's desk four years ago and found the letter revealing the truth.

'Your mother isn't the first woman to pass her child off as her sibling,' he replied at last.

'You're not stunned?' She was.

'No.' He turned back to his desk and slid a book off of the top of the stack, an ancient tome with a cracked leather cover and yellowed pages.

His movement left the path to the music room clear. Marianne could bolt out the door, leave him and her foolishness behind, but she held her ground. She wouldn't act like a coward in front of a man who'd been to war.

He flipped through the book, then held out the open page to her. 'Lady Matilda of Triano did the same thing in 1152.'

Marianne slid her hands beneath the book, running them over the uneven leather to grasp it when her fingers brushed his. She pulled back, and the tome wobbled on her forearms before she steadied it. It wasn't fear which made her recoil from him as she used to the men at Madame de Badeau's. It was the spark his touch had sent racing across her skin. She'd never experienced a reaction like this to a gentleman before.

She stepped back and fixed her attention on the beautiful drawing of a wan woman holding a rose, her blue and red gown a part of the curving and gilded initial, trying not to entertain her shocking response to Sir Warren's touch. She stole a glimpse at his hands, wondering what they'd feel like against her bare skin. She jerked her attention back to the open book, wondering what she was going on about. She'd spent too many years dodging the wandering hands of Madame de Badeau's lovers to search out any man's touch now.

'She hid her son to keep her brother-in-law from murdering the child when he seized the Duchy of Triano,' Sir Warren explained, his voice soothing her like a warm bath. 'The truth came out ten years later when the uncle lay dying and Lady Matilda revealed her son's identity to secure his rightful inheritance.'

She returned the book to him, careful to keep her

fingers away from his. 'A lovely story, but my mother's motives weren't so noble.'

'You're not to blame for what your mother did.' He set down the open book on the desk.

'You're the first stranger to think so. Lady Cartwright and the others are determined to believe I'm just as wanton and wicked as Madame de Badeau and they only think she's my sister. I'm not like her. I never have been.' It was a declaration she wished she could make in front of every family in the country and London, one she wished deep down even she believed. She was Madame de Badeau's daughter, it was possible her mother's sins were ingrained in Marianne and nothing would stop them from eventually coming out.

'I can see you're not like her. Not like most women. I recognised it the moment you insisted I help Lady Ellington and then refused to leave her side.'

'What I did was nothing,' she whispered, as unused to compliments as she was to embraces.

'It was everything. I've seen men sacrifice themselves for their fellow sailors, hold down their best friends while I sawed off a mangled limb. I've also watched cowards leave their comrades to suffer while they steal provisions, or hide in the darkness of the surgeon's deck with a minor wound to avoid fighting. I doubt Lady Cartwright or any of her other guests would have done half as much as you did for your friend.'

She stared at him, amazed by this near stranger's faith in her and how freely he offered it to her. It frightened her more than her belief in her own weakness. If it was easily given, it might easily be revoked. She eyed the door to the music room, wanting to be through it and at the keys of the piano and away from this uncertain familiarity. She'd revealed too much already, foolishly making herself vulnerable. 'If you don't mind, I'd like to play now.'

'Of course.' He pulled open the door, revealing the stately black instrument dominating the area in front of the large, bowed window at the far end of the room.

She strode to it, relief washing through her. Music was her one constant and comfort, though even this had threatened to leave her once. 'It's beautiful.'

She slid on to the bench and raised the cover on the keys. Flexing her fingers over the brilliant white ivory, she began the first chord. The pianoforte was as well tuned as it was grand and each note rang true and deep. They vibrated through her and with each stanza she played, her past, her concerns, Sir Warren and everything faded away until there was nothing but the notes. In them the only true happiness she'd ever known.

Warren didn't follow her into the room. He leaned against the door jamb and watched as she drew from the long-silent instrument beautiful music laced with a strange, almost effervescent melancholy. Lancelot came to his side and leaned against Warren's leg as Warren scratched behind the dog's ears.

The pianoforte faced the window overlooking the garden. She sat with her back to him so he couldn't see her face, but the languid way she moved in front of the keys, her arms losing their stiffness for the first time since she'd happened into his study, didn't escape his notice. The intensity of her focus and the graceful sway of her body in time to the music told him she was no longer here, but carried off by the piece to the same place he drifted to whenever a story fully gripped him. He was glad. She was too young to frown so much or to take in the world, or his compliments, with such distrustful eyes. He wished he could have brought her as much peace as her playing but, like him, her past still troubled her and she had yet to conquer it.

It wasn't the past facing him today, but the future. No matter how much he wanted to stand here and listen to her, he had to return to work. He needed the money. He left the door open to allow the notes to fill the study. As Warren settled in at his desk, Lancelot stretched out on the hearthrug and returned to his nap. Warren picked up his pen, dipped the nib in the inkwell and settled it over the last word, ready to write, to create, to weave his tale.

Nothing.

The deep notes of the piano boomed before sliding up the scale into the softer, higher octaves.

He read the last paragraph, hoping to regain the thread of the story. It wasn't so much a thread as a jumble of sentences as dull as the minutes of Parliament.

The higher notes wavered, then settled into the smooth mid-tones like water in the bottom of a bowl.

He dropped his head in his hands and rubbed his temples. Today wasn't going any better than yesterday, or last week or the past year.

He glanced over the top of the pages to where the

medieval book lay open. Lady Matilda's sad yet determined stare met his from the vellum. He reached out and ran one finger over the black lines of her face and eyes. The pensive notes of the pianoforte slid beneath the image, the despair in the lower octaves contradicted by the hope ringing in the brief tinkle of the higher ones.

He chewed the end of his pen as he listened to Miss Domville playing, his teeth finding the familiar grooves as a new story began to separate itself in his mind from his worries and frustration. He took a deep breath and closed his eyes. The image of a regal lady wearing a fine blue kirtle over a red-velvet dress slid through the mist blanketing a thick forest. Lady Matilda, one slender hand on a damp and knotted oak, paused as if finally ready to reveal what she'd been keeping from him. He rolled the scarred wood of his pen between his thumb and forefinger as he watched the elusive lady threatening to vanish into the mist-covered trees.

'Come on, out with it,' he growled, frustrated by her coquetry. He needed her to guide him and help release the steady stream of ideas being held back by this interminable block.

Behind the teasing curve of Lady Matilda's smile, the melody of Miss Domville's playing curled like smoke around him and the woman. In the vibrating notes, Lady Matilda's tale suddenly revealed itself.

He opened his eyes, slid a clean sheet of paper on to the blotter and began to write. The words flowed as fast as the notes of first one piece and then another as page after page took shape beneath his pen. He was so engrossed in the story, an hour later he failed to notice when the music faded into nothingness, the cover pulled down over the keys and soft footsteps left the music room.

The only things which remained were his story and the faint scent of peonies.

Chapter Four

Marianne played the section again and frowned. The last note wasn't right. She tried the C instead of the D, then nodded. Taking up her pen, she dipped the nib in the inkwell next to the stand and drew a quarter note on the staff. She played the section again, smiling as the stanza fell into place, the first half of her composition nearly complete. Reaching the end of it, she held her foot down on the pedal, allowing the chords to resonate off into the air.

Lady Ellington's Broadwood was a gorgeous instrument, but not as grand as Sir Warren's Érard. She wondered how rich and full the piece would sound on his instrument.

Excellent, I'm sure. She picked up the pen and changed the half note at the end to a whole one. She wasn't likely to play at Priorton Abbey again. Her skin prickled beneath the netting of the fichu covering her chest as the memory of Sir Warren listening to her story about Madame de Badeau came rushing back.

She shouldn't have confided in him. She'd been in a panic for days over her mistake, waiting for any hint of the truth of her parentage to make the rounds. There'd been nothing but silence on the matter. The only gossip she'd heard had concerned Lord Malvern's near indiscretion with a maid at Lord Cartwright's hunting party.

She replayed the stanza, holding the end longer to reflect her correction, contemplating Sir Warren's silence more than her music. With no word from anyone at Priorton since their visit, it was plain the incidents from two weeks ago had been forgotten. It irritated her as much as a missed note, even though she should be glad. She'd allowed his kindness to trick her into revealing her ugly secret. Heaven knew what other mistakes, or deeper weakness, might have been revealed if she'd had the chance to know Sir Warren better.

'Beautiful, as always, my dear.' Lady Ellington applauded as Marianne ended the piece. The pianoforte didn't face the window at Welton Place as it did at Priorton Abbey, preventing the blooming roses in the garden from distracting Marianne while she worked. 'It's a shame I'm the only one who ever gets to hear it.'

Marianne closed the red composition book, leaving it on the stand. 'You're not the only one. Lady St Onge used to listen to me play before she decided to return to London for the winter.'

'You know what I mean.' She sat down on the bench beside her. 'A letter from Theresa arrived for you.'

Marianne took the missive and flicked the edge with her fingernail, in no mood to read about her friend's happiness. It only made her lack of it more obvious.

Theresa was at Hallington Hall, the estate on the other side of Falconbridge Manor, with her young son, husband and his family. It wasn't far to travel yet Marianne had barely seen her this summer. She shouldn't have stayed away. As much as she loved Lady Ellington's she'd been restless lately for no good reason. The shortening days and cooler weather and the isolation of Welton Place added to her disquiet.

'This also came for you.' Lady Ellington handed her a package wrapped in brown paper. A prong holding a diamond in place on one of her rings snagged the securing twine before she freed it. 'It's from Priorton Abbey.'

Marianne gripped the package tight, crinkling the smooth paper. *He hasn't forgotten about me.* She eased her hold on the slender package, refusing to get her hopes up about Sir Warren's interest in her or to pine after a man. Her mother had obsessed about Lord Falconbridge and look how that had ended. 'It must be from Mrs Stevens. Sir Warren wouldn't send me anything.'

'Perhaps you charmed him with your playing.'

'It would be a change from what my presence usually inspires in people.' The knot came loose and she tugged off the twine.

'Don't be so hard on yourself. You inspire more than gossip in many people.' She squeezed Marianne's arm. 'Now open it. I want to see what it is.'

Marianne tore off the paper to reveal the back of a journal. She turned it over and read the handwritten title on the white cover plate. '*Lady Matilda's Trials*, by Sir Warren Stevens.'

She opened the front cover and a note slipped out from between the pages. She plucked it off the rug then unfolded the card and read aloud the words printed on the thick paper.

Dear Miss Domville,
Enclosed is a copy of my latest manuscript. Your lovely piano-playing was invaluable to the cre-ation of this story. I hope it's to your liking and I would very much appreciate your thoughts on it before I send it to my publisher.
Your faithful scribe,
Sir Warren

'My goodness.' Lady Ellington laid one sparkling hand on her ample bosom, rainbows from her diamonds spraying out over her dark blue dress. 'I didn't think the two of you were so well acquainted.'

'We aren't. I spent more time with his Érard than I did with him when we visited.' The spine cracked as she opened the journal. She tapped her toes against the floor, as puzzled as she was flattered by his gift.

Lady Ellington rose. 'Hurry and read it so you can give him your thoughts on it when we visit them to-morrow.'

Marianne brought her toes down hard against the parquet, leery of another meeting with him. 'Can't I simply send him a note?'

'Not for something like this.' A wicked twinkle lit

up her pale blue eyes before she strode to the door.
'You'll have to play for him again and see what else
you might inspire.'

Marianne frowned, not quite as amused by the situation as Lady Ellington, but certainly intrigued. She
ran her finger over the title on the front of the journal,
the one written by Sir Warren. He was asking her, a
person he barely knew, to critique his work. It would
be like her giving him one of her compositions to play.
For all the flowers and stupid poems Lord Bolton had
sent her, none had touched her as much as Sir Warren's simple request.

Leaving the pianoforte, Marianne wandered through
the double French doors overlooking the garden, past
where the aged gardener, Walker, knelt in front of the
rose beds. The heady scent of the summer blooms
no longer hung in the air. It had been replaced by the
crisp chill of autumn and wet dirt. She strolled along
the gravel path, passing the fountain in the middle of
Zeus and a nymph in an evocative embrace.

Too evocative. The same could be said about most
of the statues scattered throughout the garden. Marianne passed by them without a second look. The peculiarities of Lady Ellington's brother, the prior Marquess
of Falconbridge, and his taste in statuary, didn't interest her. Instead, with the journal clutched to her chest,
she wondered if maybe Lady Ellington was right and it
was time to stop hiding away from the world at Welton
Place. If a famous man like Sir Warren could see the
value in an acquaintance with her, perhaps some other
gentlemen who weren't Lord Bolton might do the same.

It was almost enough to convince her to accept Lady Ellington's offer of a Season in London, but not quite.

She reached the far side of the garden and followed the path winding up through the copse of trees to the brick orangery hidden among the oaks. Arched and latticed windows marked the front-left side while those to the right had been bricked in. She stepped through the double doors and into the comfortably furnished garden building. Sets of *bergère* chairs with generous cushions all done in the Louis XV style dominated the window side of the room. A tall screen embroidered with a mythic scene of Apollo seducing Calliope, as shocking in its depiction of love as the garden statuary, shielded a wide sofa situated in the darker half. The gaudy gilding reminded Marianne more of her mother's boudoir than it did an outbuilding. Like the garden, the orangery owed its decorations to the old Marquess, a bachelor rake she'd heard so much about from Madame de Badeau she'd often wondered if the woman hadn't bedded him too.

The orangery, despite its gaudy and erotic decorations, was, for Marianne, a small retreat from the dower house and a good place to be alone. She'd come here after more than one afternoon party to fume over the whisperings of Miss Cartwright or Lady Astley.

She chose a comfortable chair near a window and settled in to read Sir Warren's note again. His handwriting was bold, each letter crafted from slashing lines and thick strokes. It was a stark contrast to the small flourishes and graceful twirls which filled her composition book.

She read it a third time, but nothing about the words changed. Like the Smiths' daughter, who used to pore over each 'good morning' from the farmer's son hoping there was more to the salutation, Marianne was looking for a deeper meaning which wasn't there. It was silly of her to do so. She'd learned long ago at Madame de Badeau's that when a man said something it was what he meant and little more. If Sir Warren was thanking her for inspiration, then he was thanking her. It didn't mean she'd sent him into raptures. She stuffed the note in the back cover, glad not to arouse a grand passion in a man. Other people's passions had already caused her no end of troubles.

She set to reading, focusing on Sir Warren's work instead of him, determined to be worthy of his faith in her. However, with each turn of the page, each paragraph outlining Lady Matilda's story, disbelief and dismay began to undermine the peace of the orangery. By the time she reached the end of the manuscript, Marianne wanted to toss the journal in the fountain at the bottom of the hill and watch the thing turn soggy and sink. She couldn't. It was too good a story. Too bad it was hers.

'I didn't work so hard to gain Priorton to sell it off piece by piece the moment things get difficult,' Warren insisted, his boots coming down hard on the stone of the cloistered walk in the garden. Lancelot trotted beside him, panting lightly. The garden ran wild in the current fashion, leading from the back of Priorton to the tree line beyond. In the centre of it, weathered stone statues lounged between the beds of dying summer plants and wildflowers.

'Then you must let some of the field labourers go,' Mr Reed, Warren's bespectacled man of affairs warned, on Warren's heels as they returned to the house after surveying the fields. The harvest had been good this year, but not nearly as profitable as either of them had hoped, or counted on.

'No, not with winter coming. I won't see families suffer because of my mistakes.' He, his mother and Leticia had suffered because of his father's financial mistakes. His father had been a good man, but he'd been careless in the management of his school, never charging enough or collecting what was due and leaving his family near destitute when he died. After refusing to apply for relief in the very parish where his father had preached, they'd been forced to rely on Warren's reluctant bachelor uncle for support. It had been his uncle's brilliant idea for Warren to enlist and save the time and money required by a lengthy apprenticeship. At sixteen, the clean, comfortable life Warren had known had been ripped from him and replaced with gore and filth, and the need to support his sister and mother. He still hated the old salt for forcing Warren into it and resented his father for failing to leave his family with means. He wouldn't visit the same misery on other families, especially those under his care.

'The second half of the payment for your next book will cover current repairs, but after they're complete, you must stop for a while,' Mr Reed instructed.

Warren slapped some dirt off of his breeches. The

payment wasn't coming any time soon. He didn't tell Mr Reed, not wanting to send the little man into an apoplectic fit. The costs of the house were forcing him to live from one payment to the next as he'd done in the Navy. This time the sums were more considerable and the chance of ruin, starving and having nowhere to live much greater. The risks would soon be eased by the publication of *Lady Matilda's Trials* and the payment of the second half of his advance. The money would help, but it wasn't enough. Even if he received Miss Domville's thoughts on the story today, it would be some weeks before the novel's release, and more after that before money from the sales began to arrive.

Warren's feet came down hard on the stone walk as he and Mr Reed approached the house. He'd taken a chance sending Miss Domville his manuscript and asking for her opinion, but he suspected she'd be blunt in her assessment it. He hoped she was. With his mounting doubts, and Leticia no longer here to read his work, it was growing more difficult for him to judge if his tales were accomplished or piles of rubbish. He wasn't about to send Mr Berkshire a second-rate novel.

How the devil did I get myself into this predicament?

Through the arched sides of the cloister separating the garden from the wild field, he admired the peaked and turreted roofline of Priorton and the hazy sky behind it. This was everything he'd ever wanted, his dream and his sister's too, the one they'd shared in childhood. He'd achieved it for both of them, but at times it seemed more crippling than magical. For all the money he spent on Priorton, he didn't enjoy it as he should. In the spring he went to London. The rest of the year was consumed with stories, bills and repairs. It was difficult to spend an hour wandering in the garden when he must toil to pay for it all. During the long, dark hours on the orlop deck, this was what he'd imagined, what he'd strived for and now he stretched to achieve it. He hoped it didn't break him, the way his father's dream of running a vicarage school had broken him.

'You could seek a loan,' Mr Reed suggested as Warren held open the back door and waved Mr Reed inside. 'To tide you over until you receive your advance.'

'No, I've never taken money from anyone before, I won't start now. We can sell off some of the sheep.'

'With wool prices falling, it won't gain us much.'

'At least we won't have to spend money to feed them.'

They strode down the long front hallway. Through the diamond-leaded front windows Warren caught sight of Lady Ellington's carriage in the drive. He tugged open his slack cravat, then struggled to retie it, wondering if Miss Domville was with the Dowager. Last night, the memory of her flowery scent and the gentle tone of her voice had disturbed his sleep more than new story ideas.

They entered his study and Warren settled himself at his desk while Mr Reed stood before it outlining expenditures. As soon as he was finished with Mr Reed, he'd join the ladies and discover what Miss Domville thought of his manuscript. Perhaps he could convince her to play for him again and inspire another story. He needed more inspiration, especially with Mr Reed rattling on about expenses.

'You can't afford to invest any additional money in Mr Hirst, beyond what you recently advanced him,' Mr Reed cautioned. 'We've yet to see any profit from his ventures or even documents outlining your shares.'

Warren organised a stack of papers on his desk. 'I don't intend to give him any more.'

'Then you'd better tell him. I heard from one my associates in London he's using your name to push his current venture. You must distance yourself from it in case it fails. You don't want to be blamed.'

'I'll write to him at once and make it clear he's not to use me as an endorsement.' The bumbling fool. It seemed Rupert's current scheme was already faltering, and taking Warren's money with it. He should have known better and not allowed emotion to play any part in his business dealings. It wouldn't happen again.

Mr Reed opened his thin lips to say something else when the study door slid open with a bang.

Warren peered around the slender man of affairs to find Boudicca herself standing beneath the lintel in the very appealing figure of Miss Domville. So much for avoiding her until his interview with Mr Reed was complete.

'If you'll excuse us, Mr Reed,' Warren asked.

Mr Reed flipped closed his ledger and tucked it under his arm, needing no explanation for why he should go. It was clear in the storm in Miss Domville's eyes. 'Yes, of course.'

He slipped from the room, leaving Warren alone to face the fury.

'Good day, Miss Domville, it's a pleasure to see you.' Almost too pleasurable. She marched up to him, her breasts covered by a sheer chemisette and the thin silk of her gown. It was all Warren could do to rise from his chair like a gentleman and keep his eyes fixed above her chin. Damn, she was beautiful, earthy and angry. 'I'd hoped to see you today.'

'Good, because we must discuss this.' She slammed his journal on the desk, making a stack of papers curl up, then settle back down. 'How could you use my story?'

He stared at the slightly rumpled pages. 'You didn't like it?'

'No, it's a wonderful story, quite enthralling.' She leaned forward on her palms. He riveted his eyes to hers to keep his attention from sliding down and increasing the fury reddening her cheeks. 'Except you took what I told you about my mother and twisted it into a tale to amuse dairy maids and hack drivers.'

'I took something you've been ashamed of and made it into something you could be proud of. I thought you'd be pleased.'

'You were wrong.' She glowered at him like a schoolmarm ready to switch a naughty student, except she was the kind of woman who filled a young man's fantasies, not his nightmares.

'No one will see you in Lady Matilda, or think her story has anything to do with yours. I hid it too well.'

'Of course they will, especially when they realise we're acquainted with one another.' She whirled around, her blue dress fluttering about the curve of her hips as she marched to the door.

'Miss Domville, wait.' She didn't stop, but took hold of the wrought-iron handle. He couldn't let her go. 'I won't publish the story if it troubles you so much.'

She released the handle. It dropped against the door with a thud as she turned to him, as astonished by his offer as he was. 'You won't publish it?'

'I won't make money off your unease.' Even if he lost everything else, his word and his honour would still be his, he'd make sure of it. 'In fact, you may keep this copy of the manuscript.'

He held out the journal to her, his grip tight on the paper as the full weight of what he'd volunteered to do settled over him.

She returned to him and took the story out of his outstretched hand. 'And your original copy? How do I know you won't send it to your publisher after I leave?'

'I'll burn it, now, so you can be sure.'

'You'd do such a thing, for me?' She clasped the journal to her chest and for a moment he was jealous of the book resting against her soft curves.

'Yes.' He picked up the stack of loose pages and tapped them twice against his palm, hesitating before he tossed them into the grate beside him. The gesture burned him as much as the flames did the parchment. Lady Matilda's story had been a godsend after months of nothing. Now he was no better off than before. 'It was never my intention to betray your trust.'

She watched with him while his words turned to ashes. 'Then why did you write it?'

'Because, until the day you came here, I hadn't been able to write a single useful word for months. With the exception of Lady Matilda's story, I still can't.' He looked at her, noting how the light from the rising flames consuming the manuscript reflected in her clear eyes. He'd hidden his failing from everyone, from his mother to Mr Berkshire. It was a relief to finally admit it someone.

'I'm sorry, I didn't realise.' Nor did she offer to let him publish her copy of the work. He wouldn't ask her either. He'd made a pledge to her, and he would keep it, as he had all the others he'd made to himself, his mother and to Leticia's memory, no matter how much it hurt.

'It's all right. I'll write something else.'

She flicked a glance at the wads of papers scattered around his chair. 'How?'

That's what I'd like to know.

Warren watched the flames die down, their new fuel spent. Miss Domville's playing had bolstered him like Leticia's encouraging letters used to do, he'd written in the semi-darkness of the ship. The influence creativity Miss Domville's playing had exerted over finishing had left with her. In the last few day could think of Lady Matilda, he'd tried everythi from the village to reclaim it, even hiring a you but it hadn't been church to play while he'd s about her presence, the same. There'd been s as at Lady Cartwright's, which had soothed and encouraged him and he wanted more of it.

He tugged on his loose cravat as an idea as unbelievable as it was tempting began to come to him. If Miss Domville could help him overcome his block once, she could do it again. No, it was foolish to draw her into his struggles, or to tempt himself with her company. She wasn't one of the London widows eager to discreetly amuse him, but a young lady fighting for respectability. For him to suggest any relationship with her outside of a betrothal and marriage was to risk her reputation further and he shouldn't even consider it, except he needed her. With his talent failing him, he might lose everything he'd achieved and find himself as destitute as his father had been at his death. He wouldn't allow it, or be forced by weakness back to the Navy to make his living. With blank pages and bills facing him, he couldn't allow his muse to escape.

'If you agree to come here and play the piano for me, I can create another story.' He smiled with all the charisma he employed to woo patrons in London, ⁿoping she didn't dismiss the idea outright. He didn't dᵒbt, given her fierce entry into his study, she'd shrⁿ from turning him down.

Shⁿ
back, tⁿied her arms beneath her breasts and stepped strumentⁿical schoolmarm returning. 'And what in- dame de Bⁿ hope I'll play afterwards? I'm not Ma- He didn't a woman to be hired as a mistress.' achieved famⁿher for being cautious. Once he'd had shrunk signⁿmber of people he could trust

'I don't want a mistress, but a muse.' It was difficult to look at her and not think of twining his hands in her golden hair, tasting her pink lips as they parted beneath his and freeing those glorious breasts from their prim confines. He'd better not concentrate on them if he wanted to win her co-operation and keep himself free from distraction, and bankruptcy. 'I need you.'

'No one needs me.' The same worthlessness which had torn him apart the morning Leticia had died hung in Miss Domville's words. He gripped his hands hard behind his back, silently raging at himself and the world. A woman of Miss Domville's loveliness and innocence didn't deserve to feel the way he had that awful morning.

'I do. I realise it's a ridiculous request, but if I don't have something to turn into my publisher soon, I could lose everything.' Lancelot trotted to his side and sat down next to him. Warren dropped his hand on the dog's head and stroked it, the simple motion easing the anxiety of waiting for Miss Domville's answer.

'Maybe what you need isn't a new novel, but a rich wife.' She slid him a brazen glance from beneath her long eyelashes, inviting him to come closer like a si eager to dash him against the rocks. If sh him, it would be no one's fault but hi hoped the destruction waited unti his next novel.

'I'm not so mercenary a
to a wife, esp

is nothing more than a business arrangement, not a ridiculous courting ruse.'

'Good, because I have no interest in a husband.' At least they held similar views on matrimony, though it saddened more than heartened him. She was alone and isolating herself further from the world. It wasn't right. 'I also have no desire to become the talk of the countryside because of this proposed arrangement and the attention my connection to a famous author might bring.'

'Then we won't tell anyone about it, beyond those who must absolutely know. My mother will act as chaperon.'

'Even if we tried to keep it a secret, people will find out, they always do. Then what'll happen? Lady Ellington has spent a great deal of time and effort trying to rebuild my reputation. She won't throw it away by consenting to something as ridiculous as this.'

'I think it's a lovely idea.' Lady Ellington clapped her hands together, making her many gold bracelets jingle on her arm.

'...do too,' Mrs Steven concurred, exchanging a ...ile with her guest.

...ped at them. *They've all gone mad.*

...understand what he's asking for?'

...not sure what he'd requested.

...on his marvellous Érard

...m, to inspire him. It

...was the only one

'It would be lovely to have your music filling this dreary house,' Mrs Stevens added. 'All the dark wood and wrought iron is rather oppressive.'

'Mother,' Sir Warren groaned. He stood beside Marianne, Lancelot at his side.

'It's true. Miss Domville's playing would cheer it up and give me something besides the workmen to listen to all day.'

Sir Warren levelled his hand at his mother while pleading with Marianne, 'See, I'm not the only one who needs your talent.'

'I didn't say I'd stay all day, or at all,' Marianne reminded him, tripping over the word 'need'. It was the second time he'd said it, but it didn't make it any less awkward to hear than mangled French. People scorned her, they rarely needed her.

'Nonsense, you spend hours at my pianoforte at home. Why not do it here?' Lady Ellington steepled her fingers and touched them to her lips in amused scrutiny. 'Say you will, my dear. I'd so love to have your beautiful compositions heard by others.'

Marianne shook her head at Lady Ellington, waving her off further mention of the com— wouldn't decided to play for Sir Wough her failings, and a bring these was say so, she wouldn't come here and words wouldn't come out. She'd stood firm st Madame de Badeau's selection of suitors and the woman's more demeaning demands. Why couldn't she simply say 'no' to this?

Because of Sir Warren. She studied him from the corner of her eye, hesitant to face him straight on. He stroked the top of the dog's head, his ink-stained fingers ruffling the red fur. The relaxed gesture didn't hide his eagerness for her answer or settle the anxiousness in his green eyes. His talent was his sanctuary, just like hers, and he was afraid of losing it. She understood. The summer Madame de Badeau had plucked her from the Smiths' house and dropped her unprepared in London, Marianne's fingers had grown stiff, the keys awkward beneath her hands. The beautiful notes which had always comforted her had faded under the pressure of Madame de Badeau's screeching insults and the lecherous leers of her male visitors. The temporary loss of her talent had been more terrifying than when she'd left France with Madame de Badeau, then a stranger to her, or during her first few days with the Smiths. Without it, she was nothing.

'Well, Miss Domville, what do you say?' Sir Warren pressed, ending the long silence punctuated by the laughter of workmen overhead.

He didn't turned the gold ring on her small finger. just like her settled into a time, his talent would return had should stop making the to Sir Warren. It had alread Madame de Badeau and this was inviting more. another. She gentlemen and their appetites at Manother. rable to trust Sir Warren's motives to be purely innocent. However, he was offering her more than a tryst, fine dresses and a house in Mayfair, but a sense of purpose. To play for him was to use her music for something other than escaping the loneliness which swathed her, but to inspire a story, maybe even one better than Lady Matilda's.

It was dangerous and wrong to agree to this, but she'd caught the torment of his past in Lady Matilda's tale, the one he'd been willing to put aside to protect her. Sir Warren wasn't just overcoming his time in the Navy, but trying to excise it from his life. He couldn't do it without his work and she couldn't leave him to suffer without the thing which had sustained him through all his difficulties. It would make her as cruel and unfeeling as her mother and she'd vowed never to be like that witch.

Lady Ellington's carriage pulled away from Priorton Abbey, leaving Sir Warren and Mrs Stevens standing in the drive. Marianne crossed her ankles beneath her dress, refusing to peer out of the back window at the man.

What in heaven's name did I just agree to?

'I don't know how this won't result in a scandal.'

'What if it does? We've weathered them before, we'll weather them again.' Her companion rarely fretted about stories, but she'd never been this cavalier either. It, and Lady Ellington smiling from across the carriage as if she'd just purchased a new diamond ring, made Marianne suspicious.

'What are you about?' Marianne demanded, not sure what to be more irked about, her inability to refuse Sir Warren's request or Lady Ellington's encouragement of it.

'Nothing.' Lady Ellington snapped open her fan and waved it in front of her face. The warm October day was a surprise after the previous cooler ones. 'Except, I've always said your music shouldn't be hidden away.'

'Priorton Abbey isn't a concert hall.'

'But from here who knows where you may go? Perhaps to Paris now all this business with Napoleon is at an end, or even Vienna.'

'Are you eager to be rid of me?' Everyone else, especially the Smiths, had been quick to distance themselves from her when the scandal with Madame de Badeau had broken. At some point Lady Ellington and the Falconbridges would grow tired of shielding her too, especially if gossip about this silly arrangement between her and Sir Warren lit up the countryside.

'Of course not, my dear. I adore you, but you need a life of your own, to have friends your age.'

'Theresa is my age,' though in reality she hadn't seen her in quite some time. Theresa's contentment made Marianne's lack of it more stark and it was hard for her to be near her friend.

'And I adore her, but she's a wife and mother now. You need to be around other young people who wish to enjoy their time before those sorts of responsibilities come about, friends who will help you be frivolous once in a while instead of so serious. It won't happen in my sitting room.'

'But you think it'll happen at Priorton, with Sir Warren?' With the medieval swords and armour hanging on the walls, frivolous was not a word she would use to describe the old priory.

'No, he's a touch too serious. I've read his books and some of his battle scenes are quite dreadful, but at thirty he is closer to your age than I am.'

Marianne leaned back against the squabs and peered out of the carriage window. On a rise in the distance stood Falconbridge Manor. The light stone of its columns was stately against the forest of red-and-orange leaves behind it. This summer, Marianne had been more agitated than a sparrow hopping around a garden, bored with the endless quiet days. Lady Ellington was right, Welton Place was no longer enough. It didn't mean Sir Warren was the answer to her dilemma, or she the answer to his, no matter what he might claim. The man was famous and the attention paid to him would magnify her notoriety when all she sought was to disappear into obscurity. A connection to her would also taint him.

'Why would a man like Sir Warren, whose livelihood depends on the good opinion of everyone, want to entangle himself in all my scandals?'

'Because he's taken an interest in you.'

Marianne fingered the manuscript resting in her lap, refusing to entertain the hope Lady Ellington's observation sparked inside her. The day she decided she wanted a man it would be for a sensible reason like companionship or a travelling partner, not for something as foolhardy as desire. 'Because he thinks I can benefit him, or he wants my money like Lord Bolton and all the rest. It's the only reason any man would risk tying himself to me.'

'My dear, you think you're an expert on gentlemen from your time in London, but I assure you, you've learned all the wrong things from all the wrong sorts.'

She wondered what sort Sir Warren was. He'd been no different in admiring her breasts than any other man, simply more discreet about it. She adjusted the fine silk covering her generous cleavage, for the first time thankful she wasn't one of those flat-chested women she saw near the walls at dances. When his eyes had flicked down, she'd wanted to remove the chemisette and not smack him for his insolence. It wasn't her usual reaction.

'Even if I go there every day, what you're hoping for won't happen. He made sure to tell me he isn't interested in marrying.' His announcement had bothered her as much as her inability to refuse his request. Was it marriage he was against, or just marriage to her?

'You can't believe everything a man says,' Lady Ellington dismissed with a wave of her bejewelled hand. 'Randall was quite adamant about never marrying and now he and Cecelia are happily wed.'

Lord and Lady Falconbridge had fallen in love in their youth. Despite a separation of ten years and the entire Atlantic ocean, they'd found one another again, thanks, in no small part, to Lady Ellington's involvement. Now, it appeared the Dowager Countess was attempting to throw Marianne and Sir Warren together. If so, she was wasting her time. Marianne didn't share her companion's faith in love. For all the poets' writings about motherly love, Madame de Badeau hadn't been able to conjure up enough concern to even admit to being Marianne's mother, much less care for her. She doubted any sweeping ardour would change Sir Warren's stance on matrimony, not while he was struggling to save his house and his career, unless landing a rich wife was his intention, but she was sure it wasn't. Despite the outrageousness of his suggestion, nothing he'd told her today had been false, unlike all the 'confidences' Lord Bolton had tried to share with her, most of which had been in his breeches.

'Sir Warren may not be interested in marriage, but he must know a number of young gentlemen who are. It is to your benefit to become better acquainted with him.'

Marianne wasn't so convinced, but if Lady Ellington saw an advantage to this arrangement, then perhaps Marianne should too. This could be her chance to at last capture something of the normal life every other young lady in the county enjoyed, assuming their time together didn't create more problems for them both. It might, depending on whose notoriety more powerfully influenced whose.

She opened and closed her gloved fingers, wishing she were home and at the keyboard. She needed the calm of the ivory to better view this situation clearly. Sir Warren had cajoled her into this arrangement with flattery and a small measure of guilt. It didn't mean she'd allow herself to believe there was anything more to the arrangement than his need to write another book.

She'd play for him, uphold her end of the agreement and nothing more. After all, once he realised she was a liability rather than an asset, he'd drop her like a hot stone. His loss of interest would sting less if she maintained her distance.

Chapter Five

Marianne finished the Mozart and began a Haydn. She glanced over her shoulder at the open door between the music room and Sir Warren's study, wondering if he was listening. No one else was. As fast as Mrs Stevens had ushered Marianne in to the Érard this morning, she'd rushed out, pleading all sorts of responsibilities while assuring Marianne she'd be down the hall listening.

Shirking her chaperon duties is more like it.

Marianne brought her fingers down hard on the low notes. She hardly needed anyone hovering over her since Sir Warren had yet to make his appearance. If it wasn't for the jingle of Lancelot's collar whenever the dog scratched himself she wouldn't even know Sir Warren was in the next room, much less the house.

She slid her fingers along the keys and into the treble clef.

Good. I'm here for us to work, not to converse.

Except he was the only one working. She was playing pieces she could perform in her sleep while her own compositions remained neglected at home. For all the effort Sir Warren was making to find inspiration, she hoped he was getting it. She still wasn't certain what she was gaining from the bargain other than a reason to leave Welton Place every day.

Playing two higher notes, she leaned back on the bench again, trying once more to see around the corner into the other room. All she caught was the wall of bookcases and the spiral staircase leading up to the balcony.

'Are you looking for me?'

Years of practice kept her from missing the next succession of notes. She turned the other way to catch Sir Warren striding in through the main door, the dog trotting beside him, smacking his jaws as if just roused from sleep.

She trilled the keys faster before forcing herself to slow down, but she couldn't stop watching his approach. He moved with the erect discipline of an officer, his gait steady and smooth. He was without his coat again and a glimpse of his smooth chest was just visible beneath the open V of his shirt under his loose cravat. She peered at it, trying to see if his chest held the same hint of a seaman's tan which graced his face and the backs of his hands. She wondered what his darker skin would look like against the lighter skin of her thighs or her stomach.

'Why did you sneak up on me?' she retorted, playing the bass notes hard, as rattled by her lurid turn of thoughts as his unannounced arrival.

'I didn't sneak up. I walked in.' He stood beside the piano and rested his elbow on the corner near the stand. She wrinkled her nose at how the weight of his body changed the tone of the piece. It made it deeper when it was supposed to be much lighter. He straightened off the instrument. 'You don't want me to listen?'

She shrugged, never losing the pace of the concerto. 'You may if you like.'

'Good.' He leaned on the case again and she frowned. She'd have to stand over him the next time he wrote and see how he liked it. She would if it didn't mean inhaling the thick, woody scent clinging to him and the linen sleeves of his shirt.

She glanced at his ink-smudged hands lying on the Erard, thinking she should be scandalised by his lack of proper dress, but she wasn't. She wondered if this was some inward failing, or simply having spent too much time at Madame de Badeau's where the gentlemen hadn't held back from making themselves comfortable and asking her to do the same.

The dog left his master's side and trotted forward to sit beside her and rest his head on her leg, weighing it down as she worked the pedals. She jiggled her knee, trying to dislodge him but he wouldn't move.

'I'm glad you didn't change your mind.' Sir Warren's full lips curled up a touch with amusement as he watched her struggle with the dog. He snapped his fingers and pointed at the floor. The dog's eyebrows shifted as it looked from him to her and ignored his owner. 'I was afraid you would.'

'I tried to, but Lady Ellington hustled me into the

carriage with so much chatter I could barely get a word in edgewise.' She finished her piece and pushed against the dog, trying to make it shoo, but it leaned harder against her. The animal's stubbornness frustrated her as much as Sir Warren standing so close and the way her heart raced because of it. If her being here bothered Sir Warren, it didn't show. He was calm and relaxed in his stance and it helped soothe the unease she usually experienced around anyone outside the Falconbridge family. She gave up struggling with the dog and stroked its head, making it close its eyes. She was here to make friends with Sir Warren. It did her no good to be cross with his pet, or him. 'Have you made progress with your novel today?'

'Not as much as I would have liked. You will come back tomorrow, won't you?'

She was as shocked by Sir Warren's desire to be near her as Lancelot's. He was a famous writer, an accomplished man who'd built himself up from a common surgeon to baronet through his own hard work. There was no reason for him to be so concerned about her, yet he was. It flattered and terrified her all at once. It was time to place some distance between them. 'I will return. Not for you, but for the Érard.'

Warren pressed his fingertips into the hard piano case as Miss Domville stretched out one slender arm and stroked the top of the lustrous instrument. The gesture was reverent and suggestive and almost knocked him over. She wore a pale yellow gown with a contrasting blue cord tucked beneath her magnificent breasts.

What he wouldn't give to see her creamy skin against the dark wood and to elicit from her as much passion as she drew from the now-silent strings.

'Care to join me for a walk?' he asked, distracting himself from his wandering imagination yet again. This morning, after he'd heard her arrive, he hadn't been able to focus on the new story until she'd finished a very long polonaise and one nocturne. Even then, it had taken all his effort not to wander to the door to watch her or to interrupt her playing with conversation until he'd completed at least one chapter.

'I'm not sure your dog will let me go outside.' She pulled one foot out from beneath the lounging canine and rolled her ankle. The hint of the slim calf clad in a semi-sheer stocking just above the top of her half boot made Warren's need to move more pressing.

'Lancelot likes you.'

'It seems he isn't the only one.' Her flush of mirthful confidence was as teasing as it was meant to be off putting, especially when she rose and stepped over the dog, the hint of *derrière* beneath her dress drawing him along after her.

Warren hurried past her to pull open the arched door leading outside. The scent of warm earth combined with her peony perfume enveloped him as she slid past him into the daylight. The sun brightened the satin ribbons trimming her dress and made her hair glow like a halo around her face.

In two steps he was beside her while Lancelot trotted off to follow a scent. He shouldn't be up from his desk, but taking advantage of their short time together to make progress. He'd found the inspiration for a new tale in one of his medieval manuscripts last night and, although it didn't enthral him like Lady Matilda's had, it offered the hope of his finishing something within a few weeks. He still had at least two more chapters to complete before his dinner at Lord Preston's tonight. However, every flick of Miss Domville's skirts above the toes of her boots, each subtle breath which met their exercise eroded his desire to go back inside.

'Where's your mother?' she asked as she raised her hand to her forehead to shield her eyes from the sun. As she admired the stone house with its numerous jutting corners and stepped peeks, her fingers rested in a graceful arch above her brow, as enticing as when they'd stroked the Érard.

'Sewing in her room.' He pointed to a bay of windows on the second floor. 'She can see us from there. I assure you it's all very respectable.'

She tilted her head at him and pulled her lips into a disbelieving smile. 'Nothing about this arrangement is respectable.'

'But it is interesting,' he prodded, the hint of red the chill brought to her full cheeks entrancing him.

'That remains to be seen.' She strolled off down the walk, as natural among the wildflowers as at the piano. The sun caressed her pale skin while her curls danced with each of her elegant steps. This was how he'd imagined her when he'd written his novel. Except then he'd met her stride, turned her to face him and tasted her full lips.

Stop it, he commanded himself. She was here to assist him, not to tempt him, but a man would have to be dead to avoid the allure of her stunning body.

Warren hurried to join her and, as they wandered around to the back of the house, he pointed out the repairs he'd made to the windows and plasterwork, trying not to think about the cost and how much was still to be done.

'I'm glad you've left it as it is instead of knocking it down,' she remarked as they reached the centre of the garden. She rolled her shoulders and the motion raised and lowered her chest, almost to the detriment of his rational mind.

'I didn't think you liked history,' he answered with a grin to mask the more heady response coming from further down his torso.

Her blue eyes widened. 'Who told you that?'

'My mother. She said you told her you don't care for historical novels.'

'I don't, especially after the last one I read.' She shot him a teasing smile, then circled the stone sundial in the centre of the path.

'Hopefully, my next one will change your mind.' He plucked a stick off of the ground and flung it away for Lancelot to chase.

She ran one graceful finger up the edge of the sundial's gnomon. 'We'll see.'

She turned and walked off down the path.

Warren rocked back on his heels before stepping forward to follow her. He thought he couldn't work without her here. He was beginning to wonder if he could work with her here. He wasn't writing now and another day was slipping away from him. Strangely enough, the lost time didn't panic him as it had yesterday, or the many long days before. She fascinated him, as much as one of his characters, and as with them, he wanted to learn more about her.

'Lady Ellington said you wrote compositions.' He motioned her towards the cloister walk separating the somewhat orderly garden from the wild field beyond. Lancelot bolted off into the high grass, scaring up birds. 'You should work on them while you're here. This time is as much for you as it is for me.'

'I'd rather not.' She stopped and picked at a loose stone in one of the pillars. The sunlight cutting through the arches slid across the nape of her neck while the shadows caressed her straight nose and the downturned curve of her mouth. The wounded young lady beneath the confident woman revealed herself. She wasn't as worldly as all her smiles and artifices tried to make him believe and he was glad. He'd seen enough worldliness during his time in the Navy. 'Besides, they're only silly little pieces, hardly worth anyone listening to.'

'Don't demean or dismiss your talent, but hold your head up high and speak with confidence,' Warren encouraged, the way Leticia used to do with him. It disturbed him to see her think so little of herself as much as it had disturbed him to interrupt her playing.

'You don't understand.'

He leaned against one arched opening. 'You think I don't know how difficult it is to show your work to the world, to risk them laughing at it or telling you it isn't good enough?'

'You're wrong, Sir Warren. I've spent a large portion of my life listening to people tell me I'm not good enough. Criticism of my compositions would pale in comparison.'

He pushed up from the wall to stand over her. The wind caught the curls dangling by her cheeks and made them tease the unblemished skin. He kept his arms by his side despite wanting to wrap her in them and ease the tension in her lips with his. With her brows knitted together, she barely resembled the woman who'd played the pianoforte with passion. 'Don't let them trouble you, Miss Domville.'

Her eyes met his and hope rippled through them like the cool breeze between the arches. Then it vanished and she took a large step away from him. 'Why does it matter to you what bothers me and what doesn't?'

'Because you're my friend and I hope to be yours.'

'Friend? Is that what they call it?' The teasing vixen he'd glimpsed from across the sundial appeared again. There was something false about it, as when his sister used to try on his mother's dresses as a budding young lady and the gowns hadn't fitted. This wasn't the real Miss Domville, but the one meant to keep him at a distance.

'You think you're the only one who suffers alone, the only one afraid of being ridiculed?'

She raised her chin in defiance. 'What do you know of ridicule? All of England adores you.'

'And not one of them was there when I was simply Lieutenant Stevens and not Sir Warren,' he said sharply, irked by her dismissal of his struggles. 'Nor were they there after my first battle as a surgeon's assistant when I staggered up to the empty forecastle to retch overboard, afraid the grizzled old surgeon would catch me and have me drummed out for being so weak. I needed my naval surgical training to establish a practice once I was demobbed and I counted on my pay to keep my mother and sister from starving. My father hadn't had the sense to pay off his debts or save enough to keep us, leaving it to me to do. There were no fans adoring me when I used to write every night, determined to make a living without cutting into men, even while the officers laughed at me and told me I'd never succeed. The only people who were there for me were my mother and sister and my own belief in my ability to pull myself out of hell.'

'I—I'm sorry, I didn't realise,' she stammered, as stunned by his forceful words as he was. 'I thought with your fame your troubles were behind you.'

'They aren't and in some ways they've increased.' He pressed his fists against his hips and stared at the large scuff on the toe of his boot, working to rein in his irritation. It wasn't her fault she didn't know the challenges he'd faced in achieving his goals. He'd rarely discussed them with anyone, so why the hell had he told her? He looked up at her. She stood as serene as a painting, except for her eyes. Uncertainty sharpened their blue and increased the guilt building inside him. He'd told her because, deep down, he sensed she'd understand and he wanted it as much as he did her inspiration. Her not walking away told him she did. 'The problem with penning great novels is more are expected. My most ardent admirers, even my publisher, will abandon me if I don't give them what they want.'

'Then you should return to your study.' A cloud passed over the sun, covering the garden in shadows followed by a chill breeze. She clasped her arms across her chest, bracing herself against a shiver. 'Besides. I don't play well when my fingers are numb.'

She hurried back to the house, stiffness marring the elegance of her gait as she retreated inside. He wanted to call her back, to resume their walk and the quiet conversation they'd enjoyed before his outburst, but he didn't.

He strode across the cloister and swept a pile of leaves off the corner of an arch before turning and marching back to the other side. He should be glad she was pushing him away. She wasn't here for him to pour out his old sorrows to like some heroine in one of his novels, but to help him work. Except he wasn't at his desk, but pacing like a nervous animal.

He let off a sharp whistle to call Lancelot. The dog bounded up to him and the two of them made for inside. He didn't need this distraction, or to have emotion drag him into yet another risk as Leticia's memory had entangled him with Rupert. Steady industry, determination and perseverance were what he needed and nothing else, no matter how much Miss Domville irritated or captivated him.

Marianne closed the cover over the keys. Turner, the butler, had come in a few moments before to announce the arrival of Lady Ellington's carriage. She hadn't noticed how late it was until she'd looked up and seen the deepening shadows beneath the trees outside. She'd been hesitant to come here this morning. Now, she was reluctant to leave. She ran her fingers over the smooth case of the Érard. It was the piano she didn't want to leave, or so she told herself.

After the walk in the garden, she'd rushed back here to her music, eager to lose herself in the peace of the instrument. Everything Sir Warren had said had struck a chord deep inside her, one she feared. In a much more forceful way than Lady Ellington, he'd urged her to not worry about the opinions of others and live her life as she wished. It was a wonderful idea and impractical. She'd defied everyone at Lady Cartwright's to help Lady Ellington. Despite her noble motives, all it had done was garner more derision. She could well imagine how everyone would react if she suddenly decided to throw off all concerns for propriety and do as she pleased. They'd say she had at last proven she was no better than her mother.

From the adjoining room, she could hear the faint scratch of a pen nib across paper, the crackle of the fire and the even snoring of Lancelot. As she peered through the open door at the books lining the far wall, she wondered why everyone was suddenly so concerned with her being out in the world when all she wanted was to be left alone, except she was tired of being alone.

She slid off the bench and gathered up her reticule and made for the study. Even though she'd all but sneered at his past difficulties in the garden, the least she could do was bid him goodnight and thank him for a mostly pleasant day. She wasn't likely to be welcomed back tomorrow. She should be glad—it would end the risk of them becoming the subject of country gossip—but she wasn't. She wanted the chance to make amends for her misstep in the garden, even if she didn't know how.

Lancelot rose from the hearthrug and trotted over to her when she entered the study. She stroked the dog lightly on the head as she cautiously approached the desk. 'Goodnight, Sir Warren.'

He didn't look up from where he sat hunched over his paper, but waved his left hand over his head. He continued writing with his right, his pen flowing over the paper except when he dipped it with flicking jabs in the inkwell. 'Goodnight.'

Her chest tightened and she tried to tell herself his dismissal didn't matter. People did it quite regularly and she didn't care. She cared tonight because she deserved it. For all the times she'd wished for someone to see her as more than rumours, he had and she'd insulted him, then fled like a scared rabbit. No wonder he wasn't eager to engage in more confidences or conversation.

'Come, Miss Domville, I'll see you out.' Mrs Stevens startled Marianne with the stealth of her approach.

The defences she'd lowered to approach him were jerked up again. 'Apparently, I'm no longer needed here.'

She followed Mrs Stevens out of the room and

through the dimly lit front hall to the arched front door, trying not to regret leaving, or today.

'Don't be too hard on him. Warren gets in a mood when he's in the midst of one of his stories. As rude as he might be, I'm glad he's hard at work. It's been too long since I last saw him so engrossed, not since before his sister—' Her voice faded away, sadness draping her like it used to Mrs Nichols whenever a student succumbed to fever. Then it was gone, replaced by her always charming smile. 'Well, it doesn't matter. He doesn't mean any insult by it.'

'I'm not insulted at all.' She wanted to believe it was him and not her, but it was hard. He'd treated her with kindness and respect and she hadn't extended him the same courtesy. Maybe she was as unworthy of it as so many believed. 'I too dislike being interrupted when I'm composing.'

They left the warmth of the entrance hall and stepped out on to the chilly drive. The sun was low in the west and the shadow of the house fell hard over Lady Ellington's maroon-lacquered coach waiting to take Marianne home.

'I'm glad you understand. Thank you again for coming. Your help means a great deal to Warren and me.'

Mrs Stevens gave Marianne's arm a motherly squeeze and Marianne forced herself not to pull back. Relief filled her when Mrs Stevens let go.

Marianne climbed inside the carriage and settled into the seat as it pulled away. So many times, being alone in the vehicle after a trying encounter had been a relief, but not today. Her reaction to the kind woman's touch shamed her as much as her behaviour with Sir Warren. In the garden, when Sir Warren had spoken to her of his past and his pain, it was as if he'd seen inside her to the doubts she tried to hide. It unsettled her how quickly he could sympathise with her. This, as much as him standing over her in the cloister, his green eyes as dark as fine velvet, his chest so close to hers she could have laid her cheek on it, had sent her running back to the pianoforte.

No, he doesn't want my affection, but to be my friend.

He'd said as much and proven it with his willingness to confide in her once again. Instead of accepting it, she'd scoffed at it and pushed him away. It was difficult not to. She'd been betrayed too many times by people who should have cared for her to give her faith so easily.

It had been a mistake to let people's past failings influence her now. Lady Ellington was right, she needed more acquaintances her age. It would only happen if she worked to overcome her reservations to cultivate friends, instead of hiding away from them, as she'd begun to do with Theresa. Sir Warren might not be the answer to all her troubles, but he might be the beginning of the change she'd desperately sought for years. He could lead her to other people who didn't judge her and a life different from the lonely one encompassing her. Like his mother, he'd reached out to her. It was time for her to accept it and his friendship. If she dared to venture back here tomorrow, if he still wanted her to, she would.

The gentlemen and ladies gathered in Lord Preston's sitting room applauded as Warren finished reading the first chapter from his last book aloud. He bowed under their admiration, thinking he looked more like the trained elephant he'd seen in India than an accomplished writer. He craved the quiet of Priorton, but soirées like this were part of his fame and crucial to garnering more readers who could influence society in his favour. These people purchased his stories, promoted his work and some day, when he at last had enough money to think of a family, their children would be his children's companions.

'Well done, Sir Warren,' Lord Preston commended as he shook Warren's hand with his palsied one. 'I've often thought of writing. Perhaps I could give you my story and you could write it for me.'

'I couldn't do it justice, Lord Preston,' Warren answered through a stiff smile, holding back a groan. For all his fame, lands and new title, the difference between Warren and his aristocratic patrons was notable. They admired his novels, but couldn't fathom the hard work it took to write them and achieve everything they possessed by luck of birth.

'You were magnificent, Sir Warren.' The young Lady Preston, with her dark hair and conniving eyes, stood at her elderly husband's elbow, practically licking her wide lips in anticipation of devouring Warren.

He knew what she was after and it wasn't his literary flourish. 'Sir Warren, you must be thirsty after so much reading.'

She snatched Warren away from her husband and escorted him to the refreshment table at the back of the room, throwing her watching friends a haughty smile of triumph. Warren struggled to maintain his cheerful and deferential mood. This wasn't the first time a bored wife had tried to snare him and notoriety among her friends. Warren wasn't interested in becoming her prized catch.

'Try one of these, they're heavenly.' With slender fingers she plucked a pink pastry from a silver tray and held it up to Warren. 'Should you wish to savour one of my delicacies, it's easy to arrange. I could do a great deal for your career, especially among the ladies of London.'

Warren avoided her attempts to slide the treat into his mouth by taking it from her. 'I'm flattered, Lady Preston, but I don't sail my host's schooner, if you take my meaning.'

Lady Preston stared at him as if she couldn't decide whether to be angry or embarrassed. It didn't matter. Warren nodded to her, then strode away, leaving the woman to return to her friends without her conquest. He'd never seduced a woman as a means to increase his fame or profits and he wouldn't do so now, no matter how much he needed money. Lord Byron he was not, as Miss Domville was not Lady Preston.

He flicked a glance at Lady Preston who stood

clucking with her friends, her eyes as sharp as broken glass as she viewed him with the hate of disappointed plans. Miss Domville had been torn apart too many times by women like Lady Preston to be like them. Instead she was original and innocent despite all her worldly experience. She didn't blatantly flaunt her more sensual charms as Lady Preston did, but kept them reserved. It was her opinions she needed to keep to herself.

Warren returned to the men and their discussion of hunting. He struggled to focus on where the best shooting was to be found because all he could think about was his conversation in the garden with Miss Domville. While other ladies drooled over him, she was at times contemptuous. He was Sir Warren to her and nothing more, as she'd proved today when she'd walked away from him. After the return to the house, he'd considered ending the arrangement, more vexed than inspired by their encounter, until she'd started to play. For the first time in too long, the words hadn't just come to him while he'd listened, but the depth of feeling for his characters, the passion which used to grip him in the centre of each story, had returned. He'd run mad with it, as he and the other sailors used to do in port cities when they went ashore. Even while the ground had still rocked beneath their feet they'd praised and revelled in the solid land. He'd done the same with his novel. As much as Miss Domville had irritated him, she'd also inspired him once again.

'Gathering wool, Sir Warren?' Lord Preston chuckled. 'Which would be well advised considering Priorton isn't earning as it should, or so I understand.'

'The previous owner didn't manage it well which is why he was forced to sell it. I assure you, it will be one of the finest estates in the county under my management,' Warren boasted, throwing out his chest to match the surety of any titled man, refusing to allow them to belittle him or the property he'd worked so hard to acquire.

'Not too fine for a purchased estate, I hope,' the rotund Lord Astley drawled in his none-too subtle reference to Warren's humble background.

Warren riveted his superior with a look as sharp as a scalpel. 'The finest.'

He was sure of it. With Miss Domville playing for him, he'd continue to write like he had today and soon there'd be another great sensation from Sir Warren Stevens, and all Lord Preston's and Lord Astley's doubts about him would be conquered, as well as his own.

Assuming Miss Domville returned to Priorton tomorrow.

Warren plucked a glass of port off the tray of a passing footman and took a deep drink. He'd been heavy handed in his insistence she stand up to the bullies in society and he couldn't blame her for snapping back at him. She probably resented his prodding as he did all the story ideas he received from well-meaning readers. He hoped it hadn't cost him their arrangement. He needed her as much as he'd needed Leticia in the days before his first book had been published. He'd been as certain it would be a flop as Miss Domville was convinced she'd always be a social outcast. Leticia, through her letters, had helped Warren to see he was wrong. He wanted to do the same for Miss Domville and he would if she gave him another chance.

Chapter Six

Marianne brought the *étude* to a thundering close, holding down the Érard's ivory keys until the ringing notes faded away.

'Is that one of your compositions?' Sir Warren applauded as he approached. The fall of his feet on the wooden floor was as melodious as a well-played drum and the sound of it tripped through her as powerfully as his voice.

His welcome eased the tension which had marred her playing since her arrival. This morning, when no note had come to Welton Place cancelling their engagement, she'd set out for Priorton wondering what she'd find. She was glad to see him smile at her as if their tiff in the garden had never happened. Without thinking, she returned it.

'No, Sir Warren, it's Schubert.' She'd considered bringing the composition book as a kind of peace offering, but at the last minute she'd changed her mind. Every heartbreak, fear and sense of loss echoed in each note in the book. She wasn't about to allow him to hear it. Despite what she'd told him about Madame de Badeau, there were limits to how many confidences she intended to share with him.

'Please, call me Warren.' He sat down on the bench beside her, his nearness more unsettling than an out-of-tune instrument.

She shifted her hips, ready to slide away before she stopped herself. He was tempting her into confidences again and she was wary of intimacy. She'd allowed herself to grow close to the Smiths and they'd made her regret it. It remained to be seen if Warren would do the same, but there was no way to find out without keeping her promise to accept his friendship and take the risk. 'And you must call me Marianne.'

'A very pretty name.'

'A common one in France.' She shrugged, trying to shake off the delight of his compliment, but he wouldn't allow it.

'It's still pretty.'

She started another tune, a soft one which allowed her to focus on the keys and the pedal instead of him watching her. She expected him to return to his writing, but he remained beside her, listening. She glanced up at him. He offered her a pleasant smile which made her duck back into the music, afraid to stumble through the notes.

'Who taught you to play?' he asked in a soft voice which mingled with the melody more than it interrupted it.

'Piano lessons were required at the Protestant

School in France where I was raised, but once Mrs Nichols, the headmistress, noticed I had a gift for it, she spent more time with me.' For all Marianne's happy memories of the hours at the keyboard with Mrs Nichols, she couldn't forget the long nights in the dormitory. The girls used to taunt her about her lack of a mother. They'd been jealous of the extra time Mrs Nichols had spent with her, unable to see how blessed they were to have parents who cared about them. Back then they'd merely thought of Madame de Badeau as her scandalous and distant sister. They would have crucified her if they'd learned the truth. 'Once we had a recital for the parents. I was seven and I played the most important piece.' She played a few notes. The pride of having performed it for the crowd of gentlemen and ladies filling her before it faded. 'I was the only girl who had no family in attendance.'

She slid her hands off the keys, wondering why she'd told him such a thing. He didn't need to know.

'I'm sorry.' His condolence wasn't flippant but heartfelt and the tenderness of it wrapped around her like a warm pelisse. The old memory didn't seem so cold in his presence.

'It doesn't matter, I've all but forgotten it,' she lied.

He scrutinised her as though he didn't believe her, but didn't debate the matter. Instead, he spread out his fingers over the keys and began an old tune she remembered from France.

'You play?' she asked, astonished.

'No, my sister made me learn this duet a long time ago so we could perform it together.' He continued to struggle through the tune, his ink-stained fingers awkward on the keys. 'It's the only one I know. As you can see, I'm not very good at it.'

'You're doing quite well.' She joined in, taking the high octaves while he did the low ones. 'It's been years since I've played this.'

After she'd left France she'd stopped learning duets. There'd been no one to play them with.

Warren focused on the keys as he played, some of them still warm from Marianne's touch. He missed more notes than he struck and she slowed her playing to give him time to draw out the old tune from his memory. All the while he was aware of Marianne next to him, her hands coming close to his as the music drew them together.

From the corner of his eye he caught her watching him. She wore a pale pink gown, the neck high as always, but it wasn't her figure which captured him, but the lightness in her blue eyes. While they played the suspicious, wary young lady vanished, replaced by a vibrant, excited one.

'I spent hours practising this with Leticia,' he explained, 'the whole time wanting to be outside running with the boys from my father's vicarage school. It was his dream, a chance to make something of himself, though he never managed to make much of the school.'

'How very unfortunate,' she sympathised, her playing and compassion effortless.

'For all of us. The debt from it sunk us after he died. It's why I work so hard. I won't ever be in so precarious a situation again.' Warren plucked at the keys, irritation making his fingers jerky before he settled it. He intended to enjoy this time with her, not wail about the past or be pulled down by his current troubles. He'd made some mistakes this year with Priorton and it had been compounded by his inability to write, but the risk to his solvency would soon pass. With Marianne here he was already creating and would soon be as productive as before.

They continued the piece, their pace increasing as the old motions came back to him During one lively section, her arm brushed against his and he missed the next note, then stumbled over a few more before regaining his rhythm. She didn't wince or bang the keys in frustration, demanding they start again like Leticia used to do. Instead she waited for him to catch up to her.

'Does your sister still play?' Miss Domville asked, the innocent question tearing him like splinters from a shattered mast.

'No, she died over a year ago.' He choked down the hopelessness which had filled him when he'd left his sister's room, forced to admit his defeat.

'I'm sorry.' She stopped playing to lay one hand over his, the touch as light as sea spray but much warmer.

He stilled beneath her and stared at her pale skin against his. The same calm she'd inspired in him at Lady Cartwright's filled him again. It, and her fresh peony scent, stretched out to envelop him and drive away the cold memories like the sun does the clouds after a storm. No woman had ever had such a powerful effect on him and it troubled him. Things were complicated enough at present without throwing a woman into it, but he couldn't push her or her soothing presence away.

He slid his hand out from under hers and rested it on his thigh. The awkwardness of their nearness which had dissolved during the duet returned. He should let it be, encourage it and the aloofness which was a basic tenet of their agreement, but it ate at him as much as his old troubles. She'd comforted him and he wished he could give her the same relief from her troubles, help her as she was helping him. Beneath his hand, the ivory keys spread out in either direction and gave him an idea. 'Have you ever considered performing your compositions for others?'

She began to play a quiet piece, her lips curling up in a sarcastic grimace. 'I can see the advert now. The notorious sister of Madame de Badeau plays the pianoforte. It'll draw a larger crowd than the Elgin Marbles.'

'What about simply publishing them? You could become a famous author, like me.' He winked at her.

'Maybe then I can carouse with the Prince and gain a baronetcy too.'

He trilled his fingers on his leg, wanting to shoot back and tell her it was hard work which had earned him his title and nothing else, but the sideways smile she pinned him with silenced him. She was teasing him, not insulting him, and he enjoyed it as much as the sparkle of her eyes beneath her long lashes.

'If the Prince handed out titles solely based on men

carousing with him, the House of Lords would be over-flowing with newly ennobled men.'

'And their wives and lovers too.' She laughed, the sound as beautiful as her playing. For the second time today she'd surrendered to emotion instead of trying to hide it behind her wary distrust of everyone and everything. He wanted to see more of this impetuous woman, but as fast as she'd allowed the slip, she covered it again. 'It's a generous offer, Warren, but I've found the less notoriety, the better. While you may crave fame, I want nothing but to be ignored.'

It wasn't true and they both knew it, but he said nothing. It was her scandals she wanted ignored. She craved attention from people who would treat her well, the way he wished to treat her. 'You could write under a pseudonym. It's done all the time.'

'No. Despite what anyone thinks of the work, if they happen to learn it's by me, they'll shun it.'

'The world is much bigger than London. I assure you, there are musicians in Vienna who care nothing about the *ton's* gossip, and people in England who have more to consider than your past.'

'You haven't even heard my pieces. They could be awful.'

'Coming from someone with such a genuine love of music, I doubt it. Of course, you could always play them for me so I could be certain.'

She didn't answer, but stopped playing and went silent as though he'd asked her to reveal her dark-est secrets, which in a way he had. He silently urged her to overcome her hesitation as she had at the Cartwrights' when she'd refused to allow the ladies' insults to deter her from helping her friend. He didn't want those same women hindering her dream, or her faith in herself like all the laughing sailors and officers had tried to do with him.

'Let's assume your compositions are magnificent,' he continued as her silence stretched out. She hadn't refused him, but she hadn't agreed either. 'I can show them to my publisher and convince him to print them. I'll lend you the strength of my name, which is something I haven't done for even my brother-in-law.'

'Why?' She eyed him like an apple on a cart, wondering if there were worms beneath the red flesh. This wasn't how he wanted her to regard him and some day he would see to it she didn't.

'Because ten years ago Mr Berkshire took a chance on me and it made all the difference. I want to do the same for you. You don't have to decide anything today, but please consider it.' Warren didn't want to press her as he had yesterday and send her fleeing, or rejecting his offer outright. 'Publishing would give you something more to do than locking yourself away at Lady Ellington's. A real purpose.'

She opened her full lips, ready to answer when a voice from the door silenced her.

'There you two are,' Warren's mother observed as she bustled into the room.

Marianne moved away from Warren as if he was an uncoiling anchor rope about to catch her leg and drag her down. He wasn't so fast to pull away. 'Miss

Domville, Lady Ellington sent the carriage early for you today.'

'The Girls' School meeting. I almost forgot.' Marianne bounded from the bench and gathered up her reticule and pelisse like a pupil late for class. The quickness of her movements gave her a youthfulness Warren admired. It was so different from the cautious seriousness which usually stalked her.

'When I didn't hear music, I thought you'd gone to the garden,' his mother mentioned as she and Warren led Marianne to the waiting carriage.

'Doesn't your room have a view of it?' Marianne asked, casting suspicious eyes on Warren.

'Yes, but it isn't a very good one,' Warren's mother answered, not a party to Warren's small lie from yesterday.

The truth exposed, he ignored the chiding glance from his muse.

They reached the carriage where the footman held open the door. Warren followed Marianne forward to the vehicle while his mother remained behind.

'Think about what I offered.' Warren held out his hand to Marianne, ready to help her into the carriage. She stared at it, not as quick to take it as she'd been to comfort him inside. He was about to withdraw his and allow the footman to assist her when she reached out and laid her palm against his. The pressure was light and heady and he curled his fingers to capture hers. Beneath the whinny of the horse, he heard her subtle intake of breath as he bowed over the delicate skin, noting a small freckle near her thumb, tempted to press his lips to it, but he couldn't, not with his mother watching. He straightened to find her staring at him as though he'd suggested he climb in the conveyance with her. He would have if she'd invited him.

She let go and dipped inside. The footman closed the door, then took his place on the back. Warren waited for Marianne to appear at the window, but she remained hidden by the shiny side of the carriage as it set off down the drive, kicking up a small cloud of dust behind it.

'You interrupted us,' Warren muttered to his mother, more irritated than grateful as she stepped forward to join him.

'I wouldn't be a very good chaperon if I hadn't.'

Warren studied his unapologetic mother. She was enjoying this, though which aspect of this, the interrupting or Warren not being thrilled about it, he wasn't sure. 'I was telling her about Leticia and how much she used to like to play.'

His mother's smile vanished. 'Please, Warren, don't remind me.'

He didn't say more. They rarely spoke of Leticia and sometimes he wondered if his mother blamed him for what had happened, like Rupert did. If she did, she'd never say so. His mother possessed a generous heart. He hoped it was charitable enough for her to forgive her son. He still hadn't forgiven himself.

'Why do you stand by Miss Domville instead of joining with Lady Cartwright and the others?' he asked, needing to discuss something else.

His mother clasped her hands in front of her stomach as she used to do when explaining the rules to a new pupil at his father's school. 'In all my years at the vicarage, more than one young lady in a difficult circumstance came to me for advice. When I used to listen to their stories, I could always tell which ones had eagerly gone to the man and which ones had genuinely been led astray. The ruined young ladies, despite their unfortunate experience, lacked a worldliness which the eager ones couldn't hide. Miss Domville has the same innocence as those misled young ladies. Whatever she'd been accused of, she hasn't done it. I'm as sure of it as you and the Falconbridges.' His mother turned to him, as serious as the day she'd sat him down in the vicarage garden when he was fourteen to tell him of the weakness invading his father's lungs. 'Be very clear about what it is you want from her. If you break her heart, she won't recover like one of your London widows.'

Warren blanched. 'What London widows?'

She wagged one finger at him. 'Don't think I don't know what you get up to when we're in town.'

He crossed his arms over his chest, refusing to discuss his non-writing activities with his mother. 'I want nothing more from Miss Domville than her inspiration. She's well aware of it and expects nothing more from me. Maybe in a few years I'll consider taking a wife, but I won't ask a young lady to wait on my whims to see herself settled.'

His mother shook her head in disappointment. 'You're work isn't everything, Warren.'

The muscles in his neck tightened as the peace of

Marianne's presence faded. With her, for a short while, he'd been able to forget all the demands pressing down on him. They returned now with as much potency as the afternoon sun on the lawn. 'It's everything we have to live on.'

He left the tranquillity of the front garden and went back inside, passing the dull armour and swords adorning the hall as he returned to his desk. He'd vowed long ago to work hard and make enough so he and those he loved would never be in poverty, or forced to endure the same horrors he had as a young man. He couldn't allow a pretty face or some misguided need for sympathy to deter him from his goals. Even if the lady had money, if he didn't, it meant nothing. He wouldn't depend on others. He'd discovered what a mistake it was to do so during the year they'd lived with his uncle.

He entered his study and stepped over Lancelot where he lay in the centre of the room. Seating himself at his desk, Warren took up his pen. He'd had been distracted enough by Marianne already. It was time to write, even if it took him a full hour to stop tilting his head to listen for Marianne's playing. The lingering scent of her perfume kept convincing him she was mere feet away.

'We've been invited to Lady Astley's musical evening next week,' Lady Ellington announced as the carriage carried them to the Girls' School on the far side of the village.

'Must we go?' Marianne sighed. 'It's bad enough I have to face her this afternoon as a school patroness, but at her house? The woman isn't much better than Lady Cartwright. Why must she and the others always be so rude to me?'

'Lady Cartwright is one of those unhappy people who, instead of looking for ways to build herself up, rips others down. All is not well between Lady Astley and her husband and I believe Lady Preston is ashamed of her past. She might be a baroness, but I don't think she's ever been comfortable with the change from merchant's daughter to titled lady. It's difficult enough at times for those of us born to it. I can only imagine what it must be like for her, and Sir Warren.'

'He seems to have taken to it well enough.' With the exception of the Falconbridges, it was yet another argument for ignoring the society of toffs, of which Sir Warren was a part, though not really. He'd raised himself up from humble beginnings and filled his coffers every day through his work. She admired him for his accomplishments. It was more than most men she'd encountered were willing to do

'He's sure to be at the musical evening which is a good reason for you to attend.'

'Is it?' She wasn't so certain, especially not after their time alone together today.

'Or as a reason to purchase a new dress, something to play up your less musical talents.' Lady Ellington circled her hand at Marianne's abundant chest hidden beneath her fichu and the restraining influence of her stays. 'I saw the most beautiful pattern for a blue ball gown in my lady's magazine. It would bring out your eyes.'

Her eyes weren't the only thing a more revealing dress would bring out. In the past, the few men who'd seen her wear the single gown she owned which accentuated her décolletage had lost their ability to speak. Unfortunately, they had retained excellent control of their pawing hands. Yet it wasn't so much them she imagined seeing her in the dress as Warren. It was almost enough to make her agree to having it done up. 'I can't. If I wear anything too revealing, everyone will call me a tart.'

They called her one anyway, even while she dressed like a nun. Warren didn't. When he'd stood over her in the cloister and today when he'd held her hand in the drive, he'd viewed her as if she were the most magnificent thing he'd ever seen. Marianne rubbed the palm of her hand, the pressure of Warren's skin against hers still vivid. She'd arrived at Priorton this morning determined to be friendly with him, but during their time together, something more than comfort or companionship had curled between them. It was something she was hesitant to consider. He was no more interested in courting than she was, and if she allowed her emotions to run away with her, who knew what mistakes it might lead to, or what weaknesses in her it might reveal.

'We're here,' Lady Ellington announced as the carriage rocked to a stop in front of a modest two-storey brick house.

With a sigh, Marianne followed the Dowager out of the carriage, wishing she could forgo this meeting, but she couldn't. To do so would mean giving the other patronesses complete control of the school and she didn't trust them to be generous to the orphan girls being trained for service. She and Lady Ellington had helped re-found the school last year after it had almost faltered due to a lack of funds. In doing so, they'd been forced to take on other patronesses such as Lady Preston and Lady Astley who were as free with their censure as their financial help. At least with Lady Ellington involved, the other ladies were forced to maintain a touch of decorum where Marianne was concerned.

Marianne followed Lady Ellington into the school, nodding and smiling to the little girls lined up on either side of the front walk to greet them.

'Welcome, Lady Ellington and Miss Domville,' Miss Speith, the slender assistant headmistress, sang out as they stepped inside. Beside her stood Mary, the oldest girl of ten with wildly curly hair.

'Good day, Mary. Here's the sheet music I promised you.' Marianne handed her the new sheet music recently arrived from London.

'Thank you, Miss Domville.' Mary clasped the music to her chest as if it were a gold sovereign. The reaction warmed and saddened Marianne. Like her, Marianne had fed off small kindnesses as a child too. There'd been few people to offer them to her. Not even Mrs Nichols, who'd had so many girls to take care of at the Protestant School, had been attentive enough.

Marianne and Lady Ellington proceeded into the dining room in the centre of the house. Like every other room it was sparse, decorated for purpose rather than pleasure. With books needing to be purchased along with food and material for clothes, there wasn't much reason to spend money on pictures. Some day, when the school was financially secure, Marianne would see it more cheerily done up.

'Good afternoon, ladies,' Mrs Croft, the long-faced headmistress with pince-nez glasses on the bridge of her nose, greeted. Marianne and Lady Ellington took their seat at the table across from Lady Menton, Lady Preston and Lady Astley.

Once everyone was settled, Mrs Croft picked up the pen beside her and looked over the list of topics in the journal before her. 'The first item to discuss is—'

As Mrs Croft led the meeting, Marianne braced herself against the other women's narrow-eyed stares, doing her best to ignore them. She'd heard enough rumours from the servants, especially about Lady Preston, to know they were no saints and yet they dared to sneer at her. If only she had the fortitude to meet their derision by calling out their sins directly to their faces. She'd catch hell for being so bold, but it might be worth it to see Lady Preston go pale beneath her overly red hair.

'Miss Domville, if you're to be a part of these meetings we need your full attention,' Mrs Croft chided as though Marianne was one of her students.

She sat up straighter in her chair, refusing to be rebuked. 'I'm part of these meetings because my money helps fund this school.'

'And we thank you for your generosity,' Mrs Croft

mumbled before returning to her list. 'As I was saying, I think it best to forgo the Christmas boxes this year.'

'No, we can't do away with them,' Marianne protested. 'Not every girl has a family to send her presents.' If it hadn't been for Mrs Nichols giving her the gold pinky ring the Christmas she'd turned ten, Marianne never would have received one yuletide gift during all her years at the Protestant School.

'I realise it will be a disappointment...' Mrs Croft peered over her pince-nez '...but our duty is to prepare these girls for their futures. For most of them, life won't be pretty boxes of sweets at Christmas.'

Marianne gripped the arms of her chair as she struggled to remain polite. 'Some of these girls have suffered enough hardships without being denied a little treat at a festive time of year. I'll pay for the boxes myself to ensure they have them.'

'That's very generous of you, Miss Domville, but I think—'

'It's a wonderful idea,' Lady Ellington cut off Mrs Croft. 'Don't you agree, Lady Menton?'

Lady Menton paled, but was prudent enough to agree, especially with Lord Falconbridge backing her son, and Theresa's husband, for MP. 'I do.'

'I do, too,' Lady Astley mumbled, following Lady Ellington's none-too-subtle hint. The Baron's wife didn't possess so pressing a reason to align herself with Lady Ellington except the pleasure of having more illustrious guests than the local farmers and tradesmen at her musical evening. Lady Preston nodded as if it physically hurt her to agree, too awed by the Dowager's lineage to openly defy her.

'Then it's settled. Mrs Croft, you may continue with the meeting,' Lady Ellington instructed.

The headmistress scratched the item off her list with a flick of her bony wrist. 'The next issue concerns the reading-book selection.'

While she spoke, Marianne silently seethed. Despite all Marianne's hard work on behalf of the school, if Lady Ellington weren't involved, Marianne would be driven away, her money and help rejected because of rumours and suspicions. It didn't matter what good deeds she did, all of these people were determined to tear her down, except Mrs Stevens and Warren. She wished she could face her critics and prove to them once and for all she was more than the wicked woman they believed her to be.

You could publish your works.

Warren's suggestion came rushing back to her as she plucked a piece of Lancelot's red hair off her dress and dropped it on the floor.

She might have scoffed at his idea, but there'd been no deriding the sincerity behind his offer or his desire to encourage her like Lady Ellington always did. She wished it didn't mean playing her pieces for him. It was one thing to distribute music to anonymous people. Everyone played the way they wished, despite all the allegros and fortissimos written in the staff. It was quite another thing for an artist to perform their own composition exactly as it was meant to be done. It revealed the true intention behind each note, the real feeling underlining every stanza. However, he must hear them if he was to judge the quality of her work and whether it was worthy of his endorsement.

She caught Lady Preston staring at her and met her hard eyes until the woman looked away first. If everyone was so determined to condemn her no matter what she did, then she might as well do what she wanted. Warren believed she should and she was sure Lady Ellington did too. Her success would defy these women's low expectations of her and prove to them she was more than a whore's relation.

Fear slipped in to undermine her determination. For them to know she would have to publish under her real name and risk society's reaction. If Lady Preston and her surreptitious glares were any indication, it wouldn't be good, but Warren was right, London was not the centre of the world. Her success as a composer was in the future. This was now and he was giving her an opportunity she might never have again. She knew how quickly everything which she believed was sure and good and constant could change. Anyone or anything might swoop in to snatch Warren and his offer away from her. Until then, she'd seize this moment and take full advantage of it. Tomorrow she'd take her composition book to Priorton Abbey.

Chapter Seven

Warren listened to the notes drifting through the open library door. The tone of Marianne's playing was different today. It wasn't continuous, but paused here and there before starting back a few stanzas and beginning again.

She's playing her own composition.

He set his pen in the stand and grasped the arms of his chair, ready to rise before he stopped. She was working with a focus he recognised. To disturb her would mean upsetting her progress as she tried one note and then another until the succession seemed right. He settled back in his seat and struggled to follow the rhythm and predict where it might go. Then, when she played it all together, it flowed like the thread in one of his stories.

He returned to his work, his progress matching hers with words coming rapidly and filling page after page. He was so engrossed, he didn't notice the music had stopped until a voice startled him.

'Warren?' His name on her lips was even prettier than her playing.

He stood as she approached his desk, moving like a dream in the cream-coloured dress. The sleeves were sheer, revealing the curve of her arms. The high neckline covered her chest, but didn't rise to her neck, leaving a hint of her glorious cleavage visible above the gold trim of the bodice. Its colour matched the tone of her hair and the small gold bracelet encircling her wrist.

She stopped in front of his desk. Lancelot stretched and trotted over to her. She scratched behind his ears, making the dog tilt his head in delight. While her fingers mussed his hair, she peered at the book lying open on Warren's desk. 'Am I disturbing you?'

'Not at all. I heard you composing.'

'Piano concertos. They're my speciality, but difficult to write when one forgets to bring enough ink.'

So it wasn't curiosity which had drawn her in here. He was a touch disappointed as he opened a desk drawer and took out a fresh bottle. 'Lucky for you I keep a great deal on hand.'

He held out the glass jar and she reached for it, her fingers curling over his. She didn't jerk away at the meeting of their skin, but allowed the tips of her fingers to caress the back of his as she slid the bottle from his grasp. Red spread along the arches of her cheeks and a faint surprise flicked through her blue eyes. They stayed as they were for a few moments, the crackle of the fire in the grate punctuating the heavy silence.

He waited for her to make an excuse and slip away

from him like his stories sometimes did if he didn't write them down fast enough. She didn't and he was the one who drew back first, fingering the edge of the top book in the stack next to him. His mother's warning to be cautious with her rang in his ears. He should take up his pen and send her into the other room. This was a distraction, a very lovely one, but he didn't need it.

He was about to suggest they both return to their work when she leaned forward and peered at the half-filled paper on his desk. 'What are you writing?'

'My version of a Robin Hood story.'

'You enjoy the myths about him?'

'Not as much as Leticia used to.' He touched the yellowed pages of the book on castles lying open on the desk. The place was well marked from all the times Leticia had studied the illustration of the Locksley keep as a girl. It had been one of her favourites. 'She shared my love of medieval stories. When we were children, we used to dream of living in a castle some day. At least one of us achieved it.'

She rested her hand on Lancelot's head. 'How did she die?'

He patted his thigh and Lancelot left Marianne to lean against Warren's leg. He stroked the dog, not wanting to relive the morning. He already did every time he thought of his sister. Maybe silence wasn't what he needed, but to talk about it the way he used to discuss the Navy with Mr Berkshire or some of his old seamen friends. They'd listened to him and recognised what it was like to be in the midst of battle, scared for your life but still doing your duty. Yet when it had come to losing Leticia, they hadn't been as sympathetic about the trials of childbed and what it had been like for Warren to lose the most important patient he'd ever cared for. He took a deep breath, drawing on his courage the way he used to before battle. Under Marianne's gentle gaze, he couldn't hold back. 'She and my poor little niece did not survive her confinement.'

'And there was nothing you could do for them.' It wasn't an accusation, but a statement of support and tenderness which almost crushed him. He didn't deserve her or anyone else's pity for what he'd failed to do.

'No. I'd stitched captains back together, saved unconscious seamen from being pitched overboard by proving they were still alive, but there'd been nothing I could do for my sister or her poor babe.'

'It's not your fault they died,' she offered as if hearing all the regrets and second guesses which continued to torture him.

He'd spent too many nights contemplating if he should have done something different, tried some procedure he'd read about. He still wondered if he could have saved one or the other, or both of their lives if he'd been less cautious in his treatment. 'I'm not so sure. Neither is Rupert and sometimes, I suspect, my mother.'

'Not her. She's too kind.'

He closed the book on castles and the gilded title caught the sunlight from the window behind him. 'She never talks about Leticia.'

'Most mothers do so love their daughters. It must be difficult to realise she's gone.'

'It is, for both of us. Leticia was my greatest supporter. She was the one who first found Mr Berkshire. She pursued him for weeks, begging him to read my manuscripts, the ones she used to critique and edit. He finally gave in to her just so she'd stop pestering him.' He smiled at the memory of Mr Berkshire blustering on in faux outrage during their first meeting while Warren had been on leave. Leticia had beamed at the publisher's compliments about her tenaciousness and Warren's gratitude for it. The humour in the memory left him and he pressed his fingertips into the top of the desk, bracing himself against defeat. 'She believed in me when I needed it the most. Then, when she needed me, I failed her.'

'You told me the night you helped Lady Ellington there's very little medical men can do except patch people up and hope they survive.'

'Most of the time they don't.'

'But sometimes they do. I'm sure there are many sailors who are still alive because of what you did for them.' Marianne studied him like the apparition he'd once seen aboard ship in the middle of a fever—an angel of strength with a hint of vulnerability beneath her gossamer silk. A vision like Miss Domville was the reason why men believed in mermaids. They were peace.

'Yes, there are.' The faces of seamen who'd left his sick bay to return to their lives or their stations trickled through his thoughts. He had made a difference to some men, and in the end, through his hard work, to his and his mother's lives. He smiled at Marianne, amazed at how, when he'd been so determined to help her, she was the one helping him. Whatever man she decided to finally reveal her full self to would be lucky. Despite all his protestations about avoiding distraction, at this moment he very much wished to be the one she chose.

'Enough of my tales of woe.' He shoved his experiences into the dark hold in his mind and beamed at her like he did his admiring readers, refusing to ruin their time together with all his misery. 'It's your beautiful music I want to hear today.'

She cocked her head at him as if to say she wouldn't forget what he'd told her, or allow him to evade revealing more of himself in the future. 'Weren't you listening to me play while you wrote? Isn't it the whole reason I'm here?'

No, not the whole reason.

It was becoming more difficult to lie to her and himself. 'May I see your composition book?'

She clutched the ink tighter, as if he'd asked to peek under her petticoat. 'Why?'

'I'm curious. I've been listening to you all morning. I want to see what you've accomplished.'

'What have you accomplished?'

He picked up his manuscript and held it out to her. 'Five chapters. Not an entire novel, but it soon will be. I'll let you read it when it's done if you'll let me see your composition book.'

She waved away his manuscript and with an 'as you wish' shrug made for the music room, making it clear he was to follow. He didn't mind. From behind, he caught the faint outline of her figure from the light coming in the window filtering through her dress. It emphasised the tempting curve of her hips and the slenderness of her waist. She approached the Érard, set the ink next to the composition book on the stand and sat at the keyboard.

He stopped in the middle of the room. Lancelot rested at his feet while Marianne posed one foot over the pedal. Her bearing was as alluring as the arch of her neck beneath the loose blonde curls brushing the nape. He trilled his fingers on his arms where he crossed them, wanting to sweep her skin with his lips and savour the sweet melody of her sighs.

Unaware of the desire for her more than her talent making him shift on his feet, she spread out her long fingers over the keys. Her hands slid across the black and white, drawing from the instrument something of her soul. The beauty of it drowned out everything— his story, his grief, even his desire for her. Her music was no longer something to fill the background while he worked. It was everything and each note wrapped around him like he wished her shapely arms would do.

The complexity of the composition reminded him of her experiences with the world. She'd suffered more of its ugliness than she deserved, just as he had in the Navy. Her loneliness rang in the mournful bass beneath the treble. It reminded him of the creaking timbers and snapping sails during the dark nights when he used to stand at the balustrade staring out at the darkness. The overwhelming solitude of the sea crept into a man's soul like the damp did everything aboard ship. Even now, late at night when he rose to stare out at the dark gardens or stood in the midst of a London crowd, he sometimes shivered with the memory of it.

She hadn't shaken her isolation either. She knew what it was like to be alone among many, to carry sadness like buckets of seawater, never able to scrub away the past. Someone so young and innocent didn't deserve to suffer the way he had during his first days in the Navy. He would make her happy, see her smile not with stoic reserve but the unrestrained joy of a young lady. In freeing her from her past, he might forget his too.

Marianne never once turned to look at Warren, confident he was there. She couldn't tell him how difficult it had been to be torn from the Protestant School and Mrs Nichols. She couldn't express how much it seared her heart when the letter from the Smiths had arrived after Madame de Badeau's scandal. If it hadn't been for Lady Ellington holding her while she'd cried, the piece she played would be darker and uglier.

Marianne moved into a more chilling stanza, her fear even this great lady would eventually leave her echoing down the length of the piano wires. There was nothing binding Lady Ellington to her any more than there had been the Smiths or the Nichols. Unlike them, Lady Ellington wasn't paid to care for her, she just did. Marianne feared Lady Ellington's regard would one day turn to disgust and she'd be as alone and wretched as she had been in Madame de Badeau's house. Lady Ellington was the one bright light in her life, until she'd met Warren.

Moving to a softer portion of the piece, she threw a subtle glance over her shoulder. She could see nothing more than the silhouette of Warren near the windows at the edge of her vision. He listened in respectful silence, not interrupting or intruding into the undefined space which enveloped her while she played. Even without seeing his expression, she knew he didn't listen with leering amusement as though she were an overly adorned Cyprian, but because he wanted to hear what she couldn't express in words.

She almost snatched her hands off the keyboard and ceased to play. Even without seeing his expression, she knew he heard the deeper meaning beneath each carefully chosen note just as she'd empathised with his pain over his sister and all he'd endured in the Royal Navy. She might not have witnessed the smoke and bloodshed of battle, but she'd fought her own war against the vile men and women who'd demeaned her for years. Like him, she'd experienced the grief of being ripped away from someone who'd cared for her. Mrs Nichols hadn't died like Leticia, but after the Peace of Amiens had failed and the blockade had ended all correspondence with France, it was as if she had passed away.

Marianne played for his anguish and hers, but with a hope they could overcome it. She drew strength from his presence and touched each key with passion, putting all of herself into the music until at last she reached the end and the final note vibrated into nothing.

He didn't clap or compliment her, but came to sit beside her on the bench. Lancelot remained where he was on the rug. The cold tones of her piece faded under the heat of Warren's arm next to hers. She turned to him and admired the serenity which softened the lines at the corner of his mouth. They didn't speak, as raw and open to one another as if they were naked. The vulnerability didn't frighten Marianne or make her raise her defences like some kind of drawbridge to shut him out. He laid his hand over hers where it rested between them on the bench. His pulse beat a steady tune against her skin, drawing her to him like the Érard did every day.

She turned her hand over and curled her fingers around his. The peace and safety which filled her at Lady Ellington's swept through her. There was no reason to fear Warren, not with her person or her heart. With him, she wouldn't be alone. It was as terrifying as it was exhilarating, like his leaning towards her. She titled her face up to his and closed her eyes.

The meeting of their lips struck her as hard as the first time she'd heard an accomplished organist perform Beethoven's *Fifth Symphony*. She'd never willingly surrendered to a man's affection, determined to remain in control of her urges and her body in a manner Madame de Badeau had failed to master. Today, she tossed it all aside as Warren slid his hand along her jaw. She shifted closer to him, raising her arm so his free one could wrap around her waist and pull her tighter against him. The press of his chest against hers and the weight of his breath across her cheeks was as glorious as the fine silk of a new dress.

She rested her hand on his arm, marvelling at the hardness of his muscle beneath the linen. It wasn't the strength of a Navy surgeon who could wield a saw, but the writer who spent every day dedicated to his craft. He didn't work for only fame and notoriety, but for the safety of his family and a home no one could take from him. She wanted to slip into the circle of his comfort and protection, forget everything he'd told her in the other room and all she'd conveyed in her music. None of it mattered except him and the peace of his embrace.

It didn't last.

'Warren, are you in here? Your mother said you were working.' A man's voice broke the quiet. Marianne stiffened beneath Warren as the sound of boots on the adjoining study floor banged through the stillness. 'Where are you?'

'Damn it,' Warren cursed as he jumped to his feet and hurried to the far side of the instrument. He placed as much distance as he could between them before Rupert strolled in as though he owned the house.

'What are you doing here?' Rupert took in the room with amazement. 'I don't think I've ever seen you in here.'

His curious gaze fell on Marianne. Her once-languid spine had gone stiff beneath Rupert's interested gleam. There was nothing else about her, not a touch of colour in her face or the nervous casting down of her eyes to suggest there'd been anything more going on than her playing for Warren. It still wasn't enough to put Rupert off.

'Good afternoon.' Rupert bowed to her, his greeting more salacious than salutary.

'What are you doing here?' Warren demanded. No introduction was necessary. They'd met at Lady Cartwright's.

'Now there's a warm reception,' Rupert complained before he focused again on Marianne, or more correctly, her chest. 'Miss Domville, it's a pleasure to see you again. I hadn't expected it to be at Priorton.'

'Where did you expect it to be?' Her question was as sharp as it was challenging, but it failed to knock the cocky arrogance out of Rupert.

'Not with Warren.'

'Miss Domville is an accomplished pianist. Mother invited her to play the Érard.' The excuse for her being here sounded about as convincing as the ones the schoolboys used to tell his father after arriving late to lessons.

'You should come and play for me some time. I'd very much like to enjoy your well-developed talent too,' Rupert sniggered.

'Shut your mouth, Rupert.' Warren rounded the curved back of the piano and placed himself between Marianne and his brother-in-law. 'When you're in my house you'll act like a gentleman to all my guests or I'll demand the return of my funding for your venture. Do you understand?'

'I do,' he stuttered, stunned out of his smarmy regard.

'Then apologise to the lady.' He stepped aside and motioned to Marianne.

With the petulance of a schoolboy, Rupert bowed to her. 'My apologies, Miss Domville.'

She said nothing. Warren didn't blame her for not offering her acceptance. Rupert's apology wasn't heartfelt.

'Where's your mother?' Rupert glanced around, making the lack of a chaperon apparent. Warren wondered the same thing. She'd sent Rupert here, why hadn't she followed? He'd promised Marianne there'd be no scandal and he'd keep his word.

Marianne rose from the piano and collected her composition book without any stumbling rush of excuses as to why she'd been caught alone with a gentleman. Her expression was as solemn as an angel's on a gravestone. It would be Warren's headstone she'd erect for this near miss. Thankfully, his mother appeared, out of breath as though she were in a hurry.

'Here I am. The cook waylaid me with some silly thing about dinner. Rupert, you were supposed to wait for me,' she chided, adding more credence to there being nothing out of the ordinary taking place in the music room. 'Miss Domville, thank you so much for allowing me to listen to your wonderful playing. Lady Ellington's coach is waiting for you. I'll walk you to it.'

'Good day, Sir Warren.' Marianne dipped a curtsy to him, her eyes revealing little of her thoughts until she flicked a hard glance at Rupert. Without another word, she followed Warren's mother out of the room.

Once she was gone, Warren headed for his study,

doing his best to act as uninterested in her departure as she did. He wasn't sure her lack of regret was an act or a real desire to be as far away from him and his reprehensible brother-in-law as possible. He didn't know when he'd find out either. After this mishap, she wasn't likely to return. Panic reared inside him, but he quickly brought it under control. He'd been in worse fixes and overcome them. He'd deal with this as well.

Rupert followed him into his office, his steps tight.

'What are you doing here?' Warren asked again. 'You weren't supposed to come until next month', with plenty of time for Warren to arrange for Marianne to not be here and to avoid a potential scandal. His promise to her was at risk of being undermined and he wanted to pound his brother-in-law into the floor. Everything he'd gained with Marianne had been stomped on by this clod who wasn't likely to keep his mouth shut about what he'd seen. Curse the fool and himself for being so careless with Marianne.

'I have some things to discuss with you in regards to the business and they couldn't wait. I'd like to stay here for the next few days while I visit some potential investors.' He glanced back and forth between Warren and the study door. 'I thought you were worried about your reputation. Isn't it why you were hesitant to invest in me?'

'It is and it was.'

'Then what are you doing entertaining a woman like Miss Domville?'

'You mean a woman with the ear of Lord Falconbridge, the protection of his aunt, the Dowager Countess of Merrell. What should I do? Call her a harlot to her face like you did? How many copies of my book do you think the Marquess and his friends will buy then? After your insult, you can kiss any hope of patronage from that corner goodbye.'

Rupert ran his hand through his thinning hair, realising too late his mistake. 'There must be a better way to curry Lord Falconbridge's favour than entertaining a woman of her reputation.'

'Neither of us will have to worry about her reputation or ours if you don't tell anyone you saw her here.' His stomach tightened with the whiff of deceit behind the comment, but he didn't want Rupert to mention Marianne's presence to the wrong person. If Rupert had a stake in keeping her visit a secret, he was more likely to watch his stupid tongue.

'Of course I won't say anything. I don't want our venture tarnished any more than you do.'

'It's not *our* venture. It's *your* venture.' Warren rubbed his hand over Lancelot's head as the dog came to sit beside him. It didn't calm him like it usually did. 'You're to stop using my name to promote it.'

'Yes, yes, I got your letter. I need you to sign the investment papers for *my* venture,' Rupert testily clarified. 'I also need the other half of the money you promised.'

'I never promised it. The amount I already gave you will have to do.'

'Damn it, Warren, I was counting on more.' Desperation replaced the spite in his brown eyes. 'I've already spent the funds from the other investors.'

'On what?'

'Necessary expenses,' Rupert mumbled.

Warren stared at the man, disgusted. 'You squandered it, didn't you?'

'There was a ship and a captain to hire and investors to woo.'

'How many fancy dinners and bottles of wine fed your cravings instead of wooing investors or paying for crews?'

He had the gall to appear insulted. 'You're using these unfounded accusations to renege on your promise.'

'Then show me your ledgers. Bring them here and outline each expense and how it was used to further your business. I'll have Mr Reed go through it and we'll see how unfounded my accusations are.'

Rupert's jaw ground as he worked to concoct another lie, another excuse to explain his dishonesty.

'Don't bother telling me anything else,' Warren warned.

'What am I going to do without your support?'

'You have your small inheritance, which is more than I had when I first started out. Use it to save yourself or did you squander it too?'

The angry pursing of Rupert's lips told him he had. 'You have tons of money, but you deny me even the smallest help.'

'You had the chance to take my assistance, and that of everyone who believed in your venture, and do something with it. Instead you wasted it. From here on out, whether you succeed or fail is according to your own effort and will, which, from what I've seen, is sorely lacking.'

Rupert swallowed hard, staring at the floor as if Lancelot might rise up to help him win the argument. 'You wouldn't have behaved like this if Leticia were still alive.'

For the first time, Rupert's reminder didn't fill Warren with guilt. 'You're right, but she isn't.'

'And whose fault is that?' Rupert hissed.

Warren slammed his fist on the desk, making the ink jars rattle in their holders. 'Get out and don't ever step foot in this house again. You don't deserve my help.'

Rupert flung one last look of hate at Warren before turning on his heel and storming out of the room. It was then Warren noticed his mother hovering in the doorway.

Warren righted the ink jar, trying to calm the tremors of rage filling him. Even when Rupert's whole world was crumbling in on him, he still tried to blame Warren for both his failures and Leticia's death. For too long he'd allowed him to use her memory against him, to ignore the worm of a man in front of him as though she were still alive. He wouldn't allow it any longer. 'How much did you hear?'

'Enough to confirm something I've been considering for a long time.'

Warren rubbed the side of his stinging hand. 'I held on to him because he reminded me of Leticia.'

'We both did.' She came up to Warren and laid a comforting hand on his arm. 'I know I don't talk about her much and have often discouraged you from speaking of her as well. I worried about you when you went into the Navy, frightened each time the post came I'd learn you'd been killed. I didn't want to lose you. I didn't think she'd be the one to die young.'

Warren stared down at his mother, stunned. It was the first time she hadn't shied away from discussing Leticia. His openness had increased hers and it never would have happened if he hadn't told Marianne. Once again, when he'd wanted to help her, she'd been the one who'd helped him. 'I didn't know.'

'We're too much alike, not admitting to others how we really feel. Your father used to complain about it.' She offered him a light smile which quickly faded. 'You blame yourself for what happened, but I don't blame you. You did everything you could.'

Warren sighed, weary of it all. 'It wasn't enough.'

'Sometimes nothing is. I saw so much of it in all the parishes I was in with your father.' His mother touched the book on castles. 'I don't say this lightly because like you, I miss her every day, but it's time for us to recall other, better memories.'

He didn't know how to move past his sister's death any more than he knew how to rid himself of the horrors of the Navy. Leaving Leticia to the past felt too much like a betrayal of her memory and everything she'd ever done for him, yet clinging to his grief had not brought her back. He looked at the ink jar, thinking of Marianne as she'd stood here listening to him. In her quiet voice, she'd told him Leticia's death wasn't his fault and for the first time, he'd believed it. Maybe she was the one who could lead him out of this grief stealing his voice and threatening to ruin his entire life.

Lancelot's collar jingled as he scratched himself with his back paw.

'What'll you do about Miss Domville? She was very hesitant when I asked if she'd return tomorrow,' his mother asked.

Warren pinched the bridge of his nose, the promise of Marianne decreasing as the troubles of the last half-hour increased. There was nothing stopping Rupert from telling anyone his suspicions about Warren and Marianne, and Warren wouldn't put it past the weasel to say something simply out of spite. Despite the risk, Warren wouldn't pay Rupert to keep silent or allow his brother-in-law to influence him ever again. He'd find another way to protect Marianne and uphold his promise to not allow their arrangement to result in a scandal. If it did, she would need him and he would stand by her, not because he was the cause of it but because he cared for her. She had fast become more than his muse.

Marianne crept closer to the downstairs sitting room, not wanting to announce her presence to Lady Ellington and Lord Falconbridge. They must not have heard the carriage return from Priorton Abbey, but she'd seen his horse in the stable and knew he was here. Marianne leaned against the wall beside the open door to listen, the composition book clutched in her hand. She hadn't done this since she'd lived with Madame de

Badeau. Back then, she used to listen at keyholes all the time. She couldn't help it this afternoon.

'I have my reservations about this arrangement.' Lord Falconbridge's deep voice carried out from the room. 'You remember how it was with you and Uncle Edgar and how he almost dragged you down with his appalling behaviour.'

'Edgar also taught me to live my life as I please and not to allow others' opinions to influence me. I want Marianne to learn the same lesson,' Lady Ellington insisted.

'And you think Sir Warren is the one to teach it to her?'

'Yes. He's a single gentleman of good reputation and means with an interest in her. Granted, he's come up with a very complicated way of going about things, but there's a man for you,' came Lady Ellington's cheerful if not practical response. 'Look at how difficult you made things with Cecelia.'

The rumble of Lord Falconbridge's laugh filled the hallway before he sobered. 'But this arrangement could do her more harm than good. Miss Domville doesn't have our stamina for weathering storms.'

'If you hadn't created so many tempests in your youth, neither would you.' The clink of the crystal stopper in Lady Ellington's plum wine decanter drifted out of the room.

'What if you're wrong about him and he doesn't pursue her?' Lord Falconbridge pressed.

Marianne clutched the composition book against her chest, the worry she'd carried home from Priorton intensifying. Lord Falconbridge's fears weren't unfounded. Warren had said he wasn't interested in marriage and she'd still flung herself at him moments before his snake of a brother-in-law had walked in. If he hadn't called out and alerted them, who knew what he might have seen.

'I'm not wrong,' Lady Ellington insisted.

'For Miss Domville's sake, and her future here in the country, I hope so.'

Panic made it impossible for Marianne to stand here without revealing herself. She hurried away, tiptoeing up the main staircase, past Lady Ellington's impressive collection of Italian landscapes covering the stairway wall.

Once inside her room, she closed and locked the door, then slumped into the chair in front of the writing table. Yet another letter from Theresa waited for her on the blotter. She covered it with her composition book, not possessing the fortitude to open the missive and read about her friend's happiness, not when her present situation was so precarious. Beneath them lay the journal with *Lady Matilda's Trials*, another glaring example of the mistakes she was making with Warren.

She rose to pace across the room. Her lack of discretion and judgement with him was putting her place with the Falconbridges in jeopardy and there was more than her reputation at stake. For all Lord Falconbridge's and Lady Ellington's support, it had only ever been against invented and imagined scandals. Whether they'd continue to stand with her in the face of a real one of her own making, she wasn't sure. She'd been acquainted with Lord Falconbridge through her mother in the days before he'd married Cecilia. Back then, he'd been hailed as one of the most formidable rakes in London. He'd abandoned his old life and reputation when he'd married the Marchioness. He wouldn't appreciate it being revived because of Marianne's wanton behaviour, especially with his children to consider. If Marianne crossed the line of decency, he might insist the family abandon her, just like Mr Smith had.

I should have been more careful with Warren. I never should have kissed him.

She'd resisted the lechers without money and the lechers with it to rise above the filth Madame de Badeau had tried to mire her in. The kiss proved she couldn't resist Warren or his continued eroding of the distance she needed to maintain between them. Except she didn't want to stay away.

She slipped *Lady Matilda's Trials* out from beneath the letter and composition book and flipped through the pages, admiring Warren's fine handwriting filling every line. Marianne traced the large M in Lady Matilda's name, the memory of Warren's light hair curling over his proud forehead, his striking green eyes and the firmness of his body against hers stirring something inside. Their kiss today hadn't been about lust or loss of control, but compassion. She'd offered him a glimpse of her soul and instead of turning away he'd embraced her. If she pushed him out of her life, she might never discover where her heart and his might lead them, assuming he did want to pursue her. Lord

Falconbridge was right. Warren might not crave anything more from her than a dalliance. She didn't want to be punished for wanting love or affection, but she feared losing Lady Ellington over something as thin as possibility. She hoped Warren didn't make her regret being so free with him today.

She flicked the book shut. What had hope ever garnered her except more heartache? At the Protestant School, she'd hoped every Christmas for a real family, and then her real mother had snatched her away. In London, she'd hoped to return to the Smiths, but they hadn't wanted her. She pulled opened the desk drawer and shoved the journal inside then slapped it shut. Her agreement with Warren was over. She wouldn't return to Priorton Abbey or perform her compositions for anyone outside this house. She wouldn't risk losing the safety of Lady Ellington's care for the uncertainty of Warren's promises. No matter what came of today, her behaviour from this moment forward must be beyond reproach. It was the safest course, and the most disheartening.

'Lord Cartwright, thank you for meeting with me on such short notice about the business.' Rupert all but grovelled beside the Baron, who accepted a loaded gun from his footman.

'Yes, yes, of course,' the haughty man mumbled as he raised his gun and let off a shot, bringing down a pheasant. His dog took off in search of the carcase. 'I understand from my man in London Sir Warren is backing this venture of yours?'

'He believes in it so much, he's—'

'Wait a moment.' Lord Cartwright raised his gun and let off an ear-piercing shot at another pheasant flying up out of the grass. He missed. 'Damn it, Alton, something is wrong with this gun.'

'Yes, sir.' The footman exchanged the empty gun for another and laid the offending piece aside.

'What were you saying about Sir Warren?' Lord Cartwright lowered his barrel to the ground, keeping an eye on the grey sky as he listened to Rupert.

'Sir Warren has placed Priorton Abbey up for collateral against any debts the company incurs. Even if things go wrong, you can't lose your investment.' Warren might not know it, but he'd help Rupert one way or another. 'If a man like him has faith in me, surely you can. He also has the backing of the Marquess of Falconbridge through his connection with Miss Domville.'

'What's he doing associating with her?' Lord Cartwright raised his gun and fired. This time he hit his mark and another dog went running into the field.

'Sir Warren and Miss Domville are quite *intimately* acquainted.' Rupert took Lord Cartwright's empty gun and handed it to the footman before taking the loaded one and offering it to the Baron. How he hated these grand men and all their privileges. Warren thought he was one of them and better than Rupert. Rupert would show him and make him pay for insisting he beg before him like one of the serfs in his novels.

'Really?' Lord Cartwright appeared more interested

in the gossip than all Rupert's talk of investments and collateral.

'I expect the Marquess to invest heavily in the business because of it. You could make a great deal of money, enough to finance your daughter's second Season.' Rupert had heard the rumours of Lord Cartwright's mounting gambling debts and his displeasure at his daughter's failure to make a lucrative match last Season.

Lord Cartwright rubbed his thumb over the shiny brass work on his gun, allowing a few pheasants scared up by the beaters to fly away as he considered Rupert's suggestion. 'You're sure it's secure?'

Rupert tried not to scream in frustration. What did this man care if it was secure or not? With his lands and money he could stand to part with a few pounds. Even if he couldn't, with his heritage he'd be shielded from his debts in a way Rupert hadn't been when his last venture had collapsed. Even then Warren had lectured him like a child about the need for responsibility. Rupert would teach him a lesson about where his responsibilities really lay. 'Sir Warren's name and fame is a guarantee against loss.'

'All right,' Lord Cartwright said at last, handing the gun to the footman. 'I'll write to my man to deposit double the amount we discussed in your account.'

'You're too gracious, my lord.' Rupert kept the smile on his face, despite his disgust. This man had nothing but assets and lands and Rupert was forced to cajole and wheedle to get a few pounds out of him. The man should give it willingly and more, he owed it to people like Rupert, just like Warren did. Rupert would see to it they both felt the sting of being selfish, especially Warren who'd regret treating Rupert with so much disdain.

Chapter Eight

Marianne sat at the pianoforte at Welton Place, trying to reclaim the flow of the music, to allow it to carry her away like it usually did, but she couldn't. It had been a full day since Warren's brother-in-law had stumbled in on her and Warren at the Érard. Every time she passed a clutch of whispering maids, she wondered if they were talking about her. She was sure any moment now the rumours about her and Warren would begin, followed by Lord Falconbridge demanding an explanation.

She glanced at the garden where Walker was raking leaves, considering a walk, anything to settle the nervousness making her tap her foot against the floor. Potential gossip wasn't the only thing making her want to stride out of the French doors. She'd sent a note to Warren first thing this morning to tell him she wouldn't come today. She hadn't gone as far as to end their arrangement, nor had she offered a reason for her absence. After yesterday, she hardly thought one was necessary.

She'd heard nothing from Warren in response. He hadn't sent her a note, come to call or, at the very least, sent his mother for tea. Maybe he'd at last decided she was more of a detriment to him than an asset and it was best to distance himself from her. After all, he had a reputation to protect too. Her chest constricted at the thought, making her fingers clumsy on the keys when she attempted to play again. He was going to turn his back on her like everyone else. She'd been a fool to grow close to him, to reveal so much and to believe it would make a difference.

'Are you still here, my dear?' Lady Ellington strolled through the room on her way out to the garden to oversee the pruning of her roses. 'Isn't Sir Warren expecting you?'

'I don't feel like going to Priorton today.'

'Did something happen when you were last there?' Lady Ellington perched her elbow on the edge of the pianoforte.

'No.' She couldn't tell Lady Ellington about the kiss, not because the woman would dance with glee, but because she feared a completely different reaction.

'Marianne?' Lady Ellington pressed, increasing Marianne's guilt over her lack of faith in her friend. Lady Ellington had always believed in her, she shouldn't doubt her faith now.

Marianne stopped playing and picked at a small imperfection in one of the white keys 'Yes, something did happen.'

Lady Ellington stood over Marianne and listened as she told her about the brother-in-law and his coming in on them alone together and insulting her. Marianne omitted the kiss, but given the scrutinising tilt of Lady Ellington's head, it was clear she suspected something more than the two of them performing a duet. If she minded or was disappointed in Marianne for having been so weak with Warren, it was difficult to discern.

'He stood up for you against a man related to him by marriage. It says a great deal about Sir Warren's regard for you,' Lady Ellington observed.

Marianne had a better inkling of his regard for her than Lady Ellington realised, but she didn't dare say so. 'He was being polite and if Mr Hirst is still there, I don't want to place Wa— I mean Sir Warren in another difficult situation.'

Lady Ellington worked to hide her smile at Marianne's near slip. 'Sir Warren is a grown man and more than capable of deciding which situations he wants to be in and which he does not.'

'If he wanted me to come back, I'm sure he would have said something by now, but he hasn't.' Nor had she ventured from Welton Place. She wouldn't run after Warren, but deport herself with dignity.

Darby, Lady Ellington's stone-faced butler, appeared in the doorway. 'Sir Warren to see Miss Domville.'

Marianne's eyes snapped to Lady Ellington's. He was here. He'd come to see her.

Lady Ellington clapped her hands together in delight. 'One day without you and he's already sprinting over here to visit you.'

'It took him quite a few hours to sprint,' Marianne

grumbled, wishing she'd gone for a walk in the garden. It would take crossing all of the Falconbridge lands to calm her now since she couldn't very well pace a hole in the floorboards.

'You'll learn, my dear, it takes men a little longer to come around to things. Darby, show Sir Warren in at once.'

The butler left before Marianne could stop him.

'What if he isn't here to see me, but to end things?' This was what she'd wanted when she'd drafted the letter ending the agreement, the one sitting unsealed on her writing table in her room. She should have sent it and made things clear before he could come over here and clarify them for her. It would hurt less if she was to break with him instead of him breaking with her.

'If he wanted to end things he'd send a note, not come here in person.'

She hoped Lady Ellington was right. She didn't want to endure another rejection like the one the Smiths had sent her four years ago.

Marianne dropped her hands in her lap and twisted around to face the sitting-room door. She attempted to affect her usual air of indifference, but it wasn't easy. Whatever he said, she would disregard it as she did Lady Cartwright's snide remarks. She could cry over it later.

No, I won't cry.

Warren entered the room and Marianne willed the creeping smile from her lips. He wore a dark blue coat as wrinkled as his untidy cravat. His hair was combed smooth over the back of his head, but the ends possessed a wildness which matched his attire. A generous smile lightened the dark circles beneath his eyes and increased the faint flutter in her stomach. No one smiled so wide before they ended an affair as she'd seen more than once at Madame de Badeau's.

He bowed to them, clutching a notebook and writing case in his left hand. 'Good morning, Lady Ellington, Miss Domville. I'm very sorry Miss Domville was unable to come to Priorton today. I hope it isn't too presumptuous of me to ask if I may work here instead.'

He wants to be with me, to keep our arrangement.

It thrilled her as much as when new sheet music arrived from London. Dread quickly squashed it. She still had no idea what was happening with Mr Hirst and what, if anything, had come of his visit. She wanted to ask Warren about it, but with Lady Ellington present she couldn't. Whatever had taken place between them after she'd left it must not have been too awful if he was here.

'What a lovely idea,' Lady Ellington answered while Marianne remained too lost in her thoughts to speak. The Dowager guided him to the escritoire to the left of the pianoforte. It sat against the window so anyone working there could see the garden with their back to the instrument. 'I've missed having music in the house these last few days. Are you sure you can work here?'

He leaned one hand on the rounded chair back, his other hand perched on his hip and drawing his coat back to reveal his solid middle. The sensation of his body against hers, his wide hand on her neck,

his flat chest firm against hers made her skin flush at
the memory.

'I used to write aboard ship, in the middle of storms.
A foreign desk and some lovely playing won't distract
me.' His eyes met Marianne's. She kept her outward
stature as impassive as possible while inside she was
running in circles. He hadn't left her, but had sought
her out as though she were more important than rumours or brothers-in-law or anything else. However,
it had taken him a day to do so. Had he wavered during their time apart or considered not coming here? If
he held any doubts they were not in his soft eyes or
the sureness of his stance. 'I won't disturb you, will I?'

'Of course not.' She flicked through the pages of
her composition book, searching for something to play
as if he were not here. For all her excitement at his
arrival, the old caution refused to release its hold on
her. She'd been careless with him yesterday and she
wouldn't allow it to happen again.

The shift of his shoulders while he arranged his
things on the desk undermined her determination. She
studied the width of his back, noting how the wool
wrinkled and flattened with each movement, sliding
up over the curve of his buttocks as he leaned forward
to set out his ink. She gripped the book tight, wrinkling a whole note near the edge of one page. She
wanted to wrap her arms around his waist, lay her
head on his shoulder and breathe him in like the mist
in the morning.

Don't be silly.

She smoothed the wrinkled edge of her music and

set the book on the stand. Her mother had thrown herself at any man with a title and money. Marianne had never behaved so basely. Her experience with Warren was an exception, not a habit, and she wouldn't allow it to continue. She'd find out more about Mr Hirst later, then make it clear to Warren their behaviour from the other day was not to be repeated. He wanted a muse and she'd be one. He could find more physical inspiration elsewhere.

As Marianne played, Lady Ellington waved her fingers in time to the music, her smile so wide one would think she'd arranged this. She probably had. Marianne should be annoyed by her friend's meddling, but she wasn't. At least the Dowager was more conscientious in her chaperon duties than Mrs Stevens.

Marianne paused to scratch a few notes in the composition book when Lady Ellington interrupted. 'If you'll excuse me, Walker is waiting for me in the garden.'

And there went the chaperon. Marianne frowned as the breeze fluttered the hem of Lady Ellington's grey pelisse as she hurried out of the French doors to where Walker waited with his pruning shears to trim the roses.

Warren turned in his chair, about to speak, but Marianne resumed her playing, not wanting to talk. It had already landed them both in too much trouble. He didn't interrupt her as he returned to his writing.

Under the influence of her music, she began to relax and enjoy his presence. In their separate spaces, they worked in tandem as if they'd done this for years. The clink of his pen against the ink jar punctuated her notes every now and again. It didn't disturb her pace, but at times enhanced it like a harmony from an accompanying flute. It settled the tension from his presence and the other day's debacle.

The melancholy tune which had teased her last night, the one she'd been reluctant to sit down and write this morning, faded into the background as a new one came forward. It startled Marianne with its effervescence and she followed its lead, playing with a vigour she hadn't experienced since the last time she'd performed for Mrs Nichols. It wasn't the piece but Warren's presence creating the change. She didn't fight it and slid into the music, not like a cave to hide in, but as if it was a pool of cool water on a hot day.

A long time passed before Lady Ellington returned. Pollen from the last of the summer roses clung to her dark skirt as she carried them to the vase on top of the pianoforte. While she arranged the flowers, she looked back and forth between the two young people and smiled with a self-satisfaction Marianne didn't mind. When Marianne reached the end of the piece, Lady Ellington clapped.

'It's too lovely a day for you both to be inside for so long. Marianne, why don't you show Sir Warren the garden?' Lady Ellington suggested to Marianne's amazement.

The peace Marianne had enjoyed while playing ended. Why didn't Lady Ellington draw the curtains and lock them in the room together? It would be more effective.

'Yes, I need some exercise.' Warren stretched over the back of the chair, the arch of his body more appealing than the buds in the vase.

We shouldn't be alone together...we can't be trusted.

She couldn't beg Lady Ellington to stay with them like a child afraid of the dark. Warren had been brave to come here unannounced. She could summon enough courage and self-control to walk with him in the garden, in broad daylight and in plain sight of the house. It wasn't as if she were dragging him to the orangery, as tempting an idea as it might be. No, it wasn't tempting but ridiculous and it was time to compose herself like a proper lady and not some hoyden. 'All right, then.'

She rose from the piano bench and led him outside. Lady Ellington's excuse for not coming followed after them. A stiff wind whipped through the garden, blowing dead leaves off of the fading summer vines and revealing more of the provocative statuary. Marianne regretted bringing him here to walk. She should have taken him to the front of the house. Perhaps he wouldn't notice the statues.

'Lady Ellington has some very unique garden decorations,' Warren remarked as they passed a well-endowed satyr.

'The house used to belong to her brother, the prior Marquess of Falconbridge. These were his statues. For some reason, she's never got rid of them.'

'Maybe they remind her of him.' With a smile, he nodded to the naked Zeus entwined with a nymph.

'Given some of the stories she's told me about him, they probably do.' Marianne had never minded the garden decor before. Today, all the naked marble bodies in a variety of suggestive poses made the unspoken between her and Warren even louder. She still didn't know what to think of the kiss, or him. He hadn't groped her like other men, but it had still been secretive, with no promise of anything else except possible rumours. She kicked a small pebble with her boot. It didn't matter. There was no future with him or any respectable man and no reason for her to think of one.

'Your playing has had quite an effect on my story today. I couldn't write my war scene so I finished the feasting one instead. Sometimes critics accuse my novels of being too dark. I don't think they'll say the same about this one.' He laughed with an agility Marianne admired. 'I hope you don't mind the intrusion, but I needed to see you.'

'For me or my inspiration?' She stopped and faced him, needing the truth.

'Both.' He studied her, his green eyes intense like a field of fresh grass in the spring. 'I cut off my dealings with Rupert because of what he said to you.'

'You think there's more to be gained by associating with a woman like me than a man like him?' It didn't seem possible.

'Yes.' His honesty shook her expectations. Few people had ever been worried about losing her. Here was one who wouldn't let her run away. It scared her more than any rumour or scandal she'd ever faced and fuelled the hope which had been building inside her since their kiss. If they weren't standing in the centre of the garden, she might slide her hands over his broad shoulders and pull him down to her. She raised her hands anyway, resisting the inclination to cow before her worries and doubts. This morning, she'd thought he'd never want to see her again and here he was in front of her as though she were as important to him as the Prince.

He shifted closer to her as her hands settled on his shoulders, his body hard beneath her palms. He stared into her eyes with mesmerising intensity which drew them closer. She began to slide up on her toes as his arms encircled her, aching to taste him again, to restore the connection between them which had been broken the other day.

Then the squeak of a wheel sounded over the birds. She jumped back from Warren just as Walker came around the corner rolling a wheelbarrow full of dirt. He waved to them. Warren waved back without hesitation. Marianne wasn't as exuberant with her greeting.

'We always seem to attract an audience,' he joked, but she didn't laugh.

If they kept up these near misses it wouldn't be long before his decision to stand beside her was tested. She expected him to fail, almost everyone else had. It was time for them to exhibit more decorum, especially in Lady Ellington's garden. 'Walker isn't a gossip. Is Mr Hirst?'

He fiddled with the loose knot of his cravat, the gesture more telling than his words. 'I made it clear his ruining your reputation would ruin his. Besides, he saw nothing.'

'It doesn't matter. He guessed enough and it's all he or anyone needs to condemn me, and you too. You could lose patrons and people's support.' She didn't mention what she might lose. She didn't want to think about it.

'I sold books and earned money before people like the Cartwrights or even the Prince found me. I can do it again. I don't care what they think of me or what they might say.'

'Some day you will, just like the Smiths, and then I won't be as tempting to you.' She started for the house.

He caught her hand. 'You think you aren't worthy to be cared for, made to feel important and valuable, but you're wrong.'

She tried to pull away, but he wouldn't let go, his hand firm around hers. 'Experience has taught me different.'

'I'm not like them.' He drew her slowly back to him. She put up the weakest of resistance, moving step by step closer to him. She didn't want to fight him as she did the rest of the world, but believe in his affection. It was foolish, ridiculous, but her lonely heart didn't care. She wanted to lose herself in his desire for her. They stood so close her breasts brushed his chest with each of her deep breaths. He continued to hold her hand while his other smoothed the wisps of hair from her temples. 'You're a wonderful person and others are shallow and blind if they can't see it.'

He tilted his face down and she lifted her chin. His

kiss jolted her like a carriage thrown off balance in a turn. She clutched his arms to steady herself, not against him, but from the old habit of retreating. Even if she'd wanted to run away from him, his light hand against the small of her back wouldn't allow it. She folded her body into his, lost in his heady heat. She reached her fingers up to touch the hair brushing his collar, the strands as soft beneath her fingertips as his mouth. He'd come here because he didn't want to be without her. In her answering kiss she reassured him she wouldn't bolt, but would stumble with him through whatever was burgeoning between them.

'Sir Warren.' Darby's voice cut through her joy.

As fast as Warren's kiss had united them, the butler's appearance sent them flying apart. Marianne wanted to scream in frustration. She and Warren should consider sending invitations to their next meeting. It would be more convenient for all involved.

'A message has come for you from Priorton Abbey,' Darby announced. 'You're needed at your publisher's in London right away.'

Darby's message delivered, he left the couple. Marianne wanted to stomp her foot at his pretend deference. He wasn't as tight-lipped as Walker and was probably whispering what he'd seen to Lady Ellington already. The Dowager Countess would clap her ring-covered hands in glee. The picture of it settled her anger for it was exactly what she hoped her friend would do. She could now tell Lord Falconbridge there was more to Marianne and Warren's arrangement than impetuous desire or skirting scandal. What exactly it was Marianne refused to say. She was too afraid to give voice to such a thing and kill it like a seedling planted before the threat of frost had passed.

'I have to go. If Mr Berkshire has sent for me, it must be important,' he explained with notable regret.

'When will you return?' She didn't want him to leave. It was the rare person who returned to her.

'I don't know, it depends on what Mr Berkshire wants, but I'll make sure to be back in time for Lady Astley's musical evening. You will be there, won't you?'

'Yes.'

'Then I look forward to it.' He claimed her lips with a swift kiss, catching her off guard. She grasped his firm upper arms, not wanting to let go, his kiss more honest than any words. He broke from her and she wavered on her feet, unable to say anything before he touched her cheek longingly with his fingers, then turned and made for the house.

Snatches of his parting conversation with Lady Ellington carried out of the open sitting-room windows before it faded way.

Smoothing her hair and adjusting the wrinkled fichu over her chest, she returned to the house, trying not to skip back. He'd kissed her, again, and told her she was more precious to him than his brother-in-law. It hadn't happened in a darkened room, or while he was drunk, but in the open for everyone to see, eliminating doubts about his intentions, especially hers. If Darby hadn't interrupted them, who knew what other declarations he might have made.

Her cheeks burned as she caught sight of Lady Ellington waiting for her, a self-satisfied smile adorning her lips. It seems Darby had been quick to report
to his mistress.

'Too bad Sir Warren was forced to leave so soon,'
Lady Ellington lamented as Marianne stepped inside.
'It was quite nice of him to come to see you today.'

'It was.' Marianne leaned against the door jamb and
stared at the desk where his papers had sat a short
time ago. The surface was empty again, with no sign
he'd been here, but she knew, the whole house did.
He wanted her and she wanted him. She touched her
swollen lips, his kiss still lingering there and with it the
promise of what could happen when they met again. A
passion for anything beside the pianoforte was dangerous, but it didn't mean she couldn't wield a little of its
power. Perhaps it was time to play up her less musical
assets. 'I've been thinking, maybe a new gown for the
musical evening would be a good idea. Perhaps a blue
one like you mentioned the other day?'

'You mean something like this?' Lady Ellington
slid a ladies' magazine off of the table beside her and
flipped it open. She held it out to Marianne, struggling
as much as her young friend to refrain from showing
too much enthusiasm. 'It would be stunning on you.'

Marianne leaned forward, her eyebrows rising at
the cut of the neckline, not sure even the stiffest brocade could contain her. Tongues would wag if she
wore something so daring, but never in her life had she
wanted a man's consideration as she did Warren's and
she would have it. A new dress, and the fondness cre-

ated by his absence, would all but guarantee it. 'How fast do you think Madame Martine can sew the dress?'

Lady Ellington flipped closed the magazine and set it aside with a triumphant smile. 'As I've already sent her instructions to do it up based on your last measurements, I'd say very soon.'

'What was so important you had to summon me from Sussex?' Warren demanded as he strode into Mr Berkshire's London office, his legs complaining from the three-hour ride. Whatever it was, it had got his notice and was the only thing short of a fire at Priorton which could have separated him from Marianne and her glorious figure against his.

Mr Berkshire pushed himself up out of the leather chair behind his massive oak desk. He wasn't fat, but solidly built like a dockworker. Despite his size, he possessed the authority and self-assuredness of the aristocrats he flattered to secure their patronage for his authors. He also specialised in anonymous memoirs of wronged society mistresses. He had yet to betray a pen name while marketing salacious stories the public ate up. He held out a copy of the *Morning Post* to Warren. 'Read this.'

Warren took the newspaper and read the headline proclaiming the latest debate in Parliament for the Pains and Penalties Bill against Queen Charlotte. What the devil was he supposed to be reading? 'I assume you didn't bring me to London to discuss the proceedings against the Queen.'

Mr Berkshire pointed a stubby finger at the paper. 'Look at the piece about halfway down.'

Warren found the small article near the bottom, under one lamenting the rising price of wheat. Calling it an article was being generous. It was the latest tattle about a duke and his mistress. The next line made Warren start to sweat.

> *The famous novelist Sir W—has been enjoying the delights of the country and Lady P—n's vast estates. Even the dowager Countess of M's companion, a young lady of dubious background, whose notorious relation caused quite the scandal four years ago, has been snared by the Lothario's literary ways.*

The moisture on his fingers smudged the ink and blurred the last few words. The *Morning Post* was a cut-rate rag with more gossip than news, but the salacious stories it published were as popular in London as they were in Sussex. It would only be a matter of time before this one found its way to the country, and Marianne and everyone else's attention.

'What have you been getting up to at Priorton?' Mr Berkshire asked as he took his seat.

'Nothing with Lady Preston.' Warren flung the paper down on the desk.

Mr Berkshire's bushy eyebrows rose. 'Then the rest is true?'

'It's not a dalliance.' It was a great deal more. With the memory of Marianne in his arms, new stories had begun to fill his mind during the hours he'd spent on the road. It had made the endless countryside pass without notice until the smoke of London had appeared in the distance, just like the craving to be near her had carried him from Priorton this morning. When he'd received her note crying off, he'd refused to let it stand or to allow the incident with Rupert to fester and undo all the progress they'd made. He'd gone to Welton Place, expecting to be turned away, not welcomed by both Lady Ellington and especially Marianne. Writing beside her, he'd felt the excitement and potential which used to fill him with each new story return. It had hurt him to leave her and the pleasure of her kiss, but for the first time in too long he felt like the old Warren, the one who could create not only tales, but every aspect of his own life.

'Whatever it is, it's not time spent writing. It's been a year since you've given me anything new,' Mr Berkshire reminded him, illustrating how much further Warren still had to go until he was his old self.

'The repairs to Priorton have interrupted me, but I assure you, you'll have something within the month.' If Mr Berkshire doubted Warren's ability to produce, his biggest ally might find himself another author to support.

Mr Berkshire thumped the top of his desk. 'I warned you not to buy the thing. Being lord of the manor is distracting you from your real purpose. Stay here in London and work in the peace of your town house.'

'No, I need the quiet of the country and Miss Domville. She's helping me, the way Leticia used to. The rest will soon be resolved.'

Mr Berkshire leaned forward on his burly arms and spoke with more caution than he usually displayed with Warren. 'If financial issues are hindering your writing, I can always help.'

Warren shook his head. 'I've never taken money from you that I haven't earned, I won't do it now.'

'But you will earn it.' Mr Berkshire threw up his hands, unable to comprehend Warren's reluctance. Sometimes Warren didn't either, but it was who he was and he wasn't going to allow difficulty to make him change. He would fight through his troubles like he always had.

'When I do, you will pay it to me and not before.'

'Then hurry up with things. You know how fickle the public is. Wait too long and they'll forget you.'

'Not with pieces like this running in the paper.'

'Mr Steed is already taking the necessary steps to make sure the publisher of this fish wrap is silenced by the threat of a libel suit.' Mr Steed was one of the best solicitors in London. To be involved with him in a hearing was to have it in all the papers and to lose, expensively. 'Who do you think sold them the story?'

'It could have been Rupert.' He explained about their falling out. 'He's never shown this much initiative, but he has the most reason to hurt me and he needs the money.'

'Then you'd better make it clear to him that if he sells any more stories like this he'll have Mr Steed to deal with.'

'I'll see what I can do before I return to Sussex.' Warren didn't pity his brother-in-law. Rupert deserved every punishment he received.

'I think I'll come with you to the country. Get in a little hunting and see for myself what's going on there and soothe things over with Lord Preston. Can't have him turning his back on you. He's influential, it'll encourage others.' Mr Berkshire shifted back in his chair and hooked his thumbs in his waistcoat pocket.

'I don't need a chaperon,' Warren retorted. There'd be enough for him to deal with when he returned without Mr Berkshire hovering over him. Including finishing the book and explaining to Marianne why she was now in the gossip column. He'd promised her no scandal. For the second time in a week he'd failed to keep his promise. If he wanted her in his life, he'd have to win her before she found out about this. It was time to prove his faith in her and them, not because of his work, but because of his heart. He'd lost it to her and in doing so he'd regained something of the man he'd been before the tragedy of Leticia's death. His confidence in himself and his stories had returned with her tenderness and understanding. He wouldn't lose it or her.

Chapter Nine

Marianne entered Lady Astley's ballroom with a nauseating mixture of apprehension and anticipation. Everyone turned to view her, their eyes never rising above the low-cut neckline of her shimmering blue-silk gown. There was nothing vulgar about the dress, not the sleeves covering her upper arms, the length of the skirt or the silver trim beneath the bust and along the hem. However, it was far more revealing than what they'd come to expect from her. If they couldn't see her heart beating against her chest, she'd be stunned. She'd never once showed these people her fear of them. Tonight she wanted to grab Lady Ellington by her massive diamond bracelet and race back to the carriage.

As if sensing Marianne's apprehension, Lady Ellington twined her arm in the younger woman's and drew her deeper into the room. It wasn't just for Marianne's benefit she did this, but for everyone who looked to her and the Falconbridge family to set the tone. Marianne was grateful for the solidarity, but it wasn't enough to stop the women from whispering behind fans or to put an end to the men's lurid looks. These people wouldn't snub her with Lady Ellington present. They'd find more snide and cutting ways to make their disapproval clear, to try and chip away at her like an artist she'd once seen in Paris sculpting a block of granite. She wouldn't let them, not with Warren beside her, encouraging her as he always did, assuming he was here.

She looked over the guests, trying to ignore their silent insults and sneers as she searched among the men for him. It had been three days since he'd left her at Welton Place. She worried he hadn't returned in time for tonight. Then her bravery would be wasted, especially if he'd forgotten her in the rush of London and his work.

I shouldn't be so quick to doubt him.

He had yet to let her down.

At last she spied him. He stood near a gilded table with a stocky gentleman she didn't recognise. As if sensing her, he turned and his jaw dropped open. Instead of wanting to cover herself, she stood up straighter, pressing her shoulders back to give him a better view of her in the dress. He stroked her with his gaze, not just her ample chest, but her entire body. A potent thrill raced along her skin and the tips of her breasts hardened beneath her stays. This wasn't the first time she'd turned a man's head, but it was the first time she'd experienced the power of being alluring and understood why it had so obsessed Madame de Badeau. If they weren't in the middle of the classically decorated sitting room, she'd rush to close the distance between them.

Instead she stood as she always did at these gatherings, as if nothing anyone said or did could pierce her steadfast surety. Even if she was crumbling inside, they'd never know, nor would she reveal the excitement she experienced at Warren's quick stride as he made his way to her. Her heart beat so fast she could feel it in every gloved fingertip.

Warren bowed to Marianne, his pulse fluttering as fast as hers above his at last properly tied cravat. The darkness of his coat across his shoulders contrasted with the green waistcoat beneath his jacket which echoed the tone of his eyes. He wore his light hair swept back off of his forehead. It had been trimmed while he'd been in town so it no longer touched the edge of his white collar.

'Did you have a good trip to London?' Lady Ellington asked while Marianne struggled to reclaim her voice. It had been startled out of her by Warren's heated regard.

The question stiffened the corners of his smile and trouble clouded his eyes before it vanished. Marianne wondered what had happened in London. Perhaps something with his book? Whatever it was, it bothered him despite his effort to hide it.

'Very productive. In fact, I brought my publisher back with me. Allow me to introduce him.' He waved over the stocky man by the fireplace. 'Miss Domville, This is Mr William Berkshire. Mr Berkshire, this is the accomplished pianist I told you about.'

'Ah, I see.' He nodded appreciatively at Warren, who offered him a terse frown, alluding to something the two of them alone understood. She wondered what Warren had said to his publisher about her. It couldn't be the more salacious tales the bucks who visited Madame de Badeau's used to exchange. Warren wasn't so crude. It was something more disturbing, one she sensed had nothing to do with books. Perhaps Mr Berkshire had doubts about her ability to play or had balked at publishing her compositions. It could easily cause tension between the two men. 'Warren told me about your gift for music and your interest in publishing your compositions. Will you be playing tonight?'

'No, I'm not. There are very few people beside Sir Warren who are aware of my playing, or my compositions.'

'Well, if Sir Warren is as talented a judge of music as he is a writer, there'll be many who learn of your music once we're done with you.'

She smiled graciously at him and his unexpected compliment. At least he wasn't resisting Warren's efforts on Marianne's behalf. It fuelled the hope she'd nurtured since Warren had first made his offer and edged out her previous worries. Maybe she could at last create a new life and reputation for herself, one free of all the people eyeing them with disapproval while she commanded the famous author's attention.

'Mr Berkshire, no business tonight. Instead, you must tell me all the gossip from town,' Lady Ellington chided with her usual grace.

'Ah, well, there isn't much to tell,' Mr Berkshire

blustered and again there was the knowing exchange between the publisher and Warren. It didn't last as Lady Ellington pulled Mr Berkshire far enough away from Marianne and Warren to give them privacy, but remained close enough so no one could accuse her of abandoning her charge.

'Did all go well in London?' she asked, eager to learn what was going on.

'Yes. There was some difficulty with a newspaper, but nothing Mr Berkshire's solicitor won't see to,' he murmured before fixing her with an admiration to make her toes curl. At home, she'd fretted over wearing the gown and at the last minute had considered changing it. She was glad she hadn't. The heat in his eyes was worth every disparaging look from the other women. He, not them, was the only one who mattered. 'You're stunning.'

Experience warned her to pry and discover what he was hiding behind his charm, but she didn't want to break the spell of his adoration. 'Careful, if you flatter me too much it will go to my head and I'll think myself too important to play for you.'

'You could never be so arrogant. You're too kind and enchanting.' He shifted a touch closer and dropped his voice. 'I missed you while I was in London. Writing wasn't the same without you.'

His breath caressed the tops of her breasts, stoking the fire building deep inside her at the nearness of him. His breathing matched hers and she was sure his pulse did too, both of their hearts beating together like two perfectly timed duet players. If they could be alone, they might move with one another like dancers, his solid body against hers, leading her through every movement of this growing affection and intimacy, one as intoxicating as it was new to her.

'I've missed you too.' The admission felt as revealing as her gown, but she didn't want to hold back from him. The last two nights, she'd nearly licked her lips raw with the reliving of their last kiss. She cursed the rules of propriety stopping her from falling into his arms now and experiencing again the thrill of his mouth against hers.

The butler struck a small gong from the front of the room, silencing everyone. 'It's time to take your seats for the performance.'

The room drained as the guests entered the ballroom where the pianoforte had been moved to the centre at the far end. Chairs gathered from all over the house stood in neat rows and ladies and gentleman filed in to fill them up. An attractive but little-known singer from Austria was to perform tonight, accompanied by a young male pianist. The entertainment wouldn't pass muster in London, but it was perfect to while away a dull autumn evening in the country.

'Shall we?' Warren offered her his elbow.

She laid her hand on his arm and accompanied him into the room, excited to at last be able touch him in the only way allowed. As they fell behind the crowd, she considered slipping off with him to somewhere where they could be alone. She didn't want to share him, not even with the singer. It was tempting, but she wasn't so daring. She couldn't openly defy convention, not even for Warren.

He guided them to the chairs in the back row. She didn't condemn his choice. By sitting behind everyone they'd be as alone as possible in the gathering. No one could turn their heads and frown at her, or watch them and speculate. It would drive them mad, except it wasn't them she wanted to tease, but Warren. She pushed back her shoulders, raising her breasts in the magnificent gown. The corner of her lips curled into a smile when she caught Warren admiring them. Desire wasn't just trouble, but a heady power and for the first time ever, she flirted with the allure of it. With Warren, she felt safe unveiling it.

He took her hand to help her sit and it was his turn to tease her. The pressure of his fingertips through the satin of her gloves reached inside her as did his nearness. She didn't want to let go of him or look away from the passionate smile gracing his fine lips. She wanted to tilt her face to his and feel his mouth on hers again, but with everyone around them shuffling into the rows, she was forced to let go and take her seat.

Lady Ellington and Mr Berkshire settled in on his other side as the singer and her pianist took their places. Most of the audience was here for something to do in the country as opposed to hearing the music, but they were polite and welcoming as the woman began her first song.

Marianne struggled to listen, more aware of Warren's steady breathing than the singer's arias. He was as tempting as the last sweet in a box and it took all her effort to avoid laying her hand on his thigh, pressing her fingers into the firmness of it and resting her head on his shoulder. She'd never wanted to be close to someone, to touch them and be touched by them the way she did with Warren.

The singer's voice rose, drawing Marianne's attention and she settled in to listen to the song. The performer was quite accomplished as was her dark-eyed pianist, a young man who exchanged more than one knowing glance with her. Marianne felt the connection between them as she did the one between her and Warren. His thigh pressed against hers thanks to the tight packing of the chairs and their knees bumped when he shifted in his seat. It was the most he could touch her without drawing either Lady Ellington's or Mr Berkshire's attention. Marianne didn't slide away from him or turn her legs, but left her thigh against his, twisting her foot to caress his heel with hers. He slid her a sly smile and she returned it without hesitation.

The song was in French, a tale of love and the fear it wouldn't be returned. Marianne understood more than the words and the melody carrying them. To need someone was to risk being hurt as she'd learned too many times in the past. She'd needed a mother and the woman had turned her back on her. She'd needed a family and the Nichols and Smiths had cared for her only as long as they'd been paid. She craved love and something more to look forward to than a life alone. Did Warren love her, or would his regard fade the moment he wrote 'the end'? She wasn't sure. Experience was a difficult thing to shake but it didn't fill her with dread as it had in the past. He was here beside her, in front of everyone. There must be something more to it than inspiration for a story and the prospect of it lifted her spirits as much as the song.

After a lengthy programme, the woman sang her final song. The guests clapped, the sound muffled by gloves and the bored uninterest of the men.

Lady Astley rose and, as was her custom, invited others to play. A few of the older gentlemen grumbled, but were silenced by their wives. The ladies found it preferable to listen to amateurs than to trudge home to another dark evening with family around the fire.

Miss Cartwright was the first to take up the invitation. Her eagerness to play had more to do with displaying her talents to any eligible gentleman than to amuse the guests. For all Miss Cartwright's other faults, her playing wasn't one of them. She executed a concerto with admirable skill instead of the painful pickings of so many other country ladies.

At the end, Miss Cartwright stood and curtsied to the crowd.

'You should play,' Warren whispered, the caress of his words across her shoulders as startling as his suggestion. 'Give them something else to talk about beside tired old rumours or the new ones they're inventing.'

'No, they don't deserve to hear it.' It had taken enough courage to come here in the low-cut gown. She wasn't going to waste what remained of it to play for these ingrates.

'Does anyone else wish to play?' Lady Astley asked her guests.

'Yes, Miss Domville.' Warren rose, giving everyone a genuine reason to finally turn around and look at them. He held out his hand to Marianne and she wanted to smack it away. How dare he make a spectacle of her after she'd told him she wouldn't play? Her music wasn't for these people, but for her and him.

Lady Astley exchanged a desperate look with Lady Cartwright as if hoping her friend might offer a suitably polite but firm refusal of Warren's suggestion.

He didn't give her the chance. 'Come, Miss Domville. The instrument awaits.'

His encouragement gave her strength. He wasn't doing this to humiliate her, but because he believed in her and her talent. He'd told her before he'd lend her the strength of his name, to stand beside her when she at last decided to make public her talent and he was keeping his word. It was time for her to be courageous and worthy of his faith in her and at last stand up to these people. She'd knock them out of their seats with her talent and prove she was more than they believed her to be.

She placed her hand in his, rose and went with him out of the row. She held her head high as Warren escorted her up the aisle between the chairs to the pianoforte. He stopped before the instrument and let go of her as she came around the bench. The turn made the blue silk of her dress flutter around her legs before she tucked it beneath her to sit. Whispers and the shuffle of feet against the hardwood floor filled the air above

the audience as Marianne prepared to play. Warren
didn't return to his seat, but stepped to the far end of
the piano, his presence bolstering her confidence. She
focused on him as she began, forgetting everyone else.

Beyond the pianoforte, the audience's expressions
changed from scowling disapproval to slack-jawed astonishment. Warren hoped those moved by Marianne's
music would be less inclined to assist Lady Cartwright
in her attacks against Marianne, but he doubted it. An-
gels could come down from heaven and accompany
Marianne with harps and it wouldn't change most of
their opinions. Once the song ended, they'd clap away
their amazement and return to their gossip and lies.
Even if they did, Warren didn't fear for Marianne. She
was at last facing them, showing her true self instead
of allowing them to define her.

Her face was beautiful and serene as she played, her
hair warm gold beneath the candlelight which sparkled
in the diamonds gracing her earlobes and echoed in the
silk of her dress. She'd worn the stunning creation for
him, he was sure of it, revealing more of herself as she
had through her music. The first sight of her tonight
had nearly stunned all rational thought out of him, it
still did. Her magnificent breasts pressed against the
rich fabric as each movement of her arms up and down
the keyboard made the supple flesh quiver. If he could
accompany her home tonight, undo the long row of
buttons along the back and take the fullness of her in
his hands, he would, but he couldn't. At least not yet.
He picked at a small imperfection in the lacquer of

the pianoforte. His time away from her, despite the pressing issues of the newspaper and Rupert, had made more acute how much he cared for her. He loved her. The piano case vibrated under his fingers with her playing as the realisation struck him. While he'd been in London, he'd missed her melodious voice, the sense of calm he experienced in her presence and the inspiration of her being. With her he could be himself in a way he hadn't been since the summer before he'd enlisted when he'd simply been the poor sixteen-year-old son of a country vicar, not a surgeon or a famous author. He was a better man because of her, not as haunted by his past, willing to let it go and embrace a future he couldn't have imagined a few weeks ago. His path would no longer be dictated solely by his career, or fear and guilt, but by the life he might lead with her beside him. He wanted her for longer than through the completion of his novel. It was what she wanted of him which concerned him.

Regret crept along Warren's spine like the vibrations of the piano beneath his fingertips. He reached into his pocket and crinkled the cut out gossip article. He hadn't found his brother-in-law in London. His housekeeper had claimed she hadn't seen him for days and he hadn't answered one note or letter from Warren. Even the papers from Mr Steed with all their legal warnings had gone unanswered. The threat of him still lingered out there somewhere waiting to strike, but Warren would make sure it could do them no harm.

Marianne drew the enchanting piece to a close and threw Warren a glorious smile. In her radiance, all the challenges facing them faded away. He withdrew his hand from his pocket and laid it back on the piano case. He wouldn't show her the newspaper, not tonight. Let her enjoy this small triumph and her happiness. Tomorrow he'd speak with her and they'd figure out how to face the coming trouble together.

At the end of the piece, Marianne folded her hands in her lap. Silence hovered over the stunned guests until Lady Ellington, accompanied by Mr Berkshire, rose to their feet to applaud. With a mixture of enthusiasm and reluctance the other guests joined in, but they didn't stand. Lady Cartwright didn't so much as twitch. She sat in the front row, her face screwed up as tight as a book binding. Warren shifted around the piano to block Marianne from the woman's acid stare as she rose from the bench and dipped into a dignified curtsy.

'After such fine playing, there won't be anyone who wants to perform next,' Lord Astley announced before his wife could, as eager as most of the men for the music to end. There was hunting to discuss and they'd sat through enough pretty playing. 'Let's retire to the sitting room for some refreshments.'

Mr Berkshire and Lady Ellington threaded their way through the retreating guests to Marianne and Warren.

'Everything Sir Warren said about you was true and more,' Mr Berkshire exclaimed. 'Was that one of your works?'

'No.'

'Well, if you can write music with as much passion

as you play it, we'll sell thousands of copies of your compositions.'

'Do you really think so?' She didn't reject the idea as she'd done when Warren had first proposed it—her daring tonight had given her a new confidence which made her glow. Warren admired it and hoped to see more of it. She would need it if things with the newspaper story grew worse.

'I do,' Mr Berkshire concurred. 'Especially if we can arrange for you to do a few performances.'

The hint of colour in her cheeks faded, along with some of her courage. 'Perform? In public?'

'There's plenty of time to discuss and arrange it all later,' Warren interrupted. He didn't want Mr Berkshire pressing her for more than she was ready to do and making her retreat into her reserved self again.

'Of course. We must enjoy the evening.' Lady Ellington waved Mr Berkshire towards the door with one glittering hand. 'Come and taste Lady Astley's lemon curd. It's the only thing her cook doesn't ruin.'

Warren and Marianne were slow to follow. 'Well done, Marianne.'

'I can't believe I did it.' They'd spoken of Vienna once. He'd love to see her in the grand opera house there, her fine skin glowing under the candles, a young lady enjoying life instead of hiding from it.

'They noticed you tonight and for the right reason.' He longed for tomorrow when they'd be alone at Priorton Abbey and he could savour her lips and the press of her breasts against his chest. He should concern himself with all their other problems, but nothing, not his reputation as an author, his bills or the possibility of scandal could intrude on his moment.

He offered her his arm and they walked together to the sitting room as naturally as they had in the garden, even if everything they did was still dictated by the rules of propriety. Instead of joining the small groups of people gathered on the sofa or around the gaming tables, they wandered to a place near the French door leading to a balcony. More than once Warren fingered the cool brass door handle, wanting to push it open and slip with her into the night with nothing but the stars to watch them, but he didn't. He couldn't allow his eagerness to be with her to compromise her more than he feared he already had.

Marianne stood across from Warren, silently willing him to open the French doors and escort her outside. Despite the people chatting together in small circles or watching them from across the tops of their fans, she wanted to be alone with him. For the first time ever, she'd stood alone against her critics, not with Lady Ellington using her influence to defend her, or Sir Warren pressuring them, but with her own talent. When she'd played, she hadn't been here worried about ugly people and ugly words, but somewhere else. Warren had once said there was a world outside this one which didn't care about her or her scandals. Playing tonight had been the first tentative step towards finding it. 'Thank you, Warren, for encouraging me. I couldn't have done it without you.'

'You're the whole reason I came home.' He turned a

bit so his hand which he held by his side was close to hers. Hidden from the others by her body, he pressed his fingers into her palm, his touch firm and welcome like a hot stone clasped between cold hands. 'I'm glad I could inspire you, the way you've inspired me.'

'It's as if I don't fear the world so much when I'm with you, as if I can at last live as I want to, with pride instead of being ashamed like they want me to be.'

'You can and you will.' He ran his thumb across her palm, his touch as natural as the chemise against her skin. She didn't want to pull away, but to draw him closer, to tug off her glove and experience more of his bare skin against hers, to be one with him. This wasn't the lust she'd feared sitting latent inside her and ready to spring out to ruin her, but a deeper connection. He'd made her believe in herself in a way not even Lady Ellington had done and there was freedom in it, freedom to be herself, to take pride in her accomplishments and to at last open herself up to the affection and connection she'd craved her entire life.

'Promise me, no matter what happens, you'll never allow them to make you believe you are anything but the beautiful, intelligent, talented and witty woman you are,' Warren demanded.

The haunted expression from his portrait flickered through his eyes and she tightened her fingers around his, concern undermining her bliss. 'Why, what might happen?'

He hesitated, pressing his lips together as if holding back words he debated speaking. 'Anything, you know as well as I do how cruel the world can be.'

'I do.' She'd stood up to her critics tonight, but it wouldn't be the last time she'd be forced to do so. The strength she'd drawn on to cross the room, to sit at the piano and reveal her talent would have to be called on again and again. The thought didn't weary her as it had in the past. With Warren beside her she could face anything and anyone, and at last achieve victory over every low opinion of her, including her own.

Chapter Ten

'It'll cost twice what I originally told you,' the foreman announced.

Warren stopped picking his way across the attic, his hope of seeing the roof finished without additional expense vanishing. 'What?'

'These supports are rotten.' The foreman scraped a beam with a small knife and the wood flaked like pastry. 'This section won't take the weight of the new slate and needs to be replaced.'

Warren would call the man a fraud, but he'd seen enough waterlogged hospital ships to know when wood was strong and when it wasn't. 'How much?'

The foreman screwed up one side of his mouth and rubbed his scraggly chin. 'Two hundred pounds.'

'Everything is two hundred pounds.' Warren stared at the exposed beams and the cobwebs hanging in the corners of the rafters. Sunlight through the narrow attic windows revealed the thick dust covering everything. 'Will this be the last of it?'

'No such thing in a house like this, sir.' The foreman chuckled. 'But it should see to the roof, keep water from damaging more once the bad weather sets in.'

Warren pinched the bridge of his nose, frustrated and exhausted, the peace and excitement of last night rubbed away beneath the pressure of this morning and this latest setback. A lack of sleep didn't help matters. He'd been up so many times pacing, Lancelot had growled at him as if to say he was disturbing his sleep. During his numerous trips up and down the front hall, the wood overhead creaking with the cold, the suits of armour silently watching him, he'd noticed how different the house was when Marianne was here. She brightened it, filling it with her presence and her music. She made his success, Priorton, everything richer and worth having.

If only he were worth having. She'd bloomed under his belief in her last night, but in reality he hadn't deserved her thanks or her faith in him. He hadn't been honest with her about the newspaper, but today it would change. He'd greeted the sunrise ready to ride to Welton Place and tell her, to plan with her how they would handle the encroaching issue together before he'd been waylaid by the foreman. If she didn't learn of the gossip from him and see how determined he was to remain beside her until it passed, he'd lose her trust. It was time to be done with the man.

'Then make the repairs. Rain running down the stairs will only cost me more money.' Warren left the attic, dropping down each step of the narrow and curving upper staircase. When he reached the first floor, Turner, the butler, hurried up to him.

'Sir Warren, Lord Cartwright is here to see you.'

'What's he doing here?' The Baron had never deigned to visit him before, always summoning Warren to him as if he were the king. His coming to Warren so early in the day, especially after last night, made him uneasy

'He didn't say. He's waiting for you in the sitting room'

'Thank you, Turner.' Warren made his way down the wide front staircase, in no mood to face the man this morning. He didn't like Lord Cartwright, especially not his wife, but tolerated them like he did so many other titled people because of their patronage. He was beginning to think he should abide by his own advice to not care what people thought of him. There were plenty of common men in England who purchased his novels, and if Mr Berkshire could see them printed in America and Europe as he planned, there'd soon be even more. With so many more fans of his books, he could at last dismiss people like the Cartwrights. He didn't like relying on anyone, especially not haughty lords with too many friends in the *ton* who thought nothing of looking down their pedigreed noses at him and Marianne.

Warren entered the sitting room. Lord Cartwright stood in the centre of it waiting for Warren, hat in his hand.

'Good morning and welcome to Priorton. What do you think of the repairs?' Warren motioned to the updated room with the newly polished panelling, white plaster, better furnishings and fresh curtains. It was a great change from the hideous shape it had been in when he'd purchased it.

'I can't say. I've never visited here before.' Lord Cartwright waved his hat at the room, rude in his un-interest.

'What brings you here today?' Warren planted his fists on his hips, bracing himself for what he guessed wasn't going to be polite chit-chat.

'I'm very disappointed in you, Sir Warren. I've been nothing but generous in supporting you and your little stories, pushing them on my friends and introducing you to the best families in the county.'

Warren's shoulders stiffened at Lord Cartwright's condescension. 'I thank you for your support, but I be-lieve it was my own effort, more than anyone else's, which gained me entrance into last night's party, Lord Preston's and many others.'

'How dare you, a jumped-up tradesman, thumb your nose at my patronage and my family?' Lord Cart-wright's grip on his hat tightened, twisting the felt brim. 'Last night, in front of everyone, you encourage Miss Domville, a woman of dubious background, to show up my daughter at the pianoforte.'

Warren ground his teeth at the insult before the truth in the man's accusation eased his jaw. The memory of Lady Cartwright shooting daggers at Marianne after she'd played came rushing back to him. Warren had encouraged Marianne to play and her superior talent had inadvertently eclipsed Miss Cartwright's. With the gossip circulating in the *Morning Post* threatening to reach them, assuming it already hadn't, Warren might have made things worse with his rashness. Despite his guilt where Marianne was concerned, he wouldn't stand here in his own home and take Lord Cartwright's insults. 'I may not have inherited Priorton, but at least I have the fortitude to work to maintain it, not to sit at the gambling tables like certain lords do and throw it all away on chance.'

Lord Cartwright's bulbous nose turned a deep shade of red as he scowled at the blatant reference to his gambling habit and the debt he was too proud, foolish and lazy to work to pay off. 'How dare you? First you allow your mistress to insult my daughter and then you insult me.'

'Miss Domville isn't my mistress,' Warren growled, ready to call Turner and have him escort Lord Cartwright out.

'You think I haven't read the news in the *Morning Post* about the two of you?'

Warren stiffened again. People had heard. It wouldn't be long before Marianne did too. He had to reach her, to tell her and make his determination to remain beside her through it all clear.

'You've become too grand for your own good,' Lord Cartwright spat out. 'I suggest you remember your place and who are your betters.'

'And I'd suggest you remember who my friends are. When I tell Lady Ellington about your snide comments about Miss Domville and she tells Lord Falconbridge, he may not be so generous in regards to your gambling debts next time. How much was it you lost to him last winter that he forgave?'

Lord Cartwright blanched, seeing his mistake as clearly as he'd pointed out Warren's. He smashed his hat down over his grey hair and stormed out of the room. A moment later, Warren heard the jingle of equipage as the carriage carried him and his rage off. Warren wished he could so easily walk away from their exchange. It wasn't just the loss of Lord Cartwright's patronage that concerned him, but Marianne.

He raced up the stairs towards his room to change into his riding clothes and hurry to Welton Place. At the top of the stairs, he paused as two men straining under a thick beam balanced on their shoulders crossed the hall. The weight of everything settled on Warren like the wood on the workmen's shoulders. He drew in a deep breath, craving even the faintest hint of Marianne's delicate perfume to settle him but there was nothing except sawdust.

Maybe I have reached for too much.

The noise of hammers pounding and chisels scraping used to fill him with pride. Today, it sounded like his hard-earned money being spent on a foolish dream, just like his father had done with the vicarage school. Warren could have bought something more modest in London, but the opportunity to purchase Priorton, like his meeting with Mr Berkshire ten years ago, was one he hadn't been able to resist. Through hard work he'd gained everything he'd ever dreamed of as a child, all the fantasies which had carried him through the darkest moments aboard ship and after his father's death. With the same tenacity, he'd won Marianne's heart. Nothing, not even a leaking roof, would make him choose begging to the Cartwrights over Marianne. He'd write more, sleep less if necessary, but he wouldn't give up on Priorton, or Marianne.

Marianne sat on a bench in the garden with her eyes closed and her face turned to the sun to enjoy its warmth. Despite spending half the night lying in bed thinking of Warren, she was exhilarated instead of exhausted this morning. The edginess which had haunted her all summer faded in the autumn cool and it was because of last night, because of Warren.

In the middle of the night, as she'd stared at the swirls of brocade in her bed canopy illuminated by the coals in the grate, she'd begun to imagine going to London in the spring, perhaps even travelling to Austria as Lady Ellington and Warren had suggested, except every time she pictured herself in the Vienna opera house enjoying a performance, it was Warren who was at her side. In the short time they'd been together, he'd encouraged her to step into the world instead of shying from it. Bit by bit she'd taken his advice until last night when she'd plunged into it at last. In doing so, she'd soared in a way she hadn't believed possible a few months ago. It was because of him and the way he gazed at her as though she was more precious to him than his writing.

She opened her eyes and fixed on the statue of Zeus embracing the nymph, admiring the sensuous lines of Zeus's marble fingers on the nymph's plump thighs, her billowing dress revealing every curve of her as she opened her mouth to kiss the god. When Warren had admired her in the dress, Marianne had felt like the nymph, revelling in his awe of her body instead of wanting to hide it away. The thrill of it rushed through her again and for the first time she felt like one of the other young ladies who became giddy over a beau and society and the future. Warren wanted her and it was no longer for inspiration, but something much deeper. It had been there in the clasp of his hand on hers last night and his every encouraging word. Warren believed in her, and it had strengthened her belief in herself and the possibility she might have at last what she'd always craved, but never thought she'd obtain—genuine love.

'Good morning, Miss Domville.' The familiar male voice made her cringe and burst her contentment.

She turned on the bench to see Lord Bolton standing behind her, hat cocked over his forehead, his charming smile oozing confidence and making her want to retch. 'What are you doing here?'

He settled his hands on his walking stick. With a lean body, forceful jaw and dark hair, he was too handsome for his own good. 'Is that any way to greet an old friend and admirer?'

She stood, pinning him with enough spite to wilt a rose. 'You were never an old friend.'

He stared at her breasts, a lascivious smile curling up one side of his too-perfect mouth. 'But I'm still an admirer.'

'Of my money. Surely you didn't travel all the way

up from London for me to refuse you again?' She
started off down the walk, determined to be rid of him,
but in two strides of his long legs he was beside her.

'Apparently, I'm not the only one. I read an interesting story in the *Morning Post* about you and Sir Warren. Of course I didn't realise it was you until Lady
Cartwright told me over tea this morning. It was all she
could talk about, especially after his stunning performance with you at Lady Astley's musical.' His smile
widened as she stopped so fast on the walk, pebbles
shifted beneath her half-boots. 'I'm sorry I missed it,
but I was delayed by a thrown horseshoe.'

'Too bad the horse didn't throw you.' She pulled
back her shoulders, regaining her usual disdain for
him, refusing to reveal any more shock or the anxiety
creeping in beneath it. Warren had been in London.
He must have heard the stories. Was this the silent unease he and Mr Berkshire had shared last night and the
trouble with a newspaper he'd mentioned? If so, he
shouldn't have kept it from her, but told her instead of
leaving her to discover it from slime like Lord Bolton.
'Lady Cartwright should have more important things
to discuss than me, especially since her daughter is
without a husband after a very expensive Season Lord
Cartwright can ill afford.'

'I'm not surprised Miss Cartwright failed to take.
Her assets aren't as impressive as yours.' His licked
his lips as he came to stand over her. 'My offer still
stands. I'll make you a respectable wife and you'll free
me of my debts. I need an heir and I'd like to leave him

a little more than an over-mortgaged estate. You should accept me—what other decent man will have you?'

'Get out or I'll have Lord Falconbridge ruin what's left of your reputation.' She needed him gone as much as she needed to see Warren, to know if the rumours were true or another of Lord Bolton's plots to undermine her confidence. He'd been as ruthless as Madame de Badeau in trying to make her believe she needed him and the protection of his name. She hadn't believed it then, she wouldn't now, even while her faith in Warren was wavering.

He shrugged away her protest. 'You needn't bother threatening me with Lord Falconbridge's wrath. My debts have ruined my reputation as much as your sister did yours. As tainted by her as you are, 'I'm the best chance you have of regaining any respect and not ending up a spinster.'

She balled her hands at her side, struggling not to strike the smirk from his face. 'Get out.'

'If you're counting on Sir Warren to offer for you, then I recommend you don't. With the Cartwrights shunning him for his liaison with you, it won't be long before others do too. He'll give you up before he loses any more patrons, unless he thinks your money is worth the trouble. I do.' Lord Bolton twirled his walking stick as he strolled around her and made for the house. 'When Sir Warren makes a formal offer for you, I'll gladly step aside. Until then, I'll be at the Horse and Lion in the village should you change your mind.'

Marianne dropped down on to the cold stone bench in front of the fountain, the fight shocked out of her.

She'd been brave last night, defied everyone and their petty expectations of her and the only thing it had gained her was more derision. She could imagine the Cartwrights sitting around the tea table, laughing about her with Lord Bolton and gobbling up his stories of her from her time with Madame de Badeau. He'd probably made up a few more to amuse his snickering hosts. It shouldn't matter, she shouldn't care. For a brief time at the piano last night, and for hours afterwards, she hadn't. She did today because it might cost her Warren.

She stared across the garden at the statue of Zeus, Lord Bolton's warning about Warren ringing in her ears. Warren hadn't declared for her and his association with her was at last costing him patrons. No, she shouldn't lose faith in him so easily. He'd stood by her last night and had always scoffed at all her previous fears over what their time together might do to him. He wouldn't abandon her simply because one or two families shunned him. He had the Prince for an admirer and who knew what other aristocrats in London. He didn't need the Cartwrights. He also didn't need her reputation placing their patronage at risk too.

She jumped up and paced in front of the statue, barely aware of the footsteps crunching over the gravel coming up from the house. She never should have come to rely on Warren. A month ago she wouldn't have cared if he never spoke to her again—this morning it terrified her. He might leave her like nearly everyone else she'd ever been close to had done.

'Is everything all right, miss?' Darby asked, appearing strangely out of place in the garden carrying a silver salver.

'Yes, thank you,' she rushed to answer and he was deferential enough not to pry. He'd leave that to Lady Ellington after he told her he'd noticed Marianne was distressed. For the first time, Marianne didn't mind. Down the walk, through the open French doors, the curtains billowed out with the fresh breeze, revealing the pianoforte. It didn't call to her like it had in the past. She didn't want to sit there alone, but be with someone to talk and figure out what was going on in her mind and her heart. She wished Lady Ellington was here instead of off paying calls. She needed to hear her say, as she had so many times in the past, all would be well.

'This arrived for you.' Darby held out the salver to reveal a letter from Theresa.

Marianne took it, relieved to see it was a friendly missive instead of something more sinister like a parting note from Warren. She'd ignored Theresa's other letters for the past couple of weeks, but she tore this one open, craving kindly words. She shouldn't have avoided her friend or allowed her malaise to make her dismiss the people who cared about her. She might have been reluctant to admit her need for them in the past, but she couldn't today, not with the possibility of Warren ending things facing her.

She read the letter. There was a friendly chiding about Marianne not coming to visit. She said if Marianne was worried about encountering Lady Menton she need not be since the woman had gone to visit her sister for a month. Marianne could come see Theresa whenever she wished though she hoped it would be soon. She pledged her unending friendship to Marianne before ending the letter.

Marianne folded it, guilty at the way she'd neglected her friend. If Theresa didn't survive her travails, and there were many women who didn't, Marianne would lose one of the few people who genuinely cared about her. Theresa, along with her husband, had stood with her as much as the Falconbridges, even against Mr Menton's parents. With her enemies mounting yet another attack, Marianne needed all the amiable smiles and pleasant conversation she could gather.

'Darby, please summon the carriage. I'm going to visit Mrs Menton.'

'Miss Domville isn't here,' the bland Welton Place butler informed Warren.

Warren stuffed down the urgency which had gripped him since Lord Cartwright's visit, determined to remain level headed. He must talk with Marianne before the news of the scandal did its damage. 'Where is she?'

'Visiting a friend.' Lady Ellington's regal voice carried out from behind the butler. The tall man stepped aside and allowed the Dowager to come forward. There was no hint of blame in her answer. She simply announced what she knew. 'Walk with me, Sir Warren, I wish to show you my Italian landscapes.'

She took his arm and Warren allowed her to lead him into the entrance hall despite his eagerness to set off to wherever Marianne was. They stopped at the bottom of the main stairs and she gestured to the stunning collection of Italian landscape paintings hung three and four tall along the walls.

'I heard a very unsettling rumour while I was visiting friends today,' the Dowager announced as she stared up at her collection.

Warren stopped himself before he could adjust his cravat. 'Did it have to do with the column in the *Morning Post*?'

'Ah, I see you are aware of it.' She at last faced him, scrutinising him like captains used to do to their new sailors.

'Is Miss Domville?' His stomach dropped when the Dowager nodded and the large diamonds dangling from her ears brushed her cheeks.

'She had an unfortunate visit from an old suitor this morning who saw fit to inform her.'

Warren didn't know who the vile man was who'd delivered the news, but he wanted to thrash him. 'I apologise. It was never my intention to compromise Miss Domville or to make her a target for ridicule.'

'And now that she is, what do you intend to do about it? Miss Domville has not had an easy life and does not need yet another person failing her. I won't allow it and neither will Lord Falconbridge.'

If Warren had ever thought losing the Cartwrights' support would be unfortunate, he sensed it was nothing compared to garnering Lord Falconbridge's wrath. With his power and influence, the Marquess could ruin him in a way none of the other country families could dream possible. However, losing Marianne would be a greater punishment than anything Lord Falconbridge might conceive.

'I won't fail her, Lady Ellington,' he assured her, as vociferous in his declaration as Lady Ellington was in her duty to her young charge. 'I care very deeply for her and I only want to see her happy.'

Lady Ellington nodded sagely. 'Have you told her this?'

'It's why I'm here.' He opened his arms to the hallway. 'But she's not.'

She tilted her head, appraising him as if he were a new bauble to adorn her fingers. Then she straightened, the decision made. 'She's gone to visit Mrs Menton at Hallington Hall. It's an easy ride from here, just on the other side of Falconbridge Manor. Mrs Menton is very preoccupied with her baby, so I don't see how she'll pay much attention to Miss Domville.' Lady Ellington winked at him. 'Good day, Sir Warren.'

'Of course Lord Bolton is wrong,' Theresa reassured Marianne. She sat in a deep chair by the fire with Alexander, her infant son, perched on her slowly shrinking lap. The chubby-cheeked boy sucked his little fingers, his eyes wide as he listened to the ladies. Marriage and a baby had mellowed Theresa's high spirits since they'd met four years ago when Lady Falconbridge, the cousin who'd raised her, had brought her to one of Madame de Badeau's salons. It was Marianne's friendship with Theresa which had led her to betray her mother and reveal to Lord Falconbridge the plot to see Cecelia humiliated by Lord Strathmore.

'What if he's not?' Marianne stopped pacing across the flowered rug to peer out of the window. Below, the lawn slipped down from the back of the house to a copse of trees. Through their nearly bare branches the lake shimmered in the sun. 'The Astleys and the Prestons and who knows what other patrons in London may abandon him. His work fuels everything he does, it's who he is. He won't let anything jeopardise it.' *Not even me.*

'You must speak with Sir Warren. It's the only way to settle your fears.'

Fears. She hated them and how they dominated her life as much as she hated the uncertainty of waiting on Warren's response to the gossip. The entire situation felt too much like the week after she'd written to the Smiths asking to return to them. She'd waited every day for their answering letter, not even unpacking her things at Lady Ellington's, sure she'd soon be on her way to her old guardians. Their letter severing all ties with her had been a blow, one she feared Warren's reaction to gossip would be too. She wiped at her eyes, pushing away the tears building there. 'I don't know if I can face him.'

Theresa set Alexander in the cradle beside her chair. She approached her friend and laid her hands on her shoulders. Marianne didn't flinch from her touch, but was grateful for the gesture and the comfort it brought her. 'If he's placed this much effort in you, he isn't going to let you go so easily. Don't run from him, Marianne. He's good for you. A month ago you wouldn't have played for Sir Warren, or even Lady Astley's guests like you did.'

'And what has it gained me except more problems?' Marianne's shoulders sagged. 'I'm tired of fighting people.'

'It won't be for ever. Nothing lasts so long.'

'Then when will it end?' A lifetime of frustration made her clench her hands at her sides. 'When they've finally driven me from the countryside or Lady Ellington tires of constantly defending me?'

'Lady Ellington will always help you like she helped me and Adam marry, and Lord and Lady Falconbridge find each other again. She won't give up on you no matter what.'

It was difficult to believe, especially after Lord Falconbridge's warning the other day that Marianne's future here depended on Lady Ellington being right about Sir Warren's intentions. If he made his aunt choose between him and her, she felt certain she'd lose. 'And Sir Warren?'

'Give him a chance to surprise you. I think he will.'

Alexander began to fuss and rub his eyes.

The stout nurse in her starched apron appeared in the doorway. 'Time for Alexander's nap, Mrs Menton.'

'All right.' Theresa offered Marianne an apologetic look. 'I must feed him, to Lady Menton's horror. She thinks I should hire a wet nurse. Will you wait here for me?'

'No, I want to walk by the lake.' She was too agitated to sit still.

'All right, I'll come find you when I'm finished.'

Marianne picked her way downstairs, cautious in case Sir Walter was about. The baronet had been cordial enough to Marianne every other time she'd been here, but there'd been no mistaking his cool disapproval of Marianne's friendship with his daughter-in-law. It would turn to outright disdain if he'd read the newspaper and Marianne might find herself permanently banned from Hallington Hall, despite Theresa's protests.

To her relief, Marianne saw no one as she made her way through the house to the back sitting room. She stepped outside on to the stone portico and crossed it to the steps leading down to the lawn. She followed the path heading into the woods and to the lake beyond, the sense of isolation increasing as she moved further and further away from the house. A breeze blew through the trees, sending a shower of brown leaves fluttering to the ground. Marianne caught one, but the brittle thing crumbled beneath her grip like everything with Warren seemed to be doing. She tilted her hand and the pieces cascaded to the ground. If only she could release her concerns the same way, but nothing except a meeting with Warren would settle her. She wasn't sure she could face him and risk his turning away.

At last she reached the lake and stood at the shore. A stiff breeze blew across the wide expanse and drove it up to lap over the rocks dotting the sand. The surface reflected the clouds passing overhead and made her feel as lonely as the grey water.

I wish Warren was here.

A path followed the bank to a Grecian temple perched on an outcrop. Marianne followed it, then climbed the lichen-covered steps leading up to the main walkway under the temple dome. The second floor of Hallington Hall appeared over the trees. The dark stone didn't stand out against the red and orange leaves as it had nearly four years ago when she'd stood here with Theresa to admire her friend's new home. Theresa was here because she had a husband, a child and peace. Marianne had nothing.

No, I might still have Warren.

She hoped Theresa was right about him not giving up on her. At one time she would have balked at needing him, but it was clear she did. Under his influence she'd begun to live as Lady Ellington had always encouraged. She wanted more of it, more time to see what existed beyond the pianoforte and the small world she'd created for herself at Welton Place. With him beside her, helping her to disregard everyone who wanted to pull her down, she could have it, assuming he wanted to remain with her. She wouldn't be surprised if he washed his hands of her and hurried to undo the damage his relationship with her might have caused.

She leaned against the cold stone building, not sure how she would stay sane with all this uncertainty nipping at her. A duck swam by, cutting a widening V across the surface. She must see Warren and settle things, one way or another. Even if meeting him meant the end of their relationship, their brief time together proved there existed gentlemen who might care for her. It should have been a comfort, but it wasn't. She didn't want any future gentleman. She wanted Warren.

Rustling from behind the temple caught her attention. She followed the curve of the building around to the other side and out of view of the house. She expected to see a rabbit or a deer in the underbrush. She was startled by the sight of Warren emerging from the woods atop a chestnut-coloured horse, Lancelot trotting beside him.

She moved, ready to run down the steps and throw her arms around him as he dismounted, but she didn't. She wasn't sure why he was here and she wasn't going to embarrass herself by clinging to him as he bade her adieu.

'I didn't think you one for riding,' she called out to him, summoning the old Marianne, the one adept at appearing aloof no matter what the situation. It was a much more difficult thing to accomplish today than in the past.

'I wouldn't be a proper baronet if I didn't.' He flipped the horse's reins over its head to dangle on the ground.

'Do you usually ride on the Menton lands?' She fingered the outline of the slim gold ring beneath her glove, as nervous as she was thrilled to see him.

'No.' He climbed the steps to her while Lancelot wandered off, sniffing the ground as he went. 'I did it to find you. Lady Ellington said you were here.'

He came for me.

She let go of her hands and let them drop to her

sides. He hadn't told her what he wanted yet. 'You came to discuss the story in the *Morning Post*?'

'I'm sorry you had to find out about it from so dubious a source. I wanted to be the one to tell you.'

'Why? So you could at last admit our arrangement was a mistake, that I'm costing you patrons?' She ducked away to follow the curve of the building. She hated hearing the words spoken aloud, but she'd said them to avoid him doing it first and crushing her already fretting heart.

Warren's footsteps echoed in the dome of the building behind her. 'Marianne, wait.'

It was the same tone he'd used the day he'd burned his copy of *Lady Matilda's Trials*. He was asking her to listen to him, to let him make things right. She faced him, opening and closing her fists at her sides, willing to give him the chance.

He strode up to her, concern deepening the small furrow between his eyebrows. 'I'd never choose them over you. You're worth more to me than any of their praises or support. I need you in my life more than I need them.'

'As your muse.' Despite the earnestness in his voice, the doubt she'd carried for so long still haunted her.

'No, as the wonderful woman you are.' He reached out and caught her hands, his solid grip spreading through her like ripples over the surface of the lake

'What are you saying?'

'You captured me with the first note you played and every day we've been together since.' He raised his hands to her cheeks, cupping her face as his words did her heart. 'Before you'd played for me, I'd lost my talent and despaired of ever being the man and writer I was before my sister died. You've helped me to unlock the stories which were holed up inside of me and to reclaim my faith in myself. I love you and I want you to be with me for ever, to be my wife.'

Her gasp of surprise was smothered by the touch of his lips to hers. His defiance of her expectations made her head whirl as much as his mouth against hers. Warren loved and cherished her, more than patrons or stories or reputations. He wanted her with him, scandalous past and all, and she would be his, free and trusting as she'd never been with anyone before.

Lancelot's loud barks as he raced past the Grecian temple and up the path interrupted their bliss. Warren broke from her and she wavered on her feet before his tight arms steadied her.

'Will you marry me, Marianne?' he asked.

'Yes.' She laid her cheek on his chest and played with the sloppily tied cravat beneath his chin. She didn't care who found them here. Let them see the two of them united against every trial and person determined to humble them. Their nastiness couldn't separate them.

'Come.' He took her by the hand to lead her to the horse.

'Where are we going?'

'For a ride.'

She resisted his gentle tug. 'I can't leave my friend.'

'I think she'll understand.' He motioned to the woods. Theresa stood petting Lancelot beneath one of the few evergreen trees. She wiggled her fingers in good-bye with a smile as mischievous as one of Lady Ellington's, then faded back into the tree line. Lancelot raced to them with excited barks before bolting off into the woods.

Theresa had been right about Warren and so had Lady Ellington. They'd never allow her to forget it and she didn't mind. It was the most glorious thing anyone could ever hold over her.

Marianne laughed when he caught her about the waist and lifted her to sit sideways across the saddle. He gripped the leather in front of her thighs, the height of the horse and the strength of Warren overwhelming as he pulled himself up behind her. His legs were strong against hers as he tightened the reins between his hands and clicked the animal into motion.

The wind slid around them, tugging a few of her curls out of their pins as the horse carried them around the curve of the lake. At the far end, the path turned to lead them deeper into the woods. Lancelot bounded past them before veering off into the trees to chase a bird.

'I've never seen Lancelot so active.' Marianna tucked her windswept hair behind one ear, but it refused to remain there.

'Sometimes his instincts get the better of his laziness, especially when he's chasing something.'

Her instincts came alive under the pressure of Warren's chest against her shoulder, his thighs hard against her buttocks. She leaned against him, all the concerns of the last day, the Cartwrights, Lord Bolton and the past dissolving in his presence.

The path led out of the trees to follow the rolling hills. She'd never ridden this way across the Menton lands or even the edge of the Falconbridge estate. Her life was circumscribed by the dower house, Falconbridge Manor, Hallington Hall, the country families and the village. After today, she would at last break free of this small existence and its influence on her, but for now she was grateful for it. While they were here it was just the two of them, untarnished by anything or anyone.

They talked while they rode. She told him about the Protestant School and the jokes they used to play on Mrs Nichols at All Hollow's Eve. The darker memories of the lonely nights in the dormitory, or the lack of letters or gifts on her birthday or at Christmas didn't intrude to overwhelm her like they used to. The warmth of the spring sun on the flowers in the garden between the school walls and the house, and the friendship of two older girls who'd come to the school three years before she'd left were the most vivid memories today.

The same optimism filled Warren's description of his childhood at the vicarage. He laughed as he explained the pranks he and the other boys used to play on his father. His smile widened with his description of Christmas dinners with the boys who hadn't gone home for the holiday. In his words, Marianne could almost smell the excitement of the season, and the aroma of the chestnuts and spiced pudding which had filled the vicarage during their small celebrations.

'Leticia and I used to play in the ruins of the Norman keep behind the village. My mother made her a princess dress out of one of our grandmother's old gowns. She'd stand in it on the old stone parapet, calling across the field to her imaginary prince to save her.' He surveyed the rolling hills of brown grass, neither his memory nor his smile darkening with anguish over his sister's passing. Like her he was too elated to be pulled down by past sorrow.

'What did you do while you were there?' Marianne laid her head on his chest and revelled in the rumbling of his voice in her ear. His happy childhood didn't make hers seem so stark, nor did she ruminate on what she hadn't had. Instead, she imagined their future children and the care and happiness they'd enjoy. They'd never doubt her love for them, or their parents' love for one another.

'I had a rusty breastplate my father had found in the attic and a wooden sword he'd carved for me out of an old plank. I used to pretend the rocks were dragons and I'd slay them and then I'd seize their imaginary treasure hoards.' Warren guided the horse down the hill which skirted the woods above Falconbridge manor. 'Some day, when the repairs to Priorton are done, I'll commission a dragon sculpture for the garden. It'll be a sleeping one I can lay between the shrubs so our children can pretend to wake it. Maybe I'll get a winged one too for near the cloister.'

'You don't have to wait. I'll buy them for you as a wedding gift along with a stone treasure chest for them to guard.'

'No, I won't take money from you to do it. I'll earn it myself, you'll see. In fact, I want your fortune placed in trust with Lord Falconbridge administering it. No funds are to be advanced from the trust unless you and he approve.'

'But why?' She pushed up from his chest, surprised by the determined set of his chin and his green eyes fixed on the road ahead. 'I want you to be able to use it for us, for Priorton. I don't want you to worry about patrons and sales.'

'No. I won't have anyone thinking I married you for any other reason than love and I will continue to earn money with my talent just I always have, do you understand?'

'I do.' His success was important to him and she wouldn't undermine it.

'I love you, Marianne, you're the only treasure I need.' He swept his lips across hers, tempting her more than a dragon's stash of rubies or gold. He wasn't a fantasy or some imagined man hidden by the mist, but hard and hot flesh beneath her fingertips. Her insides melted under the pressure of his kiss and she reached up to lace her hands in his hair, to pull him closer and deeper into her.

The horse snorted and tossed its head, breaking their kiss.

'So much for our mighty steed.' Warren laughed as he guided the animal to where the trail ambled down through another forest. It rose again to follow the ridge behind Falconbridge Manor. Their sweet conversation continued until the roof of Welton Place peaked above the orange and yellow treetops.

Warren tugged the horse to a stop. 'I don't want to go back.'

Neither did Marianne. 'We don't have to. Turn here.'

He guided the horse to the path Marianne pointed to. It followed the slope of the hill beneath two sprawling oak trees until the red brick of the orangery came into view.

'What's this?' Warren asked, bringing the horse to a halt.

'Somewhere we won't be disturbed.'

He dismounted, then reached up for her. She held tight to his arms as he lifted her down, her skirt flaring out before his legs pinned the fabric against her thighs. She didn't let go, but studied him. The afternoon sunlight through the branches cut hard across his cheeks and played in the light hair at his temples. She ran her hand down the curve of his arm and entwined her fingers with his. She led Warren inside the orangery where the sun through the tall windows warded off the chill of the brick and the day. In this moment, she wanted to be more than his intended, but one with him.

'I see the Falconbridge family's taste in art extends to the decorative ones too.' He cleared his throat as he motioned to the gilded screen dividing the room.

Marianne closed the double doors and threw the lock. She didn't need any curious maids, or, heaven forbid, Darby, stumbling in on them. She came to stand in front of Warren and with her fingers turned his face from the erotic embroidered screen to her. 'Lady Ellington's brother used this place for trysts while keeping his regular mistress in the dower house. He was too cheap to pay for a London home.'

'And why are we here?' It was clear from his hard swallow he knew, but she appreciated him wanting her to make it clear. He wouldn't fall on her because of opportunity, but wait for her to guide them both. Today, she would be with Warren in all the ways a woman could be with a man without any interruptions. This wasn't wrong or licentious like her mother's old liaisons, but beautiful and made richer by his promise to love her for ever. 'To seal our betrothal.'

She unbuttoned her pelisse and dropped it to the floor as she slipped behind the tall screen to the windowless half of the orangery. Then she peered around the edge of it, cocking her finger at him to join her. He didn't hesitate, entering the shadows and embracing her with the same force as the embroidered Apollo taking Calliope. She followed his unrestrained passion, allowing it and hers to carry her beyond regrets, or second guesses. They couldn't wait, and she didn't want to. He loved her and the rest was all a formality.

Breaking from Warren's kiss but remaining within the circle of his arms, she leaned back and undid the small pearl buttons of her fichu. Slowly she slid it off her neck to reveal the tops of her breast before flicking it away to flutter to the floor. Warren's eyes were ablaze as he took in the length of her cleavage. He slipped his hand from around her waist and brought it up to cup one heavy mound through the fine muslin. Leaning down, he tasted her neck, his tongue making small circles on the skin as he worked his way to her décolletage. His breath against the moisture from his tongue made her shiver and her nipples peaked, the tightness of them increasing the desire for him building inside her. For the first time ever she understood what it was to want someone beyond reason and good sense. She'd never craved a man the way she did Warren, her legs weak with her need for him and the love he'd promised. It wasn't physical passion driving her forward, but the longing to finally end in his embrace the loneliness which had shadowed her for years.

As if hearing her desire, he placed his hands behind her and began to undo the long row of buttons. While his nimble fingers worked, she tasted the smooth skin of his neck, inhaling the rich cedar scent of him made more potent by the heat of the ride. His breath caressed her ear as he slipped each button free, exposing little by little the skin on her chest. There was too much between them, too many laces and linens, buttons and tapes. She wanted to feel his skin against hers, the weight of him on top of her, to be covered by his touch and his love.

When the last button finally came loose, the garment dropped before catching on the cups of the stays supporting her breasts. He shifted back from her and ran one finger along the edge of the cotton, across her skin to slip the dress free. She shivered as the muslin brushed her thighs as it dropped over her to puddle at her feet. He raised his eyebrows in admiration of her as he traced the curve of her hips and narrow waist beneath the stays. She didn't shrink from the wanting in his eyes, or knock his hand away, but stood strong in front of him. He didn't want her as some plaything to enjoy and toss away. He wanted her future, her talent and the friendship and support which had grown between them. She would give it and all of herself to him.

She tugged his coat from his torso, pushing it down to trap his arms before she rose up on her toes to press her lips to his. He tasted like fine port and she drank him in, languid under his influence. She drew back, clutching the wool, and he smiled playfully as she held him prisoner. At last she slid the coat the rest of the way off of his arms and tossed it aside to add more wrinkles to the ones already marring the wool. One by one, she undid the line of buttons on his waistcoat and soon it joined the other garments scattered around them. It didn't take her long to untie the loose knot of his cravat, her fingers as nimble with the linen as they were at the keyboard. She twisted the free ends around her hands and pulled slightly, drawing him down to her. With his body against hers, she felt the hardness of him through the stiff cotton of her stays and the chemise beneath. It urged her on, but she held back, not wanting to rush or appear like the hussy so many painted her to be. She was his alone and, after their marriage, everyone would know it.

She let go of one end of his cravat and pulled it off his neck. Then she shifted back out of his arms. He straightened to watch as she raised first one stocking-clad foot and then another to step out of the circle of her dress. Turning slowly, she exposed the laces of her stays. Glancing at him over her shoulder, she silently invited him to undo them. She would reveal everything to him, just as she'd done when she'd played her composition for him, laying bare not only her emotions but her whole being.

Warren ran his hands over her buttocks, than traced the line of the laces to her stays. Last night he'd feared he'd lost her. Today she offered him her entire self. He would be worthy of her, help her fight the rumours and work even harder to make a life for them. Row by row he slipped the laces free, letting the past and all his concerns fade with each empty eyelet. While they were together, nothing could trouble them.

At last the confining thing dropped away. He caught her chemise by the sides and drew it over her head. She turned to face him, unflinching in her nakedness, her gorgeous breasts tight and heavy above her flat stomach. He'd dreamed of seeing her like this so many times during the darkest nights in London, but not even his imagination could match reality. He reached out to caress the pointed tip of her breasts, his chest catching as they drew tighter with his touch. His fingertips dug into the generous flesh as he cupped the heavy mounds. She moaned as he took one pert nipple into his mouth to sweep it with his tongue. She tasted as good as fresh water after a long voyage, quenching the burning pain which had driven him on for too long. He'd worried about her turning away from him, but she embraced him, offering him everything as he'd given all of himself to her.

He trailed his fingers down the length of her stomach and slipped them between her thighs. She pressed her hips against his hand as he worked her pleasure, her body like the finest sand on a beach never touched by a man before. She was innocent and open, sensuous and inexperienced. He wanted to teach her and see her bloom beneath his touch. Her breathing quickened and her body tightened around his until he slid free, determined to be one with her when her pleasure came.

He leaned back to tug off his shirt, then pulled her to him again, delighting in the softness of her body against his as he claimed her mouth once more. While her tongue tasted his lips, her fingers stroked the skin of his chest, following the line of his torso to where his breeches encircled his narrow waist. He allowed her to explore his muscled body, her curiosity feeding his building need. She pulled free the fall from its buttons and he caught her hand. He stepped back to push down the buckskin and reveal himself and his desire for her.

Marianne swallowed at the sight and strength of Warren. For all the statues in the garden, nothing could have prepared her for the true majesty of a man. She wrapped her hand around his member and he tilted back his head and closed his eyes. He moaned as she stroked the hard shaft, revelling in her ability to bring him as much pleasure as he brought her. A chill slipped through the room and she let go, eager for the heat of his skin against hers. She pressed her body to his and his hot member against her stomach made her rise on her toes in delight. She wanted him as much as he wanted her and they tumbled together on to the wide sofa.

Thoughts fled from Marianne as Warren covered her, his chest hard against her softness. He settled between her thighs, his eager staff seeking entrance. She opened to him, gasping as he slid forward to claim her. He was slow and cautious, waiting until she could completely embrace him before stroking her with slow and even thrusts. They reached into her very heart as she clung to him, hands tight on the contours of his back. She'd never been so close to someone before, one with him in both body and heart, taking him deeper into herself and her life.

He slid his arms beneath her back to grip her shoulders and nuzzle her neck, his subtle groans against her skin the most stunning of music. As she began to lose herself in the flurry of their passion so did he, his thrusts growing faster and faster until he surged forward one final time, pushing her over the edge to cry out with him as they reached their pleasure together.

As the last of her quivers and his faded, Warren didn't withdraw from her, but continued to hold her tight. She'd been as much of a dream for him as Priorton or his writing. Like them she was his, completely and without hesitation. In her arms failure couldn't touch him for there was more to strive for now than money or freedom. He would be for her the one constant she could count on, the person who never left her, who believed in her as she believed in him. Together they would pursue their art and become more than their pasts. With her, he couldn't fail.

He slid off to hold her close and she rested one curving leg on his hip as he traced circles on the alabaster flesh. The filtered light from the front half of the room turned her glowing skin a gorgeous shade of cream. She stroked the line of light hair in the centre of his chest, her heavy breasts resting against his chest rising and falling with a long, contented sigh. He matched it with one of his own, catching the birds twittering outside and the peace and still of the room and their time together.

'I assume you enjoyed that.' He smiled against her temple, not regretting what they'd done. It was the sealing of their promise to one another and there was nothing sordid about it.

'Very much,' she purred, her contentment matching his.

'There'll be a great deal more of that after we're married.' Their day before the altar couldn't come fast enough for him. He wanted her at Priorton with him, her inspiration filling the house and his life.

'I hope so,' she answered with a wicked little laugh. 'Will you obtain a common licence?'

'No, we'll read the banns so everyone will hear about our marriage and how proud I am to make you my wife. I don't want anyone to think it a quick and clandestine affair.'

'It'll be difficult to wait three weeks to make afternoons like this a regular and blessed affair.' She ran her tongue over her upper lip, like one of his more sultry admirers, but the gesture was for him the man, not the famous author.

His member began to stiffen in anticipation and he cupped his hand behind her neck and drew her to him. 'We needn't wait.'

Chapter Eleven

Morning light filled the study as Warren collected his papers in preparation for the visit to the vicar. It had been difficult to leave Marianne and the pleasure of the orangery yesterday, to spend the night away from her, but the sooner he arranged for the banns, the sooner their life together could begin. He folded the note from Marianne outlining the details of her birth and parentage which the vicar would need for the licence. They'd agreed to continue with the lie of her mother being her sister. Their marriage would create enough talk without the added gossip of her true lineage.

Lancelot raised his head to the door and let out a small bark.

Rupert stood there, glaring at Warren the way he did whenever he mentioned Leticia's death. 'I told you never to come back.' Warren marched up hard on him and grabbed him by the arm. 'Get out.'

Rupert's boots scratched and banged over the black and white tiles of the entry hall as Warren pulled him along.

'Not before I show you this.' Rupert jerked away, revealing more fortitude than he had during Leticia's trials. He shoved the piece of paper he was carrying in Warren's face.

Warren batted it aside. 'I'm no longer interested in anything involving you.'

'You should be. It's the stockholder agreement laying out all the assets of the company to be sold in case of debt or default. It outlines how you were the primary backer and placed Priorton Abbey as collateral in case the business failed. Everyone who invested in this venture was convinced you believed in it enough to stake your entire reputation and all your assets on its success. When the business fails, and it will, it's not me the investors will press to recoup their losses, but you.'

Warren snatched the paper out of Rupert's hands and skimmed the print. Sweat began to pool in the small of his back as he read in black and white Priorton Abbey and all future profits from his books laid out as collateral for the business. His stomach clenched as it had the first time he'd cut into flesh, but he fought to stay on his feet and to not give in to the horror chewing out his insides. This couldn't be. It was a lie, like everything connected to Rupert.

Warren flung the paper in Rupert's face, refusing to be bested by this scum of a man. 'I never agreed to this. This is fraud. I'll see you in the Old Bailey for what you've done, not just to me, but to other innocent people.'

Rupert allowed the paper to flutter to the ground, leering at Warren in triumph. 'I'm not the one who'll be pilloried in the newspapers when the truth comes out. You deserve to suffer like all those dupes whose money I took. They have bags of it, but when I asked them for a pittance they made me grovel for it, just like you did.'

'If you wanted what they and I have, you should have worked for it. Instead you were too lazy, you always have been.'

'Spare me another of your lectures. You'll need all your strength to write and keep this pile of mouldering bricks over your head.'

Lancelot trotted to Warren's side. He didn't sit on his haunches like he normally did, but remained on all fours. The hairs on the back of his neck rose as he pointed at Rupert and growled. If the dog were an Irish Wolfhound, capable of ripping Rupert's throat out, he'd set the animal on the man, but he wasn't about to risk Lancelot being hurt for the piece of filth standing across from him. He dropped his hand on the dog's head and stroked it, steadying the animal and himself. 'I'll fight you on this and you'll lose.'

'No, I won't. When you resist the seizure of Priorton Abbey, it'll appear as if you're unwilling to pay back everyone who trusted in you. Your entire reputation, everything you strived to build these last ten years, will come crumbling down around you.'

Fear curled through Warren again. Rupert was right. Warren had watched society tear down the Duke of York for his scandal over the selling of commissions and he was one of *them*. They'd do worse to Warren, a man viewed by many as an upstart who'd invaded their ranks. They'd be glad to see him demoted, crushed beneath their heels into oblivion while they continued with their rounds of balls and gossip.

'I helped you, Rupert, I gave you money when no one else would, provided my blessing for your and Leticia's marriage and this is how you thank me?' Warren hissed, wanting to take a sword from the arms on the wall and run Rupert through.

'You never helped me, but tried to turn Leticia against me. She said I was crazy to think you didn't believe in me or I wasn't good enough for her, but I was right. I hate you now more than the day I married her, or the morning you let her die.'

Warren rammed his fist into Rupert's face and his brother-in-law crumpled to the floor. He gripped his nose, wailing in agony as Warren stood over him. 'You bastard. You will return every last pound you accepted from every investor or heaven help me I'll make sure you hang for forgery.'

Rupert smiled through the blood running down his nose and dropping on the marble. 'I can't give it back. It's gone.'

'Then you'll find a way to work to repay it.'

Rupert pushed to his feet, wobbling on his toes, but never losing his nasty smirk. 'Not me, Warren, you. The day the debtors come to auction off your entire library, this house and all the rusty junk in it, I'll be here to watch. The morning your ship sets sail because you're forced back into the Navy to make a living, I'll be there on the wharf watching you. You'll regret the way you treated me.'

'I'll regret I didn't kill you.' He snatched a medieval dagger from the wall and held up the thin, sharp blade between them. Rupert's blackened eyes widened and he lost his arrogance as he scurried out of the house like a rat, fat drops of blood trailing him across the pebbled drive.

Warren dropped the knife and it clattered against the marble floor. His floor in the house he was about to lose, along with everything else he'd built. He snatched up the investment paper and read it, wanting to throw up the way he used to after surgery. How much money had Rupert taken and from whom? Warren couldn't fathom the trouble he was in, but it was large, like a wave at sea threatening to drown him.

He crumpled the paper between his sweaty hands. Everything was being cut out from under him, but he wouldn't allow it to be taken from him without a fight. He wouldn't go back to the Navy or lose everything he'd strived so hard to create. He had to get to London and Mr Berkshire. His solicitor, Mr Steed, and his barrister partner, Mr Dyer, were the best in London. They'd find a way to undo the damage and straighten out this mess before Rupert made it known. First he had to see Marianne and tell her before she found out about it from a more dubious source.

He hurried upstairs to change, pausing on the landing. The first floor was quiet since the workers had yet to arrive to begin their day. Beams, tools and cloths dusted with sawdust littered the hall and many of the adjoining rooms. The beauty of the house was hidden beneath the construction, as his life with Marianne was fast being eclipsed by Rupert's treachery.

He leaned on the hallway wall and rested his head against the cool plaster. The wood chips and their aroma of pine reminded him of a shipyard he'd once visited while in the Navy. In the scent was the very real possibility Warren might be forced back into the stinking ships reeking of death and blood to keep himself, Marianne and his mother from starving. He wouldn't allow it to happen, but if too much was owed, if he couldn't triumph over Rupert, he might not have a choice. He must support his mother. Marianne was another matter.

He pushed away from the wall and wandered to his room with heavy steps. Marianne's wealth could save him, or he could end up squandering it in the fight against Rupert like his father had squandered all his income from the living, leaving his family with nothing. In the end, he might still be forced to re-enlist and then where would she be? Sitting at home with his mother like Leticia used to do, in near poverty, constantly worrying about whether he would return or be blown to bits. To see her life torn apart the way his, Leticia's and his mother's had been by his father's death wasn't what he wanted for Marianne or their future children. He couldn't risk visiting the horror or uncertainty of poverty on those he loved by rushing Marianne into marriage.

Warren tugged at his cravat as he entered his bedroom and began gathering up everything he'd need to make for London after he had visited Marianne. He had no idea what he'd say to her or how he'd make her see they must postpone the ceremony until things were settled one way or another, no matter how much time it took. With any luck, it wouldn't be long, but with no real knowledge of the situation he now found himself in, he couldn't say. As much as he loved her and wanted her beside him in this crisis, he wouldn't drag her down with his failure or have another scandal heaped on her because of him.

He stuffed the crinkled stock agreement in his satchel along with his notebooks then buckled it, tugging the leather to make it tight. She would resist, but he'd make her see it was for the best for both for them. He'd never relied on a woman or anyone else for financial support before and he wouldn't do so now, nor have everyone, including her, doubt the sincerity of his love by the convenient timing of their union. He hoped she would agree to wait for him.

The very real prospect she wouldn't seized him and he leaned hard on his hands against his dressing table. He stared at his reflection in the mirror, his face as ashen as after an amputation. His inability to provide for a wife and his family, to be like his father, was everything he hadn't wanted, the reason for resisting her allure during their first days together. He was nothing without Marianne, but if Rupert succeeded in ruining him, he'd be even less. She deserved happiness, not squalor or a husband stinking of blood and gunpowder. No, it wouldn't come to that, he wouldn't allow it.

He straightened, regaining control over himself

and his fears as he hung the satchel strap over one shoulder. He loved her, but he wouldn't wed her as a failure. He would be for her the strong man who'd overcome this difficulty as he had every other one in his life, a man made worthy of her hand by the industry of his own.

'I wish we had time to go to London for the trousseau,' Lady Ellington good naturedly complained as they left the milliner's shop on the village high street, 'but with the wedding breakfast and so much else to plan, there isn't time.'

'It doesn't matter. I could be wed in my riding habit for all I care.' Marianne floated down the walk beside the Dowager, oblivious to the people wishing them good day as they passed. Not long ago, she'd thought the normal life of a young lady impossible. Today, she'd shopped for her trousseau, anticipating her union with Warren and all aspects of their life together. After telling Madame Martine the reason for their visit, Marianne was sure the news of her engagement would be all over the entire countryside by evening. It would be confirmed when the banns were read and then everyone who'd ever tried to pull her down would see they no longer had any hold on her. Even if they never stopped gossiping about her, she was done caring about what they said or thought. Her life with Warren was the only thing that mattered, the rest was simply noise.

'Miss Domville,' a voice called out over the passing wagons and the men laughing in front of the tobacconists. Down the walk Mr Hirst pushed through the promenading people in an effort to reach them. 'Miss Domville.'

'Come, we have more things to do today.' Marianne took Lady Ellington by the elbow and hustled her towards the coach. She wanted nothing to do with Mr Hirst or for his nasty, leering remarks to tarnish the happy day.

'Miss Domville, please wait, I must speak to you.' Mr Hirst jumped in front of them. His crooked and swollen nose beneath two black eyes and a blood-stained cravat was as startling as his insistence. 'It's urgent, about Warren.'

'Has there been an accident?' Panic seized Marianne. All her life so many pleasant times had been torn from her by people and circumstances outside of her control. Despite her elation over the engagement and Warren's love, it wasn't difficult to imagine something happening to end it all.

'Warren did this to me.' He pointed at his nose as if he expected pity.

'Then I'm sure you deserved it.' She pushed past him to reach the carriage where the tall footman stood, watching to decide if he should intervene or not.

'Wait, I've come to warn you. Warren only wants you for your money. His business venture is failing and he doesn't want to sell Priorton to pay back the investors. He needs your wealth to keep him out of debtors' prison.' He shoved a paper at her. 'This is the stock agreement, it outlines everything.'

Marianne stopped and Lady Ellington held up her

hand for the footman to remain where he was. Marianne took the paper, covering her mouth with one hand as she read the script laying out Priorton Abbey as a guarantee against losses and the backing of the investments by Warren.

'You aren't the only wealthy woman he's tried to woo either.' Mr Hirst slid an old edition of the *Morning Post* over the stock agreement. 'Lady Preston has also been a great admirer of his work, in more ways than one. With her support and your wealth, he can save Priorton, pay back the investors and keep the scandal from reaching the papers.'

Above a none-too-subtle allusion to Warren's relationship with Marianne was also printed an alleged affair with a Lady P. It had to be Lady Preston.

Lord Bolton's warning came rushing back to her.

'He might phrase the contract in prettier terms, but in the end he's after your money and he'll woo you for it like he wooed society and the Prince to get his title and lands.'

No, she wouldn't allow scum like Lord Bolton or Mr Hirst to make her doubt Warren. Warren had visited Lady Preston's manor to read his work, but it had been at the invitation of her husband. As for his wooing her before the truth could come out, she'd been the one to lead Warren to the orangery and hurry their intimacy. He wanted the banns read and for them to take their time and for her fortune to be safeguarded against his use. He wouldn't have insisted on any of those things if he'd wanted to capture her before she could flee, or if his need for her money was as urgent as Mr Hirst implied.

'I don't believe or trust you, Mr Hirst. I suspect it was you who gave this story to the papers and it's you who wants to brand him a liar and darken his name.' She flung the *Morning Post* into the dirt, then motioned for the footman to keep Mr Hirst at bay while she climbed into the coach. Lady Ellington swiftly followed, settling into the opposite seat, lips drawn tight with her concern.

'I'm trying to help you!' Mr Hirst shouted as the footman closed the door. 'Whatever misfortune you suffer, you've brought it on yourself,'

Mr Hirst's further cries were muffled as the carriage set off, leaving the bruised man yelling in the street.

Marianne studied the wrinkled document in her hand, the ink smudging the cream tip of her glove.

'Well?' Lady Ellington asked.

She handed her the stock agreement. 'I'm not sure what to make of it. It appears genuine but I'm not convinced.'

She'd learned from Madame de Badeau how easily letters and signatures could be forged. It was how Madame de Badeau had tried to bring down Cecelia and Lord Falconbridge. Her incriminating letter had been a note, this was a legal document. It was difficult to fathom Mr Hirst being criminal enough to draw up something like this, but his accusations went against everything she knew about Warren. He was too honourable to swindle people, too intent on making his own way to be a cheat or a con.

'You must speak to Sir Warren at once,' Lady Ellington advised. 'I'm sure he'll explain everything.'

She was right, but it didn't calm her fears. It wasn't simply the document which concerned her, but what else it meant. 'If what Mr Hirst said about the business venture is true, it will soon be all over London. My presence as Warren's intended wife will increase the gossip and make him look worse. There'll be no hiding away from it, or stopping people from bringing up my past to smear him.'

'No, my dear, there won't,' Lady Ellington gravely concurred. 'As his wife, you will have to face it and support him through it all.'

Marianne rubbed at the ink stain on her glove, amazed how once again notoriety was being thrust on her through no fault of her own. She couldn't flinch or hide away from it this time. By wedding Warren, she'd have to endure whatever vicious criticism was hurled at them and more stories like the one in the newspaper, possibly worse ones. It was what she'd feared when he'd asked her to play for him and when he'd encouraged her to publish her music.

She stared out of the carriage window at the passing countryside. The quiet existence she'd always craved was about to end in a way she never could have imagined. Instead of terrifying her, or making her want to hide from society or run from Warren as it would have a short while ago, the prospect of it no longer troubled her. The strength she'd relied on to stand firm against Madame de Badeau and her male visitors, the determination which had helped her endure every disappointment from her girlhood until now, would help carry her and Warren through this crisis. She loved him and she would stand beside him and their future, whatever it might hold.

Chapter Twelve

'You wish to postpone the marriage?' Marianne whispered, the floor rocking beneath her as though she were still in the carriage.

Warren stood across the garden path from her, his words littering the gravel between them like old leaves. It reminded her of the morning Mrs Nichols had told her she'd soon be leaving the school. She'd been impassive, direct, as if Marianne leaving the only home she'd ever known were nothing more than a slight upsetting of plans. It was the same way Warren had delivered his news and it chilled her just as much.

'Only until this issue with Rupert can be settled. I must stop Rupert and make sure he doesn't get away with it.' Warren had explained everything to her, his brother-in-law's role in the affair, the risk to Priorton and Warren's innocence in the scheme.

'We needn't delay the wedding for him, or allow his treachery to ruin our plans. Besides, you'll need funds to fight him and I have those.' Her bottom lip quivered ever so slightly as she tried to speak like the brave woman she wanted to be.

'And I won't take them, nor will I rely on the riches of a wife to save me or Priorton.'

'I want you to have them, for everything of mine to be yours,' she cried, wincing at the desperation in her voice. He was pulling away and she was trying to cling to him, as her mother had clung to Lord Falconbridge. If he wanted to be free of her, she should comport herself with dignity and let him go, but she couldn't.

'No.' The word was as hard as his stance and she sensed nothing, not a rational argument or even tears, could make him change his mind.

A gentle breeze blew across the rose bushes behind her, but the hard-pruned and scraggily branches barely moved. She wished she were as untouched by the cold as they were, then Warren's words wouldn't be tearing her apart. 'Why are you pushing me away?'

Warren's chest burned at the stricken look which came over Marianne's delicate features. She appeared as his mother had the morning they'd lost Leticia, as though the world was ending. It killed him to cause her such pain, but he must. 'I won't allow you to risk your fortune or jeopardise your security because, like a fool, I trusted Rupert.'

'Liar. You don't want me because you've finally discovered how much my situation will reflect on you. Once the public sees you with a woman like me, they'll judge you much harsher than they would if it were the venture alone sinking you.' Marianne settled her shoulders, a mask of indifference sliding over her. She was retreating from him and returning to the self-preserving caution which had marked her first days at Priorton.

Desperation seized him as it had when he'd realised Leticia was dying. He couldn't allow her to slip away from him or to stop him from doing what he knew was the best for both of them. He might hate himself now as much as she did, but some day when this was behind them, they'd both see he'd done the right thing. He only had to convince her to keep faith in him and his plan. 'It isn't true. I love you too much to have your past and all the stories about you dragged through the papers and ballrooms because of me. Nor will I allow our marriage to be questioned and doubted by everyone until they weaken your belief in me.'

'It isn't them weakening it, but you. You spent so much time working to get me to rely on you, cajoling me to care for you, convincing me you loved me. Then, at the first whisper of trouble, you run away.'

'I'm not running. I still need you, nothing about that has changed, but we can't marry until I'm clear. Can't you understand?' He took her hand, but it was like holding one of Lancelot's paws. She was no longer the passionate woman who'd pulled him into the orangery and shared with him the most intimate parts of herself, and it was his fault. 'I won't drag us both into poverty.'

'You're not your father, Warren,' Marianne said in an even voice, something of the caring woman coming back into her expression.

He dropped her hand, her words like a slap he deserved. 'I will be if I fail.'

Her lips thinned with her anger. 'Then go to London and save yourself. I no longer care.'

She whirled on her heel and made for the house.

'Marianne, wait,' he called after her, but this time his entreaty didn't stop her.

'No, I won't be humiliated by you or waste my life waiting. I'm finished with you,' she cried over her shoulder before disappearing inside.

Tears blurred Marianne's eyes as she rushed into the sitting room and slammed the French doors closed behind her. She turned the lock, determined to stop him from pursuing her. The rings at the top of the curtain panels rattled in protest as she jerked them together, darkening the sitting room and turning the silent pianoforte a deeper black. She staggered to the instrument and sat down on the bench. The two brass knobs on the key cover were cold against her skin as she tried to take hold of them, but she couldn't make her trembling hands co-operate. At last she gave up, glad she couldn't play. She feared the dark and forbidding notes which might come from her. She'd loved him and he'd pushed her away just like the Smiths, like her mother, like everyone she'd ever cared about. She'd trusted him with her heart and her body and he'd made her regret it.

Tears streamed down her cheeks as a new anguish emerged from her sorrow. She dropped her hands to her stomach. Nothing there felt different and it would be a week or more before she knew how terrible a mistake she'd made with him. If a child came from their lovemaking, not even Lord Bolton would have her and the repercussions would be far greater than anything she'd ever faced before.

She rose and began to pace across the rug, refusing to glance out of the single uncovered window to the view of the orangery. Its place as a sanctuary was over, just as Lady Ellington's house might soon be denied to her too. The Falconbridge family had been steadfast in their support of her when all the rumours had been unfounded. If they were proven true, through an illegitimate child, there'd be no reason for them not to cast her out. Lord Falconbridge had already warned Lady Ellington about Marianne and Warren.

She shuddered to think what lies she'd have to resort to like her mother had to protect herself and a baby. She'd vowed never to be like her, except she was. Fresh tears stung her eyes. In the end, no wonder Warren hadn't wanted her.

'Marianne, what's wrong?' Lady Ellington appeared in the sitting room doorway. 'I heard you and Sir Warren shouting at one another in the garden and Darby tells me he left in a hurry. What happened?'

Marianne faced her friend, afraid of seeing the care and concern etching her delicate features turn into loathing and disgust. They wouldn't if Marianne kept silent about the depth of her relationship with Warren, but all the pain tearing her apart wouldn't allow it.

'I've made a horrible mistake and you'll hate me for it.' She buried her face in her hands and dropped back down on the bench, wishing she could stop crying, but she couldn't.

'I could never hate you, my dear.' Lady Ellington hurried to her, taking her in her plump arms and pressing Marianne against her chest. She stroked her back in the motherly way Marianne had craved during so many dark times in her childhood. 'Now, tell me everything.'

Lady Ellington held Marianne as the details of Marianne's conversation and relationship with Warren came spilling out. She couldn't hold the words back as she confessed her intimacy with Warren and her fears of what might happen because of it. Lady Ellington listened without interrupting as all the loneliness, abandonment, helplessness and tragedy which had marked Marianne's twenty years filled her words.

When Marianne was done, she braced herself, expecting Lady Ellington to rail at her for being so foolish and surrendering to temptation. Instead, the woman shook her head as though considering a blight on her roses. 'This is troubling.'

'I'll understand if you don't want me here any more,' Marianne choked out. Of all the places she'd ever had to leave, this one would hurt the most. Lady Ellington had been the closest thing to a mother Marianne had ever experienced.

'There's no reason for you to go anywhere.'

'But what about Lord Falconbridge? I overheard him say to you the other day my future here depended on there being no scandal with Warren.'

'That's not what he said at all, my dear. He was afraid if I was wrong about you and Sir Warren, you'd be hurt and things might become even more difficult for you in this part of the world than they already are.' Lady Ellington laid her jewelled hand on Marianne's and clasped it tight. Her eyes, which were usually so full of mirth, were serious and determined. 'I would never throw you out, not for any reason. And don't you dare worry about Randall, he wouldn't either. No matter what happens you'll always be welcome here.'

'Why? Why do you keep standing beside me when everyone else walks away?' Marianne asked with no small amount of shame, for both her behaviour and her low opinion of Lord Falconbridge.

'Because I know what it's like to be unfairly judged by others, especially for things you haven't done. My brother Edgar was a greater womaniser than King Charles II. After I lost my husband,' Lady Ellington fingered her diamond bracelet, her voice catching before she continued, 'and I came to live with him, I couldn't even talk to a gentleman without everyone thinking we were lovers and I was as wanton as Edgar. Refusing to remarry made the rumours worse, but after my husband, I couldn't wed again without love. I certainly couldn't accept any of the fortune hunters chasing after me.

'Then, one summer, when I couldn't take much more of the vicious rumours, I considered a proposal from doddery old Lord Fontgrass, thinking it would end them. When I told Edgar, he rode to Lord Fontgrass's and told him he and his proposal could go to hell. Then he came to me and, in his oh, so delicate way, said he didn't care what I or anyone thought about me and I shouldn't either. I should live as I wanted and ignore everyone else. He was right.'

Marianne shook her head. 'It can't have been so easy.'

'It wasn't, but in time when everyone realised they couldn't hurt me, they lost interest in trying. I want the same thing for you.'

'I thought I had it until this morning, but I don't.' Marianne's shoulders slumped with her sorrow. 'If there's a baby, everyone will know I'm no better than my mother and all their derision of me will at last be vindicated.'

'If there is a child, we will deal with it as we have every other issue.' Lady Ellington sat back and took Marianne by the chin and fixed her with a serious look. 'As for you being like your mother, you are nothing like her. You have a heart. She never did. You are caring and loyal to those you love, even Sir Warren. Don't give up on him or your future, Marianne. You'll regret it if you do.'

'But he doesn't want me.'

'He does. He loves you as much as you love him, I'm sure of it, but I fear he's in a difficult state right now and not thinking clearly. Like you, he's fought his battles alone for so long, he can't conceive of accepting help, but you must assist him whether he wants it or not.'

Marianne considered what she said and what Warren had told her. He hadn't called off the wedding, but asked her to wait. She'd taken it as a rejection and retreated into her old habits just like he had. If she didn't find some way to make him see his mistake, as Lady Ellington had helped her to recognise hers, she might lose him for good. She couldn't allow it or return to the lonely life she'd led before she'd met him. She did love him and she wouldn't lose him, but she would fight for their future, though she had no idea how. 'What can I do if he doesn't want my help?'

Lady Ellington shook her head, as at a loss for ideas as Marianne. 'We'll think of something, some way to assist him which won't damage his pride.'

Marianne leaned back against the piano, the sharp edge of the key cover pressing into her back. If he refused to take her money, perhaps she could speak with Mr Berkshire and arrange to purchase some of Warren's books. Maybe Lord Falconbridge could act on her behalf, but if Warren ever discovered the ruse, it would undermine his need to help himself. If only he'd written a new story, the one he'd craved when he'd first proposed their arrangement. Then he'd have his next novel and the funds it might raise.

Marianne sat up straight as the idea struck her. 'The book.'

'What book?' Lady Ellington asked as confused as Marianne was excited.

'*Lady Matilda's Trials*. It's still upstairs in my desk. It's the one he sent me after we first visited him at Priorton.' The one she'd made him burn because of her fears. It was his fears ruling them now and she wouldn't allow it, like she would no longer hide from her past and the gossip or life, but face it and live as she wished. Marianne didn't know how many people would see the truth behind Lady Matilda's story, but it was a chance she had to take. 'If I give Mr Berkshire the manuscript, Warren will have his next novel, his advance, and the chance to earn enough money to pay back the investors and the solicitors.'

Lady Ellington clutched Marianne's hands, gripped by the thrill of the scheme. 'Then we must go to London at once.'

'Well, Mr Steed, can we fight it?' Warren asked the solicitor. He sat in Mr Steed's Temple Bar offices as the illustrious solicitor read over the document. From a room on the lower floor a woman and a man screamed at one another.

Mr Dyer, the noted barrister, read over his partner's shoulder. The gentleman had a reputation for dealing with forgery cases. There were rumours Mr Dyer had gained his flair for uncovering forgers through his secret work with the Alien Office, rooting out criminals and spies, but they'd never been confirmed. Mr Berkshire paid them to keep copies of Warren's books from appearing under the names of other printers. Hopefully, they were as good at preventing Warren's name from being connected to fraud as they were at maintaining the integrity of his work.

'What do you think?' Mr Steed asked his colleague.

Warren tapped his foot, waiting for an answer. If Steed and Dyer couldn't help him, he was sunk.

'Looks like Fink's work. See the O there and the way he's spelled Lord Cartwright's name. For a forger, he can't spell worth a damn.' Mr Dyer perched his hands on his hips, drawing back the corners of his coat and emphasising his impressive height and stance. 'I'll speak with him, persuade him it's more lucrative and to his advantage to confess than to try and protect Mr Hirst. I'm sure he'll be eager to assist us. It's better than swinging for forgery.'

The man's and woman's yelling grew louder, adding to Warren's tension. 'And if Mr Fink won't give evidence against him?'

'If Mr Hirst has no other documents from you supporting his claim to an agreement, then you have a very sturdy case against him. Your reputation, which up to this point has been sterling, should help.'

Warren's reputation wasn't so sterling after his time in the country. Lord and Lady Cartwright would be all too willing to testify to his shortcomings if this issue did come to trial. He wasn't sure who else might come forward to join them, eager to get rid of this upstart in their ranks. He could well imagine Lady Preston joining the chorus of his critics, and Marianne.

Regret gripped him for what he'd done, but there was no time to entertain it.

'I also doubt Mr Hirst has the resources to fight this in court,' Mr Steed added, laying the stock agreement on the blotter of his pristine desk. 'Especially if, as you say, he's squandered the money.'

'He's probably squirrelled it away somewhere,' Mr Dyer speculated. 'He'll need it, especially since he's the one who approached the investors. Even though he's tied this to you, Sir Warren, those who lost money will remember him and sue him too. If nothing else, he will need an income to live off if he plans to leave England to escape any consequences.'

It was thin comfort. If even a part of the money existed, it would alleviate some of Warren's debt, but they still had no idea what the outstanding amount was. It might be staggering, more than whatever Rupert had hidden away, or Warren could raise without selling Priorton.

'And the court of public opinion? A trial could ruin me and everything I've worked so hard to build,' Warren reminded them.

'Then we must make sure it doesn't come to trial,' Mr Dyer said. 'We'll find a way for Mr Hirst to admit his guilt by convincing him there's no other route but to produce whatever money is left and then disappear. I understand Australia is quite charming for criminals.'

He laughed, but Warren could barely join him. He wished he had the barrister's confidence in the outcome of this issue, but he didn't. Every expectation he'd considered solid in the last few days had shifted beneath him like the sea in a storm. Priorton and his career were in danger and all his dreams of a life with Marianne were gone.

He pressed his fingertips together and stared at the tightly fitted floorboard between his boots. He'd acted like an ass with her, storming away like a stubborn child, determined not to need anyone's help but he did, especially hers. He dropped his hands and sat up. No, he'd been right to postpone the marriage. He'd promised her at the start of their relationship he wouldn't expose her to more scandal and he wouldn't, nor would he chain her to a man burdened with the risk of ruin. 'Do whatever you have to, but make sure this doesn't become public.'

'Don't worry, Sir Warren, we'll see to it justice is done,' Mr Dyer assured him before Warren took his leave.

He hailed a hack, ready to make for Mr Reed's house to discuss his finances. Together, they'd see what could be sold to raise money and what measures might be taken to save Priorton in case things were even worse than they'd imagined. A vehicle drew up to the kerb. Warren gave the driver directions then climbed inside, wrinkling his nose at the mouldy smell of the conveyance.

The brackish taste of cask water began to singe his tongue.

No, not this. I don't need this.

He pressed his fingers to his temples, trying to drive back the chilling memory of the scrape of saw against bone and the unending screams of his patients and the moans of the wounded. The rock of the carriage as it drove along made the memories worse, mimicking the roll and pitch of a ship. He opened his eyes, hoping the daylight would drive it all back, but the darkness of the hack and the mouldy stench of its seats made the visions worse.

He banged on the roof, bringing the vehicle to a halt. He staggered out, dragging in a large lungful of the foul London air. The sooty river stench was preferable to the damp and rot of the hack, but not as settling as Marianne and her fragrant flower perfume.

'Everything all right, sir?' the driver asked from atop his high seat.

Warren fished a coin out of his pocket and tossed it up to the man. 'I need to walk.'

He made off down the street, weaving through the teeming mass of people. One or two paused to study him and he prayed they wouldn't recognise him. He didn't have the stamina to smile and coddle their interest in him. Anonymity was what he craved and Marianne. He shouldn't have let her go or pushed her away. In doing so he'd destroyed everything he'd built between them, he'd caught it in the hardness of her stance and her sharp, dismissing words. She'd spent her life being rejected by people and in the end he'd proven himself no better than them.

He ducked into a nearby pub and elbowed his way through the patrons to the publican behind the counter. He thumped the top of the scarred wood. 'Brandy.'

The publican poured out a measure into a pewter glass and set it before Warren. Warren lifted the cool metal cup to his lips and threw back the burning liquid. It made his eyes water, but settled him the same way rum used to aboard ship when nothing else would ease his nerves after a battle. He motioned to the publican for another. After three more, he dropped four coins on the counter and left the dark and tobacco-filled pub for the bright and noisy London streets.

Panic didn't drive him on as it had in the hack. Like the desperate days at sea when the end of his maritime nightmare had been something out of sight over the horizon, a life with Marianne didn't seem as unfathomable as before. He more than anyone knew all hells eventually ended and when his did, he'd court her again. Regaining her trust would take more hard work than pulling in sails during a storm, but he'd do it. It was the one good thing he had to look forward to and he held on tight to it as he moved with the surge of people in the street. He'd achieved every goal he'd ever set himself to and he would win her heart again once things with Rupert were settled.

Chapter Thirteen

'Thank you for seeing me on such short notice, Mr Berkshire.' Marianne smiled at the publisher as she sat before his desk. Warren's manuscript rested on her lap, a potent reminder of the risk she was about to take and what it might gain her. 'Sir Warren would have brought this to you himself, but he's been delayed by some trouble with his brother-in-law.'

Mr Berkshire scrunched his thick eyebrows in confusion. 'We spoke before he went to see my solicitor and he told me he didn't have a completed manuscript.'

'He was being modest. He gave me this copy before he left the country and asked me to deliver it to you when I joined him in town.' She held the journal out across the desk, struggling to grip it despite the tremble in her arm. Once the story was in the publisher's hands it would only be a matter of time before it was out in the world for all to see. She hoped Warren had hidden the truth of Lady Matilda's inspiration as well as he'd claimed.

Mr Berkshire reached out and took the other end of the manuscript. He began to pull it back and she opened her fingers to let go.

'I'll be sure to get on the story at once,' Mr Berkshire assured her. 'I hope this wretched to do with his brother-in-law doesn't undermine his talent. It could end up costing Sir Warren a great deal more than his livelihood.'

She knew all too well about the cost to him and her

'Then we must make sure that doesn't happen.'

Warren crumpled up a piece of paper and threw it aside to join the many others littering the floor. He dug his elbows into the desk and scraped his fingers through his hair, wanting to cry out in frustration. After leaving Mr Reed's more morose than buoyed, he'd come home to his narrow town house in Gough Square, determined to finish this manuscript. He'd sat here the entire night trying to work, hoping it would settle the demons plaguing him. It had only made things worse. He had nothing to show for his efforts except dark circles under his eyes and wasted sheets of paper. Another expense he didn't need.

He took a deep breath, trying to calm himself without giving in to the temptation of having a drink. Fuddling his mind wouldn't help him, but perseverance would. He'd written with the pitch and roll of the ship making him sick. He'd worked beneath a single candle with the smell of dust and blood surrounding him. He could work through this. He picked up his pen, dipped it in the inkwell and poised it over the paper. A drop of ink hit the surface, feathering out on the parchment, but still nothing came to him.

He tossed down his pen before the door opened and his mother entered.

'Warren, you must eat.' She carried in a tray of cheese, cold meat and bread and set it on the corner of his desk. He'd tried to leave his mother at Priorton, but she'd insisted on accompanying him to London. She was just as worried as he was over the Rupert affair.

Warren glanced at the food, then hunched over the paper to read what little he'd managed to complete. 'I'm not hungry.'

'You won't help anyone if you make yourself sick.'

She was right. He snatched up the bread, tore off a piece and ate it. Once it was in his mouth his stomach growled and he at last acknowledged his hunger. 'I hate it when you're practical.'

'I hate it when you're pig-headed, just like your father.'

'I'm not like him.' He refused to be, at least where providing for those he loved was concerned.

His mother studied him, her head tilted to one side. 'In most ways you aren't, but you have his determination to make something of yourself.'

'Except he never did.' Warren flicked a crumb off of his paper. It landed on the floor in front of Lancelot's nose and the dog licked it up.

'He would have if he'd been granted more time.' His mother crossed her hands in front of her, regaining the stalwart but serene stance of a vicar's wife. 'I know you blame him for leaving us like he did, but try and forgive him, Warren. He was a good father to you and Leticia while he was alive.'

'Yes, he was.' Warren reached down beside his chair to scratch Lancelot's back. She was right. He should remember the father who'd cleaned up the breastplate for him and encouraged his fantasies, instead of the one he'd cursed after his death. Like Warren, he'd had his ambitions, but not enough time on earth to pursue them. His dreams had been snatched from him by death, just like Warren's were being threatened by Rupert.

Lancelot stood up among the wads of papers surrounding him and stared at the door. He wagged his tale, appearing more animated than at any other time today.

'What is it, boy?'

The bang of the front knocker echoed through the town house.

'Perhaps it's Miss Domville,' his mother offered, optimistic as always.

Warren continued to stroke the dog's back. 'She isn't one for convention, but not even she is likely to appear at the home of a single gentleman.'

'I don't know. She might surprise you.'

He wished she would. It would bolster his belief in winning her back after everything was settled.

The butler's voice echoed through the hall, followed by Mr Berkshire's. Warren's shoulders sank. It wasn't Marianne.

'Congratulations, Warren, you've done it again,' Mr Berkshire enthused as he strode into the room. Lancelot bounded up to him and received a hearty back rub. 'Mrs Stevens, you have the most talented son.'

'I know and he's persistent with it, just like his father.' She smiled warmly at Warren before leaving the men to their business.

He didn't mind the comparison because it was true. His father had given him a reason to strive and succeed. Without it, he wouldn't have achieved everything he was fighting to hold on to.

'Has Mr Steed or Mr Dyer told you something about the case?' Warren rose to greet his guest, hoping he had good news for him.

Mr Berkshire appeared stunned at the mention of the nasty business. 'No, this is about your new manuscript. I read it last night and I couldn't put it down. It's excellent. You've never written anything like it before. I think it'll outsell even your last story.'

'What new manuscript? I didn't send you one.'

'Modesty won't serve you this time.' Mr Berkshire helped himself to some of the brandy on the sideboard by the bookcase. '*Lady Matilda's Trials* is brilliant.'

Warren gaped at his friend as Berkshire sipped his drink. 'How did you get that manuscript?'

'Miss Domville brought it to me yesterday just as you told her to. It's magnificent and I want to get it into print at once.' He smacked his lips in appreciation of the fine liquor.

'Miss Domville gave you a manuscript?' It wasn't possible.

Mr Berkshire stopped mid-drink and eyed Warren over the top of the glass. 'Don't tell me she wrote it and is passing it off as yours, in which case I need to find the young lady at once. She's quite a talent. Better than you.' He laughed before he threw back the drink.

'No, I wrote it.' Warren stared down at his scrawled handwriting marring the paper on his blotter. Marianne had given Mr Berkshire the novel, the one she'd made him burn. She'd come to his aid even after his rebuke of her the other day and she was here in London. It could only mean one thing. He hadn't lost her, despite his stupidity.

Berkshire set aside the empty glass. 'Well, I can't sit here all day congratulating you. I'll have my man send over the last half of your advance. With this book finally done, can I sign you up for another? Same terms as before? I can have Steed's clerk draw up the contract this afternoon.'

Warren shook himself out of his musing. 'No, I want twice as much for the next one.'

'All right, it's yours. I'll get the manuscript to the printer right away, strike while the iron is hot as they say. Maybe we can release it before there's any more trouble with your brother-in-law?'

As fast as Warren's spirits rose, they came crashing back down. 'Are you sure you want to sign a contract with a man teetering on the verge of scandal?'

'You wouldn't be the first notorious author I've handled. Besides, might increase sales the way it did for Lady Caroline Lamb's awful tome.'

Warren tapped the top of his desk. 'If it doesn't destroy me first.'

Mr Berkshire scratched his stomach on the outside

of his waistcoat. 'It's called a pen name, my boy. People use them all the time. You could too. Then, when people forget the scandal, we find a way to out you to the papers. We could make a fortune with the story.'

'You give people too much credit for short memories.' Once the scam became public Warren would be linked to the swindle for ever. There weren't enough pen names available to save him.

'Listen, Warren, I've been in publishing a long time and if there's one thing I've learned, there's no such thing as a smooth path. No matter what happens or what you've achieved, some problem will always arise. It's the one constant you can depend on and the entire reason I engaged Mr Steed and Mr Dyer. The trick is to face each challenge and overcome it. Those who do, succeed, those who don't crumple under the pressure and quit.'

'I can see why they give up. It would be a hell of a lot easier.'

'But you won't. You never have. That's why I believed in you. Still do. Today it will be your brother-in-law, tomorrow something else. You'll get through this and your difficulties with the young lady. I have no doubt of it.'

With a nod, Berkshire took his leave.

Lancelot watched Warren from his place before the fire, mildly interested as always. Warren summoned the dog to his side and stroked the soft fur, the motion centring him and allowing him to think clearly for the first time since the sun had set the night before.

* * *

'Why you returned to London in the autumn is beyond me,' Lady St Onge complained as they sat in the morning room of Lady Ellington's Hyde Park town house taking tea.

'I told you, Miss Domville and I came to London to purchase the last of her wedding trousseau.' This was the lie they'd agreed upon before they'd left Welton Place to keep from announcing the indefinite postponement of the wedding. If all went well, Marianne and Warren would keep their date before the vicar. She prayed they did. Marianne had endured a great number of humiliations in her life. She didn't relish adding betrothed for less than a day to the long list. 'There's only so much we can secure in Sussex.'

'Too true,' Lady St Onge mumbled into her tea cup before taking a sip.

Marianne didn't touch her tea, allowing it to grow cold on the table in front of her. Despite giving the manuscript to Mr Berkshire yesterday, they'd heard nothing from Warren. His publisher must have told him of Marianne's visit by now.

'At least remove the door knocker so no one realises you're here,' Lady St Onge suggested. 'Otherwise, people will talk.'

'One would think you were old enough not to care what people think,' Lady Ellington observed as she blew the steam from her tea.

'We don't all have your years of learning to ignore it, what with your brother and nephew.' Lady St Onge set down her cup with a rattle.

Marianne wondered if they shouldn't take the knocker off the door. It would stop her from spending the rest of the day waiting for it to hit the strike plate. When the morning post had come and gone without a word from Warren, Marianne had suggested they pay a call on him, but Lady Ellington had balked. The Dowager might be one of the first to defy a convention or two, but not this one and not in London. Despite Marianne's impatient protests, Lady Ellington was certain if Marianne waited Warren would come to her. She tried to believe he would, if only to keep from going mad while she waited.

Lady Ellington offered her cousin an impish smile. 'Don't be so sanctimonious, Rosemary. You chased after Edgar like half the ladies of the *ton*, despite, or should I say because of, his scandals.'

Lady St Onge grew redder beneath her rogue and adjusted the pin holding closed her high necked gown. 'What a ridiculous thing for you to say.'

Marianne caught the hint of a smile before the grand dame smothered it. She'd have to be sure to ask Lady Ellington about it once they were alone. It was hard to imagine the prim old widow having any kind of amorous past. It was also difficult to not picture herself turning into a woman like Lady St Onge if their plan failed.

The thud of the front-door knocker echoed through the house and Marianne nearly knocked over the table with her knee as she twisted in her chair to try and see out of the front window. She exchanged a look with

Lady Ellington, who raised her chin with pride. 'That will teach you to doubt me.'

'You don't even know who it is,' Marianne shot back, secretly wanting to be proven wrong.

'It's probably Lady Rexton,' Lady St Onge added with a purse of her wrinkled lips. 'She saw your carriage and now wants to chatter on about her youngest son. As if anyone cares about him tromping through the African jungle.'

The old lady's muttering didn't last as Darby opened the front door. A deep voice rolled through the entrance hall.

'I believe it is Sir Warren.' Lady Ellington threw Marianne an *I told you so* look.

'Even more reason why you should have removed the knocker.' Lady St Onge sniffed. 'Look at the riff-raff you're attracting.'

'Rosemary, you're speaking of Marianne's betrothed,' Lady Ellington reminded in a firm voice.

'Oh, yes, I'd forgotten. Sorry, my dear,' the cantankerous woman grudgingly apologised.

Marianne didn't care what Lady St Onge said. Warren was here. He'd come to see her, just like Lady Ellington had assured her he would. It was what he'd come here to say she worried about.

She rose, adjusting the lace fichu over her chest. She shouldn't get excited. He might be about to officially end the engagement, their time apart having reinforced his decision to avoid adding her scandals to his. She faced the door, holding her breath as Warren's steady footsteps carried down the hall.

At last he stepped into the room and she swallowed hard. He appeared as serious this morning as he had in the painting at Priorton, the brim of his hat clutched tight in his ink-blackened hands. Shadows darkened the skin beneath his eyes with a weariness she felt. She'd barely slept these last few nights and she doubted he had either. Whatever had happened during their time apart, it hadn't eased his burdens or made him happy. She didn't revel in his misery, for it was hers too and with only one cure.

'Sir Warren, welcome. Will you join us for tea?' Lady Ellington greeted, unflustered by his appearance or her cousin's disapproving grimace.

'I'd like an audience with Miss Domville, please?' He fixed on Marianne as though the other two ladies didn't exist. 'Alone.'

Marianne shifted her feet forward, eager to jump up and rush into his arms, but she forced herself to remain seated, determined to retain at least some of her dignity.

'Of course. Rosemary, please join me in the sitting room.' Lady Ellington took her cousin by the arm and drew her out of the chair.

'You can't leave her alone with a gentleman. It isn't proper,' Lady St Onge protested as Lady Ellington all but dragged her from the room and closed the door behind them.

Marianne rose and laced her hands in front of her, willing her shaky legs to support her. 'It seems I'm to be bold with a gentleman once again.'

A small smile split the severity of his lips, bringing a bit of light to his eyes. It heartened her and she dropped her hands to her side as the tension between them began to ease.

'I understand you've been bold not just with me, but with my publisher. Mr Berkshire said you gave him *Lady Matilda's Trials*.'

'I did.' She couldn't discern if he was happy or angry about her decision.

'Why?'

'It's your best work and you need the money from the sale of it to fight Mr Hirst.'

'And the fact it's your story?'

'If it helps you, then let everyone read it. I no longer care what they think.' She slipped the ring on and off her finger, waiting for his response, to learn where they stood. 'Was I right to do it?'

'You were.' He set his hat down on the chair beside him and came to stand over her like the day in the cloister when he'd tried so hard to make her see she was more than gossip or her past. Much more. 'I wanted to save myself through my own industry. You giving him the story means I will, but I couldn't have done it without you. I can't continue to do it if you aren't with me. I love you, Marianne, and if you'll still have me, I want you to be my wife.'

She closed the small distance between them and laid her hand on his cheek. His skin, cool from his time outside, warmed beneath her touch. 'Through richer or poorer?'

'Through it all.' He took her by the waist and pulled her to him, his fingers digging into her sides with an intensity which echoed in her heart. 'I'm sorry I was a stubborn fool. I love you.'

'I love you, too.'

He claimed her lips with a relief as palpable as hers. This was everything she'd wanted when she and Lady Ellington had climbed into the carriage and set out for London, and the coming true of every girlish dream. All would be well between them. She was as certain of it today as she had been when they'd made love in the orangery. Their future together had nearly been ruined by their fears and misunderstandings. Neither of them would ever allow such a thing to happen again.

Warren savoured Marianne's moist lips and her curving figure against his angles. He wrapped his arms around her, not ever wanting to let go. Her love for him had been stronger than his troubles and hers, and although so many things remained unsettled or uncertain, in her embrace it didn't matter. He broke from their kiss, pressed his forehead against hers and inhaled her rich peony scent.

'Thank you for understanding.' She always had, never once laughing at his dreams, or his weaknesses. With her he'd stopped to enjoy what he'd built for himself. He wanted to share it and all with her, but there were still obstacles facing them. 'My dealings with Rupert aren't over yet.'

'Then we'll fight him together. If only the common licence didn't force us to wait seven days. We could marry at once and put all this foolishness behind us.'

She straightened his wrinkled cravat, her hands on his chest light yet heady.

'Perhaps we don't have to wait.' He took one of her hands and raised it to his mouth, pressing his lips to the pulse of her wrist and making her inhale sharply. 'The Cartwrights may not like me, but I have other friends among the peerage, including one in the Prince's employ. He might be able to intercede with the bishop on our behalf and gain us a special licence.'

'If he can't, Lady Ellington and Lord Falconbridge certainly can. It will be expensive,' she warned, but he didn't care.

'I'll pay any cost to be with you.' He lowered his face to hers, her mouth tantalisingly close to his when someone behind them cleared their throat. He groaned, wondering if on their wedding night they'd be interrupted by as many people as those who regularly intruded on their kisses. He would have to make sure their bedroom door had a lock. He didn't want anything, not servants or intrusive relatives, to interrupt their wedded bliss.

Marianne stepped out of his arms with a mirthful smile, she more than Warren finding amusement in the interruption. They turned to find Darby waiting for their attention.

'Sir Warren, this arrived for you from your town house. The messenger said you are to read it at once.'

Warren took the letter, noting the mark of Mr Steed and Mr Dyer. 'It's from the solicitor.'

He tore it open as the butler left them. He read over

the missive, the calm Marianne's sacrifice for him had brought increasing with Mr Steed's words.

'What does he say?' Marianne peered over his arm to read the letter.

'Mr Dyer has some evidence he thinks will send Rupert running from his claims and out of our lives. We have to present it to him and we'll need your help to do it.'

'I'll do anything to ensure he and his lies are destroyed.'

'I don't see why this meeting is necessary,' Rupert sneered at Warren from across the study in Warren's town house. Mr Steed and Mr Dyer watched the exchange from where they sat beneath the far window. Warren hadn't introduced them and they hadn't revealed who they were or why they were here. Rupert seemed to wonder at it as well as he glanced back and forth at the gentlemen, waiting for them to speak. 'Everything we needed to discuss was done in the country.'

'No, there's a great deal more we have to talk about.' Warren rose and came around the desk. 'I want a list of all the investors and how much each of them gave you. I also want an accounting of the money you still have, no matter how small, and with it a tally of your possessions and valuables which can be sold to raise more.'

'I won't give you any of the information, but let you swing while every investor rushes to attack you,' Rupert answered with wicked delight, his satisfaction in his victory making Warren want to blacken his eyes an even deeper shade of purple than they already were. Instead he remained calm, refusing to sink to his brother-in-law's level. 'I want you to sell Priorton to pay them back and then be thrown in debtors' prison because it still isn't enough.'

'The only one who'll go to prison is you. As for going into debt, it isn't possible. While Priorton has cost me a great deal, I'm far from broke or without resources.' Warren strolled to the door connecting the study to the adjacent sitting room.

'Of course you are. You can barely afford to pay the workmen, much less the investors.'

'On the matter of my finances, you're gravely mistaken.' Warren opened the door. Marianne strode through, the diamond engagement ring gifted to her by Lady Ellington and adorning her finger glittering in the early morning light. He took her by the hand and raised it to his lips. The memory of everything they'd shared in the orangery, and her coming to him in London, settled the anger and disgust struggling to take control of him. All would be well. Together they would make sure of it. 'I believe you already know my betrothed. We will be married by special licence tomorrow.'

Rupert gaped at them as he grasped what the coming marriage meant, but he remained stubborn in his hate. 'So, once you're done spending your money, you'll waste hers and in the end you'll both be without a house or reputations. I'll see to it the press ruins you for swindling aristocrats, then aligning yourself with the notorious relation of a whore.'

Warren's arm stiffened and he stepped forward to strike him, but Marianne's restraining hand stopped him. No, he couldn't hit the snake. They still needed a small measure of his co-operation.

'My guardian, Lord Falconbridge, is a prudent man,' Marianne replied with confidence, peering down her elegant nose at Rupert as though he were a weed in Lady Ellington's rose bed. 'As we speak, he is arranging for my money to be placed in trust where I will have access to it, but creditors will not.'

'You can't save him,' Rupert insisted, desperation beginning to undermine his determination. 'All you can do is make things worse.'

'He isn't the one who'll need to be saved, but you. You're in more danger than you think,' she replied as if explaining to him the notes on a pianoforte.

'Mr Dyer, do you care to inform Mr Rupert why it is I've asked him to join us today?' Warren at last addressed the two men.

Rupert paled at the mention of the famous barrister's name.

Mr Dyer rose and approached Rupert, who had the sense to step cautiously back.

'Mr Hirst, I've reviewed the documents you provided Sir Warren and have been briefed on what transpired between the two of you in regards to your venture,' Mr Dyer began, with the authority of a man used to addressing magistrates and lowlifes. 'Despite your claims it was Sir Warren and not you who invented this scheme, there's nothing in your possession signed by Sir Warren to prove it. Nor is there anything in writing showing he agreed to the terms you included in the stock certificate, including placing Priorton Abbey up as collateral.'

'It doesn't matter what you believe. The investors believed it and they're the ones who will crucify him.' Rupert raised one shaking finger at Warren. 'Especially once it reaches the papers and I'll make sure it does.'

'No, you won't because you won't be here,' Mr Dyer explained. 'You will be on the next ship to Australia. You'll go there to make your life over. You're to have no more contact with my client, you're not to sell the story to the papers and, if you ever set foot in England again, I'll see to it you're prosecuted for forgery, the penalty for which is death. As you know, my reputation for prosecuting such cases is unmatched.'

'You have no proof.' Rupert's voice wavered as doubt about his plan began to take hold in his feeble mind.

'You're wrong.' It was Mr Dyer's turn to go to the door. He opened it and waved in a man with a flick of his fingers. A moment later, a skinny printer with a greasy hat held between his dirty hands crept into the room.

At the sight of him, the red flush of hate in Rupert's face vanished.

'I believe you know Mr Fink,' Mr Dyer said. 'He's ready to give evidence against you in exchange for protection from prosecution. He'll testify how you employed him to draft the forged investment papers which you then presented to a number of titled men.

Once he's done testifying, I'll place every investor on the stand and have them tell the magistrate how it was you, and not Sir Warren, who convinced them to invest in the scheme. It's not Sir Warren they and the papers will crucify, but you.'

Rupert slumped against Warren's desk, knocking over the dusting-powder shaker, his plan crumbling around him and threatening to bring down his life with it. Warren didn't pity him. The man was as terrible a scandal creator as he was a businessman and deserved every punishment he'd brought upon his balding head. Then Rupert straightened himself, finding a little more fight in his weak constitution. 'You think you've won, Warren, but you haven't. There are still the debts and you might be paying Mr Dyer now, but when you have no money left, he'll stop fighting for you like any other bloodsucking barrister.'

'I'd gladly work for free to see scum like you ruined,' Mr Dyer replied, 'especially since I know you still have the investors' money.'

Panic widened Rupert's watery eyes. 'I don't. I spent it. It's gone.'

'Some of it is, but not the bulk of it,' Mr Dyer contradicted. 'Yesterday, I visited a friend of mine who owns your bank. When I explained to him the situation, he was very co-operative in showing me your false account and the money you've squirrelled away. He's more than happy to turn the funds over to me and avoid him and his bank being entangled in a forgery trial.'

Rupert looked back and forth between Mr Dyer and

Warren as though it taxed his mind to believe what was being said and to find some kind of response to it.

'It's over, Rupert,' Warren said in the same voice he'd used to tell him Leticia had passed. Today was just as tragic as then, but this time it was all Rupert's fault. He'd done this to himself and no one but he would suffer. 'Whatever you planned, it won't happen. Instead, you'll find yourself at the end of a rope.'

'Unless you co-operate with us now.' Mr Steed rose to join the conversation. He laid out a sheet of paper, picked the pen off Warren's desk and held it out to Rupert. 'Write out a list of every investor and what they're owed. Include a full accounting of your assets so we may see to their selling at once and resolve this matter. You're also to sign over your quarterly inheritance payment to me to cover any additional shortfalls in what is owed.'

'You'll leave me destitute,' Rupert wailed as though expecting sympathy after everything he'd done.

'I'll leave you to your own devices, not here in London, but in Australia,' Warren spat out, wanting him gone from his life, his house and even the country for good. 'You'll succeed or fail according to your own merits, which are badly lacking.'

'I won't go.'

'Then you force us to turn everything over to the magistrate.' Mr Steed returned the pen to its stand. 'And you will be hanged for forgery.'

Rupert lunged at the pen, snatching it and the paper up. 'All right, I'll do as you ask.'

Like one of Warren's father's reluctant students, Rupert wrote out the required information. Over the next half-hour, the solicitor and the barrister questioned him to make sure he'd told them everything. He crumpled under their scrutiny like a weathered fence, signing his name to every affidavit and legal document they placed in front of him.

At last, when the two men were satisfied, Mr Dyer approached Warren. 'We'll handle any remaining matters from here, including making sure Mr Hirst has packed his things and is on the ship when it departs.'

'Is this the end of it, then?' Warren asked in disbelief.

'It should be. I'll let you know as soon as the investors are repaid.'

'I'll cover any differences, no matter what the cost.' With his new novel in Mr Berkshire's hands, and the inspiration for the next story one of the few bright points to come from this experience, he didn't worry about affording the extra expense.

'They shouldn't be much. He took sums from some well-known men, but it appears they didn't believe in him enough to give him large amounts.'

'And the papers?'

'I doubt anyone will say anything to them. No aristocrat wants to reveal having been duped by a man like Mr Hirst.'

Marianne slid her hand in Warren's and gave it a squeeze. 'Come, there's nothing more for us to do here.'

She tugged him into the adjoining sitting room where Lancelot slept on the sofa, his head resting on one tufted arm. Warren stared at everything surrounding him, especially the painting of Priorton hanging on the wall above the dog. The last time he'd sat in here, he'd feared losing it all. Now it was safe and Marianne was at his side.

'We won and you don't look happy.' Marianne wrapped her arms around his waist and held him close. 'What's wrong?'

'Mr Berkshire gave me some advice yesterday. He said challenges never end, but how you deal with them matters.'

'Lady Ellington said something similar to me. They're both right.'

'I'm glad they are.' Contented happiness replaced his seriousness as he bent her into a kiss. They were together once more and nothing would ever come between them again.

Chapter Fourteen

'Come, my dear, I have a surprise waiting for you in the church,' Lady Ellington announced as she hustled Marianne out of the carriage.

Above them the spiked spire of St Martin in the Fields rose against the bright blue London sky. True to his word, Warren had spoken to his royal connection and had asked him to approach the bishop about the special licence. Thankfully, the bishop was a great admirer of Warren's work and had been more than happy to grant the licence, especially when presented with autographed copies of Warren's novels. The clergyman had even arranged to perform the ceremony himself at St Martin in the Fields. The hurried affair meant no banns, and no spectacle for Warren's fans, much to Mr Berkshire's lament. Having been denied a more public wedding, the publisher had insisted on inviting his most trusted newspaperman to the ceremony to publish the story in the morning paper. Marianne was glad. She wanted all of London to hear of their marriage and her love for Warren.

'But, Lady Ellington, you've done so much for me already.' Marianne followed Lady Ellington into the vestibule, holding up the hem of her blue dress to keep from tripping on it. There'd been no time for a new gown, so Marianne had chosen to wear the one from Lady Astley's. They'd added a chemisette to it to make it more appropriate for the church, otherwise nothing else about it had been altered for the solemn occasion. She hoped the sight of her in it struck Warren as powerfully as it had at the musical and made him look forward to their first night together as man and wife as much as she did.

Lady Ellington hustled Marianne to one side, out of sight of the altar and the gentlemen standing there. Then Theresa's voice rang out.

'Marianne, you're gorgeous,' Theresa gushed as she hugged her friend. 'I'm so happy the wedding is taking place before my confinement. I didn't want to miss your happy day.'

'But how did you know?' It was then she noticed Lord and Lady Falconbridge standing behind Theresa and her husband, Mr Menton. 'What are you all doing here?'

'I summoned them,' Lady Ellington explained, quite pleased with herself. 'I wanted those who care about you the most to be here on this important day.'

'We're so happy for you.' Lady Falconbridge opened her arms to embrace Marianne, hugging her as well as a woman so heavy with child could.

She didn't pull away, but wrapped her arms around the graceful woman's shoulders and returned the tight embrace. It wasn't awkward or embarrassing, but the most natural thing she could do. This was the family she'd always wanted, the one she'd craved during the long nights at the Protestant School and in London with Madame de Badeau. She thought she'd found it once with the Smiths, but they'd never cherished her like the Falconbridges, Theresa or Lady Ellington. These people would never leave her or abandon her no matter what and she loved them.

Overhead the bells began to peal and the elderly sexton appeared to announce it was time for the guests to be seated for the ceremony.

Lady Ellington drew Marianne to one side while everyone, except Lord Falconbridge, left to take their places in the pew. Lady Ellington laid her hands on Marianne's shoulders, her eyes glistening like her diamonds. 'It used to break my heart to see you try and look cheerful when news from Theresa about her husband used to arrive, or the melancholy way you watched Randall and Cecelia. Now look at you, glowing like an Advent candle.'

Lady Ellington wrapped her plump arms around Marianne and hugged her hard before stepping away to allow Lord Falconbridge to approach.

'Miss Domville, may I escort you up the aisle?' Lord Falconbridge offered Marianne his arm.

'Yes, you may.'

A few moments later, with everyone seated, Lord Falconbridge led Marianne to the top of the aisle. Mrs Stevens sat in the pew with Lady Ellington, the two of them beaming with pleasure at seeing their efforts to match the young people complete.

Warren stood at the altar with Mr Berkshire and the bishop. He wore a dark green coat which increased the intensity of his eyes as they focused on her. Beneath his chin, his cravat was better tied than usual, but still remained at a slightly haphazard angle. It matched the gaiety in his smile and the joy illuminating his face like the light coming in through the tall windows behind him. He shifted on his feet, revealing his anxiousness to take her hand. His exuberance almost made her let go of Lord Falconbridge and sprint up the aisle to meet him. Instead, she marched in a stately gait with Lord Falconbridge as the organ behind them played. Her heart raced beneath her gown. She'd thought everything lost only a short while ago, now they were together for what would soon be the rest of their lives. He loved her, despite all the stories and their mutual missteps. He was hers and she was his and neither of them would ever be alone again.

At last Lord Falconbridge handed her to Warren and took his place beside his wife in the pew. Marianne pressed her hand in Warren's and the ceremony began. She heard little of what the bishop said as he read the service. She'd watched Theresa walk down the aisle to Mr Menton, been there the morning Lord Falconbridge had married Lady Falconbridge. Each time she'd been happy for her friends while silently despairing of ever seeing her own wedding day. At last it was her turn before the altar and not with some leech like Lord Bolton, but with Warren, a man who'd always encouraged her to be more than even she'd imagined. Where might she go now with him as her husband? The idea of performing as Mr Berkshire had suggested didn't terrify her, not when she imagined Warren standing with her on the stage as he stood beside her now. She'd help him to reach even greater heights with his writing, all the while enjoying with him the love and security of a home and a true place in the world.

The promise of their life together was strong in his lips against hers as the bishop instructed them to kiss and seal the vows they'd made to one another.

After the ceremony, they returned to Lady Ellington's for the wedding breakfast. It was a rousing affair with a great deal of laughter and a few ribald remarks. For all the excited celebration, Marianne couldn't wait to be alone with Warren.

At last the time came. His carriage whisked them off to his town house, and soon they were alone in his room, indulging in the first private moment of their life together.

Warren made a show of locking the door and dropping the iron key on the table beside it. 'I refuse to be disturbed.'

'I'm surprised Mr Berkshire didn't insist on sending the newspaper man home with us after inviting him to the breakfast.' Marianne laughed as Warren stood over her and took her in his arms. He was solid and firm against her and it made her heartbeat quicken.

'Speaking of Mr Berkshire, what were you and he discussing before we left?' he murmured as he nuzzled the skin of her neck, his fingers slipping beneath the chemisette to caress the tops of her breasts.

She could barely recall the publisher's words under the pressure of Warren's touch. 'He was telling me about his plans for my compositions. He has quite a few of them.'

'Such as?' He slid a small pearl button through a hole and slipped the fine silk from her chest.

'Where I will perform my first concert.' She swept her tongue along the skin of his neck above his cravat, inhaling his strong male scent. 'I was thinking at Madame de Badeau's old town house. I still own it as part of my inheritance. It will attract people's attention and increase sales.'

Warren straightened as he examined her with a curious tilt of his head. 'Aren't you worried about society's reaction to such a questionable venue?'

'Not at all. After all, there is some advantage to scandal.'

'Indeed, there is.' He dipped her into a deep kiss and everything else faded away.

* * * * *